Innocent virgins

Passion

Falling in love has

The
innocence
Collection

Three complete novels from fabulous international bestselling authors

Penny Jordan, Carole Mortimer and Kay Thorpe

Also available:

Because every woman has her wicked side.

The

innocence

Collection

THE BLACKMAIL BABY

by
Penny Jordan

THE SECRET VIRGIN

by
Carole Mortimer

VIRGIN MISTRESS

by
Kay Thorpe

First published in Great Britain 2007
by Harlequin Mills & Boon Limited, Eton House,
18-24 Paradise Road, Richmond, Surrey TW9 1SR

The Blackmail Baby, The Secret Virgin and *Virgin Mistress* were first published in Great Britain in separate, single volumes.

ISBN 13: 978 0 263 85551 7
ISBN 10: 0 263 85551 1

024-0107

Printed and bound in Spain
by Litografia Rosés S.A., Barcelona

THE BLACKMAIL BABY

by

Penny Jordan

Penny Jordan has been writing for more than twenty years and has an outstanding record: over 130 novels published, including the phenomenally successful A PERFECT FAMILY, TO LOVE, HONOUR & BETRAY, THE PERFECT SINNER and POWER PLAY, which hit *The Sunday Times* and *New York Times* bestseller lists. Penny Jordan was born in Preston, Lancashire, and now lives in rural Cheshire.

Don't miss Penny Jordan's new novel, available in February, *Taken by the Sheikh,* from Mills & Boon Modern Romance™!

PROLOGUE

'SO YOU'RE going to go through with it? You're going to go ahead and marry Dracco, even though he doesn't love you?'

Imogen flinched as the full venom of her stepmother Lisa's words hit her. They were in Imogen's bedroom, or at least the bedroom that had been Imogen's until after her father's death. Since then Lisa had declared her intention to sell the pretty country house where Imogen had grown up and to buy herself a modern apartment in the small market town where they lived.

'Dracco has asked me to be on hand to help him entertain the clients,' Lisa had said at the time of her shock announcement about the house. 'He says he can see how much more business the company has been attracting since I became your father's hostess. Unfortunately your mother never seemed to realise just how vitally important being a good hostess was.'

She had given the openly dismissive, almost contemptuous shrug with which Imogen had become teeth-grittingly familiar whenever Lisa spoke about her late mother. Instinctively Imogen had wanted to leap to her mother's defence, but she had sufficient experience of Lisa to know better than to do so. Even so, she had not been able to stop herself from pointing out quietly, 'Mummy was ill. Otherwise, I know she would have wanted to entertain Daddy's clients for him.'

'Oh, yes, we all know that you think your precious mother was a saint.' Imogen had seen the furious look of hostility in Lisa's hard blue eyes. 'And Dracco agrees with me that you made life very difficult for your father all these years by constantly harping on about your mother, trying to make him feel guilty because he fell in love with me.'

Lisa had preened herself openly, making Imogen's stomach churn with sickening misery and anguish. Then her stepmother had continued triumphantly, 'Dracco considers that your father was very fortunate to be married to me. In fact...' She had stopped, giving Imogen a small, secret little smile that had made her heart thump heavily against her ribs. It hurt, unbearably, to hear Lisa speaking about Dracco as though a special closeness existed between them, especially when Imogen was so desperately in love with him herself!

Imogen had never truly been able to understand how her beloved father had fallen in love with a woman as cold and manipulative as Lisa. Granted, she was stunningly attractive: tall, blonde-haired, with a perfect and lushly curved body, totally unlike Imogen's own. Imogen took after her mother, who had been petite and fine-boned with the same thick dark mop of untameable blackberry curls and amazingly coloured dark violet eyes. And, where Imogen remembered her mother's eyes shining with warmth and love, Lisa's pale blue eyes were always cold.

Imogen had loved her father far too much, though, to say anything to him. Her mother had died when she was seven, and when he'd decided to remarry when she was fourteen Imogen had made up her mind to accept her new stepmother for his sake. She had adored her father and been fiercely protective of him, in her little-girl way, after her mother's death, but she had been ready to welcome into their lives anyone who could make him happy.

Lisa, though, had quickly made it plain that she was not prepared to be equally generous. She had been thirty-two when she married Imogen's father, with no particular fondness for children and even less for other members of her own sex. Right from the start of their relationship she had treated the young girl as an adversary, a rival for Imogen's father's affections and loyalty.

Lisa had been in their lives less than three months when she had told Imogen coolly that she considered it would be far better for her to go to boarding school than live at home and attend the local private school her mother had chosen before succumbing to the degenerative illness which had ultimately killed her. It had been Dracco who had stepped in then, reminding Imogen's father that his first wife had hand-picked her daughter's secondary school even when she knew she would not be alive to see Imogen attend it. It had been Dracco too who had come to that same school to break the news of her father's fatal accident to Imogen, tears sheening the normally composed and unreadable jade depths of his eyes.

That had been nearly twelve months ago. Imogen had been seventeen then, now she was eighteen, and in less than an hour's time she would be Dracco's wife.

The car that was to take her to the same small church where her parents had been married and her mother was buried was waiting outside. Inside it was her father's elderly solicitor, who was to give her away. It was to be a quiet wedding. She had pleaded fervently with Dracco for that.

So you're going to go through with it? You're going to go ahead and marry Dracco, even though he doesn't love you? Imogen's mind returned to her stepmother's deliberately painful question.

'Dracco says it's…it's for my own good…and that it's what my father would have wanted,' she answered.

'"Dracco says,"' Lisa Atkins mimicked cruelly. 'You are such a fool, Imogen. There is only one reason Dracco is marrying you and that's because of who you are. Because he wants to gain full control of the business.'

'No, that isn't true!' Imogen protested frantically. 'Dracco already runs the business,' she reminded her stepmother. 'He knows I would never try to change that.'

'*You* might not,' Lisa agreed coolly. 'But what about the man you may one day marry if Dracco doesn't step in? He may have other plans. Your father's will leaves your share in trust for you until you are thirty unless you marry before then. Oh, come on, Imogen. Surely you don't actually think that Dracco wants you?' One elegant eyebrow arched mockingly before Lisa went on, 'Dracco is a man! To him you are just a child, less than that, in fact… Dracco wants what you can give him. He has told me himself that if it wasn't for the business there is no way he'd be marrying you.'

Although she tried to stop herself, Imogen could not quite prevent the sharp gasp of pain escaping. She could see Lisa's triumphant smile, and hated herself for letting the older woman break through her defences.

In an effort to recover the ground she had lost, she began unsteadily, 'Dracco wouldn't—'

But she wasn't allowed to go any further; Lisa stopped her, saying softly, 'Dracco wouldn't what, Imogen? Dracco wouldn't confide in me? Oh, my dear, I'm afraid you are way behind the times. Dracco and I...' She paused and examined her perfectly manicured fingernails. 'Well, it should be for Dracco to tell you this and not me, but let us just say that Dracco and I have a relationship which is very special—to both of us.'

Imogen could hardly take in what she was being told. She felt sick with a numbing disbelief that this could be happening on her wedding day; the day that should have been one of the happiest of her life, but which now, thanks to Lisa's shocking revelations, was fast turning into one of the worst.

So far she had not given very much thought to the complexities of her father's will. She had been too grief-stricken by his loss to consider how his death would affect her financially. She knew, though, of course, that he had been an extremely successful and wealthy man. As an acclaimed financial adviser, John Atkins had been held in high esteem by both his clients and those he did business with. Imogen could still remember how enthusiastic and pleased he had been when he had first taken Dracco under his wing as a raw university graduate.

They had met when her father went to debate an issue at Dracco's university. Dracco had been on the opposing side and her father had been impressed not just by his debating skills but by his grasp of the whole subject, and what he had described as Dracco's raw energy and hunger to succeed.

Dracco had had a stormy childhood, abandoned by his own father and brought up by a succession of relatives after his mother had remarried and her second husband had refused to take him on. He had worked to pay his own way through university, and when he had first come to work for Imogen's father he had for a time lived with them.

It had been Dracco who had chauffeured her to school when her father was away on business; Dracco who had taught her to ride her new bike; Dracco the Dragon, as she had nicknamed him teasingly. And when her father had made him a junior partner in his business it had been Imogen Dracco had taken out to celebrate his promotion—to an ice-cream parlour in the local town.

Quite when her acceptance of him as Dracco, her father's partner and her own friend had changed, and she had begun to see him as Dracco, the man, Imogen wasn't sure.

She could remember coming out of school one day to find him waiting for her in the little scarlet sports car he had bought for himself. It had been a hot, sunny afternoon, the hood had been down, the sunlight glinting on the thick night-darkness of his hair. He had turned his head to look at her, as though sensing her presence even before she had reached him, and studied her with the intense dark greenness of his gaze.

Suddenly it had been as though she was seeing him for the first time. As though she had been struck by a thunderbolt. Her heart had started to race and then thud heavily.

She had felt sick, excited, filled with a dangerous, heady exuberance and a shocked self-consciousness.

Without knowing why, she had found that she wanted to look at his mouth. Somewhere deep inside her body an unfamiliar sensation had begun to uncurl itself; a sensation that had made her face blush bright red and her legs turn to jelly. She had felt as though she couldn't bear to be near him in case he guessed how she felt, but at the same time she couldn't bear him not to be there.

'Only a child as naïve and inexperienced as you could possibly think that Dracco wants you. A woman, a real woman, would know immediately that there was already someone else in his life. He hasn't even tried to take you to bed, has he?' Lisa challenged, before adding cruelly, 'And don't bother trying to pretend that you haven't wanted him to. That crush you have on him is painfully obvious.'

The sharp interruption of Lisa's goading voice broke into Imogen's thoughts. Instinctively she turned away from her stepmother to guard her expression, catching sight of her own reflection in the mirror as she did so. It had been Dracco who had insisted that she should wear a traditional wedding dress.

'Your father would have wanted you to,' had been his winning argument.

If there was one thing she and Dracco did share it was their mutual love for her father.

'Dracco doesn't love you. Not as a man loves a woman.'

Once again Imogen couldn't prevent a small sound of anguish escaping her lips.

Narrowing her eyes, Lisa dropped her voice to a soft, sensual purr. 'Surely even someone as sexless as you must have thought it odd that he hasn't taken you to bed? Any normal woman would guess immediately what that meant. Especially where an obviously red-blooded man like Dracco is concerned.' Lisa smiled unkindly at her. 'If you're determined to be an unwanted wife you will have to learn to conceal your feelings a little better. Surely you couldn't have imagined that there haven't been women in Dracco's life? He is, after all, a very potent man.'

Imogen prayed that she wouldn't be sick and that she wouldn't give in to her desire to run out of the room and away from Lisa's hateful, mocking voice. Of course she knew there had been other women in Dracco's life and she knew too what it felt like to be agonisingly jealous of them—after all, she had had enough practice.

Dracco with other girls; girls that he found attractive and desirable in all the ways he obviously did not view her; girls that he wanted in all the ways he did not want her, in his arms, in his bed, beneath the fierce male hardness of his body, naked, skin to skin, whilst he…

To Dracco she was nothing more than a baby, the daughter of his partner and closest friend, someone to be treated with amusement and paternalism as though twenty-odd years separated them and not a mere ten… Ten…a full decade… But soon they would be equals; soon now she would be Dracco's wife. Imogen gave a small shiver. All through her teenage years she had dreamed of her private fantasy coming true and of Dracco returning her love, telling her that he could not live without her, demanding passionately that she give herself to him and become his wife.

Of course, a tiny part of her, a voice she had refused out of fear and anguish to listen to, urged her to be cautious, to wonder why in all the things that Dracco had said to her since her father's death there had been no mention of love.

And somehow until now she had managed to ignore what that omission could mean. Until now.

There was, Imogen recognised through her shocked pain, an odd air of almost driven determination in her stepmother's manner, an air that bordered on furious desperation, but Imogen felt too weakened by her own anguish to consider why that might be.

Drawing herself up to her full height, she told Lisa with quiet dignity, 'Dracco is marrying me—'

'No,' Lisa told her furiously, 'Dracco is marrying your inheritance. Have you no pride, you little fool? Any woman worthy of the name would walk away now before it's too late, find herself a man who really wants her instead of crawling after one who doesn't; one who already has in his life the woman he really wants!'

Imogen felt as though she was inhabiting a nightmare. What further cruelty was Lisa trying to inflict on her? Whatever it was, she didn't want to hear it. She did not want to allow herself to hear it.

It was time for her to leave. Imogen started to walk past her stepmother but Lisa grabbed hold of her arm, stopping her, hissing viciously to her, 'I know what you're hoping but you're wasting your time; Dracco will never love you. He loves someone else. If you don't believe me, ask him! Ask him today, now, before he marries you, if there is someone; a woman in his life whom he loves. And ask him, if you dare, just who she is.'

* * *

A woman in Dracco's life whom he loved. Imogen's head was swimming with pain and fear as she started to walk down the aisle. She could see the back of Dracco's dark head as he waited for her to reach him. The scent of the lilies filling the church was so heady that it was making Imogen feel slightly sick and faint. How could that be true? How could he possibly even consider marrying her if he loved someone else?

Lisa had been lying… Lying, as she had done so often in the past, trying to cause trouble for Imogen; to hurt and upset her.

And as for her final comment, it had to be impossible, surely, as Lisa had been implying that she herself was the woman Dracco loved.

Totally, completely, unbearably impossible, at least so far as Imogen was concerned.

'Dearly beloved…'

Imogen felt herself start to sway. Immediately Dracco's fingers curled supportively around her arm.

Pain and longing filled her in equal measures. This should have been the happiest day of her life. She was, after all, marrying the man she loved. The man she had loved since she had first realised what love was.

'Imogen. Are you all right? For a moment in there I thought you were going to faint.'

Imogen tried to force a smile as she met the frowning concern in Dracco's gaze. Her husband's gaze. She could feel her knees threatening to buckle. She felt so odd. So…so alone and afraid.

'Dracco, there's something I want to ask you.'

They were standing outside the church whilst the bells pealed and their wedding guests chattered happily.

'Mmmm…'

Dracco was barely even looking at her, Imogen recognised miserably. They didn't seem like a newly married couple at all…like husband and wife, a pair of lovers. A sharp pain seemed to pierce her to her heart. Before she could lose her courage she demanded unevenly, 'Have you…? Is there…is there someone…a woman you love?'

He was looking at her now, Imogen recognised bitterly, concentrating all his attention on her, but not in the way she had longed for. He was frowning forbiddingly in the tense silence her nervous question had created.

Imogen could hardly bear to continue looking at him. She saw the flash of emotion glitter in the jade depths of his eyes; heard the furious anger in his voice as he demanded curtly, 'Who told you about that?'

Her heart felt as though it was breaking. It was true.

In numb despair she watched as he cursed grimly under his breath and then said more gently, 'Yes. Yes, there is. But…'

Dracco loved another woman. He loved another woman but he had still married her.

Imogen felt as though her whole world had come crashing down around her. Where was the man she had put on a pedestal; adored, trusted, loved? He didn't exist…

With a low cry of torment she turned on her heel and started to run, desperate to escape from her pain, from her stepmother's knowing triumph, but most of all from

Dracco himself, who had betrayed her and everything she had believed about him. Behind her she could hear Dracco calling her name, but that only made her run even faster. In the street beyond the church a taxi was pulling up to disgorge its passenger, and without stopping to think what she was doing Imogen ran up to it and jumped in. At any other time the way the taxi driver was goggling at her would have made her giggle, but laughing was the last thing she felt like doing right now…

'Quick,' she instructed the driver, her voice trembling. 'Please hurry.'

As she spoke she darted a quick backward glance towards the church, half expecting to see Dracco coming in pursuit of her, but the street behind her was empty.

'Don't tell me,' the taxi driver quipped jovially as he took in both his passenger's bridal array and her breathless anxiety, 'you're in a hurry to get to a wedding—right?' Laughing at his own joke, he started to negotiate the traffic.

'Wrong,' Imogen corrected him fiercely. 'I'm actually in a hurry to get away from one.'

As he swung round to stare at her, ignoring the busy traffic, Imogen could see the bemusement in his eyes.

'What?' he protested. 'A runaway bride? I never thought.'

Quickly Imogen gave him her home address, adding tersely, 'And please hurry.'

So far there was no evidence of any pursuit—no sign of either Dracco's sleek Daimler or her stepmother's Rolls-Royce.

* * *

Never had a drive seemed to last so long, nor caused her to sit on the edge of her seat, her fingers clenched into the upholstery in anxiety as she checked constantly to see if they were being followed. But at last the taxi driver was setting her down outside her home, waiting whilst she hurried inside to get the money to pay him—as a bride, there had been no need for her to have any cash with her.

Once she had paid him and soothed his unexpectedly paternal concern for her, she ran back upstairs to her room, dragging off her wedding dress with such force that the fragile fabric ripped. Just as her stepmother and Dracco between them had ripped apart her foolish dreams.

Feverishly she pulled on jeans and a top, hastily emptying the suitcase packed for the honeymoon she and Dracco were to have been taking and refilling it with clothes wrenched blindly off hangers and out of drawers.

She still hadn't really taken in what she had done; all she knew was that she had to get as far away from Dracco as she could and as fast as she could. If, as her stepmother had warned her, he had only been marrying her to gain control of the business then he would not be satisfied until he had that control. She knew how determined he could be. How focused and… A small shudder shook her body. Dracco! Dracco! How could he have done this to her? How could he have humiliated and hurt her so? Tears burning her eyes, Imogen picked up her new cream leather handbag—bought especially for her honeymoon. Inside it was her passport, and the wallet of traveller's cheques Dracco had given her earlier in the week.

'Spending-money,' he had told her with a small smile. The same smile that always made her heart lift and then beat frantically fast, whilst her insides melted and her body longed...

She had counted them after he had gone, her eyes widening as she realised just how much he had given her.

Well, that money would be put to good use now, she reflected bitterly as she allowed herself to enjoy the irony of her using the money Dracco had given her to spend on their honeymoon on funding her escape from him.

She would use it to buy herself a ticket to fly just as far away from him as she could!

'Well, there are seats left on the flight due to leave for Rio de Janeiro in half an hour,' the clerk responded in answer to Imogen's anxious enquiry.

Even whilst she listened to the clerk she couldn't stop herself from glancing nervously over her shoulder, still half expecting to see Dracco's familiar figure bearing down on her, and was chagrined to discover that there was a part of her that was almost desperately hoping that he would be.

But now it was too late. Now she was booked on to the flight for Rio. Shakily she walked over to the check-in desk and handed over her case.

Goodbye, home; goodbye, everything she knew; goodbye, love she had hoped so very very much to have.

Goodbye, Dracco!

CHAPTER ONE

Four years later

THROUGHOUT the flight from Rio Imogen had been rehearsing exactly what she was going to say, and the manner in which she was going to say it. She reminded herself as she did so that she wasn't a naïve girl of just eighteen any more, who knew virtually nothing of the real world or the shadowed, darker side of life, a girl who had been sheltered and protected by her father's love and concern. No; she was a woman now, a woman of twenty-two, who knew exactly what the real world encompassed, exactly how much pain, poverty and degradation it could hold, as well as how much love, compassion and sheer generosity of spirit.

Looking back over the last four years, it seemed almost impossible that she had anything left in common with the girl she had once been. Imogen closed her eyes and lay back in her seat, an economy-class seat, even though she could technically at least have flown home first class. You didn't do things like that when you had spent the last few years working to help destitute orphans who lived in a world where children under five would fight to the death over a scrap of bread. Now, thanks to the small private charitable organisation she worked for, some of those orphans at least were being given a roof over their heads, food, education and, most important of all in Imogen's eyes, love.

Imogen couldn't pin-point exactly when she had first started to regret turning her back on her inheritance—not in any way for her own sake, but for what it could mean to the charity she worked for and the children she so much wanted to help.

Perhaps it had begun when she had stood and watched the happiness light up the face of Sister Maria the day she had announced to them all, in a voice that trembled with thrilled gratitude, that the fund-raising they had all worked so hard on that year had raised a sum of money that was only a tithe of the income Imogen knew she could have expected from her inheritance—never mind its saleable value.

All she did know was that increasingly over recent months she had begun to question the wisdom of what she had done and just how right she was to allow pride to stand in the way of all that she could do to benefit the charity.

And, as if that weren't enough, she had begun, too, to wonder how her friends and fellow workers would view her if they knew how wilfully and indeed selfishly she was refusing to use her own assets where they could do so much good. Pride was all very well but who exactly was paying for her to have the luxury of indulging in it? These and other equally painful questions had been causing Imogen to battle within herself for far too long. And now finally she had come to a decision she felt ashamed to have taken so long in reaching.

The nuns were so kind, so gentle, so humbly grateful for every scrap of help they received. They would never blame or criticise her, Imogen knew, but she was beginning to blame and criticise herself.

During her years in Rio Imogen had learned to protect and value her privacy, to guard herself from any unwanted questions, however kindly meant. Her trust was not something she gave lightly to others any more. Her past was a taboo subject and one she discussed with no one.

She had made friends in Rio, it was true, but her past was something she had kept to herself, and the friends she had made had all been kept at something of a distance—especially the men. Falling in love, being in love—these were things that hurt too much for her to even think about, never mind risk doing. Not after Dracco. *Dracco.* Even now she still sometimes dreamed about him. Dreams that drained her so much emotionally that for days afterwards she ached with pain.

There was no one to whom she wanted to confide just how searing her sense of loss and aloneness had been when she had first arrived in the city, or just how often she had been tempted to change her mind and return home. Only her pride had stopped her—that and the letter she had sent to her father's solicitor a week after her arrival in Rio, informing him that she was disassociating herself completely from her past life. She had said that she wanted nothing to do with the inheritance her father had left her and that henceforward she wanted to be allowed to lead her own life, on her own. She had made her letter as formal as possible, stating that under no circumstances did she want any kind of contact with either her stepmother or Dracco.

She had, of course, omitted to put any address on the

letter, and as an added precaution she had used the last of the money Dracco had given her to fly to America, where she had posted her letter before returning to Rio.

In order to support herself she had found work both as an interpreter and a teacher, and it had been through that work that she had become involved with the sisters and their children's charity.

It had taken her what was now a guilt-inducing amount of time to bring herself to take the action she was now taking, and she still felt acutely ashamed to remember the look of bemused disbelief on Sister Maria's face when she had haltingly explained to her that she was not the penniless young woman she had allowed everyone to believe she was.

Sister Maria's total lack of any attempt to question or criticise her had reinforced Imogen's determination to put matters right as speedily as she could.

Initially she had believed that it would be enough simply for her to write to her father's solicitor, explaining that she had changed her mind about the income she could receive under her father's will. She had explained in the simplest possible terms how she wished to use it to benefit Rio's pitifully needy street children. It had distressed her to receive a letter back not from Henry Fairburn but from an unknown David Bryant. He had introduced himself in the letter as Henry's successor and nephew, explaining that his uncle had died and that he had taken over the business.

As to Imogen's income from the inheritance left to her by her father, the letter had continued, he considered that because of the complications of the situation it would be necessary for her to return to England to put her wishes into action, and he had advised her to lose no time in doing so.

Of course, she had baulked at the idea of returning home. But, after all, what was there really for her to fear other than her own fear?

There was certainly no need for her to fear her long-dead love for Dracco. How could there be?

There had been no contact between them whatsoever, and for all that she knew he and Lisa could now be living together in blissful happiness. They certainly deserved one another. She had never met two people who matched one another so exactly in terms of cold-bloodedness.

It was a great pity that her father had seen fit to make Dracco one of her trustees and an even greater one that Henry, her other trustee, was no longer alive. Imogen wasn't quite sure just what the full legal position with regard to her inheritance and her rights was, but no doubt this David Bryant would be able to advise her on that. And on the other crumple in the otherwise smooth surface of her life that she really ought to get ironed out?

That small and impossible-to-blank-out fact that she and Dracco were still legally, so far as she was aware, married?

Disconcertingly the only gently chiding comment Sister Maria had made when Imogen had been explaining her situation had been a soft reminder that the vows of marriage were supposed to be for life!

Foolishly she had never bothered to get their marriage annulled. She had been far too terrified in those early days that Dracco might somehow persuade her to return home and to their marriage.

Now, of course, she had no such fear, and no need for the status of a single woman either, other than as a salve to her own pride, a final step into a Dracco-free future.

She was also looking forward to, as she had promised she would, writing to Sister Maria to tell her that everything was going smoothly and that she would soon be returning to Rio.

Her stomach muscles tensed with a nervous apprehension that she told herself firmly was entirely natural as the plane began its descent into Heathrow Airport.

The Imogen who had left Heathrow four years earlier had been pretty in a soft, still-girlish way, but the woman she had become could never in a thousand years have been described as wishy-washily pretty. The hardship of a life that was lived without any kind of luxury, a life that was spent giving one hundred and fifty per cent physical commitment and two hundred and fifty per cent emotional love, had stripped Imogen's body of its late-teenage layer of protective flesh and honed her face to a delicately boned translucency. This revealed not just her stunningly perfect features and the deep, intense amethyst of her amazing eyes, but also gave her a luminosity that was almost spiritual and that made people turn to look at her not just once but a second and then a third time.

She was dressed simply in soft chinos and a white cotton shirt, but no woman could possibly live in Rio without absorbing something of the sensuality of its people, of a culture that flagrantly and unselfconsciously worshipped the female form. Brazilian clothes were cut in a way that was unique, and not even the loose fit of what she was wearing could conceal the narrowness of Imogen's waist, the high curve of her breasts, the unexpected length of her legs, but most of all the rounded curve of her bottom.

Her dark hair meant that her skin had adapted well to the South American sun, which had given her a warm, ripe, peachy glow. As she raised her hand to shield her eyes from the shaft of sunlight breaking through the grey cloud the gold watch her father had given her shortly before his death glinted in the light, emphasising the fragility of her wrist. A group of stewardesses walking past her looked enviously at the careless way she had tied the tangled thickness of her curls back off her face with an old white silk scarf.

Taking a deep breath, Imogen summoned a taxi. Once inside it, she studied the piece of paper she had removed from her purse, and gave the address written on it to the driver.

As he repeated it he commented, 'Bute Wharf. That'll be one of them new developments down by the river.'

Imogen smiled dutifully in acknowledgement of his comment but said nothing. She had asked the advice of her solicitor on where to stay, specifying that it had to be reasonably close to his office, and cheap.

To her astonishment, not only had he replied with a terse note that explained that he had made arrangements for her to stay 'at the enclosed address' but which had also enclosed a cheque to cover her air fare. A first-class fare—although she had chosen not to make use of it.

This particular Docklands area of London was unfamiliar to her and Imogen's eyes widened a little as she studied it through the taxi window: streets filled with expensive cars, young men and women dressed in designer clothing, an air about the whole area of affluence and prestige. Was this really the kind of place where she was going to find cheap accommodation? She began to panic a little, wondering if the solicitor had misunderstood her request.

The taxi was pulling up outside an impressive apartment block. Getting out, Imogen glanced up uncertainly at her surroundings, paying off the taxi and then picking up her one small case before squaring her shoulders and heading determinedly towards the entrance.

As she did so she was vaguely aware of the dark shadow of a large car gliding into the space left by the taxi, but she paid no attention to it, too busy making sure that she had the right address to concern herself with it.

Yes, the address was the same one the solicitor had given her.

A little warily Imogen walked into the luxurious atrium that was the apartment block's lobby and then stopped, drawn by some compelling force she couldn't resist to turn round and stare, and then stare again. Her breath froze in shock in her lungs as she recognised the man casually slamming the door of the car she had been so vaguely aware of before turning to stride determinedly through the entrance towards her, exclaiming coolly as he did so, 'Imo! I had hoped to meet you at the airport, but somehow I missed you.'

'Dracco!'

How weak her voice sounded, shaky and thin, the

voice of a child, a girl… Fiercely she tried to clear her throat, reminding herself that she was twenty-two and an adult, but her senses had shut down. They were concentrating exclusively on Dracco.

Four years hadn't changed him as much as she believed they had changed her, but then, he had already been an adult when she had left.

He still possessed that same aura of taut male sexual power she remembered so vividly, only now, as a woman, she was instantly, intensely aware of just how strong it was. It was like suddenly seeing something which had previously only been a hazy image brought sharply into focus, and she almost recoiled physically from the raw reality of it.

Had she forgotten just how magnetically sexy he was or had she simply never known, been too naïve to know? Well, if so, she wasn't now.

His hair was still as dark as she remembered, but cut shorter, giving him a somewhat harder edge. His eyes were harder than she remembered too. Harder and scrutinising her with a coldness that made her shiver.

'You didn't travel first class.'

'You knew that I was coming?' Try as she might, Imogen couldn't keep her appalled shock to herself.

'Of course. I'm your trustee, remember, and since the purpose of your visit is to discuss your inheritance…'

Her trustee! Well, of course she knew that, but somehow she had assumed, believed, that it would be David Bryant she would be talking to and that he would act as a negotiator between herself and Dracco. The last thing she wanted or needed was to be confronted by him like this when she was already feeling nervous and on edge. Not to mention jet-lagged.

Determined to grab back at least some small measure of control, she threw at him acidly, 'I'm surprised that Lisa isn't with you.'

'Lisa?'

She could see from his sharply incisive tone and the look he was giving her that he didn't like her pointed comment.

'This was nothing to do with Lisa,' he told her coldly.

Of course, he would want to protect his lover, Imogen acknowledged angrily.

The shocking realisation of how much she wanted to hurl at him all the accusations she had thought safely disarmed and vanquished years ago hit her nerve-endings like the kick of a mule. The old Imogen might well have given in and done so, but there had been something in the way he had looked at her when he had reminded her that he was her trustee that was warning her to tread very carefully.

Surely it was only a matter of formality for her to be able to reclaim the income she had previously rejected? It was, after all, legally hers, wasn't it?

Surely David Bryant would have told her, warned her, if this wasn't the case or if he had foreseen problems, rather than encouraging her to come all this way?

When it came to disposing of her share of the business, Imogen felt that she was on firmer ground. Since Dracco had been willing to marry her to secure it, surely it made sense that he would be delighted to be given legal control of her share of it in return for guaranteeing its income would be given to the charity?

After all, if she wished she could always sell it on the open market! Knowing that she held that power, that threat over him, helped to rally her courage.

Dracco had reached her now, and Imogen discovered that one thing hadn't changed. She still had to tilt her head right back to look up into his eyes when he stood next to her.

Too late to regret now the comfortable low-heeled pumps she was wearing.

'Come on.' As he spoke Dracco was propelling her forward, the fear of experiencing the sensation of that powerful long-fingered hand of his, placed firmly in the small of her back, causing her to hurry in the direction he was indicating.

What was the matter with her? Why on earth should she fear Dracco touching her now? Once she had feared it because then she had known that even the briefest and most non-sexual contact with him was enough to make her aching body feel as though it might explode with longing, but those days were over! All around her on the streets of Rio she had seen the living, suffering evidence of what happened when two human beings indulged in their sexual desires. She would never abandon her child—never in a million years—but then, she was not a girl, a child herself, penniless and without any means of support. No, that wasn't the point. The point was...the point was...

Dizzily, dangerously Imogen realised that she was having a hard time focusing on anything logical or sensible; that she was, in fact, finding it virtually impossible to concentrate on anything other than Dracco himself.

'It's this way.'

Automatically she followed him towards the glass-walled lift, numbly aware of the brief nod of the hovering uniformed commissionaire as he greeted Dracco with a respectful, 'Good afternoon, Mr Barrington.'

'Afternoon, Bates,' Dracco responded calmly. 'Family OK?'

'Yes, they're fine, and young Robert's over the moon about that job you got for him.'

The smile Dracco gave the doorman suddenly made him look far less formidable and reminded Imogen of the smiles he once used to give her. An almost unbearably tight pain filled her chest, which she firmly put down to the speed with which the lift was surging upwards.

'Still scared of heights? Don't look down,' Dracco told her coolly. 'Heaven knows why, but for some reason every architect in the city seems to have decided that glass-walled lifts are the in thing.'

Where once he would have made such a comment in a voice that was ruefully amused, now he sounded terse and cold. Well, there was no reason why he should show her any warmth, was there?

But why shouldn't he? She had, after all, spared him the trouble of having to pretend that he had wanted to marry her or that he cared about her, and she had given him what he really wanted at the same time. In the letter she had sent to Henry renouncing her inheritance she had given Dracco complete and total authority to use the power that came with her share of the business as he saw fit.

In doing so, she had known beyond any kind of doubt that Dracco would uphold her father's business ideals and aims. In that regard at least she had known she could trust him totally.

She had closed her eyes when the lift started to move, but unexpectedly the images, the memories suddenly tormenting her were even worse in their own way than the heights she feared. She would, she knew, never forgive Dracco for what he had tried to do; for the way he had tried to manipulate her; for the way he had abused the trust her father had placed in him.

The lift shivered to a silent stop.

'You can open your eyes now,' she heard Dracco telling her wryly.

As she edged out of the lift Imogen saw that they had stopped at the floor marked 'Penthouse Suite'.

Penthouse suite. Her solicitor had roomed her in a penthouse suite? Discomfort flickered down her spine. She just knew that this was going to be expensive.

It had taken her a long time to get used to the shared dormitory she had slept in when she had first arrived in Rio, but when she finally found her own small apartment for the first few weeks she had actually missed the presence of the other girls. Now, though, she had to admit to relishing the privacy and the luxury of having her own bathroom.

'I asked David Bryant to find me somewhere cheap and convenient for his office,' she murmured as Dracco produced a key and unlocked the apartment's door.

Imogen could see his eyebrows rise as he listened to her.

'Well, he's complied with both those instructions,' he informed her. 'His office isn't that far away, and you're staying here as my guest.'

'Your guest?'

Imogen froze on the spot, staring at him with wide eyes, whilst Dracco pushed the door to, enclosing them both in the intimacy of the empty hallway.

'Your guest?' Imogen repeated starkly. 'This is your apartment?'

'Yes,' Dracco confirmed. 'When David told me that you'd specified you wanted to stay somewhere close to his office I told him that you might as well stay here with me. After all, there's a great deal we need to discuss…and not just about your inheritance.'

He was, Imogen recognised, looking pointedly at her left hand, the hand from which she had removed the wedding ring he had placed on it, throwing it as far as she could through the open taxi window on her way to Heathrow, too blinded by tears to see where it landed, and too sick at heart to care.

'You mean…' She paused and flicked her tongue tip over her suddenly dry lips, nervously aware of Dracco's iron gaze following her every movement.

'You mean our marriage?' she guessed shakily.

'I mean our marriage,' Dracco confirmed.

'You know,' he told her conversationally as he bent to pick up her lightweight case, 'for a woman who is still a virgin, you look…decidedly unvirginal.'

Imogen tried to convince herself that the rushing sensation of faintness engulfing her was caused by the airlessness of the hallway rather than by what Dracco had said, but still she heard herself demanding huskily, 'How…how do you know?'

'That you are still a virgin?' Dracco completed for

her. 'I know everything there is to know about you, Imo… After all, you are my wife…'

His wife!

Imogen felt sick; filled with a cold, shaky disbelief and an even colder fear. This was not what she had expected; what she had steeled herself to deal with.

During the long flight from Rio she had forced herself to confront the fear that had raised its threatening head in her nightmares in the days leading up to her journey. She had been terrified that somehow, totally against her will and all logic, if she were to see Dracco again she might discover a dangerous residue of her teenage love for him had somehow survived; that it was waiting, ready to explode like a time bomb, to destroy her new life and the peace of mind she had fought so hard for. But now! Now it wasn't love that Dracco was arousing inside her but a furious mixture of anger and hostility.

So she was still a virgin—was that a crime?

'You have no right to pry into my life, to spy on me,' she began furiously, but Dracco refused to allow her to continue.

'We are still married. I am still your husband; you are still my wife,' he pointed out coldly.

Imogen turned away to conceal her expression from him. Married in the eyes of the church, perhaps, but surely not in the eyes of the law, since their marriage had never been consummated. And that certainly didn't give Dracco the right to claim her as his wife in a voice that suggested… Wearily Imogen shook her head. Now she was letting her imagination run away with her. Thinking she had heard possessiveness in Dracco's voice.

His words had given her a shock. Why on earth hadn't Dracco had the marriage set aside? He, after all, loved another woman—her stepmother!

Even after all these years it still filled her with acute nausea and disgust to think of Dracco with Lisa. Her father's wife and the man her father had loved and valued so very much. Had Dracco slept with Lisa whilst her father was still alive? Had they…? Had he…? Unstoppably all the questions she had fiercely forbidden herself to even think before suddenly stormed through her. The images they were conjuring up sickened her, causing a red-hot boiling pain in her middle.

All those years ago, Dracco had implied to her that he was marrying her to protect her, when all he had really wanted to protect had been his own interests!

Tiredly Imogen closed her eyes. She had come to England for one purpose and one purpose only and that was to claim whatever money might be owing to her. And to persuade Dracco to transfer her interest in the business into the name of the charity so that in future it could benefit direct from her inheritance. Anything else…

'I haven't come back to discuss our marriage, Dracco.' Firmly Imogen took a deep breath, determined to take control of the situation. 'I've already written to David Bryant, explaining what I want, and that is—'

'To give away your inheritance to some charity,' Dracco interrupted her grimly. 'No, Imo,' he told her curtly. 'As your trustee, there's no way I would be fulfilling my moral obligation towards you if I agreed, and as your husband…'

She ached to be able to challenge him, to throw caution to the wind and demand furiously to know just when moral obligations had become important to him. But some inner instinct warned her against going too far. This wasn't how their interview was supposed to go. She was an adult now, on an equal footing with Dracco, and not a child whom he could dictate to.

'Legally the money is mine,' she reminded him, having mentally counted to ten and calmed herself down a little.

'Was yours,' Dracco corrected her harshly. 'You insisted that you wanted nothing to do with your inheritance—and you put that insistence in writing—remember.'

Imogen took another deep breath. The situation was proving even more fraught with difficulties than she had expected.

'I did write to Uncle Henry saying that,' she agreed, pausing to ask him quietly, 'When did he die? I had no idea.'

Dracco had turned away from her, and for a moment Imogen thought that he had either not heard her question or that he did not intend to answer it, but then without turning back to her he said coldly, 'He had a heart attack shortly after…on the day of our wedding.'

Horrified, Imogen could only make a soft, anguished sound of distress.

'Apparently he hadn't been feeling well before the ceremony,' Dracco continued as though he hadn't heard her. 'When he collapsed outside the church…' He stopped whilst Imogen battled against her shock. 'I went with him to the hospital. They hoped then… But he had a second attack whilst he was in Intensive Care which proved fatal.'

'Was it...?' Too shocked to guard her thoughts, Imogen blurted out shakily, 'Was it because of me? Because I...?'

'He had been under a tremendous amount of pressure,' Dracco told her without answering her anguished plea for reassurance. 'Your father's death had caused him an immense amount of work, and it seems that there had been certain warning signs of a heart problem which he had ignored. He wasn't a young man—he was ten years older than your father.' He paused and then said abruptly, 'He asked me to tell you how proud he had been to give you away.'

Tears blurred Imogen's eyes. She had a mental image of her father's solicitor on the morning of her wedding, dressed in his morning suit, his silver-grey hair immaculately groomed. In the car on the way to the church he had taken hold of her hand and patted it a little awkwardly. He had been a widower, like her father, with no children of his own, and Imogen had always sensed a certain shyness in his manner towards her. Her father had been a very loving man and she had desperately missed the father-daughter warmth of their relationship. She had known from the look in his eyes that, like her, Henry Fairburn had been thinking about her father on that day.

She had been sad to learn of his death from his nephew, but she had never imagined...

'If you're going to throw yourself into a self-indulgent bout of emotional guilt, I shouldn't bother,' Dracco was warning her hardly. 'His heart attack was a situation waiting to happen and would have happened whether or not you had been there.'

Somehow, instead of comforting and reassuring her, Dracco's blunt words were only making her feel worse, Imogen acknowledged.

'I don't want to argue with you, Dracco,' she said quietly. 'You are a wealthy man in your own right. If you could just see the plight of these children…'

'It is a good cause, yes, involvement with the shelter. My sources inform me that—'

'Your sources?' Imogen checked him angrily. 'You have no right—'

'Surely you didn't think I would allow you to simply disappear without any trace, Imo? For your father's sake, if nothing else; I owed it to him to—'

'I can't believe that even someone like you could stoop so low. To have me watched, spied on,' Imogen breathed bitterly.

'You're overreacting,' Dracco told her laconically. 'Yes, I made enquiries to ascertain where you were and what you were doing and with whom,' he agreed. 'Anyone would have done the same in the circumstances. You were a young, naïve girl of eighteen. Anything could have happened to you.'

He was frowning broodingly and Imogen had to shake herself free of the foolish feeling that he had been genuinely concerned about her.

'It doesn't matter what you say, Dracco, I'm not going to give up,' she warned him determinedly. 'The shelter needs money so desperately, and I warn you now that I'm prepared to do whatever it takes to make sure it gets mine.'

The silence that followed her passionate outburst caused a tiny sliver of apprehension to needle its way into Imogen's nervous system. Dracco was looking at her as though…as though…

Why had she never realised as a girl how very hawkish and predatory he could look, almost demonically so? She shivered and instantly blamed her reaction on the change of continent.

'Well, you're a woman now, Imo, and not a girl and, as you must have surely come to realise, nothing in this life comes without a price. You handed your inheritance over to me of your own accord. Now you wish me to hand it back to you, and not only the income which your share of the business has earned these last four years, but the future income of that share as well.'

'It belongs to me,' Imogen insisted. 'The terms of my father's will stated that it would become mine either on my thirtieth birthday or when I married, whichever happened first.'

'Mmm…' Dracco gave her a look she could not identify.

'You have told me what it is you want me to give you, Imo, but what are you prepared to give me in exchange for my agreement—supposing, of course, that I am prepared to give it?'

Imogen started to frown. What could she give him?

'We are still married,' Dracco was reminding her yet again. 'Our marriage was never annulled.'

Imogen's face cleared. 'You want an annulment,' she guessed, ignoring the sharp, unwanted stab of pain biting into her heart and concentrating instead on clinging determinedly to the relief she wanted to feel. 'Well, of course I will agree, and—'

'No, I do not want an annulment,' Dracco cut across her hurried assent. 'Far from it.'

CHAPTER TWO

'YOU don't want an annulment?' Imogen stared at Dracco as though she couldn't believe what she had heard. 'What...what do you mean?' she demanded.

She could hear the nervous stammer in her voice and despised herself for it. Dracco couldn't mean that he wanted to remain married to her. That was impossible. And just as impossible to accept was that sharp, shocking thrill of excitement his words had given her.

Dracco watched her carefully. As Imogen's trustee, it was his moral duty to safeguard her inheritance for her, to be worthy of the trust her father had placed in him, and that was something he fully intended to do. And if in helping her he was able to progress his own personal agenda, then so much the better! And as for him telling her just why...but, no...that was totally out of the question. Fate had generously dealt some very powerful cards into his hand, and now it was up to him to play them successfully. And he intended to play them and to win!

Imogen felt a nervous tremor run through her body as she waited for Dracco's response. His expression was hard and unreadable, his eyes cold and distant.

'I hope that you don't need me to remind you of just how much your father meant to me,' he began abruptly.

'I know that you married me because of his will,' Imogen responded ambiguously. She had wanted to give Dracco a subtle warning that she was not the naïve girl who had trusted him so implicitly any longer, but even she was shocked by the swiftness with which he decoded her message. Shocked and, if she was honest, just a little bit apprehensive when she saw the immediate and fearsome blaze of anger in the look he gave her.

'And what exactly is that supposed to mean?' Dracco challenged her softly.

Imogen took a deep breath. There was no way she was going to allow him to face her down! There was too much at stake. She had a responsibility to those who were dependent on her for her help.

'I was very young when I married you, Dracco,' she told him as calmly as she could. 'My father's will, as we both know, stipulated that I should have control of my share of the business upon my marriage. Naturally, since I was so young, I would have deferred to you where matters of business were concerned, so that in effect you would have had full control of the business—and the income it generated. Of course, had you chosen to sell the business and utilise the profits from that sale on your own behalf...'

'What?'

For a moment Dracco looked almost as though she had shocked him.

'If you are trying to imply that I married you for financial gain then let me tell you you're way off the mark. In fact, I am wealthier now than your father ever was—thanks, I have to admit, to everything he taught me.'

He was speaking to her as though he were admonishing a child, Imogen decided angrily.

'So why exactly did you marry me, then?' she asked him sharply.

'You know why.' He started to turn away from her so that she couldn't see his face, his voice becoming curt.

Imogen could sense that her question had made him uneasy in some way. Because he felt guilty? Well he might!

'Yes, I do, don't I?' Imogen agreed acerbically. 'My father—'

'Your father was a man I admired more than any other man I have ever met.' Dracco cut across what she had been about to say, his tone warning her against questioning the truth of his words. 'In fact, in the early years of our friendship, I often wished that he had been *my* father. I have never met a man I have respected or loved as much as I did John Atkins, Imogen. I felt proud to have his friendship and his trust. He was everything I myself most wanted to be. He was everything that my own father was not.'

He paused, whilst Imogen silently swallowed the huge lump of emotion in her throat.

Dracco's father had left his mother whilst Dracco had still been a baby; a gambler and a womaniser, he had been killed in a drunken brawl when Dracco had been in his early teens.

'I have never lost either my admiration or my love for your father, Imo, nor the wish that he and I might share a closer, more personal tie.' He paused meaningfully whilst Imogen fidgeted with anxiety. Whatever conditions Dracco imposed on his agreement to hand over her inheritance, Imogen knew that somehow she would have to meet them. There was no way she wanted to disappoint the nuns now, nor did she intend to do anything that would prevent her being able to improve the lot of those who were dependent on the shelter.

'Your father could never be my father, Imo, but he could be the grandfather of my son—our son,' Dracco told her meaningfully.

His son…their son. Stupefied, Imogen gaped at him. She couldn't possibly have heard him correctly.

'No!' she protested frantically. 'You can't mean it.' But she could see from his expression that he did, and her heart somersaulted inside her ribcage and then banged dizzyingly against her ribs themselves.

'No,' she whispered painfully. 'I can't. I won't! This is blackmail, Dracco,' she accused him. 'If you want a child so much—'

'I don't want "a" child, Imo,' he cut across her coolly. 'Haven't you been listening to what I said? What I want is your father's grandchild. My blood linked to his, and only you can provide me with that.'

'You're mad,' Imogen gasped. 'This is like something out of the Dark Ages…it's…I won't do it!' she told him fiercely.

'Then I won't give you your money,' Dracco informed her in a voice that was dangerously soft.

'You'll have to… I'll take you to court. I'll…' Imogen began wildly, but once again Dracco stopped her, shaking his head as he told her unkindly,

'Somehow I don't think a court would agree to you giving away your birthright. Especially if it was to be implied that part of the reason your father set up his will as he did was because he feared that you were not financially astute enough to protect your own interests.'

Imogen glared furiously at him. 'You wouldn't dare,' she began, but Dracco was smiling at her, a mocking smile that didn't touch his eyes as he told her softly, 'Try me!'

Imogen shook her head in angry disbelief. This was emotional manipulation at its worst. How on earth could she ever have loved Dracco? Right now she positively hated him.

'You can't do this,' she protested, her face raw with emotion as she told him shakily, 'If you could see these children—they have nothing, Dracco. Less than nothing. They need help so badly!'

'And they can have it, Imo,' Dracco told her calmly, 'but not from your inheritance. As your trustee, I cannot allow that, but—' he paused and looked at her, his penetrating gaze holding her own and refusing to let her look away '—but,' he repeated coolly, 'as your husband,' Dracco continued with a pseudo-gentleness that made her tense her stomach muscles against whatever it was he was going to say, 'as your husband,' he stressed with deliberate emphasis, 'I would be quite prepared to promise to pay one million pounds to the shelter now, and another one million when you give birth to our child.'

If Imogen hadn't already decided she hated Dracco she knew she would have done so now. How could he be so cynical, so cruel, so corrupt? Two million pounds! He must be rich indeed if he could afford to part with so much money so easily and just so that… He had loved and revered her father, she knew that, and she could even see too why he might want to have a child who carried her father's blood. But to go about it in such a way, when he knew that he would be forcing her to have sex with him and when he knew too that he didn't love her… Imogen couldn't stop herself from shuddering with angry loathing.

'I…I need time to think,' she told him defiantly.

'To think, or to run away again? I thought this charity was all-important to you, Imo, but it seems…'

'Stop it.' Covering her ears with her hands, Imogen turned away from him.

His cruelty appalled her but she couldn't stop herself from acknowledging the truth of what he was saying. When she thought about the difference his money would make to Rio's homeless street children Imogen knew that she could not possibly put her own needs before theirs.

'So do we have a deal—two million for your charity, a wife and, hopefully, your father's grandchild for me?'

Somehow Imogen managed not to show how desperately tempted she was to refuse. Summoning all her courage, she took a deep breath and agreed huskily, 'Yes.'

Bleakly Imogen stared out of the window of Dracco's car—a sleek silver BMW now and not the Daimler she remembered him driving—as they sped through the uniquely green English countryside. She had not asked Dracco where they were going, had not addressed any questions or conversation to him at all, in fact, since she had woken up in his city apartment earlier on in the day. His apartment but thankfully not his bed; no, she had been spared that at least for now, having slept alone in his guest room.

She had no idea where they were going and had no intention of asking. All Dracco had told her once he had ascertained that she was prepared to accede to the terms he had proposed to her—an agreement she had thrown at him with flashing eyes and an angrily set mouth as she tried to remind herself that his proposition surely demeaned him far more than it demeaned her—was that he was taking her to the house that was going to be her home.

'Stop behaving like a tragedy queen, Imo,' she heard him saying drily to her. 'It doesn't suit you and, besides, there's no need.'

'No need? After what you've done,' Imogen exploded.

'After what I've done?' Dracco checked her. 'I haven't done anything other than offer you a deal.'

'A deal!' Indignation flashed from Imogen's eyes. 'You're blackmailing me into having a child with you.' Quickly she turned away from him before he could sense the emotions she was struggling to overcome. 'What's going to happen once you have your child, Dracco?'

'What do you think is going to happen?' he challenged her sharply. 'No child of mine is going to be abandoned by either of its parents, Imogen.'

'You expect me to stay married to you?'

Surely that wasn't actually relief she could feel spreading through her tensed muscles?

'What I expect is that you and I will stay married to one another for just as long as our child needs us to be.

What were you expecting?' he demanded as he skilfully negotiated a tight bend.

Imogen shook her head, not wanting him to see how relieved she was that he wasn't going to try to separate her from her child, to send her away whilst he brought it up alone. Because she knew that, no matter what she might think about Dracco himself, no matter how much she might loathe and hate him for what he was doing, she would never be able to walk away from her baby.

She frowned as she suddenly recognised the countryside they were driving through, her heart starting to beat increasingly heavily as the road dropped down into the village where she had grown up. At the end of the village street Dracco turned left. The lane started to climb steeply and, even though it had been four years since she had last travelled down it, Imogen remembered every inch of it. It had been down this road that Dracco had driven her to school; down this road that he had driven her when he had come to fetch her the day her father had died; down this road she had travelled on her way to her wedding.

'You've bought our old house.' She said it as a statement rather than a question, her voice flat as she fought to control her emotions.

'I was already negotiating for it before our wedding,' Dracco answered her unemotionally. 'It was supposed to be a surprise wedding present for you. I knew how much you hated the idea of Lisa selling it. By the time it became obvious that you weren't going to be around to collect any wedding presents from me or anyone else, it was too late to pull out of the deal.' He gave a small dismissive shrug. 'I suppose I could have put it back on the market, but...'

Dracco had turned into the house's familiar drive and for a moment, as the car crunched over the gravel and came to a halt outside the front door, Imogen almost felt that if she closed her eyes and then opened them again she would see her father come hurrying towards her.

But her father was dead, and something inside her had died now as well.

'It still looks just the same,' she told Dracco distantly as they both got out of the car. He was a stranger to her, a man she loathed, and yet tonight he would...

Whilst she fought to control the shudders of fear that rocked her Dracco was unlocking the front door.

'Well, you'll find there have been some changes,' he warned her casually. 'I left your father's room as it was, but...' He paused and turned away from her, his voice suddenly shadowed and edged with an emotion she couldn't analyse. 'I haven't really used the house much myself. However, I have made some changes to some of the other rooms.'

When she looked questioningly at him he turned to face her fully and told her bluntly, 'I didn't think that either of us would want to use the rooms that had been your parents', so I had a new master-bedroom suite built on—and the conservatory your father once told me your mother had always wanted. He didn't have the heart to add it after her death, but I thought...' He stopped, his mouth compressing, pushing open the front door without enlightening her as to what his thoughts had been.

Imogen discovered that she was shaking as she followed him inside. It had been down these stairs that she had semi-stumbled on the way to her wedding, her whole world destroyed by Lisa's cruelty, and down them too that she had run in her haste to escape from Dracco and her marriage to him.

Her tastes had changed and matured in the last few years, and she recognised with a sharp pang of pain just how old-fashioned and, yes, shabby the dark red stair carpet her mother had chosen looked. She could almost feel how unloved and desolate the whole house was. Dust motes danced in the sunshine and she could see a film of it lying on the table beneath the ornate Venetian wall mirror that her parents had bought on their honeymoon.

Her mother had been a wonderful homemaker before her illness had struck her down and suddenly Imogen discovered that her own inner eye was itching to bring the house back to life, to turn it back to the love-filled home she could remember. Irritated by her own vulnerability, she demanded sharply of Dracco, 'Why exactly have you brought me here? Apart from the obvious reason, of course.' She added acerbically, 'I have to admit that I'm surprised you don't actually want to conceive this child in my father's bed.'

She stopped in mid-sentence, shocked into silence by the look in his eyes. It was far more dangerous than any verbal warning could have been.

'I have brought you here because this will be your home from now on,' Dracco told her levelly, once he had forced her to drop her gaze from his.

'But you don't live here?' Imogen guessed, thinking about the dust she had seen.

'I haven't been doing,' Dracco agreed. 'There wasn't

any point. But now… A city apartment isn't, in my opinion, the right place to bring up a child.'

'But you will still be spending some time in the city?' Imogen pressed him. Please God, let him say that he would; let him say too that his visits here to the house, to her, and to the bed he was forcing her to share with him, would be infrequent and of short duration.

But instead of answering her directly he surprised her by asking softly, 'What exactly is it about sex that you find so threatening, Imo?'

'Nothing! I don't,' she denied quickly, knowing that her face was burning hotly with a self-consciousness that he had to have seen before she turned defensively away from him. 'It isn't the sex,' she denied doggedly, 'it's you…and the way…'

'I don't believe you,' Dracco told her. 'For a woman of your age still to be a virgin suggests…'

'Suggests what?' Imogen immediately challenged him. 'That I'm choosy about who I give my…' My love, she had been about to say, but she quickly corrected herself and said instead, 'Myself to.'

'Suggests that you're afraid of something,' Dracco continued smoothly, as though she hadn't interrupted him. 'Are you, Imo? Are you afraid?'

'No,' she denied vehemently. But she knew that she was lying. She was afraid. She was very afraid. To her the physical act of sex was inextricably linked with the emotion of love, and she was desperately, mortally afraid that…

That what? That being forced to have sex with Dracco to produce the child he wanted would somehow force her to love him again? How could it?

Last night, lying awake in Dracco's guest room, she had told herself that what she was sacrificing was nothing weighed against what the charity would be gaining and that she was too old to have any right to start feeling sorry for herself. But no amount of trying to be logical about what had happened had helped to ease the sharp, stark pain in her heart—or the fear that accompanied it.

As she moved away from Dracco and walked down the hallway, instinctively heading for her father's study, she could hear him saying wryly, 'A team of cleaners from the village comes in once a month to go over the whole place and I asked them to stock up the fridge and freezer. If their shopping is of the same calibre as their cleaning it might be as well to check the fridge. I have booked a table for dinner at Emporio's for tonight. I trust you do still like Italian food?'

'You're taking me out for dinner?' Imogen couldn't keep the cynicism out of her voice. 'Why not just take me straight to bed? Why waste time—and money? After all, you've already committed yourself to paying two million for it.'

'Stop that at once.'

Imogen gasped as Dracco crossed the distance that separated them with startling speed, taking hold of her forearms, his lean fingers biting hard into her vulnerable flesh as he gave her a small shake.

'You're my wife, Imogen, not some paid harlot. And if I choose to woo you—'

'Woo me!' Imogen could feel the hysterical laughter bubbling up inside her. 'Why on earth would you want to do that?' she challenged him acidly. 'All you really want is a child, my father's grandchild! You can achieve that without going to the expense of buying me dinner. After all, you don't care whether I'm willing or not!'

Dracco released her so quickly that Imogen felt the unwanted shock of his withdrawal from her right through her body. The shaming knowledge that a tiny part of her was actually daring to miss the warm male touch of Dracco's hands on her arms infuriated and frightened her. She told herself that it was just her memory playing tricks, reminding her of a time when she had welcomed and wanted his touch. Welcomed and wanted it! Craved it, ached for it, hungered for it and for him—that was a far more accurate description. Abruptly Imogen dragged her mind back to the present, wincing a little as she saw the furious look Dracco was giving her.

He shook his head, his mouth compressing. 'What I want, and what I intend for this child—*our* child—is that it is born if not out of mutual love then at least out of mutual pleasure.'

His words shocked her, almost thrilled her in some atavistic and explosively dangerous way.

Recklessly Imogen flung back her head and demanded, 'And how is that going to happen when there is no way I could ever want you?'

She could almost hear the seconds ticking by as Dracco looked at her. What could he see…what was he looking for? Her tongue snaked out and touched her suddenly dry lips. Dracco's diamond-hard gaze fastened on her small betraying gesture, seizing on it even more fiercely than his hands had grasped her only minutes earlier. Imogen could almost feel the physical effect of his gaze on her; on her mouth; her body; her senses!

'There is nothing you could ever do that could make

me want you, Dracco. Do you hear me?' The excited fury in her own reiteration frightened her but she refused to allow herself to acknowledge either her fear or her folly.

'Are you challenging me, Imogen?' Dracco asked her softly. 'Because if you want me to prove you wrong I can promise you that I am more than willing to do so. Very much more than willing,' he emphasised with meaningful deliberation.

Imogen's heightened senses relayed to her every aspect of what was happening: the scent of the dust in the air, the limpid warmth of the sun streaming in through the window, which in no way could match the white heat of the fury she could see burning in Dracco's eyes. She shivered, but not with cold, as feelings she had thought long dead sprang to life inside her.

'No!' she whispered painfully beneath her breath. No! It was over. Dead, done… She did not love Dracco any more and she wasn't going to allow herself to do so ever again.

Drawing a shaky breath, she met the look he was giving her.

'You couldn't,' she denied, making herself believe it.

'No? Watch me!' Dracco breathed. 'Just watch me, Imogen. And when you're lying in my bed, my arms, beneath my body, crying out for my possession, wanting me, I shall remind you of this moment.'

CHAPTER THREE

IMOGEN turned away from the window of her childhood bedroom and glanced at her watch.

Seven-thirty; soon she would have to go downstairs and join Dracco, who had warned her that unless she was ready to go out for dinner with him by eight o'clock he would personally 'escort' her downstairs.

'Why are you doing this?' she had demanded in furious frustration.

'Why are you?' he had countered with a coolness that had made her grind her teeth in impotent rage.

'You know why I'm doing it. I don't have any choice.'

'Of course you do,' he had returned promptly. 'You could choose to simply walk away if you wished to do so.'

'The shelter needs money—you know that,' Imogen had argued bitterly.

That was true, and what was also true was that she didn't think she could live with herself if she didn't do everything she could to help. Perhaps a part of her determination to do so had its roots in the fact that she felt guilty because she had withheld her financial help for so long, she acknowledged. But it had taken her a long time to stop being afraid of the power the past had over her; to stop being afraid of the love she had had for Dracco. Now she had overcome that fear!

But to allow Dracco to consummate their marriage; to have his child! Unwillingly Imogen's gaze was drawn back to her bedroom window. Did she really have the resolve, the courage to do that?

It had been from this window that she had watched so many times for her father to come home. She had knelt on the window seat, her elbows on the sill propping up her head as she strained her ears and her eyes for the familiar sound and sight of her father's car. The moment she could hear it she had dashed downstairs, ready to fling herself into his arms just as soon as she could.

Even during the dark days of her mother's final illness her father had never failed to give her the loving reassurance of his time and attention.

And then had come the darker days of his marriage to Lisa, when it had so often been Dracco she had turned to for comfort. Dracco she had waited impatiently to see arriving at the house from the sanctuary of her bedroom.

Her father had loved this house. He had once told her that to him it epitomised everything that a family home should be.

'One day you will bring your children here to see me, Imo,' he had often told her as she grew up.

He had been looking forward to becoming a grandfather.

The scene in front of Imogen's eyes began to blur.

A child. A child that was both a part of him and of herself and Dracco. Her father would have loved that so much, cherished that child so much.

A child. Dracco's child. How often had she sat at this very window and fantasised about that happening; about

Dracco loving her; about that love resulting in the birth of their baby?

Dracco loving her! Angrily Imogen shook away her threatening emotional tears. Dracco did not love her. He simply wanted to share a blood tie with her father. He had told her so.

And yet as she turned away from the bedroom window she could still see so vividly in her mind's eye the three of them walking together up the drive, Dracco, herself and, between them, the dark-haired green-eyed boy-child who shared his father's strong bone-structure and his grandfather's loving smile.

'I must be mad,' Imogen whispered reprovingly to herself as she snatched up her jacket and her bag and headed for her bedroom door.

There was no way she could ever willingly do what Dracco was forcing on her. And surely no way either that she could ever deny that fierce tug of maternal love she had felt so very sharply for the child her own treacherous imagination had conjured up.

When she opened her door she saw Dracco advancing along the landing towards her.

Unlike her, he had changed his clothes, removing the city suit he had been wearing and putting on in its place a more casual pair of cotton chinos and a short-sleeved shirt.

England must have been having a good summer, Imogen acknowledged absently as her gaze slid helplessly along the length of Dracco's bare bronzed arms. There had always been something about his arms that fascinated her, something that had sent a shower of excited girlish sensuality shivering over her skin. In those days, just the thought of Dracco's arms closing round her, holding her in the tender and protective embrace which had been all her innocent mind had then been able to conjure up, had been enough to set off that hot, aching, melting feeling in the pit of her stomach.

Later, as she grew older, it hadn't been so much Dracco's arms holding her she had fantasised about as his hands, touching her, caressing her, stroking and arousing her willing flesh with the kind of intimate and wildly dangerous touch that even in the privacy of her own bed had made her face burn with hot, guilty, excited desire.

He had, Imogen guessed, not only changed his clothes but showered as well, which made her feel uncomfortably aware of the fact that she was still wearing the clothes she had flown into Heathrow in. She had refused to allow herself to change out of a stubborn determination to show him just how unimportant either his opinion of her or his company was. Right now, however, it wasn't a sense of satisfaction in her own stubbornness she was experiencing but rather a very unwanted feeling of gritty discomfort, and general grubbiness, which caused her to reach up defensively to rake her fingers through her tangled curls.

'Too busy to have time to get changed? Never mind, I'm sure Luigi will understand,' Dracco commented.

'You've told Luigi that you...we're...'

'I've told him that you're going to be my dinner guest, yes,' Dracco confirmed. 'I just hope you still like pear and almond tart and honey ice cream.'

Ignoring his dry reference to her teenage love of her

favourite local Italian restaurant's pudding, Imogen demanded wildly, 'What else have you told him?'

Dracco gave a small shrug. 'Nothing,' he denied.

As she absorbed his response Imogen struggled to understand why instead of feeling relief that Dracco hadn't made any kind of public statement about their marriage what she actually felt was a kind of anger.

'But you are going to have to say something?' she persisted. 'We can't just suddenly start living together as a married couple.'

Dracco gave another dismissive shrug. 'As to that, I shall tell people what they will want to hear.'

'Which is?' Imogen challenged him.

'Which is that there has been a rapprochement between us, a mutual agreement with the benefit of hindsight and maturity that we wish to give our marriage a second chance.'

'A second chance?' Imogen couldn't help querying, and then wished that she had not when she saw the look Dracco was giving her.

'Most of them will assume, no doubt, that we were lovers before our marriage, and somehow I doubt that you will want people to know that you are still a virgin.'

Imogen could feel her face reddening.

'Don't flatter yourself that my virginity has anything to do with you!' She threw the words recklessly at him, unaware of just how they might be interpreted or what they might reveal. 'The fact that I haven't…that I'm… Well, that's my business and has nothing to do with anyone else.'

Dracco was already heading for the stairs and automatically Imogen walked with him.

'Just a minute,' he demanded as they reached the hallway.

Warily, Imogen waited as he reached into his pocket and withdrew a small box.

'You're going to need this,' he told her coolly. 'I notice that you aren't wearing the original. This one doesn't have the benefit of a clerical blessing, and I had to guess at the size. You're more slender than you were…'

Without giving her the opportunity to take the box from him, he flipped open the lid, revealing a gold wedding band so similar to the first one he had given her that Imogen had to suppress a superstitious feeling that it was the same ring.

And with it was something she had desperately wished she had not had to leave behind when she had run away—the engagement ring she had not been wearing on the day of her marriage that Dracco had had made for her. It incorporated in an elegant modern setting the three diamonds that had originally been in her mother's engagement ring. Those stones meant so much to her that now as she stared at it, tears stung Imogen's eyes.

'My ring,' she whispered.

'It might be a little bit too big now,' Dracco warned her as she reached for it. He forestalled her and took hold of her hand.

Imogen could feel herself starting to tremble. Against her will she went back in time; she was in church, waiting for Dracco to place his ring on her finger.

Now, as he slid the cold metal over her knuckle, she could remember exactly how she had felt, how much she had wanted to believe that their marriage was more to him than simply a business arrangement.

He was right—the engagement ring was slightly loose, she reflected shakily as he placed it on her finger. Suddenly she was finding it extraordinarily difficult to breathe properly. Her chest felt tightly constricted, her heart was hammering ferociously against her ribs. As though it was happening in slow motion, she was aware of Dracco watching her, waiting, and then lifting her hand towards his mouth.

'No.'

Imogen pulled frantically away from him as the denial was torn from her tense throat. In church he had kissed her hand, the warmth of his lips brushing her cold fingers, making her tremble violently, her whole body ablaze with the intensity of her longing for him as her lover. Yet despite that feeling she had not been able to stop herself from asking him the question that had destroyed her foolish illusions. What would have happened if she had said nothing? But no, she must not even think of asking herself that. Would she really have wanted to live in ignorance of the truth? No, of course she wouldn't!

Unable to bring herself to look at Dracco, she hurried towards the front door. The warm evening sun dazzled her for a moment as they walked outside. She could smell the scent of the roses from the rose bed close to the front door. They had been her mother's favourite flowers and for a moment a wave of nostalgia and pain pierced her. This house held so many memories, so much of her past. The thought of her own child growing up here was unbearably poignant.

Locked into her thoughts, she stood stiffly, staring unseeingly into the distance. The future, with all the hideous complications and emotional pain it now threatened, lay darkly ahead of her. Marriage in these modern times was not necessarily for life, but a child, the bond between parent and child, mother and child, that most certainly was. For her, at least.

'If you're having second thoughts, I shouldn't,' she heard Dracco telling her caustically.

Imogen frowned as the sound of Dracco's voice pierced the bubble surrounding her. For a moment it had almost seemed as though Dracco was actually afraid that she *might* change her mind. He must want this child very badly. Was that the reason he and Lisa had not married, because he had not wanted his child to be her child? Imogen didn't like herself very much for the sharp thrill of pleasure the thought gave her.

'Ah, but you have not changed at all; you are even more beautiful, even more *bella*, than ever!' Luigi was telling Imogen in a voice vibrant with emotion as he showed them to their table.

'If she has not changed then how can she be more *bella*, Luigi? Dracco was demanding drily.

'Then she was a beautiful girl,' Luigi responded with aplomb. 'Now…' His dark eyes glowed with appreciation and approval as he surveyed Imogen in the kind of way that only an Italian male could get away with. 'Now she is a beautiful woman! And what a woman! *Mamma mia!* Ah, but you are one lucky man, my friend, to have such a beautiful wife.'

So Luigi had remembered that they were married!

'Well, it is just as well that one of us can remember what she looked like after one of your lessons in how to eat spaghetti.' Dracco grinned, the dryness of his voice so at odds with the genuine amusement in his eyes that Imogen found somehow she was unable to drag her own gaze away from his face. A face that suddenly, dangerously, looked so much like the face she remembered from her teens, his eyes warm and teasing, his mouth curved into that sizzlingly sexy smile that had made her toes curl up in delight. Luigi's had always been her favourite restaurant, a place she had associated with the happy times in her life.

'I have saved you a special table.' Luigi was beaming as he led them through the busy restaurant to the table that had always been her father's favourite.

A huge lump rose in Imogen's throat. Impulsively she threw her arms around Luigi's rotund frame and gave him a swift hug.

Luigi was hugging her back enthusiastically, then he let her go with unexpected suddenness, stepping back from her whilst apologising to Dracco.

Frowning, Imogen looked from Dracco's now set face to Luigi's apologetic one, unable to fathom out quite what was happening.

'I was forgetting for a moment that you are no longer a little girl but a married woman,' Luigi told her, but it was Dracco he was looking at as he spoke.

As they sat down and Luigi hurried off to get them menus Dracco told her quietly, 'I would prefer it if you didn't flirt with other men.'

'Flirt.' Imogen repeated in disbelief. 'I wasn't flirting. I was just...' She stopped. Why was she bothering to defend herself? She had done nothing wrong. All she had done was to hug Luigi, and for Dracco to accuse her of flirting was totally ridiculous!

'You may still be a virgin, Imo,' Dracco told her, leaning across the table so that no one else could hear what he was saying, 'but that does not make you totally naïve. You're a married woman…my wife.'

'I can't believe I'm hearing this,' Imogen cut in stormily. 'I was just hugging Luigi, that's all. It was nothing at all.'

'It may be nothing to you,' Dracco stopped her grimly. 'But it's a hell of a lot more than I've ever had from you.'

'You're different,' Imogen returned smartly, and then wished she hadn't as she saw his expression. Her stomach writhed nervously.

'Yes. I am different,' Dracco agreed. 'I'm your husband.' He broke off as a young waiter brought them their menus, waiting until he had gone before telling her coldly, 'Before tomorrow night I expect you to move your things into the master bedroom.'

Imogen wondered if he knew just what effect his words had had on her, how shocked and, yes, terrified they had made her. In an effort to conceal those feelings she picked up her menu and, hiding behind it, told him flippantly, 'So much for the threatened seduction.'

When there was no immediate response she carefully lowered her menu, reflecting gleefully that she had at least scored one hit against that impenetrable, tough armour that had both repelled and attracted her for as long as she had known him. But then she saw his face, and the hand holding her menu shook betrayingly.

'Oh, that wasn't a threat, Imo. It was a promise. A promise that I shall do such things to you and for you as to make you scream my name with longing in the darkness of the night; make you ache with your need for my possession; make you—'

'No!'

The denial was strangled in Imogen's throat as the young waiter suddenly appeared and nervously asked if they were ready to order. She knew that her face was burning scarlet with colour, her thoughts a wild, chaotic stampede of disbelief and fury.

How could Dracco say such things to her one minute and the next be calmly discussing with their waiter what exactly the 'specials' were, and whether or not they had a particular wine he wanted?

'You will like this wine, Imo,' he told her calmly once they were alone. 'Your father introduced me to it. It was produced in the same year as you. And, like you…' he continued, his voice dropping to a slow, sensual rasp that licked against Imogen's raw nerve endings in the same way her tormented, traitorous imagination was telling her that his tongue might rasp against the intimate sensitivity of her skin. 'But no!' he told her softly. 'I shall not tell you now what characteristics it shares with you!'

Imogen had ordered mussels as her first course, and her mouth watered when they arrived, cooked in Luigi's special sauce. They had eaten simply and cheaply in Rio, and she was unaware of the way Dracco was watching her as she ate her food with almost childlike enjoyment.

He wondered how she would react if she knew what he was really thinking; feeling; wanting! He took a deep swallow of his wine; like Imogen herself, it had an allure that drew one back almost compulsively to it. His mouth twisted bitterly. It was probably just as well that she didn't know just what was going on inside his head, or inside his body. If she did she would probably run a mile, or rather six thousand miles or so, back to Rio.

Dracco's eyes grew bleak when they rested on Imogen's downbent head as she mopped up the last of her sauce with a piece of bread. If she hadn't come back of her own accord he had had plans in hand for bringing her home. And now that she was home it was up to him to make sure that she stayed there.

As Imogen lifted her head, as if somehow conscious that he was watching her, Dracco dropped his. Observing Dracco's hooded gaze fixed on his plate, Imogen frowned, wondering why on earth she had thought he was looking at her.

'Good; you enjoy that?' Luigi was demanding, beaming as he removed her empty plate.

'Scrumptious,' Imogen assured him, reverting to her favourite childhood word as she started to smile at him and then stopped, the smile which had begun to dimple her mouth fading as she glanced warily at Dracco. Was a married woman allowed to smile at another man? And why should she care anyway whether Dracco approved of her behaviour or not? She didn't, and there was certainly no way she was ever going to allow him to dictate to her what she did!

'Dracco, and Imogen, isn't it? I thought I recognised you. My goodness, what a surprise!'

The angry turbulence of Imogen's thoughts came to

an abrupt halt as she stared into the familiar face of one of her stepmother's closest friends.

Her stepmother and Miranda Walker had been tennis partners and had both had membership at an exclusive local health club. Imogen had liked Miranda only marginally less than she had liked her stepmother. Miranda's husband, she remembered, had spent a lot of time working abroad, but he was obviously back at home now.

It was a shock to see someone so closely and so unpleasantly connected with the past so soon after her return, although she admitted she should perhaps have expected it, as Emporio's had always been the town's most favoured restaurant.

She could almost feel the speculation emanating from Miranda as she continued to stand at their table, ignoring her husband's obvious desire to move away.

'Are we to take it that the two of you are back together?' Miranda was asking with a suggestive coyness that nauseated Imogen. 'I always did think it was rather impetuous of you to run away from him like that, darling.' She laughed as she gave Imogen a fake smile accompanied by a sharply assessing look. 'Wait until I see Lisa. Fancy her not telling me.'

When neither Imogen nor Dracco said anything Miranda demanded excitedly, 'She doesn't know, does she?' There was a pause. 'Oh, dear! She isn't going to be very pleased. She's still in the Caribbean and won't be back for another week yet, will she?' She directed this question at Dracco.

'Excuse me.' Without waiting to hear what Dracco's response was, Imogen got up and headed for the ladies' cloakroom.

It was stupid of her to feel shocked, and as for that daunting, aching pain that was draining her, well, there was no way that could be betrayal. She already knew what the score was; knew how cynically determined Dracco could be to have his cake and eat it.

As she reached the sanctuary of the rest room, and started to run restoring cool water over her wrists, she told herself that she didn't care what his relationship with Lisa was any more. After all, there was only one reason she was here with him tonight and it had nothing to do with any personal desire to be with him. It was because of the children, the shelter, that was all! Just as he was here with her not because he wanted her, but because he wanted her child.

She ought, she told herself judicially, to feel sorry for Lisa.

So far as Imogen was concerned, the whole tone of Miranda's conversation had given away the relationship between Dracco and her stepmother. Had he told Lisa what he was planning to do? Somehow Imogen rather suspected that he had not.

Carefully drying her hands, she took a deep breath. It was time for her to go back.

There was no sign of Miranda or her husband when Imogen returned to the table. Without saying anything, she sat down. Her head had started to ache badly. She felt almost as though she was about to come down with a bad case of flu; her throat felt tight and sore, she felt slightly sick, and—

Imogen gave a small gasp as the whole room spun round.

'Imogen. Are you all right?'

Somehow Dracco was standing next to her.

'No,' she told him muzzily. 'I feel sick.'

Frowning, Dracco glanced from Imogen's barely touched glass of wine to her white face.

'Let's get you outside. You might feel better in the fresh air.'

As Imogen felt him moving closer to her she instinctively shrank away from him. Listening to Miranda had underlined for her all the most unpalatable aspects of her situation that she least wanted to think about. The hands that Dracco was reaching out to her had touched Lisa, her enemy; the voice expressing distant concern for her had no doubt whispered soft, passionate words of desire and wanting to her stepmother. The act of procreation he would share with her would be a cold, mechanical, loveless thing, very different from his physical intimacy with Lisa... Imogen shuddered, unable to control her revulsion. No wonder she felt so sick.

Imogen saw in Dracco's eyes his reaction to her instinctive rejection of him. Bending his head, he muttered angrily to her, 'We're supposed to be giving our marriage a second chance. Remember?'

'You don't want to give our marriage a second chance,' Imogen managed to hiss swiftly. 'You just want...'

Somehow Dracco had shepherded her to the door, and was opening it. Greedily Imogen gulped in the fresh evening air. Her dizziness was beginning to clear, her nausea retreating.

'Want to tell me what all that was about?'

Warily she looked at Dracco. 'I felt sick, that's all. Surely it's hardly surprising in the circumstances.

Nothing's changed, has it, Dracco?' she challenged him bitterly.

'Did you expect it to have done? Don't you think that's rather naïve?'

The hard expression she could see in his eyes made her muscles clench. He wasn't even remotely ashamed of what he was doing.

'You didn't tell me that Lisa was still living locally,' she told him bitterly. He was shrugging dismissively as though he found her anger an irrelevance, and his attitude goaded her into a fiercely hostile reaction.

'Lisa was married to my father. She's—'

He interrupted her. 'I know what Lisa is, Imo.'

'You know but you don't care, do you?' Imogen couldn't stop herself from saying the words, even though she could already see the truth in his eyes.

Just as she could hear the anguish shaking through her own voice.

She heard Dracco mutter something under his breath before telling her grimly, 'You always were too damned sensitive for your own good. And too damned...' Whatever he had been about to say was lost as the restaurant door opened and another couple emerged, pausing to give them a briefly curious look, no doubt able to sense the hostility and tension crackling between them. Taking hold of Imogen's arm, Dracco informed her curtly, 'This isn't the place for a discussion of this nature,' as he propelled her to where he had parked his car.

'Let go of me,' Imogen demanded through gritted teeth as they reached it. 'I can't bear to have you touching me, Dracco. Not now. Not after...' She stopped as she saw the intensity of the fury darkening his eyes as he opened the car door for her.

Logic told her that he wasn't responsible for Miranda's appearance at the restaurant, but he was responsible for the fact that he had betrayed her father's trust and was now callously using her. How she hated him, loathed him, despised him!

She took a deep breath as she tried to close her mind against the unwelcome knowledge of just how much she herself hurt, how raw and painful her emotions felt. It was humiliating to know that he could still affect her like this, even now, as an adult.

Wrapped up in her thoughts, Imogen didn't realise that they had reached the house until Dracco leaned across her to open the car door. This close she could see the fine, soft hairs on his arm, see the taut structure of the sinew and muscle beneath his skin, smell the soap he used, clean and cool—and something else. Something that made her flesh come out in a rash of goosebumps, whilst her nostrils quivered with delicate female recognition of the potent maleness of his personal body scent, hot, musky and dangerous. Her eyes widened as she made an involuntary movement that somehow brought her body into immediate physical contact with his bare arm, her breasts pressing against it as though… Hot-faced, Imogen refused to acknowledge just what the insolent peaking of her nipples might be trying to proclaim as she pulled quickly back from him.

Ignoring him, she climbed out of the car, heading for the house. Behind her she could hear Dracco's footsteps crunching across the gravel. A sudden tremor of panic flared through her and she started to walk faster, only to realise that she couldn't get into the house without him, since she didn't possess a key.

Standing to one side, she waited for him to open the door. For the rest of her life she would hate him for what he was doing to her! Imogen could feel her hands balling into angry fists.

'Imo.'

Imogen felt Dracco's hands resting on her shoulders.

'Don't you dare touch me!' she spat furiously at him. But as she tried to pull away he refused to let her go, following the movement she made, so that she was backed up against the door.

'Imo, listen.'

'No.'

There was just time for Imogen to see the furious brilliant glitter of his eyes before his head blotted out the light as he grated angrily against her ear, 'Well, if you won't listen then perhaps this is the only way of communicating with you.'

She gasped once in outraged protest that he should dare to ignore her wishes, and then a second time, in shocked disbelief, as she felt the heat of his breath searing across her lips. And then she was not capable of gasping at all, as her breath was snatched away and with it her ability to think, and reason, and reject, because every fibre of her being, every single cell she possessed, was fully occupied in dealing with the nuclear fall-out caused by Dracco's kiss.

Its effect on her anger was like hot chocolate being poured on ice cream, she reflected dizzily, like every feeling, every pleasure, every delicious taste she had ever experienced magnified a million times over. It was like nothing she had ever dreamed of experiencing and at the same time it was exactly…exactly what she had always dreamed it might be, only more so…much more so.

Somehow the original furious anger of Dracco's kiss had turned to a sensuous, coaxing, lingering caress that involved not just their lips but their tongues as well. And their hands too, Imogen was discovering as her body melted beneath Dracco's touch, then burned, flamed and hungered…

'You kiss me like you've been aching for me for half a lifetime. Starving for me.' She could hear Dracco groaning as his hands ran fierce hot shudders of delight over her skin. He drew her body into his own, fitting her against him, fitting himself against her, into the cupped eagerness of her parted thighs.

As the full meaning of his words penetrated the sensual daze of her feelings Imogen suddenly realised what she was doing, and with a sharp cry she pulled away from him.

'I'm not starving—for anything, and certainly not for you,' she told him in passionate denial. 'But the street children of Rio are starving, Dracco, and that's why I'm here, because of them and only because of them.'

White-faced, she confronted him across the small space that now divided them.

His face was in the shadows, so that she could not see his expression, only sense his hunting immobility and know that he was watching her, making her feel vulnerable and exposed. She waited for him to voice some cutting put-down, but instead of retaliating in any way he simply turned from her and went to unlock the front door.

All the way up the stairs Imogen expected to hear him if not following her then at least commanding her to stop, but there was only silence. She didn't turn round to see why, though. She did not dare.

CHAPTER FOUR

IMOGEN was deeply asleep, lost in the most wonderful dream.

'Mmm.' Languorously she reached up to curl her hand against the firm, smooth skin at the nape of Dracco's neck. She could feel the silky thickness of his hair as she burrowed her fingertips into it, firmly drawing his head closer to her own.

'You know this is very dangerous, don't you?' Dracco was warning her in a sensually raw whisper, the sound caressing her skin with deliciously rough male warmth.

'I like danger,' Imogen responded provocatively as she looked up into the deep sea-green depths of his eyes. 'And I like it even more when that danger is you,' she added.

A small bubble of laughter gurgled in her throat as she saw the way Dracco was looking at her. It felt so good to be so at ease with him, so intimately aware of the special relationship they shared. At ease, and yet at the same time... A tiny thrill of wanton excitement shivered across her skin as she watched his eyes darken. Her own closed, her lips parting in eager anticipation of his kiss.

When it came the hot sweetness of it melted right through her body, touching every single nerve-ending, reaching into the deepest core of her, so that suddenly what they were doing was no longer a teasing game that she controlled, but a fierce, elemental need that controlled them both.

'Dracco!' Hungrily she reached out to drag him down against her naked body, driven to feel him against her, skin to skin, lips to lips, breath to breath! Helplessly her nails raked the firm flesh of his back as her body arched up against his, drawn into a tight, aching bow of longing.

As Dracco responded to her body's hungry demands he groaned her name against her lips. Imogen opened her eyes. Sunlight streamed in through her bedroom window, glinting on the gold of her wedding ring.

Dracco was holding her tightly now, his hands roving wantonly over her naked body with the powerful touch of a hungry sensualist, dipping lingeringly into her most secret places of delight, drawing from her a need to arouse him in the same way. Each kiss, each touch was taking her closer and closer to the shatteringly climactic culmination she knew was waiting for her, but as they did so somehow her joy was being overtaken by a fear that her happiness was about to be snatched away from her. A fear that made her cry out in anguish as she clung frantically to Dracco, desperately afraid that somehow she might lose him, lose his love.

'No!'

The sound of her own sharp moan of panic brought Imogen immediately out of her dream. For a few seconds she was still so wrapped up in it that it took her several deep breaths to realise just where she was. When she did she sat up in bed, reaching for her bedside light, illuminating the bedroom in a soft peachy glow. But nothing could warm the cold tentacles of dread reaching out to wrap themselves around her heart. She had been dreaming about Dracco, dreaming that he…that she… that they… Closing her eyes, Imogen hugged her arms around her body in an instinctive gesture of protection.

'Imogen, what's wrong? I heard you cry out.'

The sound of Dracco's voice as he thrust open her bedroom door and strode into her room made Imogen open her eyes immediately.

'Nothing. Nothing's wrong,' she denied tensely.

There was no way she could disclose to Dracco the content of her dream, nor exactly why she had given that anguished moan of distress.

'I heard you cry out,' Dracco persisted.

He was walking towards her bed as he spoke, and he was still fully dressed, although he had unbuttoned the top few buttons of his shirt and on the flesh they exposed Imogen could see the tangled criss-crossed darkness of his body hair.

Unable to drag her gaze away from it, she felt her stomach lurch. In her dream he had been totally naked. In her dream she had touched his skin, drawn her fingertips through that silky male covering of fine dark hair whilst her whole body quivered in thrilled sensual pleasure… Imogen shuddered.

What was happening to her? It had been years since she had fantasised about touching Dracco like that. She had been a mere girl then, sleeping in this very same bedroom. Was that it? Was it because she was sleeping in the room that had been hers as a girl that she had dreamed so inappropriately of the kind of intimacy with Dracco she most certainly no longer wanted? She was just beginning to relax into the security of finding a logical explanation for what had happened when she suddenly remembered how in her dream she had seen sunlight shining on her wedding ring.

A second shudder, even more apparent than her first, galvanised her body, bringing Dracco to the side of her bed, where he frowned down at her.

'Perhaps we should get Dr Armstrong to take a look at you,' he told her. 'You felt sick earlier on; now you're shivering.'

Imogen could feel her self-control starting to slip.

'There's nothing wrong with me. Apart from the fact that I'm being blackmailed into having sex with a man I don't want so that he can have the son he does want. But,' she added with angry sarcasm, 'I'm sure you aren't going to tell Dr Armstrong that. You're very good at not telling people things they ought to know, aren't you, Dracco?'

'And just what the hell do you mean?' he demanded.

'Work it out for yourself,' Imogen challenged him. When he continued to frown at her she flung at him bitterly, 'Somehow I don't imagine you've told Lisa about your plans for me. For the child you want me—*us*—to have,' she emphasised savagely. 'And...'

She took a deep breath, intending to remind him that he had also neglected to tell her, when he had originally proposed marriage to her, that he was already in love with her stepmother, but before she could do so he was interrupting her, exclaiming, 'No, I haven't. Why should I?'

How could he stand there and say that? Furiously Imogen confronted him.

'Why?' Imogen repeated in disbelief. Shaking her

head, she changed tack slightly, unable to trust herself to say what she was really feeling and settling instead for a quietly contemptuous, 'She's bound to find out, you know. Miranda will tell her.'

To her own shock she discovered that she was holding her breath, waiting, almost as though she was hoping that he would tell her Lisa was nothing to him now, that it was over between them. Was she really so frighteningly stupid, so crazily vulnerable?

'Our marriage, our relationship and the plans we make within it have nothing whatsoever to do with Lisa.'

'And you don't care what she thinks or feels about the situation?' Imogen challenged.

'My desire to have a child with your father's genes doesn't impact in any way at all on Lisa's life.'

'Nor on your relationship with her?' Imogen couldn't stop herself from persisting. There was a brief pause before Dracco answered.

'I know how you feel about Lisa, Imo, but you're an adult now. My relationship with her, as you term it, is what it is and cannot be changed. My feelings towards her haven't changed either, you know,' he told her as gently as he could.

Dracco frowned as he watched the look of anguished disbelief darkening Imogen's eyes. He knew how bitterly unhappy her stepmother had made her, and, as he had just told her, he liked Lisa as little now as he had done when John had first married her. In Dracco's eyes she was a shallow, selfish, greedy woman, but that did not alter the fact that, just as he had a responsibility towards Imogen, he also had a responsibility as one of the executors of Imogen's late father's will to ensure that Lisa received the biannual allowance she was entitled to. It was obvious, though, that Imogen was in no mood to listen to such logic.

Imogen felt as though someone was squeezing her lungs in a frighteningly painful grasp, making it almost impossible for her to breathe, but not impossible for her to feel. Oh, no, she could still do that! But why could she, when for the last four years she had believed that she no longer cared, that Dracco no longer had the power to hurt her, that her love for him had died along with her trust and respect?

'I think I hate you, Dracco,' she whispered savagely, correcting herself to tell him, 'No, I know I hate you.'

He was turning away from her and going to stand in front of her bedroom window, looking out into the darkness beyond it.

'Fine, you can hate me all you like,' he told her coolly, 'but you will still give me my son, Imo.'

Without giving her the opportunity to retaliate, he strode through her still open bedroom door, pulling it shut behind him.

As she glared at it, Imogen was not surprised to discover that she was shaking from head to foot—with burning hot rage. How could he; how dared he stand there and tell her he expected her to bear his child when he had just admitted that there was another woman in his life? And not just any 'other' woman, but her stepmother Lisa!

Of course, it was impossible for her to go back to sleep. A glance at her watch told her that it was only just gone midnight and she realised that Dracco must have heard her cry out on his own way to bed. How could she have allowed herself to dream about him like that? What part of her subconscious had produced those treacherous images? And why was the discovery that Dracco still loved Lisa making her feel not just that she wanted to hurl her furious contempt at him for his betrayal of her own youthful adoration, but also so filled with pain and despair?

Anyone would think that she still loved him, she derided herself warningly. And of course she did not!

If only she were back in Rio. There she had been safe; there she had been far too busy to think about Dracco. She made a small restless movement in her bed as her conscience prodded her for the lie she was telling herself. 'All right, then,' she muttered beneath her breath, 'so I did think about him occasionally.'

You thought about him and you dreamed about him, that same voice reminded her relentlessly. You know you did.

'Yes, yes, all right,' she conceded, 'but those were not dreams, they were nightmares, and I had quite definitely stopped loving him. Quite definitely!

'You've got half an hour to have breakfast and then we're leaving for London.'

As she heard what Dracco was saying to her for a moment Imogen's hopes rose. Had he changed his mind after what she had said to him last night? Was he taking her back to London in order to put her on a plane to Rio?

Oh, please...please! she begged fate fervently as she

told Dracco automatically, 'I don't eat breakfast. I'll go up and pack.'

'Pack?' Dracco's eyebrows lifted as he drawled the single word laconically, shaking his head as he did so. 'We're going to see our solicitor, Imo, and it won't involve an overnight stay, although I dare say you might want to wear something a little more formal,' he added as he flicked a disparaging glance at her well-worn outfit.

Immediately Imogen was on the defensive. 'If you don't like my clothes, Dracco—' she began, and then was forced to stop, as without allowing her to finish Dracco cut in smoothly,

'I can buy you some new ones? My feelings exactly, Imo, and that's what I intend to do, once our business with David is concluded. I don't doubt that you trust me, just as I do you, but I thought it might give you some degree of reassurance if I committed myself legally to our...agreement. I intend to take your adherence to your part on trust. What do you mean, you don't eat breakfast?' he suddenly questioned her with a frown.

The lightning speed with which he changed subjects threw Imogen into total confusion. And distracted her from the shock of discovering that he intended to put the proposal he had made to her on a legal footing.

The proposal he had made to her? The blackmail he was forcing on her, she corrected herself fiercely as she heard him saying, 'No wonder you're so slender. Have some of these.'

Imogen's eyes widened as he reached out and picked up a packet of cereal from the table, shaking some into the bowl in front of her.

'Fruit Munchies with chocolate chips,' he told her humorously. 'You used to love them.'

'That was when I was thirteen,' Imogen reminded him, but Dracco wasn't paying any attention.

Instead he poured milk onto her cereal, before warning her, 'We don't leave this house until you have eaten, Imo.'

'Why? Are you afraid that people will think you're starving me as well as blackmailing me?' she demanded acerbically.

'Blackmailing you?' He gave her a sharply incisive look, but before he could continue the telephone started to ring. 'Excuse me,' he told her. 'This is probably a business call I was expecting. I'll take it in the study. I shan't be long.'

After he had gone Imogen stared at the bowl in front of her. She wasn't going to eat the cereal, of course she wasn't, but somehow she was dipping her spoon into it. In Rio she had eaten sparingly, knowing how little food the children they were dealing with had to eat.

She was over halfway through by the time Dracco returned, and, although she pushed the bowl away from her without finishing its contents, she had to admit that she had rather enjoyed the cereal.

Dracco's solicitor had an office in the same block that housed the offices which had originally been her father's and which were now, of course, exclusively Dracco's.

A sharp pang gripped Imogen as she remembered how often she had visited the office with her father. She still missed him, not with the savage intensity she had suffered immediately after his death any longer, but with a sadness that had become a small, familiar shadow in her life.

As he guided her towards the lift Dracco said quietly to her, 'I've lost count of the number of times I've thought about moving. I still expect to see your father here, coming out of the lift, opening the office door. I still miss him and I dare say I always will.'

His words were so in tune with her thoughts that Imogen couldn't speak without betraying her emotions. Instead she turned her face away from Dracco so that he couldn't see it. How could he speak so about her father and yet at the same time have betrayed him by falling in love with his wife?

Imogen continued to ignore Dracco as the lift bore them upwards. When it stopped and the door opened he touched her arm, and immediately Imogen flinched.

Despairingly she wondered how on earth she would be able to keep her part of the bargain and provide him with a child when she couldn't even bear him to touch her!

You managed to bear it very well when he kissed you last night, a small inner voice told her, adding, 'And what about that dream? Then you weren't just bearing it.

'No,' Imogen protested out loud, covering her ears with her hands.

'What is it?' Dracco demanded sharply. Are you feeling ill again? I really do think you need to be checked out by Dr Armstrong. You could have picked up something on the flight.'

'I'm fine,' Imogen choked. She could see an office door ahead of them.

There was still time for her to change her mind. Still time for her to decide that she was not strong enough to make such a sacrifice and to fly straight back to Rio. All it would take was one sentence, but even whilst she longed to speak it, to tell Dracco that she had changed her mind, Imogen's pride refused to allow her to do so. Her pride and the deep inner knowledge that she would never forgive herself for her selfishness if she did.

Dracco pushed open the office door, ushering her inside ahead of him. A smiling receptionist greeted them. It was obvious that she knew Dracco well and was more than a touch in awe of him.

'David shouldn't be long,' she told Dracco, glancing at her watch. 'He was called out to a meeting with a client. He didn't want to go, really, knowing that you were coming in, but it was an urgent case.'

She seemed almost to be apologising, Imogen recognised as the other woman turned to smile a little uncertainly at her. She was about her own age, Imogen guessed, brunette with hazel eyes and very obviously pregnant.

Shakily Imogen averted her gaze from the other woman's body. She was still saying something to Dracco, but then she stopped as the office door opened and a slightly thick-set young man with an open, honest face came in.

'Oh, there you are, darling,' she said with obvious relief. 'I was just explaining to Dracco that you'd had to go out.'

As she reached up to kiss him briefly Imogen noticed the wedding ring she was wearing and guessed that they were husband and wife even before Dracco had introduced them to her as David and Charlotte Bryant.

'Mrs Barrington.' David Bryant smiled as he shook Imogen's hand. 'I've heard an awful lot about you. My uncle Henry was a great fan of yours and of course he and your father were very close friends. He often used to talk to my mother about you. She was his sister. I know how much it would have meant to him to learn that you and Dracco are…have decided… That you are reconciled.' He stopped, colouring up and looking slightly uncomfortable, whilst Imogen automatically asked him to call her by her Christian name. It irked her that Dracco had been so sure of her reaction that he had already told David Bryant that they were 'reconciled'.

She must not allow herself to forget that Dracco was a master manipulator, she warned herself as she thanked Charlotte Bryant for the cup of coffee she had just made her.

'Yes,' the other woman was confirming quietly, 'David's mother often talks about her brother to us. I know she is particularly grateful to you, Dracco, for everything you did when he had his fatal heart attack, going with him to the hospital, staying with him.'

'It was the least I could do,' Imogen heard Dracco saying curtly, almost as though he didn't want the subject to be discussed.

Imogen shivered. If Henry had not had his heart attack, would Dracco have come after her and stopped her from leaving? She had believed he had let her go out of indifference and relief, but now it seemed that she might have been wrong. Had she been wrong about anything else?

David and Charlotte Bryant obviously thought a lot of Dracco, but then they didn't know him the way she did!

'So what now? A celebratory glass of champagne? We aren't too far from one of the city's new hotels, and, since it's time for lunch...'

Imogen stared at Dracco in disbelief as they stepped out of the office block and into the sunshine.

'You might feel you have something to celebrate,' she told him wildly, 'but I most certainly don't.'

'No? I've just signed a legally binding document agreeing to give your charity over one million pounds. I should have thought that was sufficient cause for celebration,' Dracco was telling her with deceptive mildness as he caught hold of her arm and drew her against his side.

Immediately Imogen tried to pull away, but Dracco refused to let go of her.

'That might be—under different circumstances,' Imogen retaliated, 'but, since I've just sold the use of my body to you in return for it...'

She could see Dracco's mouth thinning and see too the warning glint in his rapidly darkening eyes.

'You loved your father, didn't you, Imo?' he asked her grimly.

'You know I did,' Imogen responded immediately.

'How do you think he would have reacted to being a grandfather, to knowing that his genes, your mother's and your own were being passed on to a new generation?'

For a moment Imogen was too shaken by his question

to answer, but when she did her voice trembled with the intensity of her feelings.

'How dare you do this to me, Dracco?' she demanded. 'How dare you use my father to blackmail me?'

'You keep throwing that accusation in my face. Be very careful that I don't throw it back at you.'

'By doing what?' she challenged him recklessly.

But instead of answering her he said calmly, 'Since you don't want any lunch, we might as well head straight for Knightsbridge and get you kitted out with some new clothes.'

'I don't want any new clothes,' Imogen started to say, but Dracco wasn't listening to her, his attention concentrated on the taxi he was hailing.

He was still holding onto Imogen's arm, his fingers curling firmly around it, and as a group of passers-by jostled against her she automatically moved closer to him. The cool wool of his suit jacket brushed against her bare arm. As she looked up she could see the faint shadow on his jaw where he had shaved earlier. There was a maleness about Dracco, she acknowledged with a faint inner tremor, a strong, dangerous sense of power that was like an unseen aura. Unseen but not unfelt. She could feel it now as he urged her into the stationary taxi. She could feel it and she was afraid of it—and of herself.

'And just remember,' Dracco was warning her as the taxi lurched into motion, 'from tonight you and I will be sharing a bedroom. And a bed.'

Ignoring him, Imogen stared out of the taxi window, praying that she would get pregnant quickly—no, not just quickly but immediately, she amended hurriedly.

Straight away, the first time, so that it would be the

only time. Would Dracco wait to see if…? Or would he…? Her mind shied away from the questions bubbling inside her head. She certainly had no fear of sex as such. These were not, after all, Victorian times, when a virgin bride was simply not told anything about what lay ahead of her. In Rio children well below the age of puberty sold themselves on the streets in order to eat and were shockingly graphic about what could be demanded of them. If providing Dracco with a child saved only one of those children…

Dracco's child. Her child. Unable to stop herself, Imogen turned to look at him. Just as she had been, he was gazing out of the taxi window, his face averted from her. Imogen cleared her throat to speak but did not get the chance. The taxi was drawing up outside a department store.

'No, that's enough—more than enough,' Imogen protested helplessly as she surveyed the full rail of clothes the store's senior personal shopper had produced.

They—Dracco, herself, the shopper and a hovering alterationist—were all in the store's elegant personal shopping suite, where Dracco and Imogen had been escorted following Dracco's production of a discreetly logoed charge card and request for a selection of clothes for Imogen to choose from.

Initially dizzy from the mouth-watering variety of outfits the personal shopper had produced, Imogen was now beginning to feel slightly nauseous in a way that reminded her of how her teenage self had sometimes felt after the consumption of a mega-sized knickerbocker glory.

Tempting though the clothes were, Imogen's conscience was causing her to experience a sense of disquiet. Just how many small stomachs would the cost of such luxurious clothes fill? And thinking of stomachs, small and otherwise, raised another consideration…

Yearningly Imogen looked at the trendy pair of designer jeans she had just tried on. The assistant had explained how they were cut to fit and flatter the female body, and they had hugged Imogen's hips and bottom in a way that had made her reluctant to come out of the cubicle until the shopper had insisted. When she had done, she'd felt acutely self-conscious standing in front of Dracco wearing them, guessing what he must be thinking—that they were far too sexy for a woman like her!

'They're not really me,' she said now, shaking her head, but Dracco, it seemed, had other ideas.

'Why not?' he asked her. 'I like them.' As he spoke Imogen was infuriatingly aware of the disparaging look he was giving the outfit she had put back on.

Lisa had always worn very fashionable, sexy clothes, and no doubt as he looked at her Dracco was mentally comparing her to his mistress.

Did he perhaps think that by dressing her in sexy clothes she would somehow become more desirable to him, more the kind of woman he wanted?

Imogen had never forgotten the disparaging comments Lisa had made to her on the morning of her marriage, and somehow since then she had favoured loose-fitting clothes that cloaked rather than emphasised her figure.

'They're very popular—and very sexy.' The shopper was smiling encouragingly.

Until he had decided that he wanted a child with her Dracco had shown no sexual interest in her whatsoever. Before their marriage he had never even kissed her properly, and yet now he apparently wanted to buy her the kind of clothes that subtly enhanced a woman's sexuality. Why? Because that would make her more acceptable to him in bed? More like Lisa?

'No,' she insisted, ignoring the jeans the shopper was still holding. 'They're very expensive and I wouldn't get much wear out of them.'

'We'll take them.' Dracco was smiling as he spoke to the assistant. 'If it's that social conscience of yours that's troubling you,' he told Imogen as he turned towards her, 'then let me remind you that it's my money you'll be spending, and…'

'Your money?' Immediately Imogen started to frown, anger taking the place of her earlier self-consciousness. 'I can afford to buy my own clothes, Dracco,' she told him fiercely. 'I did have a salary for my work for the charity, albeit a small one!'

Discreetly the personal shopper had moved out of earshot.

'I know you can,' Dracco agreed, 'but surely it's a husband's privilege to be allowed to indulge his wife?'

Thoroughly angry now, Imogen glared at him. 'If you really want to "indulge me", as you put it, there are other ways!'

To her disbelief, she could see that Dracco was actually starting to smile.

'You haven't really changed at all, have you, Imo?' he challenged her ruefully. 'I can remember how much it amused your father—and infuriated Lisa—when you insisted that you'd rather he bought some winter feed for the ponies tethered illegally on the village common than buy you a Christmas-party dress.'

To her own mortification, Imogen felt emotional tears start to prick the backs of her eyes.

Yes, she could remember that incident as well. Her father had been amused, and in the end she had not only got his agreement to provide winter feed for the ponies, but she had also, at Lisa's furious insistence, got a new party dress as well. She had hated that dress, it had been babyish, pink, with frills and a big full skirt, not suitable for a teenager at all.

Lisa—was Dracco thinking of her now? Was he wishing that Lisa was here with him; that she was the one he was buying a new wardrobe for that she would wear for his delectation—both in bed and out of it? Imogen forced herself to take a deep, calming breath.

'Anyway,' she told Dracco, 'there isn't much point in you buying me these kind of clothes.' When Dracco raised one eyebrow interrogatively she flushed a little as she was forced to explain huskily, 'They're all very fitted, and I won't... I shan't... I shall probably soon be needing things with more room in them,' she told him, unable to stop herself from giving him an indignant look when the enlightenment finally dawned in his eyes.

'If you're trying to say that you'll soon be needing maternity outfits, then, yes, I agree,' he said in obvious amusement. 'But I think our reconciliation alone is going to cause enough speculation without us adding to it by you appearing in public in maternity gear.' Giving her an oblique look, he added softly, 'I must say, you've surprised me, Imo; I hadn't realised you were so actively looking forward to the consummation of our agreement!'

'That isn't what I meant. I'm not!' Imogen hissed in immediate denial. She couldn't believe his sudden and unexpected lightheartedness. It was almost as though he was teasing her, and enjoying doing so as well. 'I just don't want to see money being wasted on clothes that—'

'Will it make you feel better if I agree to match pound for pound everything I spend on you with an additional donation to the shelter?' Dracco asked.

Imogen opened her mouth and then closed it again. She didn't want to see him like this, to remember how wonderful and special she had once believed he was. To make up for her own foolish weakness she gave him a mutely hostile look before telling him frostily, 'That's bribery.'

'It's your decision,' Dracco replied. 'Just remember that the less you spend on yourself, the less I give to the shelter.'

The personal shopper was moving determinedly back towards them, obviously having decided that they had had enough time to sort out their differences. Was there anything Dracco would not do to get his own way? Imogen wondered helplessly.

Whether it was because of Dracco's comment, the personal shopper's skilled salesmanship, or her own unexpected pleasure in the clothes she tried on, Imogen didn't know, but when she finally left the suite she was the slightly guilty owner of a much larger new wardrobe than she had planned—and the shelter was in line to get a substantial extra 'bonus'.

'I take it that on this occasion you won't want to celebrate a successful conclusion to our activities at the Soda Fountain,' Dracco drawled as they left the store with half a dozen large carrier bags.

For some reason, his reference to a favourite rendezvous for her schoolgirl treats on her visits to her father's office filled her with a welling sense of emotion. So much so that she stopped dead in the street, causing Dracco's smile to change to a frown as he watched her.

Imogen felt as though she wanted to run and hide.

Just for one betraying millisecond of time she had caught herself actually wishing that things could be different, that she and Dracco were genuinely making an attempt to start afresh with one another and that the planned conception of their child, her father's grandchild, was an event they were undertaking in a mutual mood of love and joy.

What on earth was happening to her? Did it really only take the mention of the Soda Fountain to wipe away the betrayals that lay between them? Surely she wasn't really so foolish and so vulnerable?

Her head lifted, her pride responding to the challenge she had given it. Managing a valiant smile, she told Dracco coolly, 'Somehow I doubt that indulging in calorie-laden snacks and these clothes—' she swung her carrier bags meaningfully '—go together.'

'You could do with putting a bit of weight on,' Dracco informed her, still frowning.

Of course he would think that! Lisa was far more voluptuously shaped than she was. 'Well, if you have your way I expect I soon shall be,' Imogen returned, and then caught her bottom lip in her teeth, her face burning a hot, self-conscious pink.

For a moment Dracco said nothing, simply studying her with a hooded gaze whilst more than one woman passer-by paused to look interestedly at him.

'If that's meant to be an invitation—' he began.

Immediately Imogen stopped him, shaking her head vigorously as she denied any such intention. 'The day I invite you to take me to bed,' she told him furiously, 'is—'

'Be careful, Imo,' Dracco told her softly. 'I've already warned you about challenging me.'

CHAPTER FIVE

ALMOST childishly Imogen kept her eyes tightly closed, even though she had been awake for well over ten minutes, knowing already what she would see the moment she opened them.

Outside the bedroom window she could hear a blackbird carolling noisily. Fighting to ignore the sensation of despair in the pit of her stomach, Imogen opened her eyes and stared across her pillow to the one that should have borne the imprint of Dracco's dark head. But, just like the huge double bed itself, it showed no evidence of Dracco's presence.

It was five days now since they had returned from London, almost a week, and still nothing had happened; still Dracco had not…they had not…

All right, so he had been away on business for three of those nights, but she had moved into the master suite the evening of their return from the shopping trip filled with trepidation. Dracco had never come anywhere near the room, or her, preferring instead to sleep downstairs on the sofa in his study, apparently because he was in the middle of a very important business deal which necessitated him making and receiving calls from other continents.

'There was no point in me coming upstairs and disturbing you, not when I knew I'd got these calls coming through,' he had explained carelessly to her the next day when she had eventually seen him. 'You weren't disappointed, I hope?'

Imogen had not known what to reply. And she had told herself that she was only too pleased to hear that he would be going away for a few days.

But in his absence, no doubt because she had had the unfamiliar luxury of time to think about such things, she had found herself questioning just why he had not as yet made any attempt to ensure that she gave him the child he wanted; the child that was, after all, the reason for them being here together.

Yesterday, when he had returned without warning late in the afternoon, she had been convinced that the event she was dreading was imminent, but once again Dracco had left her to sleep alone.

Because he didn't want her? Because he only wanted the child she could give him? Because in reality the woman he truly wanted was Lisa?

The pristine pillow next to her own began to blur. Wrathfully Imogen told herself that she didn't care and blinked away the tears. She was not going to cry!

No, instead of wanting to cry she ought to be asking herself why she was being so illogical. After all, by rights she should have been pleased.

Once she had showered and dressed, Imogen made her way downstairs. She had grown up in this house. Absently she ran her fingertips along the smooth rich wood of the carved banister rail. Hidden in its carving were tiny little animals; Imogen could remember her mother showing them to her. When her mother had been alive this house had been a home, the kind of home she would have wanted to give her own child, but her mother's death and her father's remarriage had changed that and had turned it into a place she had needed to seek refuge from.

And the person she had sought that refuge with most often had been Dracco! Dracco. Where was he? The study door was closed. Tentatively Imogen hovered outside it and then, taking a deep breath, she reached for the handle and turned it.

Inside the room the computer hummed softly, its screen illuminating the semi-darkness. Frowning, her housewifely instincts aroused, Imogen started to make her way towards the window to release the closed blind and let the sunlight in, but then, abruptly, she stopped as she saw Dracco's sleeping form sprawled uncomfortably on the narrow sofa.

He was still wearing the clothes he had arrived home in the previous afternoon—a lightweight suit, the jacket of which was lying on a chair. At some stage he had obviously started to unbutton his shirt, and as her eyes adjusted to the half-light of the room Imogen could see the deep dark 'V' of exposed flesh stretching from his throat all the way down to where his trousers lay low on his hips.

Her muscles contracted in helpless reaction, a silent, tortured contortion that sliced through her body. She made an involuntary movement towards him and then stopped. In the shuttered heat of the room his fine, silky body hair lay in damp whorls against his flesh; his chest rose and fell with his breathing. Even relaxed, his muscles had an imposing male tautness that drew and held her gaze. Once, as a girl, she had yearned to touch

Dracco's body, her imagination, her senses, her deepest self driven crazy with excitement and longing.

In Rio, whenever she had fallen into the trap of thinking about Dracco, or remembering how she had felt about him, she had told herself sternly that her imaginings had been those of a hormone-fevered adolescent with no bearing whatsoever on reality. She had assured herself too that as an adult she would look scornfully on the reactions of the girl she had been, that she would be safely beyond such foolish feelings.

She had been wrong, Imogen recognised dizzily. Right now the effect the sight of Dracco was having on her was—

'Imo?'

Imogen jumped as though she had been stung as Dracco suddenly said her name. How long had he been awake, watching her watching him? Guilty heat stained her skin and she started to back towards the door.

'I…I wasn't sure if you were in here,' she began huskily.

'I had some work to do,' Dracco told her casually as he sat up and grimaced slightly as he flexed his body. 'I remember feeling tired.'

'It can't have been very comfortable for you, sleeping on the sofa,' Imogen told him.

She barely knew what she was saying; all she could think about was the extraordinary and very definitely unwanted surge of feeling that had filled her whilst she had been looking at him.

'Mmm…it could have been worse,' Dracco responded.

For some reason the way he was looking at her made

her face burn even hotter. What exactly was he implying? That sleeping on the sofa was preferable to sleeping with her? He was the one who had insisted that he didn't want their marriage annulled! Imogen turned round and reached for the door handle.

She was opening the door when Dracco said abruptly from behind her, 'If you like we could go out later. Drive to the coast?'

Once such an invitation would have filled her with incandescent joy, and no power on earth would have prevented her from accepting it. Perhaps it was because she could remember that feeling so vividly that she felt she had to punish herself. Imogen didn't know, but she could hear the anger and the pain in her voice as she replied pointedly, shaking her head, 'No, I don't like. There's only one reason I'm here, Dracco, and it doesn't have anything to do with trips to the coast.'

She was gone before he could retaliate, closing the door behind her as she hurried into the kitchen.

A solitary morning followed by an afternoon deadheading roses had not done anything to improve her mood, Imogen recognised as she sucked irritably on her thorn-pricked thumb while hurrying upstairs.

'Imo.'

She froze as Dracco suddenly appeared at the top of the stairs. He was virtually naked, a towel wrapped casually around his hips whilst he rubbed absently at his wet hair with another.

'I saw you coming in from the garden from the bedroom window,' he began, 'and I thought—'

'That you ought to warn me that you were wandering

around half-naked, just in case I got the wrong idea?' Imogen supplied grittily for him. 'You were the one who threatened to seduce me, Dracco, not the other way around,' she couldn't resist pointing out.

'Actually, what I wanted to discuss with you is the fact that you're going to need some form of transport. I was thinking perhaps of a small four-wheel drive. They seem very popular with mothers.' His voice dropped to a dangerous softness that brought up the hairs on the nape of Imogen's neck in sensual awareness as intensely as though he had physically reached out and touched her, when he added smoothly, 'However, since you have raised the subject...'

'I have not raised anything,' Imogen objected immediately, and then went bright red, whilst Dracco continued to look at her with that detached hooded gaze of his that was so unreadable.

'And am I to take that as an indication that you do want to raise...something?' Dracco queried dangerously gently.

'You're the one who insisted that our marriage was to continue and that...you wanted me to...that you wanted a child,' Imogen told him wildly.

'And if I remember correctly you were the one who said that there was no point in me attempting to seduce you,' Dracco pointed out. 'However, if you're trying to tell me that you've changed your mind...?'

Changed her mind? No! Never! She would die before she did that! But for some reason Imogen found it impossible to voice that fierce denial. Perhaps, she decided, it was because her attention was concentrated not on her own thoughts but on the precarious way in which Dracco had wrapped the towel around his hips, so loosely that…

Imogen discovered that she couldn't drag her fascinated gaze away from it. And nor, it seemed, could she resist allowing that same gaze to skim helplessly over the flat muscular plane of Dracco's belly with its dark arrowing of hair that disappeared beneath the soft whiteness of his towel. She found that, as badly as she wanted to swallow, for some reason she could not.

'Imo.'

There was a smooth, liquid sensuality in the way Dracco mouthed her name, a spellbinding dark magic that somehow paralysed her so that she couldn't move until his fingers curled round her wrist as he firmly tugged her towards him.

'You smell of fresh air and sunshine,' she heard him whisper against her hair. 'And roses.'

'You smell of…you,' Imogen whispered helplessly back. Her eyes, already huge in the delicate triangle of her face, widened even further when she saw the look that leapt fiercely to life in Dracco's own eyes. The look of a hunter, a male animal, aroused, dangerous, silently waiting to pounce.

'Have you any idea just how provocative that remark is?' he asked her with a soft savagery that made her whole body shudder.

As she shook her head he mouthed her denial for her, questioning, 'No?' His hand moved to hold the side of her neck, tipping it back, his thumb rimming the shape of her ear, sending a shower of pleasure darting over her skin. The warmth of his breath as he bent his head towards her scorched her senses. His fingers, stroking the delicate, sensitive flesh just beneath her hairline, made her tremble wildly without knowing why she should do so.

'You don't know just what it does to a man when you tell him that you can recognise his personal scent? Shall I tell you? Show you?'

He had closed the distance between them, enclosing her with his body, so that she could feel its heat—and more. Automatically she tensed against her awareness of his arousal, a virgin's shocked reaction to a man's sexuality, but beneath that reaction, running hot and wild, was a river of flooding sensation.

'No.' Her denial slid from her lips into the infinitesimal space between them, and was lost for ever as Dracco's mouth brushed hers—the briefest of touches, and yet somehow so sensual and commanding that Imogen automatically felt her toes starting to curl.

'More? You want more?' she heard Dracco murmuring, even though she could have sworn she had said nothing. Perhaps it was her body that had given her away, her lips? 'Like this, Imo?' Dracco was asking her, his voice so soft and low that she had to strain to hear it, just as she was having to strain to reach out for the feel of his mouth against her own. 'Your mouth should taste sweet and virginal and not all dark enchantment, the mouth of a sorceress no man can resist. Are you a sorceress, Imo?'

Dizzily Imogen tried to listen to what he was saying, but there was a sharp, fierce ache in her body. Beneath her thin top she could feel her breasts swelling, her nipples tight, hurting with the need to have Dracco touch them, stroke them, suck them.

She shuddered wildly, her eyes suddenly wantonly feral as her female instincts overwhelmed her. It was as though time had telescoped backwards, as though somehow she was feeling once again what she had felt as a teenager, only now she was feeling those desires and needs with all the authority and power of a truly mature woman.

Somehow, too, her body considered Dracco to be its mate, a mate from whom it had been parted for far too long! Denied far too long!

Urgently she wound her arms around Dracco's body, holding him to her, her gaze smouldering passionately into his.

'Do you want me?' he asked her softly. 'When, Imo?' he demanded when her body shuddered in response. 'Now?'

Imogen felt her body jolt against his as though it had received a charge of electricity. 'Yes,' she responded hoarsely. 'Yes, now,' she told him. 'Now, Dracco!' she repeated urgently, raising herself up on her tiptoes and pressing her mouth passionately against his.

For a second there was no response, and then Dracco opened his mouth on hers, the fierce drive of his tongue into the intimate sweetness she was willingly offering shattering all her teenage preconceptions about what such a kiss would be.

It was like drowning, dying, being turned inside-out, giving something of herself so intimate that she felt as though he was totally possessing her, and yet at the same time filling her with such an aching hunger that she felt as though she would die unless he satisfied it. And she knew only he, only Dracco alone, could satisfy her.

Beneath her hands she could feel the sleek, hard warmth of his bare skin, the breadth of his shoulders tapering down into the narrowness of his waist. The barrier of his towel frustrated her and beneath the increasingly demanding thrust of Dracco's seeking tongue she made a small, angry sound of protest.

Immediately he released her, staring down into the desire-hazed darkness of her eyes with a gaze so green and luminous that it made her heart turn over.

'What is it?' he asked her rawly. 'Too much—too soon?'

He was holding one of her hands in his own, and as she turned away, unable to answer his question, his fingers suddenly tightened almost painfully on hers, causing her to look quickly back at him.

'This doesn't say that you don't want me, Imo,' he told her, and her breath caught on a frantic gasp of mingled shock and pleasure as he ran his fingertip over the jutting outline of her breast, pausing deliberately to circle her nipple, erect and aroused beneath the fine fabric of her top.

Without waiting for her to answer him, he turned towards the master suite, firmly drawing her with him. Imogen didn't try to resist. She didn't want to resist.

The bedroom was dappled with evening sunlight; it shone through the voile curtaining, giving the peaceful cream comfort of the room a golden gleam.

As a new extension to the original house, this room did not share the air of sad shabbiness that had so struck at Imogen's emotions when she had first walked into her childhood home. In her parents' day this room had simply not existed, and Imogen acknowledged her sense of relief and release that this bedroom held no painful memories for her, and that she was coming to it as an adult woman.

'This room suits you, Imo,' Dracco was telling her quietly whilst his thumb ran lazily up and down the inside of her bare arm, the effect of his touch on her so devastatingly erotic that she found it almost impossible to focus on what he was saying.

'Cream is your colour. Cream and gold.' He leaned forward, his lips caressing the side of her neck, his fingers so swift and deft on the fastening of her top that she was barely aware of the fact that he had slid it off her shoulder until she felt the heat of his mouth caressing her there.

A hundred thousand fiery darts of pleasure thrilled over her skin. She heard the sound of her own low, aching moan filling the room; a counterpoint to the rapidly increasing rate of their breathing.

Dracco's hands were sliding beneath her top, easing it off her body. A delicious shivery sensation shimmered over her skin.

'Cream, and honey-gold,' Imogen heard Dracco saying thickly as he freed her breasts from the confines of her bra and gently kneaded them, playing tenderly with the stiff peaks of her nipples in a way that made her writhe hotly in his embrace. She closed her eyes and bit into her bottom lip as she fought to suppress the raw moan of appreciative delight she could feel building up inside her.

'Beautiful! You are so very beautiful, even more perfect than I knew. So perfect that I can hardly bear to look at you. Do you know what it does to me, Imo, seeing you like this?' she could hear Dracco demanding as he looked down at her naked breasts and then back up into her eyes.

The expression she could see in the depths of those eyes both shocked and thrilled her.

Dracco wanted her. She could see it; feel it in his body; hear it in his voice.

That knowledge was all she needed to loosen the last faint threads of inhibition binding her and set herself free to be the woman she had always known she could be—with Dracco.

As his hands came to her waist, so narrow that her trousers slid down from it to lie loosely on her hips, Imogen raised herself up on her tiptoes. She still wasn't quite brave enough to look down at Dracco's body. Miraculously his towel was still in place, but he had not made any attempt to disguise how aroused he was.

When she reached to wrap her arms around him Dracco held her slightly away from him. He whispered thickly, 'Let me see all of you, Imo.'

Although his words made her tremble, she didn't try to resist as he carefully removed her trousers, unzipping them to let them fall to the floor and then lifting her out of them, holding her right there against his own body. She was pressed deep into his hard masculinity, thigh to thigh, hip to hip, groin to groin, whilst he kissed her with a slow passion that burned and smouldered potently.

Imogen ached to open her legs and wrap them tightly around him, to lure and coax him by any means she could to take the gift she was so wantonly ready to give him. Just the thought of feeling him sliding powerfully into her was enough to make her shudder again wildly, her eyes stormily dark with longing.

How could she have lived so long without this, without him? It was a question she couldn't even begin to answer.

Mutely she let him slide her down to the floor, his hands smoothing the flesh of her back, her waist, her buttocks, cupping the soft feminine cheeks, his fingers splayed over them.

Imogen could hear the frantic high-pitched sound of her sharp protest that he should arouse her so intensely and tormentingly without satisfying her, but it was something she heard from a distance, her whole being concentrated on the increasingly urgent necessity of feeling him, having him touch her with the full intimacy of a lover.

Her nails clawed his naked back, echoing the intensity of what she was feeling. Impatiently she tugged at the soft fabric of the towel covering his body.

Against her ear she could hear him asking, 'Imo, are you sure this is what you want? Because if it isn't and you don't tell me now...'

How could he even ask her such a question? Couldn't he tell? See? Feel?

'I want you, Dracco,' she told him. 'I want you now.'

It was like nothing she had ever imagined, and so much—so much more than everything she had ever dared to hope for. Tears of emotion stung her eyes at the look on Dracco's face as he studied her naked body, his gaze absorbed, hungry, fiercely hungry, in direct contrast to the tender touch of his hands.

When he kissed her breasts, each one in turn and then

each nipple, slowly laving the aching peaks, she shivered in mute ecstasy. The slow trail of his tongue-tip down over her belly had the same effect on her skin as red wine might have had on her blood—a hot, sensual rush of pleasure that took control of her senses. To call the effect he was having on her mind-blowing fell so far short of the reality of what he was doing to her that it was almost an insult. When his tongue rimmed her navel, and dipped gently into it, she moaned out loud in bewildered pleasure.

Never in a thousand lifetimes had she imagined this kind of intimacy with him, and never had it even crossed her mind that she would be the one urging him on with her hands, with the hoarse cry of her voice and with the frantic writhing of her body. Through her half-closed eyes she could still see the full, powerful maleness of him. She ached to reach out and touch him, but the sensation of him gently parting the outer covering of her sex made her forget everything but her intense need for him.

Instincts she hadn't known she possessed were driving her, possessing her now, insisting that the mere touch of his fingers was not enough, not what her body really needed, even though their careful touch was making her shudder from head to foot.

'Dracco,' she whispered, pleading.

Immediately he was beside her, looking deep into her eyes as he demanded hoarsely, 'What is it? Do you want me to stop?'

'No, it isn't that,' Imogen denied immediately. Helplessly her gaze, hot and fevered with longing, jolted over his body. 'I want you, Dracco,' she told him fiercely. 'You… With me. Inside me.'

For a moment the triumphant blaze in his eyes shocked her. It was as though she had said something, given him something he had hungered for for a very long time. But it was too late to try to analyse what she thought she might have seen; Dracco was gathering her up in his arms, holding her, positioning her, moving over her and then finally and oh, so blissfully into her.

The high, wild sound of her cry of longing mingled with the harshly guttural groan of Dracco's male growl of possession. Their bodies moved together in an urgent harmony that felt so right, so natural that it seemed to Imogen she had finally found a vitally important missing piece of her life and herself.

And then there was no room for thought, no room for anything other than absorbing the feel of Dracco's body, the hot, musky scent of his skin, the physical reality of him here with her and within her as he drove them both to that place she knew she would die if she did not reach it.

But she did reach it, reached it and exploded in a million tiny pieces of piercingly intense release to lie exhausted in Dracco's protective arms. She was dazed with satisfaction and an awed disbelief that it was possible to experience something so spectacularly wonderful as sleep claimed her.

CHAPTER SIX

IMOGEN opened her eyes and stretched luxuriously. Dracco might not still be in the bed beside her but she could still smell his scent, feel the warm place where his body had been, feel the secret, special, place within herself where he had been.

Rolling over, she looked towards the window. It was a wonderful day. How could it not be? The revelations of the previous night still clung to her, filling her emotions with the same golden glow the sun brought through the window, its brightness softened into a mellow gilding by the voile curtains.

And so it was with her own feelings; they too were softened, gilded by the wondrous power of love, the love she had rediscovered in the breathless passages of the night when Dracco had held her, touching not just her body and her senses but also the deepest and most precious part of her.

They might not have spoken of love, but they had breathed it, shared it, given and bequeathed it to one another, surely? There was no way she could be mistaken about that.

She turned her head and studied the pillow next to her own, the pillow that still bore the imprint of Dracco's head. It was a new and sweet thing for her, this soft heaviness within her body, this small ache of satisfaction and remembered pleasure.

She had so many plans for her future, their future; so many hopes. Joy trembled uncertainly within her. She didn't want to question what she was feeling, nor to analyse the past. She didn't, Imogen recognised, want anything to intrude on the special memories and pleasures she and Dracco had created together.

She and Dracco together…

And perhaps, just perhaps, memories weren't all they had created!

A fierce quickening sensation gripped her body. A child.

'I want your father's grandchild,' Dracco had told her. And now her body was telling her that it wanted Dracco's child.

Somewhere outside the warmth of the bed, beyond the sunlight of the bedroom, lay certain sharply informed realities, but Imogen was in no mood to acknowledge them. What did they matter now? she taunted in silent mental recklessness. What, after last night, could matter more than what she and Dracco had shared? What she had discovered?

The love he had denied her as a girl had been there for her last night. She was sure of it.

The muslin voile curtains moved in the breeze, throwing small shadows across the room that were as ephemeral and as easily despatched as her unwanted doubts.

She loved Dracco. She couldn't not love him and have shared with him, as she had done yesterday, that deepest and most intimate sense of herself. And he surely could not have touched her, aroused her, savoured and satisfied her in the way that he had if he had not cared about her? Loved her in return?

Love. It was such a small word to cover such an infinity of emotion. Did she even truthfully know what it was? She had gone from loving Dracco to hating him, and then last night… Imogen took a deep breath, willing herself to think logically and realistically, but it was no use. Every time she tried to do so all she could see was Dracco's face, all she could feel was his touch, all she could hear was the immeasurably sweet sound of his breathing.

She was twenty-two and a woman, she reminded herself fiercely, and, even though physically she might have been a virgin, she was mature enough to know that sex, however good it might be, wasn't love.

Her heart refused to acknowledge such unworthy thoughts. What she and Dracco had shared had gone way beyond mere sex. It wasn't just one another's bodies they had touched; they had touched one another's hearts, one another's souls. Whatever had happened to them individually in their lives before last night no longer mattered. Her whole body was quivering, singing in the sweet, intoxicating aftermath of love. All she really wanted was to be with Dracco! To drink in the reality of him, breathe in the scent of him.

Imogen smiled ruefully at her own giddiness. She and Dracco needed to talk, to face one another and their shared past.

She took another deep breath. Surely in the light of what had already happened between them they were both adult enough to discuss everything? Their future and their past?

It was time to get up, for her to face the day—and Dracco.

* * *

Her foot poised on the topmost stair, Imogen paused and looked down through the banister into the hallway towards the closed door to what had once been her father's study and was now her husband's. Her husband, Dracco! The melting, delicious warmth just thinking such a thought gave her was a revelation. Dracco. Her husband. The father of her child…their child. A sensation not unlike the delicate touch of a skilled musician on a treasured instrument trembled across her skin.

Suddenly she couldn't wait to see him, to be with him, to reach up and pull that dark head down toward her, to feel those male lips caressing hers.

Light-heartedly she quickened her footsteps.

The study door was closed and Imogen paused outside it, suddenly feeling slightly nervous. Her senses felt preternaturally heightened; she could almost smell and taste the dust motes dancing on the sun-warmed air. The enormity of the moment and what it might portend made her heart beat unsteadily. On the other side of that door lay not just Dracco, but also her future. Their future, and potentially the future of their child.

Instinctively she touched her stomach. It was too soon to know if yesterday…

She gave a small gasp as the study door opened. Dracco was standing within the opening watching her, frowning at her. Her own forehead automatically started to mimic the expression she could see on his, although, whilst his frown was one of impatience and distance, hers was one of questioning concern.

'Imo.'

Even the way he said her name had a certain harshness

about it, Imogen recognised as her glance slid from his face to his body. He was wearing a formidably businesslike dark suit, the jacket unfastened over a crisp white shirt, and as she watched him he shot back his cuff to look at his watch.

One did not need to be an expert at interpreting body language to recognise his impatience.

'You look as though you're very busy. I had hoped that we might be able to talk,' she began.

'Talk? What about?'

It was not a promising start, Imogen acknowledged, but she was not a teenager gazing star-struck at an idol any more. She and Dracco were equals now.

'About us, and last night,' she responded calmly.

Imogen was proud of the way she managed to keep her gaze steady under the pressure of the look Dracco gave her.

'Last night?'

If anything his voice had become even more curt, carrying an edge to it that warned Imogen she was trespassing on a no-go area. But, as Imogen had discovered in the years she had been away, she possessed her own brand of strength and courage, and the issue that lay between them was not one she was going to allow to be ignored.

Moving closer to him, she reiterated softly, 'Yes, Dracco, last night. You do remember last night, don't you?' As she spoke the gentle mockery in her voice gave way to a soft liquid tenderness that shone in her eyes and curled her mouth. 'Last night, when you made love to me. You do remember that, don't you?' she teased.

'What I remember is that we had sex.'

The brutality of the cold words ripped into the shining delicate warmth of Imogen's hopes and dreams.

Now it was her turn to repeat Dracco's words.

'Sex.' She could hear the stammering anxiety in her voice, the desire to be reassured, but Dracco was already turning away from her, looking irritably towards the front door, as though he couldn't wait to escape.

'Dracco,' she protested, and she could hear the pain trembling through her voice. 'It wasn't just sex. It was...'

Helpless in the face of his remoteness, she couldn't bring herself to say the word 'love', to expose it and herself to the savage pain of his contemptuous dismissal. Instead her voice trailed away on an unsteady protest that held echoes of her childhood insecurity as she told him, 'It was more than that.'

'It was sex, Imo,' Dracco overrode her tersely. His head was turned away from her but she could see his profile, see the bleak downward turn of his mouth, the grimness in his expression, which warned her that he wanted the conversation brought to an end.

But there was a stubbornness in her that refused to allow her to let go, and, as though he sensed it, she heard him draw in his breath in open exasperation before he turned fully towards her. His gaze, clinical, cold, rejecting, swept her from head to toe.

'Sex, that's all,' he repeated. 'No more and no less.'

All the fiery passion that was so much a part of her nature rose up inside Imogen.

What she had felt with him, for him, last night was too important to be swept aside. She believed in her feelings and her instincts, even if Dracco didn't, and she was prepared to fight and fight hard if she had to to have them recognised.

'I'm twenty-two years old, Dracco; I've been independent for the last four years. You might remember me as a naïve teenager, but the woman you held in your arms last night, the woman you made love with—'

'Was a naïve virgin,' Dracco cut across her impassioned speech. He was watching her with almost clinical detachment to see how she reacted, how she recovered from the cutting edge of his blow. 'It's true that I do remember you as a child, Imogen. A very immature and romantic young teenager, who idealised the physical relationship between men and women, and who could only allow it into her life wrapped in the pretty packaging of ''love''. You claim to be mature. But a mature woman would never have clung to her virginity the way you have to yours.'

The cruelty of his clinical dissection of her took Imogen's breath away. It was as though he was determined to strip every last bit of emotion from what they had shared and turn it into something cold and meaningless.

'Psychologically for you,' he continued ruthlessly, 'the mere fact that you have had sex with me—and enjoyed it—means that you have to convince yourself that the physical arousal and desire you felt had to be the product of ''love''. Loving someone, Imo, means knowing them, accepting them, valuing them as they are. You and I do not...'

Imogen was not prepared to listen to any more. Boldly she stepped up to him; so close to him in fact that she was virtually touching him. As she put her hand on his arm she felt his muscles lock against her touch.

'Imo, I've got an appointment I have to keep, and I'm already dangerously close to being late for it.'

Willing him to allow her through the barriers he had thrown up against her, Imogen leaned into him, whispering, 'Dracco, please… Last night must have meant something to you. I—'

'It meant a great deal.' Imogen felt tears begin to sting her eyes. But her relief was short-lived.

Instead of reassuring her as she longed for him to do, Dracco told her crisply, 'It meant that, if we are lucky, nine months from now we shall have a child—I shall have a son or daughter who carries your father's blood, which is, after all, what this is about.'

He couldn't have made it any plainer to her that she meant nothing to him, Imogen recognised, as he sidestepped her.

Her vision blurred as she stared towards the stairs she had come down less than half an hour ago, her hopes so high, her belief so sure!

Dracco had reached the front door.

Somehow she managed to make herself turn towards him. 'And if…if we aren't lucky?' she challenged him desperately.

There was a small pause before he told her quietly, 'Then in that case we shall just have to try again until we are.'

As he opened the door and walked through it Imogen felt a shudder tear through her body as though it and she were being ripped apart. How could she endure that? The cold lovelessness of the act of sex with a man who did not love her but whom she…

She didn't cry. She couldn't! The pain was like a wound inflicted so deep within her body that it destroyed internally without any outward evidence of the injury.

Dracco got down the drive and as far as the main road without giving in to his emotions, but once there he recognised that, feeling as he did right now, he was a danger to himself and to others.

Cursing sharply beneath his breath, he pulled off the road and stopped his car.

He had lied to Imo about the urgency of his appointment. He was on his way to see David Bryant to sign the new will he had had the other man draw up.

'You want to make Imogen and any child she might conceive the main beneficiaries of your estate?' David had commented when Dracco informed him of his wishes. 'We're talking about a very large inheritance, Dracco. You say you want Imogen to have full control of it?' He had paused uncertainly. 'It is customary where such a large amount is concerned to appoint trustees or set up a trust fund.'

'There is no one I trust more than Imogen,' Dracco had responded firmly.

Imogen would never know just what last night had done to him, the sheer unbearable immensity of the guilt and remorse it had brought him—and the pleasure! So much pleasure that it was impossible to quantify it. How could he measure something that had been so longed and hungered for? How could he estimate the breadth and depth of how he had felt when after a virtually sleepless night he had leaned over in the first minutes of the new day to look down into her sleeping face?

Even in her sleep she had been smiling, her lips curved in soft, sensuous warmth. The tears of release and fulfilment she had cried in his arms had gone, but their salty trail had lain gently crystallised on her skin. Beneath the bedclothes she'd been naked, and the temptation to run his hand possessively down her body from the top of her head right the way to her toes, just for the luxurious pleasure of knowing she was there, had almost overwhelmed him.

He knew he had given her pleasure—would have known it even if she had not cried it out to him in a voice of shocked, delighted wonder—simply from the way her body had responded to him, fitted itself around him, accepted and embraced his touch upon it and within it.

But he had always known that there would be pleasure between them; had known it from the moment he had looked beyond the shy awkwardness of the girl she'd been and seen the woman she would become. She had desired him then with all the innocent hunger of a young girl's awakening sexuality and he had known it, and known too that he was equally drawn by longing to her as she was to him. The only difference had been that he'd been an adult and she had not. An adult male with an adult male's needs for a mate, a woman.

Dracco closed his eyes and breathed in, filling his lungs.

What he had told her about wanting her father's blood to run in the veins of his own child had been true, but it was only a small part of the truth.

John Atkins had been an astute and loving father. He had seen as clearly as Dracco had himself the growing intensity of Imogen's youthful crush on Dracco.

'She imagines herself in love with you,' John had told him in a no-holds-barred man-to-man conversation he had instituted shortly before Imogen's sixteenth birthday.

'I know,' Dracco had concurred. 'I love her, John,' he had told his friend and mentor rawly, 'and I know too that she is far too young as yet—'

'Dracco,' John Atkins had interrupted him immediately, 'I don't dispute your feelings, but, as Imogen's father, I would ask you to give me your word that you will allow her to have time to grow up and experience life before you tell her of your love. If you love her you'll understand why I'm asking you this.'

And of course Dracco had, even though the thought of having to stand to one side and watch whilst the girl he loved grew into womanhood with someone else had torn him apart.

'If you and Imogen should eventually become a couple,' John Atkins had continued emotionally, 'and I can promise you that there is nothing that would give me more pleasure, Dracco, it has to be as two equals, adults, not now whilst Imogen, for all she thinks she is passionately in love with you, is still little more than a child. I know how hard what I'm asking of you is going to be but, for Imogen's own sake and for the sake of the love I hope you may one day share, will you promise to say nothing of your feelings to her until she is twenty-one?'

Twenty-one. Five years! But Dracco had known why John was demanding such a promise from him, and he had given it. Had Imogen been his daughter he would have done exactly the same thing.

He had told himself after her father's death that he owed it to his friend and mentor to protect his only daughter, if necessary against himself, but then circumstances had left him with no choice other than to marry Imogen, for her own sake.

How he had agonised over that decision, ultimately seeking the advice of Henry Fairburn, John's solicitor and oldest friend.

He had told himself that he would not break his word to John, that he would somehow find the strength to make sure that his marriage to Imogen was in name only and that she knew nothing of his feelings for her.

But then as they'd left the church she had asked him if there was someone he loved, and he had known that she knew the truth, had seen in her eyes that she already knew the answer to her own question. Her reaction to it had made it plain how she felt.

After all, there was no more obvious a way of stating that someone's love was not wanted than to run away from them.

Lisa had taunted him about it, saying that he should have left Imogen to play teenage sex games with someone of her own age, claiming that the thought of having sex with a real live man had probably terrified her.

'A real man needs a real woman, Dracco,' she had told him, her hand on his arm, stroking it suggestively. He had shrugged her off, barely able to conceal either his dislike or his pain at losing Imogen.

Out of guilt and remorse and pain he had managed to

stop himself from going after Imogen and bringing her back.

How could he possibly have claimed to love her and then forced her to accept that love when she didn't want it?

And then David Bryant had told him about the letter he had received from her, and, almost as though he was watching himself from a distance, a part of Dracco had looked on in grim contempt whilst he set about making plans to…

To what? Couldn't he even admit to himself what he had done? Well, perhaps it was time he did. He had manoeuvred and manipulated Imogen into coming back to him. And the result had far exceeded even the most fevered scenarios conjured up by the long lonely nights of wanting her.

To hear that note of wonderment in her voice earlier when she had talked about last night, about them 'making love', had made him want to take hold of her right there and show her that last night had been a mere fraction of what they could share together. But what he wanted from her was a lot more than the orgasm-induced emotion of physical satisfaction. What he wanted was her love, a love that matched his own; a love that went way beyond the giving and taking of pleasure in bed. Yes, it was satisfying to know that physically Imo wanted him, but it was a bitter, tainted pleasure. It was her love he wanted, not her body, and how the hell could he ever win that after what he had done?

Even now Dracco found it hard to explain to himself why he had overreacted so uncharacteristically when Imogen had assumed that he wanted a divorce.

Yes, of course he wanted her to have his child, and, yes, he very much wanted to share a blood tie with the man who had meant so much to him, but to use that as an excuse to force Imo to consummate their marriage… There was no acceptable explanation for what he had done.

Dracco opened his eyes. He had kept track of Imogen all the time they had been apart, knowing that it was what her father would have expected him to do.

He had never for one moment intended… But somehow things had got out of hand; and he had found it far harder to control his feelings than he had expected. The reality of dealing with a fully grown woman and not a girl had brought it home to him how dangerously vulnerable he actually was.

He had tried to keep as much physical distance between them as he could, working away from home, sleeping downstairs in the study. But last night all those plans had been crushed out of existence, along with his self-control. Last night he had done the very thing he had promised himself he would never, ever do under any circumstances.

And now Imo was telling him that she loved him. Not because she did—dammit—but because he was her first lover, her only lover. For a woman as idealistic as Imogen, that meant she could not allow herself the physical pleasure they had shared without convincing herself that she must love him. But she hadn't loved him when she had run away from him on the day of their marriage.

He had seen the hurt in her eyes when she had turned away in the hallway just now, and he had ached to take her in his arms and tell her just how he felt about her, just what she did to him, had always done to him.

Right now he didn't know which was causing him the greater pain—his love for her or his guilt.

Dracco closed his eyes again. He had no idea how long he had been sitting here in his car, and neither did he care. He was back in the study of the house he had just left, Imo's father's study. It was the morning of Imo's seventeenth birthday, the morning she had run downstairs to him and begged him shyly for a birthday kiss, when he had known that he had to plead with his mentor and friend to release him from his promise.

'Yes, I know how hard it is, Dracco,' John Atkins had accepted gently when Dracco had finished his terse little speech. 'But Imogen is only seventeen.'

'Seventeen going on a thousand,' Dracco had groaned. 'She looks at me sometimes with all the knowledge of every woman that ever lived in her eyes, and then at other times…' He had paused and shaken his head. 'At other times she looks at me with the unknowing innocence of a child.'

'And it is the innocence and the future of that child I would ask you to protect and respect, Dracco,' Imogen's father had responded gently, getting to his feet and coming to Dracco's side, placing his hand on Dracco's arm in a benign, almost fatherly gesture.

He had paused before continuing in a sterner voice, 'If you love her you will want her to give you her love as a woman, not take from her the naïve love of a child.'

His words had hit home, and Dracco had acknowledged their truth.

'Nothing will ever change the way I feel about her,'

he had told the older man fiercely. 'But for her sake I will do as you ask, and I will wait.'

'It is nearly as hard for me as it for you, Dracco,' Imogen's father had told him gently. 'When I said I love you as a son that is exactly what I meant, and I can think of no greater pleasure than having you marry my daughter unless it is that of holding your children. But Imo is far too young yet to be burdened by a man's love. She needs time and space to grow up properly.'

Dracco hated himself for what he had done last night. He felt corrupted by his own emotions, his love, his desire, the constant, aching need for Imogen that had flared into a fiercely unstoppable conflagration the moment he had touched her.

He could feel it still now, knew he would feel it forever, just as he would love her forever.

It was over an hour since he had stopped his car. Reaching for his mobile, Dracco put a call through to David Bryant to explain that he was going to be late for their meeting.

Tugging viciously at the nettles growing in amongst the roses she could remember her mother planting, Imogen muttered an angry protest as she felt them stinging her through the thickness of the gardening gloves she had found in the old-fashioned potting shed.

Dracco's rejection of her love and the scorn with which he had reacted to it and to her, instead of making her question the validity of her feelings had somehow had totally the opposite effect and brought out in her a passionate strength she had not guessed she possessed.

How dared he try to tell her that she did not know

what love was? She tugged furiously on another nettle, giving a small sound of triumph as she threw it into the wheelbarrow without getting stung.

How dared he imply that she was some kind of naïve ninny who thought that just because she had sex with a man she must be in love with him?

Another nettle joined its fellows.

And as for his comments about her virginity... Well, it just so happened that the reason she had not...that she was still...had been still...had nothing to do with naïveté or timidity; it was simply that she had never met a man she had wanted enough.

Imogen yelped in pain as her momentary loss of concentration, whilst she battled against the dangerous images her brain was sending, resulted in a sharp reminder that nettles, carelessly handled, could and did sting.

'Ouch,' she protested out loud, as she inspected the swiftly lifting rash on the palm of her hand.

Like Dracco, it had caught her off guard and the result was pain. Well, this time at least she could retaliate, she decided grimly as she bent towards the offending weed and very determinedly removed it from the soil.

'Now see how you like that!' she told the nettle triumphantly.

'Excuse me.'

The sound of a hesitant male voice behind her caused her to spin round, her face pink with confusion at being caught conversing with the vegetation.

'It stung me,' she said rather lamely to the young man who was standing several feet away from her.

'My wife hates nettles,' he responded easily. 'Her

brothers hid her doll in a nettle patch when she was a little girl.'

'Oh, how unkind of them.'

'Well, I suspect she might have deserved it,' he told her, his voice ruefully candid. 'She had buried all their toy soldiers in a pile of builders' sand. The builder wasn't too pleased when it ruined his concrete. Her excuse was that they had been overwhelmed by a sandstorm in the desert.

'I was looking for Dracco,' he went on. 'I rang the bell but no one answered and then I saw you here in the garden. You must be his wife.'

'Yes, yes, I am,' Imogen responded. Who was this young man, and how did he know that Dracco was married?

As though he guessed what she was thinking, her unexpected visitor quickly explained, 'I'm Robert Bates—I work for Dracco. He left a message at the office, saying that…that he had got married, and asking me to bring him some papers he wanted.'

He was looking rather pleased with his deductive powers, and Imogen couldn't resist gently teasing him.

'And because of that you assumed that I must be Dracco's wife?'

'Not just because of that,' she was told sturdily. 'He has a photograph of you on his desk, and I recognised you from it straight away. Your father started the business, didn't he? Dracco told me about him.'

Now Imogen was surprised. Dracco had a photograph of her? She remembered that her father had had one taken on her seventeenth birthday; presumably Dracco must have inherited it. However, before she could reply her visitor was saying something she found even more surprising.

'I know that your father started the business, but Dracco is the one who made it the success it is today.' As he spoke Imogen could hear the admiration and respect in the younger man's voice. 'I couldn't believe my luck when he took me on. I didn't have the qualifications or the background.' He flushed a little whilst Imogen watched him in silence. 'I certainly didn't deserve the faith he's shown in me. The night we met I was sitting in a bar, full of self-pity and drinking myself into oblivion. Natasha, my wife now but my girlfriend as she was then, had just told me that her parents had threatened her that if she married me they were going to stop her trust fund.

'We met at university and I knew straight away that she was the one for me, and she said she felt the same, but what I didn't know then was that Natasha's family had money—and ambitions.' His voice grew slightly bitter. 'And those ambitions did not include a son-in-law with no family connections, no money and no prospects. Oh, Tasha said that it didn't matter, but of course it did. I couldn't give her the kind of life she'd grown up with, the kind of future she deserved; I couldn't even get a job. And then I met Dracco.

'He gave me a job, and time off so that I could get my Masters in business studies; he let me and Tasha live rent-free in a flat above the offices. He even went to see Tasha's parents, and God knows what he said to them but…' He broke off and gave Imogen an embarrassed look. 'I don't know why I'm telling you all this. After all, you already know exactly what kind of man Dracco is—you're married to him.'

He paused and then added hesitantly, 'Once when I asked him why he had helped me he said it was because I reminded him of what he himself had once been, and of everything that your father had done for him. He said that he wanted to pass on the good deed your father had done, to honour his memory and to show his gratitude for it. He said that your father had taught him the value of true generosity of spirit and the importance of self-respect.'

Imogen felt sharp tears sting her eyes in the small silence that followed. When she was sure she had full control of herself she offered, 'I'll give Dracco the papers if you want to leave them with me. But first let's go up to the house. I'm ready for a cup of tea; would you like one?'

'No, I'd better not. I promised Tasha I'd be home early. It's our wedding anniversary today, and her parents are taking us out to dinner!'

After her unexpected visitor had driven away Imogen couldn't help thinking about what he had said to her.

She had come out into the garden after Dracco's departure, ready to hate him all over again, but now she had been shown a compassionate side of him that made her feel uncertain.

Her hand felt acutely painful where the nettles had stung her. She had always been sensitive to their sting and an unpleasant tingling numbness now accompanied the raised rash, swelling the palm of her hand and her fingers.

She massaged it absently, thinking about her father.

She had always known how much he had thought of Dracco, and he had been held in high esteem by his peers for his shrewd judgement. She wished that he were here now for her to turn to.

Dracco still hadn't come back. And when he did... She quickly calculated how long it might be before she would know if she was pregnant.

And if she wasn't? Her face burned with mortified colour as she recognised that the bumping of her heart against her ribs at the thought of a repetition of the previous night was quite definitely not caused by dread or revulsion. Far from it. But Dracco did not love her and, according to him, she could not love him.

Who had he been thinking of whilst he touched her body, whilst he aroused it, entered it, possessed and filled it with the gift of immortality?

Imogen willed the acid sting of the tears burning her eyes not to fall.

As a child she had cried over her loss of her father's love to Lisa. As a woman there was no way she was going to cry over the loss of Dracco's love to her stepmother. No way at all!

Imogen sighed as she heard someone pressing impatiently and repeatedly on the front doorbell. Today was quite obviously her day for visitors.

Running lightly downstairs, she pulled open the front door, to reveal the features of her uninvited guest.

'Lisa!' It was impossible for Imogen to keep the shock out of her voice.

Her stepmother was wearing a pair of white Capri pants, her face and body tanned from her Caribbean holiday. Glaring at Imogen, she stepped into the hallway without waiting for an invitation and demanded sharply, 'Where's Dracco? I need to speak to him. Is he in the study?' She was walking towards the door before Imogen could stop her.

'No, he isn't,' Imogen told her as calmly as she could.

Seeing her stepmother here in the house which her presence had made so unhappy would have been bad enough, but knowing what Imogen now knew made that pain a thousand times worse.

'Then where is he?' Lisa was asking her angrily.

'He's out on business,' Imogen told her reluctantly. She would have preferred not to have to answer her at all. She would have preferred, in fact, to have enough belief in Dracco's support to insist that Lisa leave the house immediately.

'You mean he's sleeping at the apartment in London because he can't bear to have to sleep here with you?' Lisa taunted aggressively. 'It's a pity you were always so pathetically antagonistic towards me, Imogen. Had you not been you might have learned one or two things of value. Such as the fact that there is nothing that a man abhors more than a woman who doesn't have the pride to accept it when he makes it obvious he doesn't want her. And Dracco doesn't want you, Imogen. He never has wanted you. On the other hand, of course, he did want the business. And who can blame him? I certainly don't. Miranda warned me that you had come crawling back to him. Somehow I wasn't totally surprised. But it won't do you any good.'

Imogen had heard enough. She wasn't a shy, grieving teenager any more, who instinctively believed she had to be polite to grown-ups no matter how offensive and rude they were to her. It was high time that Lisa had a taste of her own medicine and Imogen was in just the mood to hand it out to her! After all, what had she got to lose? Dracco had already told her that he didn't love her. That they had only had sex!

If in punishing Lisa she punished Dracco as well, so much the better. He deserved it—they both did! Imogen couldn't remember ever feeling so furiously, gloriously angry!

She was a woman betrayed, a woman scorned, and those who had done the betraying and the scorning had just better watch out. They were going to find out that she could give as good as she got!

'As a matter of fact, it was Dracco who insisted on giving our marriage a second chance, not me,' she told Lisa with pseudo-sweetness. If she hadn't been enjoying herself so much she might almost have been shocked by the savage sense of satisfaction it gave her to say the words that were responsible for the brief look of fury she saw in Lisa's eyes. 'And it isn't just my share of the business he wants, Lisa,' she continued recklessly, only distantly aware of just how dangerous the surge of euphoria sweeping her up into its enticing embrace might be.

'Well, it can't possibly be your body!' Lisa retaliated nastily. 'If it was he'd be here with you now.'

'Perhaps I should leave it to him to tell you just what he wants from our marriage,' Imogen suggested serenely. She was almost enjoying the effect her words were having on her stepmother, who was staring at her as though she was seeing her properly for the first time. 'Unless, of course, he has already told you?'

Lisa gave a dismissive shrug. 'Dracco and I don't discuss you, Imogen, we have far more important things to talk about.'

Imogen could feel her self-control cracking as the euphoria left her as suddenly as it had swept her up, leaving in its wake a wash of anguished pain. 'Yes,' she agreed bitterly. 'Such as the way the pair of you deceived my father.'

She could see from the smirk the other woman was giving that she had allowed her emotions to betray her.

'You're making assumptions, accusations that you simply can't prove, Imogen.'

'I don't have to prove them,' Imogen retorted. 'Both you and Dracco have already shown me how true they are. Your affair—'

'Dracco told you we had an affair?' Lisa stopped her. For some reason she was frowning, as though she didn't believe what Imogen was telling her. But then unexpectedly she smiled, as though she was actually pleased to be revealed as a woman who had broken her marriage vows.

'He didn't need to tell me. You did that…on my wedding day,' Imogen reminded her grimly.

Lisa's smile widened. 'Yes, so I did. Poor little Imogen; you were so naïve, so stupid… Umm… Well, if Dracco is at the office I suppose I'd better go and see him there. I'm sure he'll appreciate the privacy for our reunion,' she purred tauntingly. 'It's been almost a month since he last saw me, and a month for a man of

Dracco's sexual appetite is a very long time. Don't expect him home too soon, will you, Mrs Barrington?'

She was walking through the door before Imogen could frame any kind of suitably cutting retort.

So it was true. Dracco was still seeing Lisa. He still loved her.

She wasn't going to cry, Imogen told herself with fierce pride. She wasn't!

CHAPTER SEVEN

'IMO, are you all right?'

'I'm fine, thank you,' Imogen responded, her voice as carefully devoid of any emotion as she could make it.

'Then why aren't you eating your dinner?' Dracco demanded sharply.

They had been living together as man and wife for just over a month, and Imogen had used the vast oasis of time Dracco's absences in London on business gave her. He had put his bank account at her disposal to set about restoring and refurbishing the house—it helped to keep her surface busy, during the day at least. At night, those long, lonely, aching nights when her thoughts and feelings couldn't be kept at bay, she felt as though she had entered a painful form of purgatory.

Not once since she had called at the house demanding to see him had he mentioned Lisa, and Imogen was stubbornly, bitterly determined not to be the one to bring up her name. Because she was afraid that if she did she would not be able to conceal what she really felt?

Lisa's cruel taunts had hit home. Had Dracco told Lisa just what he wanted from their marriage? There was no way Imogen could have borne to know that the man she loved was contemplating having a child with another woman, even a woman he did not love, but then Lisa had never been in the least bit maternal.

'Because I'm not hungry.' Imogen answered Dracco's

question coolly, lifting her gaze to meet his down the length of the pretty table she had seen in an antique shop and bought for a sum that had given her a vicious slam of guilt that was only slightly appeased by the pleasure it gave her to run her fingertips over the old satiny polished, wood.

A little to her own surprise, she had slipped back into life here in their small market town with unexpected ease. It was true that she had not made any close friends in Rio for her to miss. Her past had made it difficult for her to talk openly with her co-workers, and Dracco's rejection of her had left painful scars that had damaged her self-confidence.

She still thought about Rio, of course, and the children. After all, it was because of her determination to help them that she was trapped in this unbearable nightmare situation. One day she would go back, but right now there were issues closer to hand that were absorbing her time and attention!

'What is it, Dracco?' she challenged him. 'Were you hoping I was going to say I wasn't eating it because I felt sick? Because I'm pregnant?' She shook her head and gave him an unkind smile. 'I'm sorry to disappoint you, but I'm afraid that I'm not. Poor you, you're going to have to force yourself to have sex with me all over again.' She gave a small, brittle laugh as fragile as the crystal in the wine glasses they were drinking out of.

She scarcely recognised herself in the embittered woman she felt she was becoming. Was this what sex did to you when it was denied to you? When you were given a taste of what it could be and then not allowed to taste it again?

Imogen had no way of knowing; after all, as Dracco had said himself, what did she know about sex? She had been a naïve virgin when he had taken her to bed, a fool who confused sex with love and who believed that love mattered.

'Perhaps we should be more scientific and work out exactly when there is the optimum chance of me conceiving. After all, neither of us wants to have sex unnecessarily.' Somehow she managed to produce a sweetly disdainful little smile as she made this suggestion.

'You're lying to me, Imo!'

For a moment she was so caught off guard that she looked at him in shock. He was only guessing. He couldn't possibly know… She wasn't even properly sure herself… That unfamiliar bout of dizziness and the fact that she could not bear her normal cup of strong coffee in the morning was all the evidence she had to go on as yet.

'You want sex, and right now you want it so badly that I could take you right here, and, believe me, I'm sorely tempted to do just that, if only to prove it to you.'

Imogen went limp with relief. He didn't know. He hadn't meant what she had thought he meant at all. And then the reality of what he was saying pierced the blanket of her relief in tiny shocking darts of electric expectancy.

'You're wrong. I don't want you.'

What on earth was she doing, pushing him to the point where he would have no choice but to…?

Imogen gave a small gasp as Dracco got up from his seat and started to walk purposefully towards her.

'I've warned you before about challenging me, Imo,' he reminded her.

He had reached her now and pulled her easily to her feet and up against his body, holding her there as he looked down into her eyes, his mouth curling with insolence whilst his gaze lingered with deliberate intent on her mouth and then her throat, where her pulse was beating frantically fast, before dropping to her breasts.

It had been a hot day and she was wearing a thin top, against which her nipples had suddenly started to push with impatient eagerness.

Very carefully Dracco flattened the fabric against one of them, studying the openly erect outline in a way that made the heat flaming her face nothing to the heat burning inside her body.

'But then, this is exactly what you wanted me to do, isn't it?' he asked her softly.

Her denial never got beyond her throat, because suddenly Dracco was covering her mouth with his, kissing her with a fierce, smothering passion that her own senses leapt to meet.

It was almost as though they were fighting a battle that each was determined to win, anger searing and sizzling through both of them.

As his mouth possessed hers Imogen made an attempt to bite at it, forestalled by the fierce thrust of his tongue between her parted lips. She could feel its smooth roughness against the edge of her teeth and then its hot, dominating slide against her own tongue.

Something inside her started to melt. She gave a keening moan, her fingers curling into the thin cotton shirt he was wearing. As though she had crushed a flower in her fingers, she could smell the hot scent of him her grip had released. It dizzied her, sending a wave of longing melting through her, a slow, sweet melt of butter-soft pleasure.

'Dracco!'

She felt his mouth take his name from her as her lips formed it; knew he had absorbed and recognised the need that pierced her with such shocking sweetness.

Behind her closed eyelids she could see his naked body already, remember it in intimate and erotic detail, every bone, every muscle, every heart-wrenchingly perfect inch of him.

'I want you so much.'

The words were drawn from her as painfully as tears. She was powerless to suppress them and even more powerless to suppress her love for him. But it wasn't love. Dracco had told her that. It was just sex!

Her whole body shuddered.

Did Lisa make him react like this? Did he make her want him like this?

The savagery of her feelings lacerated her pride, but somehow she couldn't withstand the pressure of her need.

'Take me to bed, Dracco,' she urged him.

Because she wanted him or because she wanted to prove to herself that she was woman enough to overpower his resistance? That what Lisa had done she too could do?

She felt him hesitate.

'You were the one who wanted this,' she reminded him. 'You're the one who wants me to have your child.'

She knew, of course, that when she returned to sanity,

when the madness of her longing and misery left her, she would despise herself for using such a weapon, for demeaning herself. But right now, what did such things matter? Right now she wanted him so much…too much.

This time it was different. This time she was anticipating every touch, every sensation, savagely hungry for him, her body rising up to meet him and demanding more. More!

But then abruptly, like someone who had fed themselves on rich confectionery, she suddenly felt nauseated by what she was doing, appalled and disgusted by her own greed and lack of self-control.

This was sex, she reminded herself. Sex, not love. Was she really so lacking in self-control, in self-respect, that she could be satisfied with a physical act given without any kind of emotional grace?

'What is it?'

She could feel Dracco's hands holding her stiffening body as he leaned over her in the summer darkness.

'I've changed my mind.'

She could feel the sharpness of his indrawn breath.

'Am I allowed to ask why?'

She could hear the tension underlying the outwardly silky words.

'You wouldn't understand.' Any minute now she was going to cry. Defensively she turned her head away from him.

'Try me.'

Was it her imagination or was his voice softer, gentler? His hands on her arms certainly were. She could feel him rubbing her skin, soothing it, stroking it as though in some way he was trying to reassure and comfort her. A touch could say so much more than words. A touch couldn't lie…could it? Or was it more that her lack of experience was making her read too much into it?

She felt drained, defeated, overwhelmed by her emotions.

'I don't want it to be just sex between us, Dracco.'

There was a long silence whilst she waited for him to answer, during which Imogen asked herself furiously why on earth she had made such an admission.

'No? Then what do you want it to be?'

His hands were on her shoulders now, cupping them, working up delicately towards her throat, gently massaging away her tension.

Imogen gave a small gasp as she felt the tiny quivers of sensation darting over her skin. The pulse at the base of her throat had started to beat fast again. Dracco placed his thumb on it, measuring it, and then lifted his hand to her lips, rubbing against her bottom lip very slowly.

'Tell me, Imogen,' he demanded huskily, his voice a soft, sensual enticement. 'What is it you want from me?'

Her whole body was trembling now. It was those two little words 'from me' that had done it.

'I want you, Dracco!' she told him helplessly. 'I want you.'

And then she was reaching for his mouth with her own, devouring it with tiny, longing-filled little kisses interspersed with soft, whispery moans.

It wasn't the way it had been before. It was sharper, sweeter, deeper, with her not merely responding but actively drawing her own response from him! Touching him with fingers that trembled slightly and then grew more confident as she saw the naked agony of wanting delineating every aspect of his expression. He wanted her touch, needed it, yearned for it so much that he was prepared to walk across burning coals to get to it and her. It gave Imogen a wave of shockingly savage pleasure to see it.

She rode that pleasure like a surfer, telling herself that she was the one controlling it and Dracco, until suddenly it crested, splintering her into a thousand diamond darts of tormentingly hot need which only the sure thrust of Dracco's body within her own could satisfy.

Only when it was over and she was sure that Dracco was asleep did she allow herself to cry, to grieve for what Dracco had not given her—his love.

It didn't matter what Dracco said, what male logic he tried to superimpose on her feelings to validate his own lack of love for her and force an emotional distance between them, Imogen knew she loved him. She didn't want to and it galled and lacerated her sensitive pride to know that she did.

She had lost count of the time she had wasted trying to rationalise her emotions, trying to list mentally all the reasons she had for not loving him. Her heart just wasn't prepared to listen to them. Not even when she tormented it with the strongest antidote of all—not even when she reminded it about Lisa!

Imogen hesitated as she stopped her car outside the house, next to Dracco's. He had told her only the previous evening that he intended to work as much as he could in future from home.

'With modern technology I don't really need a London base any more, and, besides...' He had glanced with deliberate emphasis at her stomach as he spoke. Imogen had felt a now familiar fluttering of guilty panic invade her body.

Sometimes it was almost as though he already knew and he was deliberately directing the conversation down an avenue that would give her no choice but to tell him of her own growing conviction that she had conceived their child.

But she didn't want to do so. Not yet. And, anyway, she had nothing official to go on. Only her own awed belief that she was carrying a new life. She could quite easily have found out one way or the other, but she didn't want to do so, and she didn't want to question just why not either.

Was it because she wanted to punish him? Or was it because a part of her hoped that his desire to father their child would keep him close to her and away from Lisa?

She was beginning to hate what her love for him was making her do, the kind of woman it was turning her into. What had happened to her moral beliefs, her pride?

They were having a truly golden summer weather-wise, and in their local town this morning she had bumped into a friend from her schooldays. They had had coffee together, exchanging recent histories. Lulu, her friend, had been living with her partner since they had left university. She had recently been headhunted for a job, which would mean her relocating to New York.

'I envy you,' she had confessed to Imogen. 'You've done things the right way around, explored the world and then settled down. I can't bear the thought of losing Mac, but I want to do something with my life. I want to see something of the world, to explore it and my own talents.'

'Won't Mac go with you?' Imogen had asked her sympathetically.

'Not a chance,' Lulu had told her ruefully. 'He wants us to get married, have babies.' She had pulled a wry face. 'I've got three brothers and five step-siblings, the youngest of whom is still in nappies... Right now the thought of a baby...'

'Do you love him?' Imogen had asked her quietly.

The look Lulu had given her in response to her question had spoken volumes.

'You're right,' Lulu had agreed ruefully. 'I'm just going to have to accustom myself to the thought of frequent transatlantic travel—and finding a good nanny.'

They had parted, agreeing that they must make a regular date to meet up, and Imogen had driven back to the house reflecting on how good it felt to have started to develop a network of supportive friends.

A new interior-design business had opened in the town, and Imogen had arranged for the young women who ran it to call at the house one day so that they could discuss some ideas Imogen had for redecorating.

As she walked through the back door Dracco came into the kitchen. As always when she saw him Imogen's feelings were mixed and very emotional. She loved and wanted him so much, and yet at the same time she dreaded being with him because of the pain it gave her to know that he did not return her feelings.

'I thought we might have lunch out today,' Dracco

announced, casually removing the supermarket bags she was carrying and starting to put away their contents for her.

'I...I thought you were working?' she responded uncertainly.

Dracco paused in the act of opening the fridge door.

'I am, but I can take a couple of hours off. You mentioned that you'd like to do something with the garden; there's a particularly good garden centre with its own design team, a specialist outfit that has an excellent reputation, about ten miles away.'

Imogen chewed on her bottom lip. It was true that she did want to redesign the garden. With the needs of an active toddler to consider, the notion of a safe enclosed play area close to the house quite naturally appealed to her.

She and Dracco hadn't been out together as a couple since the early days of their reunion, nearly two months ago now. She chewed harder on her lip. He was spending more time at home, though.

'There's a very good restaurant where we could have lunch down by the river,' Dracco was saying.

If she was to refuse to go with him he might be tempted to ask Lisa. The sheer savagery of the jealousy that gored her made her catch her breath. What was the matter? She ought to hate and despise him for what he was doing, for what he was, instead of... What she was feeling was totally illogical! But then, when had love ever been anything else?

Helplessly Imogen watched him. She could feel the sheer intensity of her love melting her resistance.

'When were you thinking of leaving?' she asked him.

'Now,' Dracco told her promptly, putting the last of the groceries away and then coming towards her. 'Ready?'

His hand was beneath her elbow, guiding her back towards the door. What was the point of denying herself the opportunity of being with him when she wanted it so much? When she wanted him so much, she acknowledged with a small, sensual shudder of pleasure at his touch.

'No, not a pond.'

Imogen could feel the sharp look Dracco gave her as she shook her head in rejection of the garden designer's suggestion for a water feature in the patio area proposed for the garden.

'But you love the garden's existing formal fish pond,' Dracco reminded her with a small frown.

'Yes, I do,' Imogen agreed. She could feel her face starting to burn self-consciously as both men looked at her, waiting for her to explain her rejection. 'I was thinking that a pond so close to the house might not be a good idea,' she began hesitantly, pausing before continuing, 'Small children can drown so easily and quickly in even a few inches of water.'

The young garden designer gave a small, approving nod.

'Of course. I should have realised. And there are some totally child-safe alternatives that we could discuss—water bubbling over pebbles; that sort of thing.'

As she listened to him Imogen was conscious of Dracco's silence and his concentrated gaze, although he waited until she had thanked the designer for his suggestions and moved out of his earshot before bending his head to murmur speculatively in her ear, 'There isn't anything you want to tell me, is there, Imo?'

'No.' Imogen knew she sounded both defensive and flustered. 'When there is something...anything...to tell you then I will.'

'I'm sure that you will,' Dracco agreed urbanely. 'After all, there's no way you're going to put yourself in the position of having to have sex again with me—unnecessarily—is there? Mmm?'

Imogen gave him a seethingly angry look. How dared he torment her like this, mocking her for her vulnerability to him, for her desire for him?

He had taken to coming to bed later, so late, in fact, that by the time he eventually did so she had fallen into an exhausted sleep.

And she knew why, of course. He didn't want to sleep with her because he really wanted Lisa. How could he be so cruel, so uncaring of her feelings? Surely he must know just how much he was hurting her?

Their lunch, followed by a walk along the river, and then well over an hour here at the garden centre had left her feeling unusually tired. She had noticed increasingly over the last few days a lassitude which tended to overwhelm her during the afternoons, sometimes to such an extent that she had actually fallen asleep. Luckily the hot, sunny spell of weather they were having meant that she could lie in the garden on a sun lounger and doze off to sleep under the pretext of sunbathing.

Now, as they walked back to Dracco's car, Imogen could feel her footsteps lagging, and despite her frantic attempts to do so she couldn't quite manage to smother a sleepy yawn.

Dracco, of course, saw it and stopped in mid-stride to frown down at her and demand, 'Tired?'

'It disturbs my sleep when you come to bed so late,' Imogen parried.

'If that's meant to be a hint that you'd like me to come to bed earlier...?'

'It isn't,' Imogen denied immediately. 'Why should I want you to? I'm not the one who forced this marriage on you, Dracco.'

Before he could retaliate she hurried ahead of him, and then ignored him when he caught up with her just as she reached the car.

A young family of three small children and their father were playing with a ball, and as she watched them Imogen was suddenly reminded of the street children in Rio. Not that these well-fed and obviously very much loved children in front of her were anything like Rio's unwanted orphans, but seeing them made her think about her old life and the people she had shared it with.

Unexpectedly she suddenly ached for the stalwart comfort of Sister Maria's calm wisdom.

Imogen woke up with a start. She had actually gone to bed after their return from the garden centre, claiming not totally untruthfully that she had a headache. Having showered and re-dressed, she headed lethargically for the stairs. Soon now she was going to have to put her suspicions to the test, not that she really had any doubts that she was pregnant, but once that knowledge was 'official' then she was honour-bound to make it known to Dracco.

Normally a couple looked forward to the arrival of a child, especially a wanted child, as an event that would bring them closer together, but in their case Imogen was certain that it would have totally the opposite effect. Once she had given him the child he wanted there would be no room in Dracco's life for her.

Halfway down the stairs, where they turned at a right angle to themselves, there was a small half-landing with a tall, deep window that overlooked the driveway. The stained glass in it had a soft-hued richness which had always delighted Imogen. She stopped automatically to look through it and then froze as she recognised the familiar figure of her stepmother picking her way from her car to the front door on spindly high-heeled sandals.

So far as she knew, Lisa had not visited the house since their confrontation.

Instinctively Imogen stepped back out of sight as Lisa rang the front-doorbell. She heard the study door open and held her breath as she listened to Dracco's strong masculine footsteps and felt the small surge of early-evening air waft into the hallway as he opened the door.

'Lisa.' His voice was expressionless, but in a way that dragged sharp, poisoned nails of anguish across Imogen's heart.

Since Lisa's previous visit to the house Imogen had not confronted the role she knew her stepmother had played and she suspected continued to play in Dracco's life. But her awareness of it shadowed every aspect of their life together. Lying awake on her own in their bed at night she had tormented herself with the knowledge that Dracco was staying away from her because he really wanted to be with Lisa.

She had known exactly why Dracco had not wanted her love, and why he had been so insistent that all they had done together was to have sex, a physical coupling devoid of emotion. He kept his love only for Lisa. And yet, knowing that, she had still wanted him, responded to him, stupidly allowed herself to believe in the impossible fantasy that she, Imogen, had to mean something to him, that he couldn't possibly be with her if she didn't. She had even been so desperate for his love that she had allowed him to mock her for her own helpless desire for him.

Every time he taunted her about it she sensed some deep, hidden, ambivalent feeling behind his words. Because he resented her for taking what should only be given to the woman he loved?

Imogen could feel herself starting to shiver and then to shudder, deep, racking manifestations of her traumatic emotional pain. She could hear Lisa saying with soft seductiveness, 'I knew you'd be expecting me.'

And then the study door was closing, shutting her out, enclosing both of them in their own private world.

If she closed her eyes Imogen could see them in it...could see the way the late-afternoon sun would illuminate dust motes of gold through the long sash windows either side of the traditional fireplace her father had insisted on keeping. The desk, an antique partners' desk at which she could vividly remember both her father and Dracco sitting, working amicably together, was in one corner of the room. Behind it were floor-to-ceiling bookcases. To one side of the fireplace was a large leather chair, and in front of it a narrow sofa, long enough for her to lie down on at full stretch, something which she had done often in the early days after her mother's death.

Was Dracco laying Lisa down on that sofa now, slowly, lovingly, longingly undressing her whilst she...?

Imogen gave a low, tortured moan of pure anguish.

She wanted to scream, to cry, to claw at her very flesh for so foolishly and wantonly betraying her, to tear her treacherous heart out of her body, to sear and seal her emotions so she would never feel again, but most of all she wanted to run as far and as fast away from Dracco as she could. Just as she had done once before.

But she wasn't a mere girl any more and answerable only to herself. She was a woman now, with responsibilities. Briefly, her hand brushed her stomach. A single tear rolled down her cheek. Imogen lifted her head.

She was Dracco's wife. He had married her of his own free will. She was carrying his child, their child. This house held so many precious happy memories for her of her life with her own parents. Her mother and her father. She fully intended that her child would enjoy the security of being loved by both its parents. No matter what the personal cost to herself.

And if that meant outfacing Lisa, standing her ground and claiming her rights as Dracco's wife, then that was exactly what she was going to do.

Lisa might have his love, but she was the one who would have his child!

CHAPTER EIGHT

'YOU'RE very quiet; is something wrong?'

'I was just thinking about the past and my father—and Lisa,' Imogen responded with deliberate emphasis, shaking her head as Dracco indicated the bottle of wine he had just opened.

She had visited her doctor earlier in the day and had had her pregnancy confirmed.

Whilst she suspected that the odd glass of red wine would not do her baby any harm, she was not prepared to take any risks. Already he or she was infinitely precious to her, and part of the reason she had been thinking about her father. He would have so loved being a grandfather, especially when Dracco, whom he had valued so much, was that baby's father.

But then, unlike her, her father had not known the truth about the man he had treated as a son. He had not known how Dracco had betrayed him with his own wife.

'Lisa never really loved my father. She only married him for his money.'

It must be the confirmation of her pregnancy that was making her feel so emotional, Imogen decided, that and the fact that her baby's father didn't love her. There had been another woman in the surgery at the same time as Imogen, very heavily pregnant and accompanied by her partner, who had watched her with such a look of tenderness and adoration that Imogen had felt her eyes sting. When the woman's hand had rested against her stomach he had lifted it to his lips, kissing it before replacing it on her belly and then covering it with his own.

'Lisa was a lot younger than your father, Imo.'

'Oh, of course you would take her side, wouldn't you?' Imogen stormed.

Dracco had been about to raise the glass of wine he had just poured himself to his lips, but now he put it down, frowning as he did so.

'I have no idea what all this is about, Imo,' he began austerely. 'You know—'

'I know that I saw Lisa here in this house and that you haven't said one word about her visit to me,' Imogen told him trenchantly.

'You saw her?' Dracco's frown deepened, his voice sharpening.

'Yes. What did you do, Dracco? Ring her up and tell her that it was safe to come over? That I was asleep? That you were tired of making love—oh, I'm sorry, having *sex*—with a woman you didn't really want and certainly didn't love? A woman who wasn't her? Well, this is my home, Dracco, and just so long as it is there is no way I intend to tolerate you entertaining your…your mistress in it…'

Imogen broke off and took a deep breath to steady her voice, but before she could continue Dracco was demanding tersely, 'What on earth are you talking about?'

Imogen couldn't believe his gall. It left her breathless, mute with a fury that visibly shook her body.

'You know perfectly well what I'm talking about,' she

threw at him when she could finally speak. 'I'm talking about the affair you are having with Lisa, the affair you were having with her when she was married to my father and which you have continued to have with her even though both of you have married elsewhere.'

She could see the muscles clenching in Dracco's jaw. He didn't like what she was saying—well, tough! How did he think she felt? How did he think her father would have felt?

'You think I'm having an affair with Lisa?'

He had to be working very hard to project such a convincing air of stunned disbelief, Imogen acknowledged, which just showed how important it was for him to keep his relationship with Lisa a secret.

'No, Dracco,' she told him calmly, 'I don't think you are having an affair with my stepmother; I know you are. Lisa told me so herself, on the morning of our wedding.'

There was a long, tense pause before Dracco asked grimly, 'Is that why you ran away?'

'What do *you* think?' Imogen responded bitterly, shaking her head before he could say anything else and telling him, 'That's it, Dracco. I'm not prepared to discuss it any further.' She felt amazed and awed by her own unexpected self-control—and the way she had taken charge of the whole situation. 'What's past is past, and it's the future that concerns me now. A future which you have forced on us both. I want to make it clear that I will not tolerate Lisa's presence here in this house. Not whilst I am expected to live here!'

Now she was going to tell him about the baby, their baby. And she was going to beg him, no, demand that he think about the effect his continued relationship with Lisa would have on the child he claimed he wanted so much! But before she could begin to speak the telephone suddenly rang.

Dracco turned away from her as he picked up the receiver, quite patently not wanting Imogen to overhear anything of the call. Because it was from Lisa? Suppressing her instinctive urge to wrench the phone from him and break the connection between them, Imogen turned instead and hurried into the hallway.

Where was her bravery now? she derided herself as she battled against her own emotions. Why wasn't she challenging Dracco? Was it because she was desperately afraid that she would lose, that he would choose Lisa above their baby?

There was no way she could allow herself to become the pathetic, unwanted, cheated-on wife of a man who found his pleasure with and gave his love to another woman, she reminded herself determinedly.

And if Dracco chose to ignore the demands she intended to make, the battle lines she intended to draw? Imogen could feel herself start to tremble. Her earlier buoyant surge of exhilaration had drained away, leaving her feeling afraid and vulnerable, not for herself but for her baby, who deserved surely to be loved by both its parents.

'Imo.'

She froze as Dracco came out into the hall and called her name.

'I've got to go to London, but when I come back there are things that you and I need to discuss, certain misconceptions you appear to have that need to be addressed and corrected.'

'I see. When will you be back?' She held her breath, even though she suspected she already knew the answer.

'I'm not sure.' Dracco's tone was cautious. 'I may have to stay overnight.'

May? Imogen only just managed to stop herself from laughing bitterly out loud. Even if the formality of his language hadn't been enough to tell her how furiously angry he was, the look on his face did, but Imogen had far more to concern her than Dracco's anger. Like, for instance, the source of that telephone call he had been so anxious for her not to overhear. It had to have been from Lisa! And now he was going to London to see her and no doubt spend the night with her!

She hated herself for not having the courage to challenge him. Was this what love did to you? Made you vulnerable? Afraid? Being unable to put her suspicions into words made her feel humiliated and ashamed.

Now, more than at any other time, surely, she ought to be able to turn to Dracco for his support and protection.

But she didn't seem to matter to him!

The sight of his own grim-faced expression as he glanced in his driving mirror only reinforced what Dracco already felt. It had stunned him to hear Imogen accusing him of having an affair with Lisa. Lisa might consider herself to be beautiful and desirable, but so far as Dracco was concerned she was ugly, ugly inside with malice, greed and selfishness. He had always suspected that Imogen's father had regretted marrying her, although he had been far too loyal to say so. His mouth tightened on the memory of the accusation Imogen had flung at him that he had been having an affair with Lisa whilst she was married to her father. Did Imogen really believe he was capable of that kind of disloyalty?

On the morning of their marriage when Imo had demanded to know if there was a woman in his life whom he loved he had assumed that she had been talking about herself. The horror and rejection in her voice and her eyes when he'd told her of his feelings had made him curse himself under his breath for what he had done to her.

The youthful infatuation she had had for him had quite plainly been destroyed by the unwanted reality of his love for her, a love which he had already been guiltily conscious she was really too young to be burdened with.

When she had run away from him that belief had been compounded. Dracco's eyes darkened with remembered pain. He had been on the verge of running after her when Henry had collapsed, and in the panic which had ensued everyone had automatically looked to him to take charge.

By the time he had been free to go after Imo it had been too late. She had already left the country.

He had tracked her down, of course, his concern for her as great as his searing anguish at losing her.

He had kept track of her ever since—for her sake and for what he owed her father. And it was for Imogen's sake that he was driving to London now, when he would far rather have been at home with her, explaining to her, reassuring her that Lisa was the last woman he would ever be interested in. Because there was and could only ever be one woman he loved and that woman was Imo herself.

However, his telephone call had been from the same agency he had used to keep track of Imogen during her absence, and they had rung to inform him as a matter of urgency that it looked as though the shelter was going to be closed down.

It seemed that the man who owned the building and the land on which the shelter stood wanted to sell the land on, and he was using strong-arms tactics to try to frighten the sisters into giving up their lease on the property.

Dracco knew just how much the shelter meant to Imogen, and he wanted to do everything he could to help save it, even if that meant helping to find and finance new premises for it.

He was driving to London so that he could, without Imogen discovering what was happening, negotiate some way of keeping the shelter open. No matter what it cost him.

Despairingly Imogen stood in the empty silence of the hallway. Dracco had left her to go to Lisa. What was she going to do?

She felt weak, defeated, frightened and alone. Her earlier confidence and bravado had completely left her. She desperately wanted to be with people who cared about her, people she felt secure with. Suddenly she missed Rio, and the sisters, the people she had known there—desperately.

What was going to happen to her and, more important, what was going to happen to her baby?

He or she needed to be loved. To be with people who cared—and for the right reasons!

Imogen knew exactly what she had to do!

This time there was no urgency, no sense of flight or desperation, just a chilling, calm acceptance of what had to be.

She packed carefully, and even managed to be controlled enough to ring ahead to Heathrow to book her seat on the first available flight to Rio.

It was leaving just before midnight, and she had plenty of time to get there.

Midnight. No doubt by then Dracco would be with Lisa in London at his apartment. In bed with her, no doubt, swearing eternal love to her.

Clutching her body, Imogen raced to the bathroom, her stomach churning with nausea.

'She has that effect on me too,' she comforted her still flat stomach sadly. 'He doesn't deserve you, my darling, no matter how much he wants you. I'm going to take us both somewhere we can be happy together without him.'

Even as she whispered the words to the new life growing inside her Imogen was aware of a small inner voice she couldn't quite silence that was objecting to what she was saying. It reminded her that although Dracco might not love her, that did not mean that he would not love his child, and that she had no real right to make decisions that would separate that child from Dracco forever.

She did not want to listen to that kind of criticism and she wasn't going to.

The taxi she had ordered arrived. She was travelling light—everything Dracco had bought for her, except this time her rings, she was leaving behind.

One small tear glittered in her eye as she closed the front door behind her. Refusing to look back, she got in the taxi.

Dracco grimaced, rubbing his hand over his tired eyes as he replaced the telephone receiver and switched on the computer on his desk.

He had managed, he hoped, to avert the crisis with the shelter—Dracco had managed to persuade the landowner to sell the shelter and the land to him, at a vastly inflated price, of course, but he didn't regret having to pay for it, not knowing how happy it would make Imogen. However, there were still certain ends he had to tie up, e-mails he had to send, people he had to contact—lawyers, accountants, bankers—but first…

He checked his watch; Imogen should still be up, and suddenly he desperately needed to hear her voice. He had hated having to leave her without talking through the whole ridiculous misunderstanding about Lisa, but he had felt that he needed time to explain everything properly to her. However, right now his need to speak to her was overwhelming everything else. He could at least tell her how much he loved her.

Dracco frowned. He had made three attempts to telephone Imogen without success. She could, of course, be asleep, or simply refusing to answer the telephone, but instinctively he knew that there was a more serious reason for her silence.

Without wasting time analysing his feelings, he reached for his car keys and headed for the door.

Heathrow was busy. Imogen had plenty of time before she needed to check in.

To distract herself from the pain of what she was having to do, she tried to make mental plans for the practicalities she would need to address once she arrived in Rio. Initially she would have to book into a hotel. Someone had now taken over her old apartment but even if they hadn't with a baby to consider she would have had to find somewhere more suitable to live, preferably a small house with its own garden.

She would also, no doubt, have to make arrangements to retain enough of the income from her share of the business to support herself and the baby, and perhaps even go back to teaching as well, instead of working full-time for the shelter.

At least there would be one advantage to her returning to Rio: her son or daughter would be bilingual. And yet for some reason, instead of making her smile, this recognition made her eyes fill with hot, acid tears.

It was nearly time to check in. Automatically she picked up her bag, and then realised that she needed to visit the ladies' cloakroom—a small side-effect of her pregnancy.

There was a little girl leaving the cloakroom at the same time as Imogen; blonde-haired and dressed in trendy denims, she appeared to be on her own, and instinctively Imogen kept a protective eye on her.

As they emerged onto the concourse the little girl ran towards a man who was standing several yards away.

Imogen could hear the love in her voice as she exclaimed, 'Daddy!' And she could see too the answering love in the man's eyes as he held tightly on to her, swinging her up into his arms.

'Come on, we'd better get you on your flight. If you

miss it your mother will never let you come and see me again.'

Now Imogen could hear pain and anger in his voice and, transfixed, she stood where she was watching them anxiously.

'I don't want to go back. I want to stay here with you,' the little girl was saying, and Imogen could hear the tears in her voice and see more in her father's eyes as he shook his head and started to carry her towards the departure gate.

Imogen felt as though she had been struck a mortal blow. One day would her child be like that little girl? Less than half a dozen yards away from her she could see another small family group, two adults—a man and a woman—and two children this time, two children with parents who loved them. Did she really want any less than that for her child?

If she went back to Rio now, and brought her child up alone, denying him or her to Dracco and denying him to them in return, what would her child ultimately think of her? Would he or she understand or would they blame her? Or, even worse in Imogen's eyes, would they simply suffer in silence, longing for the father they did not have?

She thought about the relationship she had had with her own parents, especially with her father. There was no way she could deny her child the right to have that magical, wonderful bond, to experience the love she had experienced. Dracco would love their child, his child; Imogen knew that instinctively. She took one step and then another, slowly at first, and then more quickly until she was almost running. She stopped only when the stitch in her side commanded her to, and her lungs were full of the sharp, acrid smell of the diesel fumes of the taxis outside the airport building.

It normally took two hours for Dracco to drive home from London—less when he did so late at night, but on this occasion he was unlucky. On this particular night an extra-wide load of dangerous chemicals was travelling along the motorway ahead of him at a speed which meant that it took Dracco over three hours to reach home.

When he did so he found the house in darkness and Imogen gone. Gone without any kind of explanation, any note.

Her hairbrush and a bottle of the perfume she always wore were still on her dressing-table. The perfume bottle had fallen over and Dracco could smell Imogen's familiar scent all around him.

He closed his eyes, his throat tight with emotion, raw with helpless anguish and fear. He could still see the look in her eyes when she had accused him of loving Lisa. Dear God, how could any woman be so blind? And how could any man be so stupid?

Why? Why hadn't he stopped to tell her the truth? Why the hell had he gone off like that, leaving her alone and vulnerable?

She believed him to be guilty of the worst kind of disloyalty, to her and to her father. And there were other issues at stake, such as the way he had treated her, the things he had said to her—and the things he hadn't said.

CHAPTER NINE

IMOGEN felt her heart starting to thump nervously as her taxi pulled into the drive. It was one in the morning, but all the house lights were on and Dracco's car was parked outside.

He had come back. He wasn't spending the night in London with Lisa!

As she got out of the taxi she had to fight against the feeling of dizziness filling her.

She was becoming used now to that disconcerting feeling of giddiness she sometimes experienced, especially when she first got up. But at least she wasn't actually being sick.

'You're a very good baby,' she whispered unsteadily to her stomach as she paid off the taxi and fought to hold on to her courage, 'a very good baby, and your mummy and your daddy are going to love you so very much.'

Had she been a fool to come back? From her own point of view, probably, she acknowledged as she opened the front door. But if Dracco dared to think that he could supplant her in her baby's life with Lisa then she was going to make sure he soon learned otherwise. She and the baby came as a package…a twosome, and if he wanted to make that a threesome then he had to take the pair of them together.

It was amazing, the strength and determination that

being a mother could give you, she acknowledged wryly as she came to an unsteady halt in the hallway, her heart pounding.

The study door started to open and Dracco came out. He looked as though he had undergone the most soul-destroying trauma. Dracco, whom she had never seen looking less than totally in control. His shirt was crumpled, and he needed a shave. His eyes were even slightly bloodshot!

Refusing to give in to the longing weakening her body, Imogen reminded herself of the decision she had just made and, drawing herself up, she fixed him with a look of angry distaste before demanding accusingly, 'I don't suppose I need to ask who you went to London to see?'

Dracco was looking at her with the kind of blank-eyed shock more appropriate, surely, to a man who had seen a ghost than one who had returned home from a rendezvous with his lover.

'Imo! You've come back. Oh, thank God, thank God!'

His voice sounded cracked, hoarse, and the look in his eyes as he strode towards her suddenly made her heart flip over inside her chest. Instinctively she backed away from him.

'I'm tired, Dracco,' she told him. 'I want to go to bed.'

'We need to talk.' He was insistent but Imogen shook her head. She knew she was far closer to emotional exhaustion than she dared to admit. If they started to talk now, to argue, she knew she wouldn't have the strength to say the things she wanted to say.

'No, not now,' she refused sharply. 'Not now, Dracco. Tomorrow.'

As much as he ached to beg her to listen to him, to find out where she had gone and why she had returned, to tell her how much he loved her and plead with her never, ever to leave him again, Dracco could see how vulnerable she was, and he wanted to protect her, to put her needs before his own.

'Very well,' he agreed heavily. 'But,' he told her, and, even though he gave her a wry smile, Imogen sensed that he meant it, 'I shall be locking all the doors and keeping the keys, Imo. So no more running away. I want you to promise me that.'

'I promise,' Imogen conceded tiredly as she headed for the stairs, praying that Dracco wouldn't make any attempt to follow her.

When he didn't, and when she finally closed the door of her old childhood bedroom behind her a part of her was weakly disappointed that he hadn't followed her. That he hadn't taken her in his arms and…and what? Face facts, she told herself wearily as she prepared for bed. Grow up, Imo. He doesn't love you. He loves Lisa.

'Can you answer that?' Imogen asked Dracco. 'I'm going to put the kettle on.'

Imogen had just arrived downstairs in the kitchen, having overslept, to find Dracco already there.

As he had said himself, they needed to talk, and the most important thing they had to talk about was the fact that she was carrying his child. Their baby!

Did she have the strength to concentrate on that all-important fact and to negotiate an acknowledgement from Dracco that their child had to come first—with both of them?

As he answered the phone Dracco kept on looking at Imogen, greedily, hungrily, absorbing the reality of her presence. He loved her so much!

What had happened? Why had she come back? Absorbed in his own thoughts, he took several seconds to realise what the caller on the other end of the telephone line was saying to him.

'Yes, I'll pass that message on to her,' he agreed quietly, his gaze still fixed on Imogen, who had turned away from the kettle to look at him.

He was watching her as though he had never seen her before, as though he was… Dizzy with the implausibility, the impossibility, surely, of what she seemed to be seeing in his eyes, Imogen stood still.

Silently Dracco replaced the receiver.

'What is it?' Imogen asked him uncertainly.

'That was the doctor's surgery,' Dracco announced with heavy quietness. 'They wanted to tell you that they've made an appointment for you at the hospital for your first antenatal clinic. You're pregnant with my child, and you didn't tell me!'

For the first time in her life Imogen did something she didn't think women did except in novels—she fainted!

When she came round she was lying on the sofa in the study, with Dracco leaning over her.

In the few seconds it had taken him to assimilate the information that Imogen was pregnant he had come from hope to despair as he recognised the reason why she had decided not to leave him. Imogen had her father's old-fashioned morals. She would not be able to leave him and take from him the child he had bargained with her to have. He had known that all along, and believed too that it would be impossible for her to leave her child either, which would mean that she would have to stay with him.

But now suddenly the realisation that she was here because she had conceived his child, rather than because she wanted to be, left a sour taste in his mouth.

Imogen shivered slightly, nervously aware of the way that Dracco was watching her and of the brooding, almost despairing look in his eyes. Because he had changed his mind? He didn't want a child by her any more?

'You're pregnant.' Dracco's voice was flat and empty of any expression for her to read.

'Yes,' she acknowledged. Please, God, don't let her cry, but this wasn't how such news should be broken—or received. So what had she expected, she challenged herself as her senses started to clear, a fanfare of trumpets proclaiming an ode to joy? Dracco gathering her up in his arms, his eyes full of tender worship and adoration?

Maybe that was unrealistic, but some expression of pleasure wouldn't have gone amiss, for their baby's sake if not for her own.

'Is that why you didn't leave—why you came back?'

'Yes,' she conceded as she swung her feet to the floor and then stood up. There was no way she intended to have this discussion with Dracco whilst in the disadvantageous position of lying down as he stood over her.

She intended to ensure that from now on whenever they met in the arena of conflict that she suspected wearily was going to be their marriage it was going to be on equal terms.

'I wanted to leave you, Dracco. You're having an affair with…with Lisa.' She stopped, her voice unsteady. 'But there was this little girl with her father, and suddenly I couldn't!'

Imogen turned away, but not before Dracco had seen the sheen of her tears in her eyes.

'Imo.'

Imogen tensed as Dracco grasped her hands in his, refusing to let her go, even though she tried desperately to pull away from him. She could feel his thumbs caressing the vulnerable undersides of her wrists in a way that sent hot shivers of pleasure racing up her arms.

'I don't know where you've got the idea that I'm having an affair with Lisa, but I can assure you that nothing could be further from the truth.'

That he could lie to her so uncaringly infuriated Imogen. Did he really think she was that much of a fool?

'No?' she challenged him. 'Then why did you go to London last night?'

Dracco shook his head, mentally cursing beneath his breath. Until everything was finally legalised, every 'i' dotted, every 't' crossed, he didn't want to tell her what had been going on, just in case something should go wrong.

'I can't tell you that, I'm afraid, Imo, but I can promise you that it wasn't to see Lisa.'

Imogen curled her lip in acid contempt as she pulled herself free of him.

'I don't believe you. Lisa told me on the morning of our wedding that you loved her. She challenged me to ask you about it. And she's confirmed her relationship with you to me since. I don't know which of you I despise the most. I suppose it must be you, if only because I never liked Lisa, whilst you...'

Imogen paused and then swallowed. What did it matter what she admitted to Dracco now about her past feelings for him? After all, she was pretty sure he must have known all about her foolish teenage crush on him.

Determinedly she looked up into his eyes and told him as calmly as she could, 'I adored you, Dracco. I put you up on a pedestal. I believed in you and I...' She stopped, appalled to discover how emotional she was becoming. 'After losing my parents, discovering how wrong I was about you was the most hurtful and traumatic thing I have ever experienced.'

She wasn't being totally honest with him, Imogen acknowledged as she looked away from him. The deaths of her mother and father had hurt, but after the immediacy of her shock and loss had worn off she had been left with the comforting knowledge that they had loved her.

In recognising Dracco's treachery she had been left with no such comfort whatsoever!

Dracco surveyed Imogen's downbent head for several seconds whilst he struggled to control the urgency of his longing to take her in his arms and hold her there until he had convinced her just how wrong she was.

'Do you really think I would have betrayed your father's trust like that?' he asked Imogen quietly.

'When love is involved other loyalties can sometimes cease to matter,' Imogen responded emptily.

Talking like this was stirring up so many painful memories inside her; too many.

'What I can't understand or forgive, Dracco, is that you were willing to marry me just for the sake of the business, even though you loved Lisa. And the way you lied to me about it... You did lie to me, didn't you?' she challenged him.

Dracco turned to stare out of the study window.

'Yes,' he admitted. 'I did. But not in the way that you think, Imo.' He heard her gasp and turned round just in time to see her almost running out of the room.

Oh, she was such a fool, Imogen derided herself as she hurried into the garden. She had to be to allow herself to still feel so much hurt over Dracco's behaviour towards her.

Instinctively she headed for her mother's rose garden, seeking its solace and comfort.

How could she possibly love a man who could so easily lie, and not just to her? Look at the way he had denied Lisa! Her hand stilled on the rose she had been touching.

What did she mean, love? She did not love Dracco.

Liar, a knowing inner voice taunted her. Of course you do; you've never stopped loving him and you never will!

'No!' A sharp pain slid through her heart. No, it couldn't be true. But of course she knew that it was.

Dracco frowned. Should he go after Imogen, make her listen whilst he tried to explain just how wrong she was and why? If he did, would she listen? He might have got what he had wanted for so long, Dracco acknowledged, but there was no real satisfaction in knowing that he was forcing Imogen to stay with him. Her presence in his life through force was not what he wanted; not in his life, or his bed. No, what he wanted was for her to be with him because she wanted to be, because she loved him.

His telephone rang and he went automatically to answer it, forcing himself to concentrate on what the client on the other end of the line was saying to him.

An unfamiliar car was coming up the drive, and Imogen shaded her eyes from the sun as it stopped and the driver got out. She smiled as she recognised David Bryant, Dracco's solicitor.

He was smiling back at her.

'How is your wife?' she asked him.

'Very pregnant and very hot.' He laughed. 'She hasn't got very long to go now, though. She wants Dracco to be one of the baby's godparents: she thinks the story of his love for you is very romantic.'

Imogen looked at him.

'I hope you don't mind me telling her,' he added uncertainly. 'My mother told me about it; she had heard it from my uncle. He thought a lot of Dracco, and of course Dracco consulted him after your father's death about what he should do. My uncle knew that your father made Dracco promise not to tell you about his feelings for you until you were over twenty-one. But he could see that your father's untimely death had changed things, and that you desperately needed someone in your life to protect you. According to my mother, my uncle fully endorsed Dracco's decision to ask you to marry him so that he could protect you and your inheritance.'

He avoided looking at Imogen as he continued, looking embarrassed, 'Of course, I don't know the whole situation—my mother has always maintained that you ran away because you were young and afraid, and suffering from young girl's wedding nerves—but it must have been hard for Dracco to lose you like that when he loved you so much.'

There was just the faintest hint of a gentle accusation in his voice.

'Still, at least it's all worked out well for you both now. My mother claims that she always knew that you'd be reconciled. Is Dracco in, by the way? I've got some papers for him to sign.' He was looking a bit self-conscious now, as though aware he'd said too much.

Her head was spinning with the shock of his revelations. Automatically she nodded and then watched as he walked towards the house. Then, very slowly and thoughtfully, she followed him.

Wearily Dracco got up from behind his desk. The house felt still and silent. Dracco had spent the hours since David Bryant had left thinking about the past—and the future—and questioning the role he had played in Imogen's life. Meanwhile he had mentally drawn up two tables, one listing the reasons why they should stay married and the other listing those why they shouldn't.

And from Imogen's point of view that list weighed heavily in favour of him setting her free, giving back to her the right to make her own decisions and choices.

He and Imogen needed to talk and there was no point in putting off what had to be said.

He found her upstairs in her old bedroom. She was sitting on the window seat with her knees drawn up into her body and her arms wrapped around them, a pose he remembered from her childhood.

Silently Imogen watched as Dracco came into her bedroom. She had come here after she had left the rose garden, moving like someone in a dream, needing somewhere safe to retreat to, somewhere she could examine and analyse her chaotic thoughts in peace.

David Bryant's comments had given her a tantalising glimpse into a situation she had never known existed; a situation, moreover, which totally changed her own interpretation of past events.

It wasn't hard for her to accept that her father would have guessed how she had felt about Dracco; after all, she had never tried to keep it a secret. But David's inference that Dracco had loved her and that her father had made him promise to keep that love a secret…

Ask him if there is a woman whom he loves, Lisa had challenged her on her wedding day, and she had done just that, and Dracco…

Could she have got it wrong, made a huge misjudgement and been encouraged to make it by Lisa? What if she had? What if the someone Dracco had loved had been not Lisa but her?

Her heart somersaulted and thudded so heavily against her chest wall that her whole body shook with the agitation of her emotions.

'Imogen.'

The sound of her full name on Dracco's lips when he

nearly always called her 'Imo' seemed somehow portentous.

She took a deep breath, her gaze searching his face, looking for some clue as to what he might be feeling, something to guide her, show her, but there was nothing. She would have to rely on her own intuition, her own need.

'Why did you marry me, Dracco?'

She could see that it wasn't the question he had been expecting. Even so, she noticed how he turned slightly away from her before he answered it, almost as though he didn't want her to be able to see his expression.

'You know why,' was his careful response.

'I certainly thought I knew why,' Imogen agreed quietly, getting off the window seat and coming to stand in front of him so that she could see his face. 'I was in the garden when David Bryant arrived. He told me…' She paused, wondering if she had the courage to go on. And then she thought of her baby, their baby, and knew that what she was doing wasn't just for herself, that it wasn't just her own future that was at stake, or her own happiness.

'Is it true that my father made you promise not to tell me you loved me until I was over twenty-one?' she challenged him.

At first she thought that he wasn't going to reply, and that alone was enough to make her heart start to hammer with fierce pleasure. After all, if what David had told her wasn't true then Dracco would have denied it immediately, wouldn't he?

'Is it, Dracco?' she persisted.

'Yes,' Dracco admitted tersely.

Dracco had loved her… Joy sang through her whole body, a glorious, empowering surge of deep female wonderment.

'Your father knew how I felt about you,' he told her. 'I couldn't have hidden it from him; it was hard enough hiding it from you, especially when…' He paused, his eyes dark and bleak, as though he was looking into a secret place that haunted him. 'He said that even though you had a teenage crush on me you were far too young to commit yourself to any kind of relationship with me, any kind of future. He said that such a relationship would be unfair to you, unbalanced, untenable, and that you needed time to grow up, to learn something of life and yourself.

'He knew that my feelings wouldn't change, but he was concerned that you should have the opportunity to change yours, and I agreed with him. Not that it was easy, not with you.' He broke off and shook his head. 'I ached for you so badly that sometimes…' He stopped. 'And then your father died.

'I didn't want to break my promise to him, but I had no choice. I talked to Henry about it, and he urged me to go ahead. He said that under the circumstances your father would have understood. You were only eighteen and so damned innocent; I knew that.' He stopped again. 'As it was, I hardly dared trust myself around you, but I had to honour at least part of my promise to your father. And so…'

'And so you planned for our marriage to be in name only,' Imogen supplied softly for him.

'Yes. I told myself that somehow I would find a way of waiting until you were twenty-one. You wanted to go to university. But then when we came out of the church you told me that you knew how I felt about you, and then…' he paused and looked directly at her '…then you ran away, leaving me in no doubt as to what you felt about being loved by me.'

'I didn't run away because you loved me, Dracco,' Imogen told him shakily. 'I ran away because I thought you loved someone else—Lisa. That was what she'd implied to me. She said there was someone in your life. She challenged me to ask you. If I had thought for one minute that you loved me then…'

'Then what?' Dracco asked her softly.

'Then.' Betrayingly Imogen's hand strayed towards her stomach as she tried to draw air into her lungs. 'Then right now this baby would probably be our third and not our first. Why didn't you tell me?' she demanded emotionally. 'You must have known how I felt about you.'

She ached for the years they had lost, the love she had gone without, the pain she had endured.

'You know why. I had promised your father, and I agreed with everything he had said. You were too young. I knew for your own sake I had to let you go. Not that I ever really did,' he admitted. 'I kept tabs on you the whole time you were in Rio, and when you came back—'

'You rejected me when I tried to tell you I loved you,' Imogen interrupted him sadly.

'Imo, I hated myself for the way I'd forced you into my bed, and because I wanted so much more from you than just sex. Too much more,' he groaned. 'Everything, all of you, just as I wanted you to accept and love all of me.'

She trembled wildly as he reached for her, allowing him to draw her into his arms, against his body.

'Kiss me, Dracco,' she demanded, lifting her face towards him, 'just to prove to me that this is really happening.'

Tenderly his lips brushed hers, but it wasn't enough for Imogen. She placed her hand on his jaw, maintaining the kiss, prolonging it, running her tongue-tip along the firm outline of his lips, tormenting and teasing them until Dracco gave a raw groan and gathered her even closer, close enough for her to feel his arousal.

'I felt so guilty about what I was doing,' Dracco admitted. 'I had forced you into a situation where you had no option other than to go to bed with me.' He stopped as he saw that Imogen was shaking her head.

'I could have refused if I'd really wanted to. Deep down inside it was what I wanted, you were what I wanted, even though initially I wouldn't admit it even to myself. That first morning after we'd made love...' she paused and shook her head in bemusement '...I felt as though finally my life was complete, Dracco, as though finally I was complete. But when I tried to tell you you rejected me, and then I remembered about Lisa.'

'Lisa never meant anything to me. I detested her both for the way she treated you and the way she abused your father's love.'

'She wanted you, though,' Imogen told him.

Dracco grimaced. 'Yes.'

Imogen waited. She knew that if he had tried to deny Lisa's desire for him she would have felt reluctant to trust him completely.

'She came on to me both during her marriage to your

father and afterwards, and I suspect that in implying to you that she and I...well, I suspect it was her way of hurting you and getting back at me. She knew how I felt about you. Although how on earth you could believe that I could ever be remotely interested in her...!'

One arm was holding her close to his side whilst his free hand lazily caressed her throat.

'She came here to see you,' Imogen pointed out.

'She gets biannual payments from your father's estate, and she wanted to try to persuade me to increase them. I told her that she was wasting her time. Just as we're wasting time now,' he whispered to her, adding, 'You don't know just how much I want to take you to bed.'

'Don't I?' Imogen teased him, moving closer to him with a small, blissful sigh as his hand cupped her breast, slowly kneading it whilst he started to kiss the soft, vulnerable flesh of her throat.

Tiny, delicious darts of pleasure rushed over her skin, making her shiver visibly and moan his name into the thick darkness of his hair. She could feel him drawing her towards her bedroom door.

'Right now, what I want more than anything I've ever wanted in the whole of my life is to lay you down on my bed, our bed, and...

'There's a bed in here,' Imogen reminded him, gesturing towards the narrow bed of her girlhood.

Immediately his eyes darkened. Shaking his head, he told her steadily, 'No...this room was yours as a child, Imo...a girl...and it isn't that child or that girl that I want to make love with now, much as I loved them both. It's you, the woman, my woman, I want to hold in my arms.'

As he very gently drew her through the bedroom door and closed it behind them Imogen felt her eyes smart slightly with tears.

Blinking them away, she touched his mouth with her fingertips. Soon now she would be kissing it, kissing him, touching him every way and being touched by him. As her breathing started to quicken with loving longing she suddenly remembered something.

'Well, if you weren't with Lisa last night, where exactly were you?'

The sombreness of his expression sent a tiny prickle of anxiety tingling down her spine.

Dracco took a deep breath. Now that David had brought the papers to him the future of the shelter was secure, and he could tell Imogen what had been happening without subjecting her to any anxiety. Very slowly he did so.

When he had finished she went quiet, and then Dracco saw the tears burning her eyes.

With a low groan he wrapped her in his arms, rocking her protectively.

'I shouldn't have told you. I've upset you and that's the last thing I wanted to do.'

'No, no, it isn't that,' Imogen reassured him shakily.

'Then what is it?' Dracco demanded.

'It's just knowing that you would do something like that for me, to make me happy. Me… You didn't know then about the baby.'

'Imo, there isn't anything I wouldn't do for you,' Dracco told her seriously, 'any sacrifice I wouldn't make.'

* * *

'Well, was it as good as you were expecting?' Dracco asked softly.

They had just woken up and Dracco was propped up on one elbow as he looked down at her.

Stretching luxuriously, revelling in the sensuality of his naked body next to her own, Imogen told him truthfully, 'No. It was even better…but just to make sure…'

As she traced the line of his jaw and reached up to kiss him Dracco groaned against her mouth.

'Come here, you wonderfully wanton woman,' he demanded as he wrapped his arms around her, 'my wonderfully wanton woman, my wife…my love…my life!'

EPILOGUE

'SHUSH...' Tenderly Imogen rocked her three-month-old son in her arms before turning proudly to listen to Dracco's short speech.

They had flown out to Rio early in the week, especially for the ceremony. Several of the sisters were crying openly as Dracco presented them with his cheque, and Imogen felt rather emotional herself, remembering just what he had done.

Alexander John had been less than three hours old when Dracco had come into her room at the hospital—the room that he had only left an hour earlier, having stayed with her throughout her labour—holding out to her an envelope, plus a small jeweller's box.

She had opened the box first, assuming that the envelope simply held a card, her eyes shining with shocked delight when she had seen the beautiful antique diamond ring Dracco had given her.

Whilst he'd slid it onto her finger he had told her, 'Before you open the envelope, let me tell you that it is not a gift from me to you, or even on account of you, infinitely beloved and precious though you are to me.'

Bemused, Imogen had waited.

'This is a gift on behalf of Alexander to those children who may not receive the love he is guaranteed.'

Imogen had been conscious of Dracco watching her

as she opened the envelope and removed the cheque inside it.

It had been made out to the shelter in Rio, and when Imogen had seen the amount of it her hand had trembled.

'Dracco…I know we made a bargain,' she had begun, 'but my feelings for you, our love…'

'You weren't listening properly to me,' he chided her gently. 'This has nothing to do with that, Imo. This is not so much payment of a debt but recognition of a gift. Your gift of love to me, mine to you, ours to our son, your father's to both of us.'

She had cried then, tears of joy and love and gratitude for everything she had been given, but most of all for Dracco himself and for their child.

And now here she was, watching as Dracco formally handed over his cheque to Sister Maria.

She had been talking to one of her old colleagues, who had informed her that it was only thanks to Dracco's timely intervention that the shelter had been saved. They all thought that he was wonderful and that she was very lucky to be married to him, and Imogen fully agreed! In her arms, Alexander gurgled and smiled up at her. Hugging him, she kissed him. He was the image of Dracco, apart from the fact that he had her father's nose.

Dracco, his speech over, was walking towards her. Imogen smiled lovingly at him. Suddenly she couldn't wait for them to be alone together.

As though he had guessed what she was thinking as he reached her, Dracco drew her into his side, bending his head to kiss her. The love in his eyes as he looked at her made her heart flood with joy. He was everything she had ever wanted and everything she would ever want.

'I love you,' she whispered emotionally to him as he released her mouth.

'I love you too, Imo,' he responded tenderly. 'I always have and I always will.'

THE SECRET VIRGIN

by

Carole Mortimer

Carole Mortimer was born in England, the youngest of three children. She began writing in 1978, and has now written over one hundred books for Harlequin Mills & Boon. Carole has four sons, Matthew, Joshua, Timothy and Peter, and a bearded collie called Merlyn. She says, 'I'm happily married to Peter senior; we're best friends as well as lovers, which is probably the best recipe for a successful relationship. We live on the Isle of Man.'

Don't miss Carole Mortimer's new novels.
Out in February comes
***Pregnant by the Millionaire* and in April,**
***Wife by Contract, Mistress by Demand*, both**
from Mills & Boon Modern Romance™!

My husband,
Peter

CHAPTER ONE

'JONATHAN MCGUIRE! Would Mr Jonathan McGuire, recently arrived from Heathrow, please come to the information desk?' The message rang out clearly over the airport tannoy system.

Tory stood frowningly beside the desk as the receptionist gave out the message, waiting to see if Jonathan McGuire would respond to it.

She had stood at the door to the baggage reclaim area a few minutes ago, as it opened and closed to allow the people from the Heathrow flight to the Isle of Man to leave once they had collected their cases, a small board held up in front of her with the name of 'Mr J McGuire' clearly written on it. But the last passenger from that flight had gone now, with no sign of Jonathan McGuire.

Maybe he had missed the flight?

Or maybe—

'I'm Jonathan McGuire.'

Tory blinked, and not just at the sound of that huskily attractive American drawl. *This* was Jonathan McGuire?

This man had been one of the first to leave the baggage reclaim area. Tory had noticed him because he was so tall, easily a foot taller than her own five feet two inches in her bare feet, and also because as he'd looked at her, and then through her, with flinty grey eyes, she hadn't been able to help noticing he was one of the most arrogantly attractive men she had ever set eyes on!

His face was ruggedly tanned, and there were those flinty grey eyes, a straight nose, and an unsmiling mouth above a square jaw. The dark grey jacket and white shirt, teamed with the faded blue denims that he wore, emphasised the width of his shoulders, the narrow waist and long, muscular legs. She guessed his age to be somewhere around low-to-mid-thirties. Which was another surprise. Somehow she had had the impression he was Madison's younger, not older, brother.

In fact, he looked nothing like Tory had expected blonde-haired, green-eyed Madison's brother to look!

Which was probably the reason why she had missed him earlier.

But that didn't explain why he hadn't approached her; his name was written very clearly on the board she had held up…

Tory stepped forward before the receptionist could respond. 'I was asked to meet you, Mr McGuire,' she told him lightly, smiling welcomingly.

Those flinty grey eyes were turned on her piercingly, no answering smile on those harshly chiselled features. 'By whom?' he prompted guardedly.

She frowned as his reply, her smile fading; she really hadn't thought, when she'd made the offer to come to the airport this morning, that giving Jonathan McGuire a lift to his sister's home was going to be as difficult as it was turning out to be.

'By your sister,' she murmured, deciding that devastating good-looks didn't go any further than skin deep on this man.

Which was a shame. She had always found Madison one of the easiest people to get along with, had expected her brother to be the same. But he not only didn't look like his sister, he had none of her warm charm, either!

'Madison?' he repeated irritatedly. 'And exactly what is your connection to my sister?' He looked at her critically.

Tory tried to see herself through his eyes: a little over five feet tall, boyishly slender, her almost black hair cut in deliberate ragged layers to fall silkily onto her shoulders, her elfin features bare of make-up; she had dark blue eyes, an upturned freckle-covered nose, a wide mouth and a determined chin. The only thing she had in common with the tall, glamorously beautiful Madison McGuire at the moment was her age; they were both twenty-four!

Her frown deepened as she sensed Jonathan McGuire's criticism of her looks. She liked Madison, was quite happy to do a favour for the other woman, but her brother was turning out to be quite another proposition!

Her second smile wasn't as openly friendly as the first. 'My parents own the farm next to Madison and Gideon's house, keep an eye on things for them while they're away.'

'And?'

Tory was very aware of the avidly listening receptionist. Not that she could blame her. Anyone would think Tory was trying to rob the man instead of offering him a lift!

'Madison telephoned last night and asked me to—'

He scowled. 'Damn it, I asked Gideon not to tell anyone where I was going!'

'Madison is his wife…' Tory pointed out ruefully.

The other couple had fallen in love while filming together on the island a couple of years previously. Madison had been the leading lady, Gideon the director of the film, a film that had won them both Oscars the following year. Consequently the two of them had great affection for the Isle of Man and had bought a home here, which they visited often with their now six-month-old daughter, Keilly.

'She may be,' Jonathan McGuire grated harshly. 'But I specifically asked Gideon—'

'Look,' Tory cut in quietly, aware they were still being

overheard, 'I suggest we go across to my car and continue this conversation there?' She raised dark brows.

He shot the receptionist an irritated look before turning on his heel without another word and walking over to the trolley that contained his luggage, which he had left parked at the bottom of some stairs.

Tory gave the receptionist a rueful shrug of her shoulders before following him, noting as she did so that as well as a suitcase there was a guitar case on the trolley Jonathan McGuire now pushed towards the automatically opening exit doors.

'Do you play?' she asked interestedly, falling into step at his side as they walked towards the car park. It was just as well that she had always walked fast herself; it took two of her strides to one of his much longer ones to keep up with him!

He looked at her blankly. 'Sorry?'

Tory somehow doubted that he was sorry at all, thought he was probably very rarely sorry for anything he did. But obviously someone had at least taught him some manners. 'I couldn't help noticing the guitar case.' She nodded towards it.

He continued to look at her with those expressionless grey eyes. 'So?'

Tory drew in a deep breath. 'Look, Mr McGuire, I suggest that the two of us start again.' She came to an abrupt halt on the pavement. 'My name is Tory Buchanan.' She held out her hand. 'I'm very pleased to welcome you to the Isle of Man.'

Jonathan McGuire still looked blankly at the slenderness of her hand for several long seconds, and then he slowly raised his own hand to grip hers. 'I've been to the island before,' he bit out economically, having released her hand after only the briefest of touches.

He had? Of course, she spent a lot of time away from the island herself, so it wasn't so surprising that she might have missed his visit. But, nevertheless, she had gained the impression on the telephone last night, as she'd spoken to Madison, that Jonathan McGuire wasn't familiar with the island, or the location of Madison and Gideon's house. In fact, that was the main reason Madison had asked if someone would be able to go to the airport to meet him.

His mouth twisted derisively. 'It was a very brief visit,' he drawled.

One he had no intention of talking about, his slightly challenging tone implied.

Well, that was okay; Tory had already decided that, good-looking as Jonathan McGuire might be, her favour towards Madison ended the moment she had dropped her brother off at the house! He was darkly cold and arrogant, when she had imagined him to be a golden-haired fun person, like Madison was herself. As far as Tory was concerned, Jonathan McGuire could keep his cold arrogance to himself!

'My car is parked over here.' She indicated they should turn to the left as they entered the car park. 'Actually, it's my father's,' she explained as she unlocked the back of the Land Rover, slightly muddy from where her father drove it around the fields that made up his farm. 'My mother and father have taken the car today to attend a wedding this morning,' she somehow felt she had to add. Although why she should feel that way she had no idea; this man's ungrateful attitude meant she owed him no explanations.

She didn't offer to help as he lifted his luggage into the back, getting in behind the wheel as she waited for him to stroll round and get into the passenger seat beside her before starting the engine. Ten years old, the engine roared protestingly for a few seconds before settling down to its normal erratic clonking noise, and she accelerated the vehicle towards the exit.

'Weren't you invited?'

'Invited where?' Tory turned briefly from feeding her ticket into the machine at the exit, the barrier instantly lifting to allow them to drive out; as she had only arrived at the airport half an hour ago she hadn't had to pay a parking fee.

'To the wedding,' Jonathan McGuire continued, perfectly relaxed in the seat next to her.

So he had been listening, after all! 'I was,' she returned.

'But...?'

'But a friend asked me to do her a favour instead,' Tory said quickly, deliberately not looking at him as she concentrated on her driving.

She sensed him looking at her through narrowed lids, nonetheless. Well, let him look. She had been invited to the wedding, but when Madison had asked if someone could meet her brother at the airport and take him to the house, Tory had been only too happy to offer to be the one to do it. After all, it was Tory's mother's niece who was getting married. Admittedly, the bride was Tory's cousin too, but she could still go to the reception later this afternoon.

'I play.'

Tory gave him a brief, puzzled glance. She seemed to have missed something somewhere!

'The guitar,' he explained. 'You asked if I play. I do.'

'Ah.' She nodded her understanding. 'What sort of music do you play?' she continued interestedly.

There was a brief silence, causing Tory to glance at him once again. His closed expression told her she had—once more!—ventured into forbidden territory. The problem with this man was that every subject seemed to have the potential of an unexplored minefield!

'Usually whatever I feel like playing,' he rasped dismissively.

Tory sighed at the deliberate snub, turning her attention back to her driving. She had only been trying to make polite conversation, for goodness' sake. Obviously a nicety wasted on Jonathan McGuire.

Only another half an hour or so and she could deposit him at his sister's home—and hopefully not see him again for the remainder of his visit. She just hoped he made it another brief one!

She tried to remember the little Madison had said about her brother during their call the previous evening. Madison had called him 'Jonny'; she remembered that. Tory couldn't ever imagine calling this remotely cold man by such an intimately friendly name!

But she could see that he looked wealthy enough; his clothes were obviously of good quality, and she could tell at a glance that his case and the guitar case were the best that money could buy. And, as Madison's brother, he must also be son of Susan Delaney—a woman had become an acting legend in her own lifetime, and a woman Tory had met several times and liked immensely, when she'd visited Madison and Gideon on the island. Perhaps Jonathan McGuire took after his father—because he was certainly nothing like his charming sister and mother!

Tory decided to forget about her less-than-gracious passenger and enjoy the drive instead. It was a lovely day, the early June weather warm and sunny, wild garlic, blue- and whitebells still in flower along the roadside, the vivid yellow-orange of the gorse so bright against fresh green foliage that it almost hurt the eyes to look at it.

Not even the taciturn Jonathan McGuire could spoil her enjoyment of a beautiful day like today!

As they approached the end of the long stretch of road, with the leaves of the trees either side of the road meeting overhead like a green arch, she automatically raised her hand.

'Hi, fairies,' the man at her side murmured softly.

Tory turned to look at him, blue eyes wide with surprise. He *had* been here before.

They had just driven over the Fairy Bridge, marked by a white wall either side of the road. It was considered bad luck not to show the 'little people' who lived under the bridge due respect by saying hello to them.

Perhaps Jonathan McGuire felt in need of good luck…?

Damn it, she was starting to feel intrigued by the man, in spite of herself. He was American, for one thing; what did a single American male, of only thirty-two or thirty-three, want from a small community like the Isle of Man? Beautiful as the island was, almost crime-free too, with a population of less than eighty thousand, it certainly couldn't be considered a fashionable holiday spot for single thirty-odd-year-old males!

She knew the same could be said of a young woman of only twenty-four as well, but it was completely different in her own case. She had been born here; her family were all here. Whereas Jonathan McGuire seemed to be getting away from his own family!

Yes, she *was* intrigued!

That was the last thing she wanted at the moment. She had come back home to do some thinking herself, to make some decisions of her own. She certainly didn't need a man like the remote Jonathan McGuire in that already complicated equation.

'I see you're aware of some of the quainter island traditions,' she remarked conversationally.

'I did tell you I had been here before,' he bit out, staring uninterestedly out of the window at his side.

She really didn't know why she was bothering. She—

'What the hell was that?' Jonathan McGuire gave a shocked gasp as a streak of red shot noisily past the Land Rover.

Tory smiled, completely unperturbed. 'Obviously you aren't aware of all the island traditions,' she drawled mockingly as another blaze of colour shot past them, blue this time, and if anything noisier than the red one. 'Ever heard of the TT Races? The Tourist Trophy?' she enlarged dryly.

She had been starting to wonder, despite his rather jaded behaviour, if perhaps the races could be the reason he was here, his completely unreadable expression told her that it wasn't.

Jonathan McGuire was frowning darkly. 'I take it those—motorbikes have something to do with that?'

'They certainly do.' Tory couldn't hold back her smile any longer. 'And I'm afraid you've chosen to visit the island at the beginning of Race Week.'

'I know I'm going to regret this,' he admitted with obvious reluctance, 'but what is Race Week? In fact, what is the Tourist Trophy?'

'Motorbike racing. The main races are next week,' she told him happily, completely unconcerned as several more motorbikes overtook them at blurringly fast speeds.

TT Fortnight, as the practice week and race week were generally known, had been taking place on the island for almost a hundred years, and while a lot of inhabitants still found it intrusive on their usual peace and quiet, Tory actually loved the atmosphere of those two weeks, when forty to fifty thousand people, usually accompanied by at least twenty-five thousand motorbikes, literally invaded the island, all intent on having fun and enjoying the racing.

'Not today?' Jonathan McGuire said.

'Oh, they haven't started racing yet today,' Tory assured him.

'You could have fooled me!' he muttered disgustedly.

She smiled. 'They close the roads off when the races are actually taking place.'

'They race on the roads?' He was obviously amazed at the idea.

Tory grinned. 'Not over the whole island, obviously—'

'Oh, obviously,' Jonathan responded. 'Madison didn't tell me about this.' He scowled once more.

'Madison isn't supposed to know you're here—remember?' Tory couldn't help returning wryly.

There was a brief silence. 'Touché, Miss Buchanan,' he finally drawled admiringly.

'Tory,' she instantly came back, surprised he had actually remembered her name; he had given the impression of being completely uninterested in anything outside himself. But perhaps she was being unfair to him... 'As we're going to be neighbours for a while...'

Those already flinty grey eyes iced over. 'I have no intention of socialising during my stay here,' he grated.

Tory drew in a sharp breath at his rudeness, instantly regretting her impulse to be friendly. 'I don't think I said I intended inviting you to a party—Mr McGuire,' she snapped coldly. Or, indeed, to anything else!

Another twenty minutes or so and she could say goodbye to this—this arrogant bastard. It couldn't pass soon enough for her!

She had intended taking him the scenic route through Douglas, along the promenade, where the horse trams travelled backwards and forwards every few minutes, and where the electric tram began its journey up to the north of the island to its final destination, Snaefell, the only mountain the island boasted.

But after the last few seconds' conversation he could jolly well take the less attractive route, past the Grandstand, along through Onchan, and then out towards Laxey! She was in no mood herself to play the gracious hostess and point out the places of interest.

She hadn't particularly wanted to go to her cousin Denise's wedding, had welcomed this excuse not to have to actually attend the service. But if she had known how uncommunicative—in fact positively rude!—the alternative was going to be, then she would have opted for attending the wedding!

'I've never seen so many bikes in one place,' Jonathan McGuire remarked incredulously as they drove past the Grandstand, with row upon row of the powerful machines parked there as the race fans gathered just to soak in the atmosphere before the race this afternoon.

'I shouldn't worry,' Tory told him abruptly. 'Madison and Gideon's house is well away from any of the roads, and my mother went shopping this morning, so you should have enough food that you won't need to go out again for some time if you don't want to.' And, after what he had said, she was sure he wouldn't want to!

Again there was a brief silence before Jonathan McGuire answered her. 'That was very kind of your mother.'

Tory's mouth tightened at his surprise at such a gesture from a complete stranger. 'She's a very kind woman. Besides,' she continued levelly, 'we're all very fond of Madison and Gideon. And Keilly is adorable,' she added affectionately.

'Yes, she is, isn't she?' he agreed huskily.

It was the first time during their acquaintance—very brief

acquaintance!—that Tory had heard anything like softness in his tone. But then, how could anyone, least of all her uncle, not be enchanted by the beautiful golden-haired Keilly?

'Not far to go now,' she realised with satisfaction, leaving Onchan behind them and driving out into the countryside once again.

She always felt refreshed, renewed, when she spent time on the island; there was a feeling of having time stand still. At the moment, with important decisions in front of her, that was something she desperately needed.

Unlike the arrogantly rude Jonathan McGuire, who was definitely something she didn't need!

'This is a very beautiful island.'

Tory was becoming used to his sudden, seemingly unconnected statements, and didn't even bother to look at him this time. 'It is,' she agreed.

'What work do you do here?'

She stiffened slightly. For a man who obviously didn't like personal questions himself, he was becoming a little too curious about her own life.

She shrugged. 'Running a farm is a full-time family concern,' she answered evasively.

Dressed as she was, in a light blue tee shirt and faded denims, the latter mud-spattered from where it had rained the day before, her face bare of make-up, she definitely had the look of someone straight off the farm.

The fact that farming wasn't what she did was none of this man's business.

'I suppose it is,' he responded, before once again turning to look out of the window.

It seemed that pleasantries were over for the day!

'What work do you do, Mr McGuire?' she prompted lightly.

'My family is in casinos in Reno.'

That was about as helpful as her own remark about farming being a full-time family concern—it actually told her precisely nothing!

'We have a casino on the island,' she said in friendly reply. 'Perhaps you would like to see it while you're here?' Although she couldn't imagine why; it was a completely soulless place, and the people who went there seemed to be either curious tourists or hardened gamblers—neither of which particularly interested Tory.

'Are you asking me out after all, Tory?' He raised mocking dark brows.

She gave him a startled glance, relaxing slightly as she saw the laughter lurking in dark grey eyes. So the man did have a sense of humour, after all!

'No, I'm not,' she assured him ruefully. 'Casinos hold no appeal for me, I'm afraid,' she added slightly apologetically. After all, it was his family business.

'Me neither,' he rejoined, that brief show of humour completely gone.

Tory waited for him to continue, and when he didn't she decided that had to be the end of that subject, too.

In the circumstances, it had been rather an odd thing to say. But then Jonathan McGuire, she was quickly coming to realise, was an enigma.

'Here we are,' she said with a certain amount of relief a few minutes later as she turned the Land Rover down the Tarmacked driveway that led to the Byrne house.

Even though she had lived in the adjoining farm most of her life, Tory could still appreciate the beauty of this particular spot, high up in the hills, completely away from everything and everyone, though the village of Laxey, with its huge black and red waterwheel, was still visible down in the valley.

The Byrne home had been the original farmhouse once—it and the adjoining acre of land having been purchased from Tory's parents a year ago. The house was now completely refurbished, looking splendidly grand in the sunlight, its pale lemon and white paint gleaming brightly.

Tory parked the vehicle in front of the house before getting down onto the Tarmac to go round and drop the tailboard, relieved the journey was over at last. With any luck she wouldn't have to see Jonathan McGuire again.

He put his bag and the guitar case down before turning to look at her. 'I'm sorry I haven't been very good company,' he told her gruffly. 'My only excuse is that I wasn't expecting anyone at the airport to meet me.'

Which was no excuse. Madison had taken the trouble to call them the evening before, obviously concerned as to her brother's comfort. Tory's mother had been shopping for him this morning. And Tory herself had taken time out to go and collect him.

'Do you have a key?' she prompted briskly, reaching into her denims' pocket for the spare Madison and Gideon always left with her parents when they were away.

Jonathan McGuire reached into his own denims' pocket and pulled out a duplicate silver key. 'Compliments of Gideon,' he offered lazily.

'Fine.' She put her own key back in her pocket. 'If there's anything else you need, I'm sure my parents would be only too pleased to help.' She gestured across the neighbouring field to the white farmhouse and accompanying barns and sheds that could be seen in the distance.

He reached out and grasped her arm as she would have turned away and got back into the Land Rover. 'But not you?' He demanded.

Tory was very aware of that hand on the bareness of her arm, the skin warm and firm to the touch. She looked up at him with dark blue eyes, shaking her head, her shaggy dark mane of hair moving softly against her shoulders. 'I may not be here. Like you, I'm only visiting.'

He frowned. 'But I thought you said—'

'You'll find food in the fridge, and bread in the bin.' She knew that because, although her mother had done the shopping, Tory had actually brought it over to the house and unpacked it. 'There's also one of my mother's apple pies in the cupboard.' She pulled out of his grasp, stepping lightly back into the Land Rover, anxious to be on her way now. 'The car is parked in the garage round the back of the house; the keys are hanging up next to the fridge. Oh, and Madison always leaves a list of relevant telephone numbers next to the phone.' She turned on the ignition, reaching out to close the door behind her.

Jonathan McGuire also reached out to grasp the door, preventing it from closing. 'Is yours there?' he asked softly. *Now* he decided to start being charming! Well, charm she had had, in plenty—and she certainly didn't want or need it from this man!

Her pointed chin rose challengingly. 'My parents' number is there, if you should need it.'

His head tilted to one side as he gave her a considering look. 'I haven't been very polite to you, have I…?'

Tory met his gaze unblinkingly for several seconds. 'No,' she finally replied.

Jonathan McGuire did blink, and when he raised his lids again that earlier humour was gleaming there once more. 'Tell me, do you get on well with my sister Madison?'

'Very,' she confirmed evenly.

'I thought you might.' He grinned suddenly.

It was like looking at a different person, Tory realised with a startled jolt. He looked years younger now he wasn't scowling grimly, his teeth white and even against his tanned skin, laughter lines crinkling beside his mouth and eyes—eyes that had now taken on a silver sheen rather than that flinty grey.

Tory wrenched her gaze away from his. 'I really do have to go now, Mr McGuire.' She pulled pointedly on the door he still held, relieved when, after only the slightest of hesitations, he decided to let go of it, allowing her to slam it shut. She wound the window down beside her. 'Just one more thing. If you do intend using the car while you're here, I shouldn't go out anywhere tomorrow; it's Mad Sunday.'

'Mad what?' he questioned suspiciously.

'Sunday,' she repeated.

'Well, I realise it's Sunday,' he said slowly. 'But what's mad about it?'

Tory grinned herself now. 'You remember all those motorbikes you saw at the Grandstand earlier? Well,' she continued at his confirming nod, 'those bikes, and about twenty thousand more, will be circling the TT course tomorrow—with only the mountain road being one-way. Mad Sunday!'

She put the vehicle into gear, released the handbrake and accelerated away, her last glimpse of Jonathan McGuire as she glanced in the driving mirror the totally dazed look on his face.

She couldn't help smiling to herself. If Jonathan McGuire had come to the island for peace and quiet—and she had a definite feeling that he had!—then he had chosen the wrong week to do it.

And in her opinion, after the hard time he had given her, it couldn't have happened to a nicer person!

CHAPTER TWO

HER mood wasn't particularly improved when she got back to the farm to find that Rupert had left a message on the answer-machine!

The machine itself had been her gift to her parents the previous summer, mainly so that she could leave messages on it herself, no matter where she was or what time zone she might be in, ensuring that her parents would always know she was okay.

But Tory had it switched on most of the time when she was at home, enabling her to pick and choose which calls she wanted to take.

She most certainly would not have taken this one from Rupert!

She had specifically told him she did not want him to call her while she was here. But in his usual high-handed fashion he had taken absolutely no notice of her.

'Hello, darling,' his charming, educated voice greeted smoothly, enabling Tory to actually visualise him as he sat back in his brown leather chair, leather-shod feet up on the desk, looking immaculate in his designer-label suit and tailored shirt, silk tie knotted perfectly. 'Just wanted to see if you're ready to come home yet. We all miss you.'

Tory turned off the machine with a definitive click. Damn him, she *was* home. And as for missing her—!

Her mouth tightened. No doubt they *were* missing her, but Rupert especially; she had helped put those leather shoes on his feet, the designer-label suit and tailored shirt on his back. In fact, she was his main meal ticket.

Oh, hell!

She dropped down into one of the kitchen chairs, elbows on the oak table as she rested her chin on her hands. The last thing she wanted was to become bitter and twisted. But what was she going to do?

That was what she had come here a week ago to find out. She was nearer the answer, she realised, she knew what she wanted to do. But if she did it all hell was going to break loose. She—

'Give us a hand, would you, love?' her father puffed as he pushed open the kitchen door, arm around her mother's waist as he helped her badly limping form into the room.

Tory jumped concernedly to her feet, rushing over to her mother's other side so the two of them could guide her over to one of the kitchen chairs. Her mother's left ankle was tightly bandaged; a pained expression was on her face.

'What on earth happened?' Tory gasped once they had her mother safely settled in the chair.

'I fell over coming out of the church.' Her mother was the one to answer, self-disgustedly, looking very summery in her floral pink and white suit with matching pink hat.

'And not a drop had passed her lips!' Tory's father, barely five feet six in height, his face ruddily weathered by the sun and wind, grinned his relief at having got back home without further mishap.

'Vanity, that's what did it. I should never have worn these high-heeled shoes,' her mother said heavily, giving the offending white shoes a glare—the one still on her foot and the other held in her hand—obviously very annoyed with herself for having fallen over in the first place. 'I don't remember when I last wore shoes like this. We've been stuck at the hospital the last half-hour while they X-rayed my ankle. Nothing's broken, thank goodness, but it's a nasty sprain.'

'I'll get you both a cup of tea,' Tory offered concernedly, Rupert's call forgotten in the face of this family crisis.

No matter how much her father might be smiling with affection at her mother's clumsiness, it *was* a crisis. Her mother was as much an essential part of running the farm as her father was, and now that she was no longer mobile…

'Good idea, love,' her father replied, also sitting down at the kitchen table now.

The whole family spent a lot of time in this room. All of their meals were eaten around this table, and they often lingered here, after they had cleared away in the evenings, to just sit and chat.

'How did the wedding go?' Tory moved swiftly around the room making the tea.

Her mother's expression instantly softened, her face as weathered by the elements as her husband's, but rounder, as was her plump body. 'Beautiful.' She smiled reminiscently. 'I do love a good wedding.'

'Denise looked well enough,' her father added less enthusiastically, obviously uncomfortable in the shirt and suit he had been persuaded into wearing for the occasion. 'Although I still can't say I'm too keen on that young man she's married.'

'Wait until it's your turn, Tory.' Her mother gave her a knowing look. 'No man is going to be good enough for you, either!'

'You have that about right, Thelma,' Tory's father agreed gruffly. 'Because no man *is* good enough for our Tory!'

Tory gave them both an affectionate smile as she handed them their cups of tea. 'I wouldn't worry about that too much if I were you; I don't intend marrying for years yet.' If ever!

Not that she had always felt that way. Until a short time

ago she had had the same hopes and dreams as other women her age: a husband, children, a warm family home like the one she had grown up in.

But that had all changed now.

As had Rupert. But too late—fortunately! After years of saying marriage wasn't for him, Rupert had suddenly done an about-face a few weeks ago, and now urged her to marry him every opportunity he had.

Maybe if he had felt that way a few years ago Tory would have accepted, she acknowledged. But not any more. Rupert was no longer a golden-haired god to her. In fact, as she now knew only too well, he had feet of clay. She just thanked goodness he hadn't asked her to marry him a couple of years ago; then she would have made the biggest mistake of her life by accepting him!

'Well, I'm glad the wedding went well.' She smiled. 'Although it's a shame about your ankle, Mum.'

'My own fault,' her mother dismissed. 'How did you get on with Madison's brother Jonny?' she asked interestedly.

Tory grimaced as she sat down at the table with her own cup of tea. 'If I tell you I still called him Mr McGuire when I dropped him off at the house—' and dropping him off a cliff might have been a better idea! '—perhaps that will tell you how well I got on with him!'

'Oh, dear,' her mother responded worriedly. 'And the Byrnes are such a nice couple.'

International film star and director they might be, Oscar winners at that, and Madison's mother the world-renowned actress Susan Delaney and Gideon's late father the English actor, John Byrne—having been as famous himself before his early death thirty or so years ago—but to Tory's parents, Madison and Gideon were just 'the Byrnes'.

The island was home to several actors, a well-known television chef, several famous musicians and singers, as well as a handful of successful writers, amongst several lesser known millionaires. The islanders just took it in their stride if they happened to find themselves standing next to one of them in the till queue at the supermarket! After all, they all had to eat, too.

'I didn't—' She broke off abruptly as the telephone began to ring.

Damn—she had forgotten to switch the answer-machine back on after listening to Rupert's message earlier. And it didn't need two guesses to know that it would be Rupert calling again.

Damn, damn, damn!

'Would you like me to get that?' her father offered gently as he saw the displeased look on her face.

Coming back here to give herself room to think was one thing. Letting her father fight her battles for her was something else entirely.

'It's okay.' She stood up, snatching up the receiver. 'Yes?' she snapped uncompromisingly.

There was a brief pause on the other end of the line, before, 'How did you know it was me?'

Not Rupert! 'I didn't,' she answered Jonathan McGuire in a slightly sheepish voice, turning away from the curious glances of her parents in the hope that they wouldn't see her uncomfortable blush.

'Who else has upset you today?' he mused mockingly, that American drawl even more distinct over a telephone line.

'No one in particular,' she said brightly. What did he want? He had left her in no doubt when she parted from him an hour ago that he wanted to be left alone.

'You're very good at that, aren't you?' he said admiringly.

Tory hesitated. 'At what?'

'The evasive answer,' he came back instantly.

She gave a startled laugh. 'And that coming from the expert at evasive answers!' She knew less about Jonathan McGuire after spending almost forty minutes in his company than she had before she met him!

A throaty chuckle resounded down the telephone line. 'Okay, so you aren't going to tell me who else has upset you today,' he accepted. 'I won't keep you long,' he added more briskly, 'I know you must be anxious to go to your cousin's wedding. I—that's actually the reason I'm phoning.'

Tory blinked. 'You aren't suggesting you would like to come with me?' she said disbelievingly.

She could just imagine the family speculation if she arrived at her cousin Denise's wedding reception with a tall, dark American in tow! Not that she intended going at all now that her mother and father weren't going to be there, but surely Jonathan McGuire couldn't be—

'Hell, no!' he instantly disabused her of that illusion. 'I—having had time to—think about things—I realise I owe you an apology for my behaviour earlier—'

'I thought you had already made one,' Tory said guardedly.

'For not thanking you for taking time out of your day to pick me up at the airport,' he completed determinedly. 'I—thank you.'

Ouch, she bet that hurt.

'You're welcome,' she returned lightly.

There was a deep sigh at the other end of the line. 'I'm not usually as rude as I was today—'

'Don't tell me—you're usually ruder!' she teased.

'You aren't making this easy for me, are you,' he responded irritably.

Well, she wasn't sure what 'this' was...! He had apologised, she had accepted that apology, so what was he still doing on the line?

'Do you think I should?' she returned warily.

After all, everything he had said was true; she had taken time out of her day, missed her cousin's wedding, just so that she could go to the airport and pick him up. Only to be faced with his rude uncooperativeness. The fact that she had been glad of the excuse not to go to the wedding was irrelevant.

'Probably not,' he accepted with resignation. 'When you see your mother could you also thank her for the pie? I was hungry when I got here, so I've already eaten a piece; it's delicious.'

It certainly was, her mother was one of the best pastry-makers on the island. Luckily Tory seemed to have a metabolism that could handle her mother's wonderful cooking, which didn't just stop at pastry, otherwise she might have ended up a very chubby child and an even fatter adult!

'Why don't you tell her yourself?' Tory declared, suddenly seeing a way of ending this conversation without appearing rude herself. 'She's sitting right here.' She held the receiver out to her mother before Jonathan McGuire could make any response—positive or negative—to her suggestion.

Tory moved to kiss her father lightly on the cheek. 'I'm just popping over to the studio for a while,' she told him softly. 'Give me a yell if you need me for anything,' she added with a glance towards her mother, the pleased flush to her mother's cheeks as she listened to Jonathan McGuire telling Tory that he must be repeating his praise of her mother's pastry.

Tory gave a smile as she left the farmhouse. The way to a man's heart might be through his stomach, but the way to her mother's was to show appreciation for her cooking.

It looked as if Jonathan McGuire was succeeding in charming one member of the Buchanan family at least.

Her smiled faded as she crossed the yard and entered the outhouse that her father had allowed her to convert into a studio. She stopped just inside the door, looking around her, feeling— What…? Everywhere she looked there was evidence of her success. And once that had been all she wanted. She had left the island six years ago in search of that dream. But after five years at the top she had realised it wasn't enough. She wanted more.

She had taken a risk six years ago, put all her hopes in her own ability, and she had been successful. Did she now have the courage, while still at the top, to take a sideways step in that career?

Rupert thought she was mad even to consider taking the step that had consumed her thoughts over the last few months. But then Rupert had his own reasons for keeping her exactly where she was, doing what she was doing. It suited his own agenda.

But did it still suit hers?

If she knew the answer to that then she wouldn't still be here on the island.

She wouldn't have had to meet the rudely taciturn Jonathan McGuire today either!

'Arrogant. Self-interested. Inconsiderate!' Tory muttered to herself as she checked the contents of the saucepans bubbling away on top of the Aga.

'Bad sign that, love,' her father observed as he came into the kitchen from outside, back in his comfortable work clothes today, looking much more at ease. 'Talking to yourself,' he explained at Tory's questioning look.

She made a face. 'Lunch should be ready in fifteen minutes.'

That was the reason she was talking to herself. Oh, not because, as her mother was incapacitated, she was the one actually cooking the Sunday lunch; she had always been happy to do her share of work about the farm, easily fell back into doing that when she was home.

No, cooking lunch wasn't the problem—it was the fact that Jonathan McGuire was invited to eat it that was irritating her!

He had given her every indication yesterday that he was doing a Greta Garbo—wanted to be alone—and yet before he had finished talking to her mother on the telephone the previous day he had accepted an invitation to come to Sunday lunch.

Tory had been all for eating in the kitchen as they usually did, but her mother had insisted that they open up the rarely used dining room at the back of the house in honour of their guest.

Honour!

Tory didn't feel in the least honoured. Sunday lunch was always an especially enjoyable family occasion, with the afternoon spent relaxing in front of the television or reading the newspapers. If eating in the dining room was an example of how this Sunday was going to go, then her father could forget about his television and Tory her newspapers; neither was allowed when they had guests. Their only hope was that this guest wouldn't linger long after lunch!

She couldn't even begin to imagine what had made Jonathan McGuire accept the invitation in the first place. So much for his claim that he didn't intend socialising while he was here!

She gave an impatient glance at her wristwatch. 'If our guest doesn't arrive soon, he's going to miss lunch altogether,' she muttered irritably.

'I'm sure—' Her father broke off what he had been about

to say as the sound of a vehicle arriving outside in the yard could clearly be heard. 'Talk of the devil.' He grinned. 'I had better go up and get some clean clothes on, at least.' He looked down ruefully at his muddy working overalls. 'Or your mother won't be too happy with me!' He was whistling as he left the room to go upstairs.

With her mother lying down in the sitting room, resting her ankle until lunch was ready, and her father upstairs changing, it was left to Tory to go in answer to the ringing of the front doorbell. A rarely used front doorbell! It was much more friendly in this island community to use the side or back door.

It took Tory several minutes to pull back the heavy bolts at the top and bottom of the door, before using the key to unlock it, and the hinges creaked from lack of use when she finally managed to open it.

'You don't have the Fort Knox gold in there, do you?' Jonathan McGuire drawled, obviously having heard the grating of the bolts and unlocking of the door.

At least, Tory assumed it was him; most of him seemed to be hidden behind a large bunch of yellow chrysanthemums wrapped in tissue paper, only his long denim-clad legs revealed beneath them.

'Very funny,' Tory snapped, stepping back to let him inside. 'But for future reference, could you use the back door?' she added with pointed sarcasm as she went through the drawn-out process of replacing the bolts and turning the lock.

The chrysanthemums were slowly lowered to reveal Jonathan McGuire's handsome face. 'Sorry,' he grimaced.

He didn't look either as tired, or grim, as he had yesterday. In fact, he looked dangerously attractive, Tory decided, the darkness of his hair still damp from a recent shower and inclined to curl, those grey eyes warm, the sculptured mouth smiling.

Tory didn't give him an answering smile. 'This way,' she told him abruptly, leading the way down the hallway back to the kitchen.

They might be going to eat in the dining room soon, but for the moment he would have to put up with the informality of the kitchen; she couldn't play hostess to him *and* cook the meal any other way!

'You really shouldn't have bothered, Mr McGuire.' She nodded in the direction of the flowers he still held; he must have called in to the shop in the village this morning.

'Er—I'm afraid they aren't for you,' he admitted. 'They're for your mother; my own mother told me to always take flowers to give to my hostess.'

How to feel small in one easy lesson!

'I'm sure my mother will be thrilled,' Tory replied, her cheeks flushed with embarrassment now. That would teach her not to try to be clever!

'These are for you.' He reached into his jacket pocket and pulled out a box of chocolates. 'Flowers for the hostess, chocolates for the daughter.' He gave a rueful shrug at this second lesson in good manners obviously taught to him by his mother.

As peace offerings went, it was a very small box of chocolates. But it had the advantage of being her favourite brand.

'Thank you,' Tory accepted, their fingers lightly touching as she took the box from him.

Ouch!

Something like an electric shock made her hand tingle, before it travelled up her arm, the feeling slowly defusing but leaving her feeling slightly breathless.

What was *that*?

She shook her head before turning to put the chocolates down on the side. 'Can I offer you a drink before lunch, Mr McGuire?' she enquired, still slightly dizzied by her reaction to just the briefest touch of his fingers against hers.

He gave no indication of being so affected himself, putting the flowers down on the table to reveal he once again wore a jacket and shirt with his denims, the jacket black this time, the shirt light blue.

'If you're having a drink then I'll join you,' he said. 'On the condition you stop calling me Mr McGuire—Tory.'

'Jonathan,' she bit out, accompanied by a terse nod of her head. There was no way she could call him Jonny! 'We have sherry, or there's a bottle of white wine cooling in the fridge. I hope you like chicken.'

For all she knew he could be a vegetarian—although it would be singularly stupid on his part not to have mentioned that fact to her mother on the telephone the previous day.

'Love it.' He had opened the fridge door and taken out the bottle of white wine. 'Do you have a corkscrew for this?'

'Make yourself at home, why don't you?' Tory mumbled to herself as she searched through the drawer for the corkscrew, turning to check the vegetables again as he opened the bottle and poured some wine into two of the glasses sitting on the side.

'Mr McGuire,' her father greeted him a few seconds later as he came into the kitchen, holding out his hand. 'Dan Buchanan. Come through to the sitting room and meet my wife. Everything okay with you, Tory?' He quirked questioning brows.

Fine—now that he had come down to take over entertaining their guest! 'I'll give you a shout when I've served the meal,' she said.

Jonathan gave her a quick glance. 'I hope I haven't put you to too much trouble on my behalf…?'

'Not in the least,' Tory assured him airily. 'We were having a roast lunch anyway,' she told him, knowing by the narrowing of those silver-grey eyes that Jonathan McGuire, at least, hadn't missed the intended slight.

'I'm afraid my wife fell over yesterday and sprained her ankle,' her father told their guest. 'But Tory cooks almost as well as her mother.'

'Almost?' Tory deliberately rose to her father's teasing; it was part of what she most enjoyed about being at home. Her parents were such genuine down-to-earth people. Unlike the crowd she was surrounded by in London!

'The proof will be in the eating.' Her father gave Jonathan a conspiratorial wink. 'Let's go through, Jonathan, and say hello to Thelma; she's been looking forward to meeting you.'

Which put her mother in the minority as far as Tory was concerned. Gifts of flowers and chocolates did not alter the fact that the man was incredibly rude.

Although there was no sign of that rudeness as the four of them sat down to lunch, her mother helped into the dining room by Jonathan McGuire's solicitous hand under her elbow.

Probably another lesson in manners taught him by his mother, Tory decided disgruntledly.

Now who was being rude and uncooperative?

So she was. But she just couldn't get past the man she had met yesterday. Even if Jonathan's next words did make it seem that he was determined to wipe out that image today…

'This is delicious,' he told her after tasting the succulent chicken and accompanying vegetables. He was seated next to Tory at the table, her parents facing them. 'School

Sunday lunches were never as good as this!' he commented. 'I grew up believing English cooking had to be the worst in the world!'

Tory's brows rose over surprised blue eyes. 'You went to school in England?' How strange, when his parents were both American.

He met her gaze steadily for several long seconds. 'English education, paradoxically, is the best in the world,' he finally answered.

'And your parents obviously wanted the best for you,' she acknowledged sardonically.

His eyes narrowed speculatively for several seconds before he turned to her mother. 'I had no idea when I accepted your invitation yesterday, Thelma, that you had hurt your ankle, that it would be Tory I was making extra work for,' he said.

If he was trying to make her feel guilty, then he was succeeding!

Though if she were truthful with herself, it wasn't really Jonathan she was annoyed with today. Rupert had telephoned again this morning, shortly before the other man arrived, annoying her intensely with his certainty that she would be back in London soon, ready to begin another round of work and mindless parties.

'It really was no trouble,' she assured Jonathan awkwardly; after all, he was her parents' guest, and she really wasn't being very welcoming. 'I'm glad you're enjoying it. There's one of Mum's cherry pies for dessert,' she added.

'If I'm not careful I shall be putting on weight while I'm here,' he came back satirically.

Tory doubted that very much. Jonathan had the build of an athlete, without looking muscle-bound—something she found most unattractive in a man.

Not that she wanted to find Jonathan McGuire attractive!

She was having enough trouble trying to sort her own life out, without complicating it with an attraction that was going nowhere. Not that Jonathan had given any indication that he found her in the least attractive anyway!

Could she possibly be a bit irritated with him because of that, too?

Maybe, she conceded. Although she never made anything of her looks when she was at home, always wore denims and tee shirts for convenience's sake—she never knew when her father was going to ask her to go and help him on the farm. And she never bothered with make-up when she was here, either; it was a relief not to always have to look perfect.

But, even so, Jonathan McGuire hadn't given any indication that he had even noticed she was female, let alone an attractive one!

'How are Madison and Gideon?' her mother asked interestedly. 'And the adorable Keilly, of course,' she added indulgently.

'I can see my niece has been breaking hearts this side of the Atlantic, too,' Jonathan recognised. 'Maddie and Gideon are fine. They're visiting Maddie's godfather and his wife at the moment; Edgar and Claire have a four-month-old son. Actually, I believe Claire is Manx,' he continued thoughtfully. 'Her name was Christian before she married Edgar,' he explained helpfully.

'A good Manx name,' Tory's father said approvingly.

'So I believe,' Jonathan replied. 'It's the name they've given the baby.'

'I can't say we know a Claire Christian…do we, Thelma?' Tory's father said.

'Sorry.' Her mother smiled apologetically. 'I expect your parents are thrilled about little Keilly, aren't they? Is it their first grandchild?'

'They are. And it is. So far…' Jonathan confirmed dryly.

Tory gave him a thoughtful glance. Her own parents might not think any man was good enough to marry her, but that didn't stop them wanting grandchildren of their own. Could Jonathan's parents, now that they had one grandchild, possibly be putting the same emotional pressure on him? Probably, she decided. It seemed to be the way with parents that they wanted to see their children happily settled.

Although if Jonathan had reached the age of thirty-two or thirty-three without succumbing to matrimony, and he had come alone on his visit to the island, it didn't look as if it was a possibility in the near future!

'And Gideon's parents?' her mother continued happily. 'I expect they're thrilled, too?'

Jonathan's expression didn't change, and yet Tory felt other, subtle changes in him as he sat next to her, his body tense now, a certain wariness in his eyes.

Because her mother had mentioned Gideon's parents? Or because she had mentioned Gideon himself? Did the two men not get on?

She found the latter hard to believe. The two men were very alike. Gideon was also forceful, very self-possessed—like this man, to the point of arrogance. Or perhaps Jonathan just didn't think Gideon was good enough for Madison? Tory believed older brothers could be like that, too.

Not that Tory had any siblings of her own, older or younger, but she could imagine Jonathan being quite protective of his 'little sister'…

'Gideon's parents are both dead,' Jonathan finally answered harshly, putting his knife and fork down on his almost empty plate. 'And now I really think I should be going; I've interrupted your Sunday afternoon for long enough,' he added, with what seemed to Tory a deliberately forced softening of his tone.

Her mother looked surprised. 'But we haven't had dessert yet,' she protested with light rebuke.

Tory knew only too well, no one was allowed to leave without eating her mother's desserts!

She stood up. 'Would you like to help me clear the plates, Jonathan?' she suggested. 'Then you can sample Mum's cherry pie and tell her which one you prefer—the apple or the cherry.' She smiled at her blushing mother.

Perhaps it wasn't quite the thing to do to ask the guest to help clear away, but it had seemed to Tory that Jonathan needed a brief respite from a conversation that seemed to be getting a little too personal for his liking. Or comfort!

Not that she could say what could possibly make him feel uncomfortable talking about his sister and her husband; she just knew that it was.

Unless it was just that he had had enough of their provincial company for one day. After all, being based in Reno, involved in the running of casinos, he would obviously be used to a much more sophisticated form of entertainment. And company!

'Thank you for that,' he said quietly once they reached the kitchen, putting the plates he carried down on the side.

Tory looked at the muscled width of his back as he stood turned away from her, once again wondering why a man like him had decided to bury himself on the Isle of Man for an indefinite period, and once again coming up with no answer!

Or perhaps, like her, he just needed some time and space to be able to think...?

Also, like her, he wasn't about to discuss what he was thinking about with a third party...

He turned sharply, as if sensing her puzzled gaze on him,

his expression immediately guarded. 'I meant, of course, for helping me avoid insulting your mother by missing out on dessert,' he explained.

Oh, sure he did! 'Of course,' she repeated dryly, still not absolutely sure of his reason for saying he was leaving a few minutes ago. If it was because she and her parents simply bored him, then he was rude! But, then, she had already known that, hadn't she?

He gave her a piercingly searching look, a look Tory withstood with calm indifference. He was wasting his time trying to disconcert her in that particular way; she was more than used to being in the spotlight.

Jonathan was the first one to break away from their locked gazes. 'Would you like me to carry anything through for you?' he offered distantly.

'The cream.' She opened the fridge and took the jug of cream out. 'Unless you would prefer ice-cream? I believe Americans prefer it with their dessert?'

During the last five years she had been to America at least a dozen times herself, and had always noticed this preference with pie. Although Jonathan McGuire probably thought she had just watched a lot of American programmes on the television!

He gave a slight inclination of his head. 'You believe correctly,' he drawled.

She took the ice-cream from the freezer, carrying through that and the pie while Jonathan carried all the other things.

Her father turned to smile at them both as they came into the room. 'I was just saying to your mother, Tory; perhaps Jonathan would like you to take him out for a ride this afternoon?'

Tory gave her father an irritated frown. She did not want to spend any more time in Jonathan McGuire's company than she had to. Besides, he was their guest, not hers.

She wasn't daft; she knew exactly what her father was up to. There was a good war film on the television this afternoon, and her father didn't want to miss it! If he could manage to persuade Jonathan to go out with Tory, then he would be able to watch it.

Jonathan looked puzzled. 'But I thought you told me it was best to stay in this afternoon?' he reminded Tory. 'Something to do with the bikes on the TT course?' he added.

'Well, that's exactly what I'm talking about,' her father told him jovially. 'Tory hasn't been round the course herself for a couple of years; I'm sure she would love to take you. Wouldn't you love?' he pressed hopefully. 'It's an experience everyone should have once in their lifetime!' he assured Jonathan.

'You ride a motorbike?' Jonathan no longer looked puzzled—he looked astounded.

Tory bristled at his disbelieving expression. She had been born on the island, lived here all her life until six years ago, still spent as much time here as work and other commitments would allow, and motorbikes were a fact of the island, whether you liked them or not. Five years ago Tory had bought her own motorbike, on the basis that if you couldn't beat them, you joined them!

'Yes, I ride a motorbike,' she confirmed stiffly. 'I'll take you out on it when we've finished lunch. If you would like to go?'

If you dare! her tone implied.

CHAPTER THREE

'How ever did we get ourselves into this?' Jonathan exclaimed as she handed him the second helmet before leaving the house, the two of them striding across the yard to the shed where Tory kept her bike.

She had been wondering that herself all the time she was in her bedroom putting on her leathers, forgoing dessert herself to leave Jonathan downstairs with her parents to enjoy his.

But she knew exactly why she had behaved in the way that she had; Jonathan's scornful reaction to hearing she rode a motorbike had clearly indicated he didn't believe she was big enough to handle a pushbike, let alone a machine powerful enough to take the two of them around the TT course.

'Don't you know?' she derided, already starting to feel hot in the black leathers as the warm sun shone down on them.

Dark brows rose over grey eyes. 'Do you?'

Tory nodded grimly. 'You were dared into it—by me! And I was goaded into it—by you!'

Jonathan grimaced. 'Very commendable!' he responded mockingly. 'Just how long is this TT course?' he asked slowly.

'Almost thirty-eight miles.' She unlocked the shed, throwing back the doors.

'Thirty-eight—! I think maybe I should have forgone that second helping of pie your mother pressed on me!' he said with feeling.

Tory turned to chuckle softly at his expression. 'Frightened you might shortly see it again?'

'God, I hope not,' he groaned.

Tory went into the shed to get her bike, needing all her strength to push it outside into the yard, sparing Jonathan a brief glance from beneath lowered lashes once she had done so. She wasn't disappointed; he was staring open-mouthed at the powerful machine.

Bright red, with a 750cc engine, it was an extremely powerful, as well as beautiful, bike.

'Can you really ride that thing?' he queried suspiciously.

Her mouth tightened. Had he forgotten that it was exactly this sort of attitude that had got them into this in the first place? Obviously not a man who learnt his lesson the first time around!

She got on the leather seat, putting her helmet on before starting the powerful engine. 'Get on,' she told him firmly. 'We'll go down to the Grandstand where the races start from. And for goodness' sake, hold on!' she ordered warningly.

She held the bike steady as Jonathan got on behind her, tensing slightly as his arms curved about her waist. Well, she was the one who had told him to hold on!

But it wasn't too difficult once they were on the TT course itself, with the sun beating down, the breeze whistling past them, and with the comradeship of the other bikers, to almost forget she had Jonathan McGuire as a passenger. Only the occasional tightening of his grip about her waist reminded her.

She had forgotten the thrill of this ride too, felt totally exhilarated as the miles passed beneath them.

As they approached the Grandstand after the first lap of the circuit she felt a dig in her ribs, and turned slightly to see what Jonathan wanted, only to find him pointing towards the parking area where thousands of bikers were already gathered.

Disappointed, she throttled down before turning into an empty space and switching off the engine, taking off her helmet to shake her dark hair loose about her shoulders before turning to look at Jonathan.

A very green-looking Jonathan!

'Are you okay?' she gasped concernedly as he got off the bike, staggering slightly.

He ripped off his own helmet, taking in huge gulps of air now that he was back on *terra firma*. 'Do I look all right?' he snarled through gritted teeth.

Actually, he looked terrible, Tory decided as she swung off the bike too, putting it on its stand before turning back to him. 'I—'

'Tory! Hey, Tory!'

They both turned to the leather-clad figure limping towards them, a grin of pure pleasure splitting the ruggedly hewn features of the newcomer.

'Terry!' Tory greeted with equal pleasure before being gathered up into a bear hug.

'It's great to see you back on the island.' Terry moved back slightly to look down at her, still grinning. 'Back on the bike, too.' He nodded his approval 'We missed you here last year,' he said wistfully.

She grinned. 'Work commitments.'

Terry grinned back. 'How's it going?'

'Oh, you know—'

'I hate to interrupt this moving reunion—' the sarcasm in Jonathan's tone completely belied his words '—but could one of you point me in the direction of a public convenience?'

Terry gave Tory an 'is he with you?' look, before answering the other man. 'Over there, mate.' He waved in the direction of the Grandstand.

'Thank you.' Jonathan gave a terse nod, his face set in grim lines as he strode off in the direction indicated.

'Friend of yours?' Terry said meaningfully.

'Sort of,' Tory replied, watching Jonathan until he disappeared into the Gents. 'I don't think he's too impressed with our TT course,' she understated, not sure that Jonathan hadn't excused himself so that he could be sick! 'If he isn't back in ten minutes, perhaps you had better go and see if he's all right,' she suggested.

Terry chuckled. 'He's American, isn't he?'

'Mmm,' she confirmed vaguely, feeling slightly guilty that she hadn't realised Jonathan wasn't enjoying the ride as much as she was. 'How are Jane and the family?' She changed the subject as she turned back to Terry.

'All well,' he responded. 'We all missed you at the wedding yesterday.'

As her cousin—in fact, Denise's older brother—of course Terry and his family would also have been at the ceremony. 'I'm sorry I missed it, too,' she said, not altogether truthfully. 'But I had—other commitments.'

That 'commitment'—she was glad to see!—was making his way back to them through the crowd at this very moment, no longer looking quite as green as he had when Tory had first looked at him after their ride.

'How is Aunty Thelma today?' Terry enquired.

'Hobbling about,' Tory assured him, happier now that she knew Jonathan wasn't collapsed in a heap somewhere. 'You know Mum,' she opined, 'you can't keep her down for long!'

'That's true,' Terry acknowledged affectionately. 'I have to say,' he went on thoughtfully as he gave the approaching

Jonathan McGuire a glance, 'he's a definite improvement on the other one you brought home.'

The 'other one', Tory knew, being Rupert! But then Rupert, with his rakish London sophistication, on the one, never to be repeated occasion he had accompanied her to the island, hadn't set out to win any points for charm. He had been deliberately condescending, to her family and friends alike.

But, by the same token, Jonathan McGuire was not someone she had brought home!

'So, what do you think of our TT course?' Terry turned to ask the other man as he rejoined them, giving Tory no opportunity to refute her cousin's mistaken impression concerning her relationship to Jonathan.

Terry had always had a wicked sense of humour, Tory remembered with an inward groan. Admittedly Jonathan wasn't green any more, but he was certainly still very white.

'Jonathan McGuire. Terry Bridson.' She introduced the two men quickly as she saw that Jonathan's eyes were once again the flinty grey colour that warned of impending danger to anyone who crossed him, and Terry's teasing definitely came under that heading!

She watched as the two men shook hands, Terry still grinning, Jonathan managing a grimace of a smile in return.

'Your TT course is—interesting,' Jonathan ventured. 'What other forms of torture do you have for the unsuspecting tourist?'

The latter was added so mildly that the sarcasm underlying the remark didn't sink in with Tory for several seconds.

Terry, however, roared with laughter, slapping the other man companionably on the back. 'We call it fun here on the island.' He grinned.

'Hmm,' Jonathan responded non-committally. 'Are you one of the competitors?'

'Not any more.' Terry sobered. 'I came off a few years ago.' He slapped his damaged knee, the reason for his pronounced limp. 'I don't have the agility to be a competitor any more.'

'Much to his family's relief,' Tory put in firmly.

Terry shrugged. 'There is that, I suppose.' But the wistfulness could clearly be heard in his voice. 'Are you staying on the island long, Jonathan? Or are you just here for TT?'

From the look on his face, Jonathan didn't care if he never looked at another motorbike in his lifetime!

'I'm unsure of the length of my stay,' he answered the other man, that guarded tone back in his voice.

'If you're still here next week, maybe you and Tory would like to come out for a quiet drink.' Terry seemed completely oblivious to the other man's non-committal answer. 'This week is out, I'm afraid. For obvious reasons.' He looked about them, the noise of bike engines, chatter and laughter almost deafening.

So was next week, as far as Tory was concerned. She had no wish to be linked as the other half of a couple with Jonathan McGuire! Especially where her family was concerned.

'We had better be getting back.' She touched her cousin's arm in apology. 'And we'll take a raincheck on next week,' she added as she pulled her helmet back on. 'Neither of us is sure of our plans at the moment.'

'Fine,' Terry said. 'But give me a ring before you go back to London. Nice to meet you, Jonathan,' he finished, before limping back to the group of friends he had been talking with when they had arrived.

Tory looked at the still ashen-faced Jonathan. 'Do you

feel up to riding back to the farm on the bike? I promise I'll go slowly.'

He briefly shut his eyes and then opened them again as he pulled his own helmet back on. 'This has got to be the maddest thing I've ever done in my life,' he said.

She gave him a mischievous look. 'It beats hot-air ballooning, hang-gliding and parachuting!'

'I've never done any of those, either.'

'You haven't lived!' Tory told him with feeling, having done—and enjoyed—all three.

He looked at her, unimpressed. 'I'm only just beginning to realise that…' He climbed back on the pillion seat. 'I'll enjoy this if it kills me!' he announced determinedly.

She laughed, lifting up a hand in farewell to Terry and his friends, several of whom she recognised, before accelerating the bike back into the stream of other bikes—but heading towards the coastal road, away from the actual course.

Jonathan didn't have her in quite such a death-grip this time, and was much more relaxed behind her now, seeming to actually be enjoying the uninterrupted views of the Irish sea, the sheer cliffs rising up from it in places, the hillsides covered in the vivid yellow-orange gorse.

Tory didn't head straight back to the farm, taking the road into Laxey instead, going down the road that led to the beach. It was crowded of course, but the sun, the sand, the bracing sea air, were all quite invigorating.

'Come on, I'll buy you an ice-cream,' she told the no longer white-faced Jonathan once she had parked the bike, leaving their helmets locked to the side of the machine.

Jonathan shook his head a few minutes later as they walked along side by side, eating the vanilla ice-creams in their cornets. Dozens of people were milling about, either on the beach itself or walking along as they were. 'Maddie and Gideon are never going to believe this. Gideon assured me this is one of the most peaceful places on earth!'

'Fifty weeks of the year it is. Well...possibly a little less than that; we also have the Manx Grand Prix and the Southern One Hundred—also motorcycle races,' Tory told him ruefully. 'But by Monday of next week the majority of these people will have gone home.'

'Home where?' he questioned.

'Europe mostly, mainly Germany. But we get people from all over the world, including the States. Believe it or not, most of the bikers are actually accountants, lawyers, white collar workers; they just let their hair down on the Isle of Man for two weeks of the year. They just want to watch the races and in between have a good time,' she explained affectionately. 'For instance, it's going to be absolutely wild in Douglas this evening.'

'That's the capital, isn't it? Jonathan asked.

'It is now, but years ago it used to be Castletown.'

Jonathan looked at her over the top of his ice-cream. 'Were you issuing an invitation just now?' he murmured huskily.

Tory gave him a startled glance. An invitation—?

'To join in this evening's fun in Douglas,' Jonathan drawled at her puzzled expression.

Of course she hadn't been issuing an invitation! She was just very proud of her island home, wanted other people to love it as much as she did.

She should have known what sort of person Rupert was three years ago when he'd come here with her; he had absolutely hated the island, had called it a provincial wilderness!

'Or perhaps I should invite you as my guest,' Jonathan continued at her lack of response. 'It seems only fair as you've taken me out this afternoon.'

'Drive down in the car, you mean,' Tory said knowingly.

He gave a rueful smile. 'That's exactly what I mean!'

'And what happened to that not intending to socialise while you're here that you mentioned yesterday?' she reminded pointedly.

He had only been here a little over twenty-four hours, and so far he had been to her parents' home for lunch, been taken out for a bike ride by her, and now he was asking her to spend the evening with him, too.

But she did not want to go out with Jonathan this evening, or any other evening for that matter. She was no more interested in socialising than he had told her he was yesterday…especially not with him!

Why especially not with him…?

Oh, shut up, she told that inner voice crossly. It was obvious why not; the man was arrogant, rude, didn't belong here any more than Rupert did!

The latter might be true, she conceded slowly, but the arrogance and rudeness hadn't been as noticeable today…

'I really am sorry I was so rude and uncooperative yesterday,' Jonathan grated, seeming to pick up on at least some of her thoughts. 'My only excuse—and it really isn't good enough—is that I had flown overnight from the States before getting on the Isle of Man plane a couple of hours later. Consequently, I was more than a little jet-lagged!'

She knew just how unpleasant that could be, had often arrived abroad completely disorientated, half the time not even knowing where she was!

'I didn't know that,' she said quietly, her ice-cream finished now.

'Why should you? I— Here,' he reached out and gently ran his fingertip along the side of her mouth. 'Hey, it was only ice-cream,' he defended at her reaction.

Tory had jumped as if someone had hit her, at once feeling the heated colour in her cheeks at her over-the-top reaction. 'Sorry,' she muttered awkwardly, wiping her mouth with a tissue now. 'I—I wondered what you were doing.'

Jonathan raised dark brows. 'What did you think I was doing?'

They had stopped walking now, were standing close together on the pavement, Tory not quite managing to meet Jonathan's searching gaze.

What *had* she thought he was doing?

More to the point, why? Jonathan hadn't shown by so much as a smile that he found her in the least attractive, so why had her imagination jumped several steps ahead and imagined he was about to kiss her a couple of minutes ago?

Which he obviously hadn't been!

She gave a bright, meaningless smile to cover up her embarrassment. 'I guess I'm a little jumpy myself at the moment,' she excused lightly, deliberately not answering his question. 'If you're sure you feel up to it, I'm quite happy to show you Douglas on the evening of Mad Sunday.'

Jonathan looked serious. 'You're starting to make me feel nervous now…'

Tory laughed at his worried expression. 'No, honestly, you'll enjoy it,' she said with certainty. 'It's just a lot of people having a lot of fun.'

Though she wasn't sure she was going to be one of them, she decided later that afternoon, as she bathed and washed her hair ready for going out that evening. The last time she had been on the island for TT she had spent most of racing week with Terry and his friends. Being in the company of Jonathan McGuire was a different proposition completely!

What was he going to make of the bikers doing fantastic wheelies up and down Douglas promenade, some of them wearing only underpants to protect their modesty? The pints and pints of beer being consumed by the crowds as they watched and cheered their antics? The impromptu parties? The bungee-jumping over the sea? The rock band playing on the quay?

If he had thought the drive around the TT course was 'interesting', then he was going to find this evening even more so!

'You look very nice, love,' her father told her as she joined them in the kitchen.

She must have changed her clothes half a dozen times before settling on the bright red tee shirt and black jeans, and she still wasn't sure she had chosen the right things to wear. Normally she would have gone to Douglas on her bike, and, like most of the revellers, she would have been in her biking leathers. But as Jonathan was driving them into Douglas…

He had thanked her very politely for taking him out when she'd returned him to the Byrnes' house earlier, had expressed pleasure in the drive back along the coast road—and promptly added, as he'd handed her the helmet back with obvious relief, that he didn't care if he never went on a motorbike again in his life—ever!

Tory had laughed, had still been smiling when she'd reached home a few minutes later—her father, as she had suspected, having very much enjoyed his war film in their absence!

'I'll do this, Mum,' she assured her mother now as she took over getting the Sunday tea: scones she had baked earlier that morning, fresh cream, and strawberry jam her mother had made a couple of months ago, also getting out a fruit cake her mother had made earlier in the week.

'Aren't you joining us, Tory?' her mother asked as Tory joined them with only a cup of tea in front of her. 'I hope you aren't dieting again, love,' she added worriedly. 'You really worried me the last time you did that.'

Rupert had decided a couple of years ago that she could do with losing a few pounds. Those 'few pounds' had resulted in even her size eights hanging loosely on her!

Her mother's answer to that, the next time Tory had gone home, had been to prepare all her favourite foods and make sure she ate them, ensuring that Tory was back to her original weight by the time she'd returned to London. Much to Rupert's annoyance!

'No, I'm not dieting, Mum,' she assured her wryly. 'Jonathan is taking me into Douglas this evening, and so—'

'Jonathan is?' her father echoed, brows raised speculatively.

Tory gave an inward sigh. Her parents, she knew, were no different from any others, and saw every man over twenty-five and under forty-five as a prospective son-in-law. She just wished that Jonathan McGuire didn't fit that particular criteria. Because he certainly wasn't suitable in any other way!

'Jonathan is,' she confirmed. 'So we'll probably pick up a snack to eat in Douglas somewhere.' There would be lots of places selling food this evening, from basic hotdogs to Chinese food.

'That'll be nice, love,' her father commented non-committally as he helped himself to the jam and cream to go with his scones.

She gave him a reproving look for his deliberate understatement. 'It won't be nice at all,' she bit out impatiently. 'But without appearing rude to Madison, as well as her brother, I could hardly refuse his invitation!'

'Of course you couldn't, Tory,' her mother agreed. 'He seems a very pleasant young man?' she continued questioningly. Indeed, the flowers he had brought her earlier were now in pride of place in the sitting room.

Jonathan McGuire was not pleasant! A lot of other things, perhaps, but nothing as wishy-washy as pleasant!

'Any more war films on tonight, Dad?' Tory turned to him teasingly, unable to answer her mother.

'No.' His eyes twinkled at their shared joke concerning this afternoon. 'But there is a John Wayne film on later.'

Another of her father's favourites, she acknowledged unbegrudgingly. Her father, and her mother, worked extremely hard on the farm, especially this time of the year, and watching the television in the evenings was one of their avenues of entertainment.

Her cup of tea finished, Tory stood up abruptly. 'Jonathan was going to pick me up in about half an hour, but it's such a lovely sunny evening I think I'll walk over.' And she would avoid any more searching questions concerning Jonathan!

She picked up a black denim jacket in case it got cooler later that evening, hooking her thumb into it before throwing it over one shoulder.

'Have you got your key to get in? We'll probably be in bed when you get home,' her mother prompted.

'I'm not expecting to be that late,' Tory said firmly; she knew her parents liked to be in bed early, but a couple of hours in Douglas should be enough. More than enough when it was spent with Jonathan McGuire!

'Take your key just in case,' her father advised.

Tory had to admit that she felt a little disgruntled as she witnessed the knowing look that passed between her parents before she left the house. They were wasting their time if they imagined there was anything in the least romantic between Jonathan McGuire and herself; as far as Tory was concerned she was just being polite to the brother of a friend and neighbour!

'The lady doth protest too much, methinks…'

Where had that little taunting voice inside her come from? Wherever it was, she wished it would go straight back again!

Jonathan was good-looking, there was no doubting that. He was also extremely self-confident—but no longer arrogant? that little voice mocked again—much to Tory's increasing irritation! He had a certain charm, when he chose to exert it. He also hadn't been in the least concerned at admitting his aversion to the ride round the TT course earlier, so he wasn't pompously self-important, either.

There was also the way she had reacted to his touching her earlier, to remove the ice-cream from the side of her mouth…

She had made light of it at the time, but as it wasn't the first time it had happened—there had also been that tingling up her arm the previous day when they'd shaken hands—there was no doubting the fact that his merest touch sent little shock waves through her body.

But what did that mean?

She had been without a man in her life for too long; that was what it meant, she told herself sharply.

That was Rupert's fault again. His possessive attitude tended to frighten away any prospective boyfriends, in fact most people considered *he* was her boyfriend, to the point where she hadn't even been asked out by another man for over eighteen months.

No doubt Rupert, for all he hated the island, wouldn't have been agreeable to her coming here on her own either if he had thought there was the remotest possibility of her meeting any eligible men!

Oh, damn Rupert, she told herself crossly. He had had his chance a couple of years ago—and he had blown it!

She waved to the people camping in the neighbouring field as she strolled across to Jonathan's house; the island hotels and boarding houses simply couldn't accommodate a sudden influx of almost fifty thousand people, and a lot of visitors chose to bring tents and simply camp out. Tory's father had been letting them use the west field for as long as she could remember, laying on water and toilet facilities for them so that their stay could be as comfortable as possible, so much so that they usually had the same people come back to stay year after year.

The Byrne house looked mellowly welcoming in the early evening sunlight, the warmth of it's colours reflecting warmly.

It was only as Tory approached the front of the house that she became aware of the sound of music playing, the gentle strum of a guitar carried hauntingly in the still evening air.

Jonathan McGuire?

He had been less than forthcoming when she'd questioned him yesterday about the guitar, only finally grudgingly admitting that he played; if that was him playing now, then he played very well!

Tory made her way quietly round the side of the house, loath to disturb him when he wasn't even aware that anyone was listening; after all, he had said he would pick her up at seven o'clock—had no idea she would walk over instead.

He was sitting on the back balcony of the house, the guitar resting comfortably on his knee, long, artistic hands moving easily over the strings of the guitar as he played, the sound absolutely beautiful to the senses.

Tory hadn't really noticed his hands before, but now she

saw they were long and slender, brushing against the strings of the guitar almost in a loving caress.

She tried to place the tune, but it wasn't one she was familiar with. Nevertheless, it was poignantly beautiful, seeming to conjure up pictures in the mind of love found and then love lost, of heartbreak. To her surprise, Tory felt the sting of tears in her eyes…

It was—

'What the hell do you think you're doing, sneaking around, spying on me like this?'

That angrily rasping voice brought her back to a sudden awareness of her surroundings, blinking rapidly as she tried to clear the mesmerising beauty of the tune Jonathan had been playing from her brain.

Jonathan had stopped playing now, had risen indignantly to his feet, was glaring across the terrace at her with undisguised fury.

Oh, help!

CHAPTER FOUR

'I ASKED you what you're doing here.' His voice was icily cold.

Tory swallowed hard, sure she had never seen anyone this angry before. 'According to you, I was spying on you,' she finally said huskily. 'Except I wasn't spying on you at all. I decided to walk over. I—you were obviously—busy. I didn't like to disturb you,' she finished with a lame shrug.

Jonathan continued to look at her through narrowed grey eyes, obviously not too impressed with her explanation.

'You were right—you can play,' she said admiringly, giving a pained wince as his scowl only seemed to darken at these words.

But she was only telling the truth; he *could* play, quite beautifully, in fact.

'Have you ever thought of taking it up professionally?' she went on at his continued defensive silence. If he didn't say something soon—! Even his unmistakable anger was better than this coldly remote non-communication.

He gave her a flintily scathing glance before bending down to put his guitar away in the case, clicking the locks down decisively. 'And just what would you know about it?' he grated straightening to glare across at her dismissively.

She raised dark brows at his obvious scorn. Not only defensive, but back to being his rude self again. Oh, well, at least she knew where she stood with that!

'Absolutely nothing.' She confirmed what he wanted to

hear. 'But it sounded okay to me,' she added with sarcastic challenge.

His mouth twisted mockingly. 'Well, for your information, it was terrible. I take it you're ready to go into Douglas?' He eyed her casual clothes.

Obviously she was—but after his behaviour just now, she had the feeling he had changed his mind about taking her!

'If you are?' She gave a determined inclination of her head.

'Just give me a couple of minutes,' he rasped, picking up the guitar case and striding back into the house.

Take a seat. Would you like a drink while you're waiting? Obviously her unexpected arrival had robbed Jonathan of those manners he had said his mother taught him!

Tory sat down in the cane chair Jonathan had recently vacated, staring out across the fields stretching up towards the hills.

What was so awful about her having heard him play the guitar, for goodness' sake? She couldn't believe it was shyness on Jonathan's part; the man didn't have an un-self-confident bone in his arrogant body!

All she had done was take a stroll over here on a pleasant early-summer evening, but Jonathan had taken exception to having an unseen audience.

His mood hadn't improved in the slightest when he rejoined her on the terrace, also wearing black denims, but his tee shirt was black, too.

'You may need a jacket later,' Tory advised. 'The evenings can become quite cool.'

This good weather wasn't usually long-lasting on the Isle of Man. Situated in the Irish Sea, between England and Ireland, the island was also in the gulf stream, ensuring that they didn't have the really cold, icy weather England often did, but also meaning that in the summer months they rarely had temperatures that exceeded the mid-eighties. And it wasn't summer yet. In fact, TT Fortnight was known for its inclement weather!

Jonathan turned back into the house to collect a jacket, silent as they drove into Douglas, driving the Jaguar saloon car that belonged to the Byrnes as if he were actually in a race!

Tory sighed as they dropped down onto Douglas promenade, instantly caught up in a heavy flow of traffic. 'Perhaps this isn't such a good idea, after all,' she commented.

Jonathan gave her a brief glance. 'We'll be out of this jam in a few minutes,' he replied.

'I wasn't referring to this.' She waved a hand at the traffic and horse trams also travelling up and down in the middle of the road. 'You're still annoyed about earlier,' she continued at his enquiring look. 'I have no idea why, but it's clear you are.' She sighed again. 'And the evening of Mad Sunday in Douglas is for enjoying.'

Not tiptoeing around someone else's annoyance—especially when it seemed rather ridiculous to her!

'And you won't enjoy it with me in this mood,' Jonathan accepted grimly. 'I'm sorry, but you—you caught me in an unguarded moment earlier. Playing the guitar has only ever been for my own enjoyment before.'

She gave a half-smile. 'I don't think I've ever heard the tune before that you were playing; does it have any words?'

She knew by the way his eyes suddenly took on that flinty sheen that she had once again stepped on forbidden ground. Was there *any* subject that wasn't sensitive to this man?

His mouth thinned. 'If you thought my playing was bad, then you should hear me sing; tuneless doesn't even come into it!' He'd successfully avoided answering her question.

But she hadn't thought his playing was bad, and she had

said as much at the time. Besides, she didn't believe him about the singing. And with good reason. He hadn't had any music in front of him earlier, could obviously play a tune by ear. And if he could do that, then she was sure he wouldn't sing out of tune either.

'I think you're probably being modest,' she answered him non-committally.

He turned to grin at her. 'I think you're humouring me, Miss Buchanan!'

She relaxed slightly at this show of humour. 'I think I'm trying to—Mr McGuire! Turn to the right up here,' she advised quickly. 'We'll find somewhere to park in one of the back streets.'

Easier said than done, they discovered during the next ten minutes of looking, but finally managed to find a parking spot near the museum.

'The walk will do us good,' Tory said uncomplainingly as they set off towards the noise of people enjoying themselves.

Jonathan took a light hold of her arm as they came out onto the main street to be confronted by thousands of people milling about. 'If I lose you now, I'll never find my way back to the car,' he offered by way of explanation as she looked up at him questioningly.

'If we happen to lose each other, just remember we're parked near the museum,' Tory hold him.

But still Jonathan kept that light hold, his hand warm against the bare flesh of her upper arm. As it became more and more crowded, the further they walked, Tory accepted that the contact was necessary if they were not to get separated.

Even if it was doing strange things to her pulse-rate! How could just the touch of his hand on her arm possibly produce this heat inside her, make her legs feel slightly weak, too?

They stood and watched the bungee-jumping for a few minutes—a brief respite for Tory from the warmth of that hand!—laughing along with everyone else in the watching crowd when the second soul brave enough to try it ended up dunking her head in the sea below.

'I hope she hadn't just done her hair,' Tory said ruefully as the girl continued to bob up and down for several minutes.

'Have you ever tried that?' Jonathan asked as he looked up to where the cage for the start of the jump was situated, high above them.

Tory shook her head. 'I'm all for trying out new things—but I'm not stupid!'

Jonathan chuckled softly. 'I never for a moment thought you were.'

Just nosy and inquisitive!

Oh, well, Tory inwardly sighed; he was entitled to his opinion—even if it was wrong!

She turned to him. 'Have you ever tried English fish and chips?'

'Surely they would be Manx fish and chips?' he came back teasingly. 'And by chips I take it you mean fries?'

Tory had read a quote somewhere once, stating that England and America were two countries divided by a common language—and, from her own visits to the States, she was inclined to agree with that sentiment.

'You take it right.' She smiled. 'Although these chips are nothing like the thin fries you have in America. And the fish has batter on it. Probably not good for one's cholesterol levels, if you happen to be health-conscious.' She wrinkled her nose. 'But delicious to eat! Unfortunately, supposedly on the grounds of hygiene, they're no longer able to serve it in newspaper, but it still tastes good.'

'Lead me to it.' Jonathan took hold of her arm once again. 'After that huge lunch you gave me, I thought I was never going to feel hungry again, but I'm actually starving,' he realised. 'Must be all this sea air.'

'And I thought it was the bike ride this afternoon that had convinced you you would never feel hungry again!' She looked at him from beneath lowered lashes.

Jonathan shook his head at the memory. 'I've decided never to repeat the experience!'

Tory laughed huskily. 'You would probably feel differently if you had been the driver rather than the passenger.'

'Maybe.' But he didn't sound convinced. 'Is that live music I can hear?' He listened for a moment.

They were walking down the road beside the quay now, the crowd getting larger the further they walked. Tory could actually hear the rock band playing up on the temporary stage now, although she wasn't tall enough to see over the heads of the people in front of her. Jonathan, with his extra foot in height, seemed to be having no such trouble.

'They're good,' she offered after several minutes.

'This time I have to agree with you,' Jonathan drawled.

As opposed to her opinion earlier, concerning his guitar playing...!

She gave him a sceptical glance. 'We can get some food just along here.' She eased her way through the crowd until she got to the other side, waiting for Jonathan to join her before going inside the fish and chip shop.

No doubt this was going to be yet another culture shock for him, Tory decided as they joined the queue.

His life in Reno, involved in the running of casinos, must be so much more sophisticated. Although he had turned down the suggestion that he might like to see the island's casino while he was here...

'Is that compulsory?' Jonathan asked a few minutes later, the two of them back outside, watching Tory as she ate her food with her fingers.

She grinned up at him. 'Try it,' she invited laughingly; he had probably never eaten food with his fingers in his life before!

They were standing slightly on the edge of the listening crowd now; part of it, and yet somehow separate.

'If my family could see me now,' Jonathan muttered, before picking up a piece of the fish and putting it in his mouth.

That he liked what he was eating was obvious; there was a look of pure enjoyment on his face now as he began to eat the chips, too.

'Your mother is extremely beautiful,' Tory told him admiringly.

'She is,' he agreed. 'And Madison is very like her.'

Tory nodded. 'Then you must take after your father.' After all, Susan Delaney and Madison McGuire were both beautiful blondes.

'Probably,' Jonathan snapped, his expression once again as forbidding as the one he'd worn at the airport yesterday.

What had she said wrong now? Did Jonathan not get on with his father? Could that be the reason for this complete getaway to the Isle of Man?

'Which of your parents do *you* most resemble?' he demanded harshly.

Tory smiled; both her parents tended towards plumpness. What had once been her father's blond hair was now a wispy grey; her mother was also blonde, although, as she was only too happy to admit, it needed a little help from a bottle to be that colour nowadays.

'Neither of them,' she answered affectionately. 'I—'

'—joined by our very own Victory Canan!' the voice over the loudspeaker suddenly shouted.

Tory had been so engrossed in her conversation with Jonathan that she hadn't even realised the band had stopped playing, let alone that the MC had taken over the microphone.

'Victory!' the man called again, looking straight at her. 'Come and join us on the stage?' He held out a hand appealingly.

Tory didn't dare even glance at Jonathan as the crowd all turned to look at her too now, most with excited interest, some with obvious awe.

Neither was an emotion she particularly wanted at this moment!

'Victory Canan...?' Jonathan softly repeated at her side, eyes narrowed on her in cold assessment. 'You're *the* Victory Canan?'

The Victory Canan...

Somehow Jonathan managed to put a wealth of insult into those three words.

Yes...she was *the* Victory Canan! Jonathan had asked her earlier what she knew about music; the honest answer to that was...she knew a lot! Voted woman vocalist of the world for the third year running, with award after award given to her at a recent music awards ceremony, she would have had to be singularly stupid not to!

Even if Jonathan hadn't recognised her, he had definitely heard of her.

She moistened dry lips, at the same time tasting the food she had so recently enjoyed, which, as she looked up at Jonathan's harshly accusing expression, now lay heavily on her stomach.

Although she couldn't understand why!

Obviously he hadn't expected to be met by *the* Victory Canan when she'd come to taxi him to his sister's home, but that didn't alter the fact that he hadn't recognised her, either.

Or did he think she should have greeted him with the words, 'Hey, by the way, I'm actually Victory Canan, the singer. I suppose you've heard of me?'

For one thing, she wasn't that conceited, and for another, she came back to the island to enjoy the privacy that so many other well-known people could enjoy in peace on the Isle of Man! Here she could be completely herself, could walk down Strand Street, the main shopping street in Douglas, and merely have people say hello to her, or simply wish her well. She was one of those well-known people who could do her shopping locally and have absolutely no notice taken of her!

She put the rest of her uneaten fish and chips in a nearby bin before looking up at Jonathan once again. His gaze was steely, his jaw set coldly.

'You don't look much like your photographs!' he told her scathingly.

That wasn't surprising! Six years ago, when she'd first gone to London, she had developed an image for herself—an image that had adorned the front of newspapers intermittently for the last five years. An image she was becoming more and more glad to leave behind her when she came home...

Her mouth twisted wryly. 'There isn't a lot of call on the Isle of Man for coloured leathers, moussed hair, and streaks to match whatever colour clothes I happen to be wearing at the time!' Her make-up was much more dramatic on stage, too; her face usually deliberately pale, with dark eye make-up, burgundy lipstick.

It was an image she left behind her when she came home.

In fact, she was surprised that the MC had recognised her; no one else seemed to have done until he'd called out her name.

But as she glanced back towards the stage she knew the answer to that particular puzzle, too; her cousin Terry was standing on the steps grinning at her, having spotted her in the crowd even if she hadn't seen him.

'Thanks!' she mouthed at him over the crowd, glaring her displeasure at his having revealed her presence.

She turned back to Jonathan, holding up her hands defensively. 'Look—'

'I take it Madison and Gideon know exactly who you are?' he said tautly.

She sighed. 'Yes, but—'

'I think your public wants you,' Jonathan cut in harshly as someone nearby began to clap, and the rest of the huge crowd quickly joined in.

'Jonathan—'

'You had better go,' he bit out coldly. The whistles and shouts were becoming louder by the second.

She gave him an impatient glare. 'I can explain—'

'There's nothing to explain—Victory,' he added scornfully—pointedly. 'And don't worry about me. I'm sure I can manage to find my own way back to the car! Near the museum, I think you said?'

In other words, he wasn't about to wait for her while she went up on stage to give the crowd the song they were asking for!

Her eyes flashed deeply blue. 'And just how am I supposed to get home?'

He looked about them at the warmly welcoming crowd, their faces alight with expectation. 'I'm sure one of your numerous fans will be only to happy to offer you a lift home! Terry, perhaps?' he suggested scathingly, obviously having seen the other man too now.

'Strange, I always thought it polite to leave with the person you arrived with.' Tory spat the words out angrily. 'Obviously we have different views on that!'

'Obviously,' he returned abruptly, his expression completely unbending. 'I'm sure you're very good at what you do, but I can't claim to have ever been a fan!' he finished insultingly.

The crowd had taken up a chant of her name now, the noise around them deafening.

'I had better not delay you any further then, had I?' she told him witheringly, before turning on her heel, her public smile on her face as she made her way up to the stage, much to the delight of the now cheering crowd.

'Do you know "Easy Street"?' she murmured to the group on stage, hoping they wouldn't mind this impromptu invasion of what was actually their show.

'Know it, love? We sing it.' The drummer smiled. 'But nowhere near as well as you do!'

She laughed her relief. 'Then let's do it!'

She became a complete professional as she launched into the song that had taken her to the top five years ago, knowing by the crowd's reaction that they were completely with her, singing and clapping along to the music.

All except one man...

Her last sight of Jonathan, after he'd given a last contemptuous glance in her direction, was as he turned on his heel and marched away, pushing his way through the rapidly growing crowd, as word of the presence of Victory Canan singing on stage spread like wildfire.

Well, damn him, she decided frustratedly.

Damn him to hell!

She wasn't going to apologise for who and what she was

to anyone, least of all the arrogant Jonathan McGuire. He could either take it or leave it.

He had chosen to leave it!

And her…

CHAPTER FIVE

'WHAT did you think you were doing, singing in some quayside concert in the middle of nowhere?'

Tory held the telephone receiver away from her ear, waiting for Rupert to stop shouting. Which he did—eventually.

'I thought,' she finally answered him in measured tones, determined not to lose her own temper, 'that I was exercising my own free will.'

Rupert might have set himself up as her keeper, but that was exactly what it was: a self-appointed role. And it wasn't one she was happy to let him take. Not any more.

'Some local reporter must have thought all his dreams had come true in one night. He sold the story and photographs of your impromptu concert the night before last to the daily newspapers over here,' Rupert continued in a disgruntled voice. '"Winner for Victory", "Impromptu Victory Concert", "A Home Win for Victory",' he quoted disgustedly.

Tory gave a wince at the terrible puns on her name. 'I thought you once told me any publicity was good publicity,' she reminded him dryly. 'Besides, all I did was sing a few songs.'

'According to the newspapers you were on stage for almost an hour and a half!' Rupert protested.

That was true. What had started out as singing one song to please the crowd had turned into a full-blown concert. The group had been more than pleased to back her as the audience shouted out for her to sing song after song. She had been amazed herself at the time that had elapsed when she'd finally managed to leave the stage.

Terry, for his sins, had been the one to drive her home later that night on the back of his bike, in apology for 'dropping her in it', he had admitted sheepishly.

Not that she had really minded. Except for the fact that Jonathan had walked off in disgust on learning she was Victory Canan in her professional life it had been a very enjoyable evening—the most fun she had had singing for years, she realised…

Jonathan's reaction to her professional persona was his own problem, she had decided as she lay in bed the night before, thinking about it. He could have no idea how refreshing it was not to be Victory Canan for even the few days of her visit here!

'Time passes quickly when you're having fun,' she told Rupert now.

'Did you get paid for it?' Rupert barked.

'Don't be ridiculous!' she snapped back, angry colour in her cheeks now, despite her earlier decision to remain calm. 'I was simply a member of the public asked to sing to a very appreciative audience.'

'Of course they were appreciative—you're Victory Canan, for goodness' sake!' Rupert was furious at the thought of her making an appearance on stage without consulting him first.

Victory Canan could ask thousands of pounds for a single performance, was worth millions in her own right from the sales of her records. Yes, she was Victory Canan, she acknowledged heavily.

Then she remembered her grinning, self-satisfied cousin, two nights ago, the couple of drinks she had shared with him and a few of his biker friends after the concert, and smiled herself now. 'Over here on the island I'm just Tory Buchanan.'

'Obviously,' Rupert retorted tightly. 'Every newspaper is questioning whether the ''soft flyaway hair'' and no make-up could possibly be a new image for you!'

Ah. Now they were getting to what was really bothering Rupert.

Her decision to leave London over a week ago had been made for two reasons: one she needed the rest and, two, she was tired of the rough, tough Victory Canan image! Rupert was more than aware of that.

'It isn't an image, Rupert,' she told him softly. 'It's the real me.' The real her that seemed, this last year or so, to have become buried under the pressure of being Victory Canan for almost fifty weeks of the year. Her bookings had sometimes seemed never-ending.

She had told Rupert before she left London that she wanted to change that image. Even the songs that she sang. Needless to say, Rupert had been absolutely horrified at the idea, and Tory knew exactly why that was.

Six years ago, raw and inexperienced, she had approached several agencies with the idea of asking them to manage her. Rupert, an Oxford graduate, new to the business himself, had been the only one willing to take the risk.

Looking back now, she could see he'd really had nothing to lose. If she were to be a success, then he would also bathe in that fame and glory, financially, of course. And it would benefit his agency to have a big star on its books. If she bombed he would lose nothing.

But she hadn't bombed. Had gone on from those first few performances Rupert had arranged for her to become a very marketable commodity. And now Rupert was very aware that changing her image, and performance, might make her less so...

'And who was the man, Tory?' Rupert curtly interrupted her musings.

'Man?' she echoed. 'What man?'

'"Miss Canan arrived at the concert with a tall, dark, mystery man".' Rupert was quoting from another of those newspapers. 'So who was he, Tory?' he repeated fiercely.

Her hand tightened about the telephone receiver. Someone had noticed that she'd arrived with Jonathan that night...?

Jonathan, if he saw any of those newspapers, was going to love this, she realised, and there was every possibility that he would, she acknowledged wearily; the island published a couple of its own newspapers, but the British dailies were delivered over here every day, too. In fact, the majority of the island's population had probably already received theirs, and so had seen the headlines about her concert and her 'mystery man'.

Not that the description didn't suit Jonathan perfectly. She had spent several hours in his company, and the little she did know about him had been dragged out of him!

'He's a friend of the family,' she told Rupert truthfully—if evasively!

'What sort of friend?' Rupert prompted shrewdly.

Until a couple of years ago Tory had made the mistake of being romantically involved with Rupert; it was a mistake she had paid for as, even after the personal relationship had fizzled out, Rupert seemed to think he had more than a professional claim on her.

'Male, obviously,' she returned impatiently.

'Oh, obviously,' Rupert echoed sarcastically. 'If there's a romance in the offing, Tory, then—'

'There isn't,' she snapped resentfully. 'I told you, he's a friend, nothing more.' After the other night, she wasn't even sure about that any more!

'The agency should handle all the publicity,' Rupert continued as if she hadn't interrupted him. 'You—'

'There isn't going to be any publicity!' Tory told him frustratedly. 'I—he's gone. Left the island,' she invented wildly.

Because if Rupert had picked up on that brief mention of a 'tall, dark, mystery man', then she was sure the world press would pick up on it, too—and try to follow up on it! She could just imagine Jonathan's horror—and fury!—if any of those reporters managed to track him down!

'He isn't a local, then?' The frown could be heard in Rupert's voice.

Her lips quivered wryly; she was well aware of Rupert's opinion of the island and its inhabitants. 'No, he isn't a local,' she confirmed.

There was a brief—and welcome!—silence on Rupert's end of the line. 'But even so—' he eventually began.

'Even so nothing,' Tory responded firmly. 'There's no story to write because there is no mystery man. Jonathan is—'

'Jonathan who?' Rupert instantly pounced.

Tory briefly wondered what his reaction would be if she were to tell him that Jonathan was actually the son of the legendary American actress Susan Delaney, and brother of Oscar-winning actress Madison McGuire. No doubt Rupert would come up with some lucrative publicity based on that information!

Which was precisely the reason he wasn't going to be given it!

'Just Jonathan, Rupert,' she replied levelly, wishing she hadn't even made that slight slip-up. 'Now, it's barely nine o'clock in the morning, Rupert, and I have things to do—as, I'm sure, do you.'

She had been up for hours, as it happened; life on a farm

this size began very early in the morning. With her mother incapacitated, a lot of the outside chores were left to Tory.

'Okay, Tory.' Rupert gave in irritably. 'But when are you coming home?'

Her mouth firmed. 'I am home.'

'You know what I meant,' he growled. 'Your mini-European tour begins in just under two weeks' time, and we still have a lot to—'

'I'm on holiday, Rupert—remember?' she jumped in. 'I'll think about the tour some time next week.' About Paris. And Amsterdam. And Berlin. And Zurich. And Rome. And all those nameless, characterless hotels she would have to stay in along the way!

'But—'

'Goodbye, Rupert,' she announced, before putting the receiver down.

She switched on the answer-machine. If, as Rupert had so angrily pointed out, the press were hot on the trail of a story, she did not intend to take any of their telephone calls.

Which left her with the problem of whether or not she ought to warn Jonathan of what was to come! He had left her in no doubt the other night as to exactly what he thought of her—and Victory Canan!—but that didn't alter the fact that if the world press started prowling about, as she suspected they might, then they would only have to add two and two together to realise that the 'tall, dark, mystery man' of the other night was actually Tory's tall, dark next-door neighbour!

As if in answer to her quandary the telephone began to ring next to her. The answer-machine went into action—to receive a message from the first of the overseas reporters to have tracked her down!

She had no choice; she would have to go and warn Jonathan!

It wasn't something she particularly relished doing. After the other night she could take a guess at what her reception was going to be, and what she had to tell Jonathan wasn't exactly going to endear her to him, either.

She turned as her father entered the house, having been up in the top fields the last couple of hours, checking on the sheep they had grazing there.

'Hello, love,' he greeted warmly, reaching under his arm to bring out the newspaper he had picked up on his drive home. 'You've made the front page again,' he told her happily, spreading the paper out on the kitchen table. '"A Home Win for Victory",' he read out with satisfaction.

Tory pulled a face. 'So I've already been told.'

'It's a good picture of you, too.' Her father hadn't looked up, so he hadn't noticed her less-than-pleased expression. 'For once it actually looks like the Tory your mother and I know and love!'

She couldn't resist strolling over to take a look, instantly understanding why Rupert was so angry about the picture in the newspapers.

'Sexy and sultry' were the words usually used to describe Victory Canan in her body-hugging leather clothes; the woman in this picture looked more like the girl next-door! She had obviously been enjoying herself when it was taken, laughing into the unseen camera, her hair having almost an ebony sheen to it, her eyes glowing, her cheeks flushed, a pale pink gloss on her lips. Anyone less like the sultry Victory Canan she couldn't imagine.

'Rupert isn't pleased,' she told her father distractedly, reading the article that went along with the picture.

Her father grimaced; the dislike was mutual between the two men. 'Been on the phone already, has he?' he asked knowingly.

'Hmm,' she confirmed vaguely, still reading the newspaper. Yes, there it was; 'Victory was accompanied by a tall, dark mystery man'!

She really didn't have a choice; she would have to go over and warn the 'mystery man'.

'Dad, I have to go out for a few minutes,' she told him awkwardly. 'If anyone rings—reporters, anyone like that—do *not* mention Jonathan's name. In fact, tell them I'm not here, either!' she added desperately as the telephone began to ring again.

'Ah.' Her father was still bent over the newspaper, having come to the part that mentioned her companion for the evening, too. He looked up, a sympathetic look on his face. 'How do you think Jonathan is going to react to that?'

'Well, considering he came to the island for peace, quiet and privacy—not very well!' she understated.

Her father chuckled. 'You had better get over there pretty smartish, then, hadn't you?'

Tory decided to go over on the bike. At least this time Jonathan wouldn't be able to accuse her of sneaking up on him; he simply couldn't miss the sound of the bike engine!

There was no sound of music from the back terrace this morning, so she went to the front door and rang the bell. And waited.

After almost five minutes of waiting, and despite the fact that the car was parked in the open garage, she decided Jonathan couldn't be at home, and turned to walk back to the bike. She would have to come back later. As long as no reporters had tracked her to the house by then. Otherwise she wouldn't be able to come back without leading the press to Jonathan's door. And he—

'Yes?'

She froze at the sound of that harshly challenging voice, turning slowly back towards the house.

Jonathan now stood in the open doorway, dark hair wet,

a dark blue robe pulled on over what appeared to be complete nakedness beneath, tanned legs bare beneath its knee-length hem, his feet also bare.

'I was taking a shower when I heard you arrive,' he told her. 'To what do I owe the honour of this visit?'

Tory didn't need to be told he was still angry at the public way he had found out she was actually Victory Canan; his mocking expression as he looked her up and down in the black leathers said it all for him.

'The honour is all mine,' she returned dryly, instantly stung into being defensive. 'I—could I talk to you for a few minutes?'

'I thought you already were,' he drawled.

'Privately,' she said firmly.

He looked about them. Apart from her parents' farm and a couple of hundred sheep, uninhabited countryside surrounded them, and his gaze was scornful as it returned to her. 'I don't think the sheep are going to pose any problem to that, do you?' He didn't even try to disguise his sarcasm.

Tory drew in a deep breath, her hand tightening about the strap of the crash helmet she carried. She sighed. 'You could try offering me a cup of coffee,' she felt stung into reproving.

'Is what you have to say going to take long enough for that?'

Her cheeks coloured resentfully. She hadn't had to come here today, could have just left him to the vultures. At least that way she wouldn't have had to put up with his rudeness—again!

He stepped back, opening the door wider. 'Would you like to come in for coffee—Victory?' he mocked.

'Thank you,' she accepted stiffly, marching past him into the house and going straight to the kitchen at the back, having sat there with Madison dozens of times drinking coffee as the two of them cooed over baby Keilly. There would certainly be no such cooing today!

She tried not to watch Jonathan as he moved about the kitchen getting the coffee ready. It wasn't that she had never seen a man dressed only in a robe before, it was just that this man happened to be Jonathan McGuire!

He looked somehow younger with his hair still damp and inclined to curl, and what she could see of his chest seemed as tanned as his bare legs and feet. Perhaps he didn't spend all his life in the false brightness of casinos!

He stopped what he was doing for a moment, looking across at her with assessing eyes. 'I suppose there must be thousands of people—make that millions!—who would be only too happy to be making coffee for Victory Canan,' he commented.

But not him, Tory acknowledged inwardly. Jonathan looked as if he would rather be doing anything else but making her coffee—preferably strangling her!

'Make that millions of *men*,' he corrected.

Tory shot him a narrow-eyed glare. 'I do have female fans, too!'

'Really?' He raised sceptical dark brows. 'I can't think why.'

Her cheeks flushed fiery red as she desperately tried to hang on to her temper—it really wouldn't help anything if they ended up in a slanging match! 'Possibly because I actually can sing. I'm also a polished performer,' she defended resentfully.

'Really?' he came back again. 'I wouldn't know. As I told you; I've never been a fan.'

He wasn't about to make this easy for her, was he? Okay, so he felt he had been duped, made a fool of, but that was only his version of what had happened. Hers was completely different; there had been no deliberate act to deceive on her part; she was simply Tory Buchanan, Dan and Thelma Buchanan's daughter, when she came back to the island.

'Thanks.' She accepted the mug of coffee he put in front of her.

'I suppose, considering who you are, it really should be in bone china cups, but—'

'Will you just stop this, Jonathan?' she cut in wearily, eyes flashing deeply blue. 'You've been to the farm; you know it isn't like that. Hey, I even cooked lunch for you on Sunday!'

His mouth tightened as he sat opposite her at the kitchen table. 'Amazing,' he drawled, making no effort to disguise his sarcasm.

Tory took a sip of the black, unsweetened coffee before answering—at the moment she felt more in need of raw caffeine than putting Jonathan McGuire in his place!

'It's a sight more than you've done for me,' she eventually exclaimed.

'True,' he replied thoughtfully. 'How did the concert go the other night?' He changed the subject mildly.

Tory shot him another resentful glare, knowing he wasn't really interested. If he had been then he wouldn't have left the way he had!

'See for yourself,' she declared, pulling the front page of her father's newspaper from the back pocket of her leathers to throw it down on the table in front of Jonathan; her father had been only to happy to loan it to her in the circumstances!

Jonathan's expression, as he read the article accompanying Tory's photograph, slowly changed from disdain to frowning concentration, to scowling anger!

Tory waited for that anger to reach verbal proportions.

Jonathan stood up abruptly, taking the newspaper with

him as he read the article a second time. 'Wonderful!' he finally looked up from the page to rasp angrily. 'Just wonderful!' He flung the newspaper back down onto the table, hands clenched furiously at his sides.

Tory swallowed hard. 'I—'

'Not one word, Victory,' he bit out tautly. 'Not one damned, single word—or I'm likely to strangle you first and think about the consequences afterwards!'

That was what she had thought earlier—but he looked as if he were more than capable of doing exactly that now!

Anyone would think she had done this on purpose! Whereas in actual fact she was no more thrilled at having her privacy invaded in this way than he was.

Although that chilling glitter to the narrowed grey eyes, the thin, angry line of his mouth, angrily clenched jaw, didn't give the indication he was in the least concerned at how *she* felt!

'I—'

'I said, not a word, Victory,' he reminded her through gritted teeth.

'"I" isn't a word. It's a—'

'Don't say I didn't warn you, Victory. Twice!' Jonathan muttered, even as he pulled her roughly to her feet.

And straight into his arms. Knocking the breath from her body. Not that she would have been able to breathe anyway, when his mouth had just savagely taken possession of hers…!

She was being kissed by Jonathan McGuire!

Thoroughly.

Completely.

Contemptuously…!

Tory wrenched her mouth free of his. Not an easy feat when she was held so tightly in his arms she could feel every muscle and sinew of his body pressed firmly against hers.

'Stop it.' She pushed ineffectually at the steel bands about her that were Jonathan's arms. 'Jonathan—'

'I have no intention of stopping anything, Victory—'

'My name is Tory!' she protested, still pushing at his arms.

Those steel bands tightened even more. 'You're Victory Canan,' he grated. 'I still can't believe I didn't recognise you!' He shook his head in self-disgust as he looked down at her. 'I've been reading about your exploits in the newspapers for years. The wild parties. The men. The—'

'Doesn't the half-truth in that newspaper—' she gestured towards the kitchen table, where he had thrown the newspaper down in his anger '—indicate how much credence you should give those other stories?'

Yes, there had been parties—it was part of her image to be seen at parties with the rich and famous. Yes, there had been men—but not in the way Jonathan was implying; she simply didn't have time the way her life was now to give to a relationship. Rupert had been her last serious involvement, and in the last two years there had simply been a succession of male escorts to take her to parties, to be seen with—nothing else.

It was that very image he was talking about that she wanted to rid herself of...!

Although she could see by Jonathan's savage expression that he didn't want to hear any of that, that he wouldn't believe her if she told him how lonely it was at the top.

She wouldn't have believed it herself six years ago, when she had gone off to London in search of fame and success—a bit like Dick Whittington, who had believed the streets of London were paved with gold! Well, they were, if you had the talent—and luck—to succeed, but she had

had no idea of the personal price she would have to pay for such success.

To Rupert, as she had eventually learnt to her emotional cost, she was just a vehicle for his own success.

To other men—those that dared to approach her, that was—she was a trophy to wear on their arm for a while. The real Tory was of no interest to them whatsoever.

But Jonathan, furiously angry Jonathan, who believed he had been taken for a fool, wasn't in any sort of mood to listen to that!

He stared at her contemptuously. 'If only half those stories are true…!'

On the surface, all of them were true. But in actual fact none of them were. Because none of them told the story of her isolation, her loneliness, of how night after night—when she wasn't away somewhere performing!—she went home alone to her sumptuous apartment, having long passed the stage of relishing her privacy, now only feeling her solitude, the silence that simply went on and on, hour after hour, night after night.

Only here, back on the island, with her parents, could she find contentment of spirit as well as a release from that exhausting loneliness.

She sighed heavily, giving a weary shrug. 'Perhaps it's true what they say; people will only believe what they want to believe.'

Jonathan's face darkened. 'Are you accusing me of being prejudiced where you're concerned?' he said sternly.

She gave a humourless smile. 'I'm accusing you of treating me like every other person does—except my parents, family and my island friends—and that's as nothing more than a money-spinning sex symbol!' She spat the last words out disgustedly.

He looked down at her with knowing eyes. 'Poor little rich girl, is that it?'

She flinched at his unmistakable scorn. 'You have no idea,' she replied.

'Tell me about it,' he encouraged.

She was still held in his arms, still pressed against the lean length of his body; she was having trouble thinking straight at all! Let alone making sense of it all.

When she was younger, before she'd gone to London, like all teenagers she had read magazine articles about how the rich and famous bemoaned the loneliness they had found along with their success, quoting that old cliché that money couldn't buy you happiness—and she had believed they were all talking a lot of nonsense. Except it wasn't. She had been lonelier for real friendship in the last six years than she ever had before.

Jonathan watched her with narrowed eyes as the emotions flickered and flittered across her face, looking more puzzled now than angry.

Tory looked up at him from beneath lowered lashes, tears poised on the edge of those lashes. For some reason this man's opinion mattered to her—and at the moment he felt only contempt for her.

Jonathan suddenly put her away from him and looked down at her with flinty grey eyes. 'Tell me,' he said, 'does this act usually work?'

Tory blinked, taken aback by this sudden—and unwarranted!—renewal of attack. 'I don't know what you mean…'

'Sure you do,' Jonathan attacked, hands thrust deeply into the pockets of his robe. 'And, you know, for a few moments there it almost worked. I was actually starting to feel sorry for you. But for the tears, I just might have believed you. They were a little over the top, I'm afraid.'

Tory blinked back the offending tears once again. Act? Act…! How dared he? Just who did he think he was?

'Indeed?' Her voice shook with anger now, and she bent down to grab her helmet up from where she had put it on the kitchen floor earlier.

Jonathan nodded. 'Where women are concerned, they usually come into play when all else fails.'

Her eyes flashed deeply blue. 'Then I won't bore you with my act any longer!'

'Oh, I'm not bored, Victory,' he assured her. 'In fact, for a few moments I was completely entertained.'

Tory had no wish to know which few moments he was referring to. 'Nevertheless, it's time I was going,' she told him frostily. 'I hope you enjoy the rest of your stay, Mr McGuire,' she added insincerely, turning to march out of the kitchen, her head high.

Arrogant, insulting…!

She had come over here today out of a sense of obligation, had felt she at least owed it to Jonathan to let him know of the repercussions he might encounter from Sunday evening.

Now, as far as she was concerned, he could take care of himself!

She was sure it was something he was good at!

CHAPTER SIX

'I THINK you should hear this one, love.' Tory's father, in the process of listening to the messages that had been left on the answer-machine throughout the day, turned to speak to her as she entered the kitchen.

Tory looked over at him with dull, lifeless eyes. Her anger towards Jonathan McGuire had stayed with her on the drive home, and through most of the afternoon. Now it was early evening and she was feeling decidedly deflated.

Jonathan had been rude the day she'd met him at the airport, and intermittently so since then, but she believed he had been deliberately hurtful this morning.

Why? That was what was puzzling her now.

He had wanted to believe the worst of her, seemed to enjoy insulting her and mocking what he had hinted were her crocodile tears.

Again, she asked herself, why?

'Okay, Dad,' she agreed wearily as she sat down at the kitchen table to listen.

Although she couldn't imagine what was going to be so different about this call; most of the daily newspapers had already phoned her, and without exception they had all wanted to know more about the mystery man who had accompanied her on Sunday evening. Curiosity she had no intention of satisfying!

'Tory? Jonathan—Jonathan McGuire.' The message began to play back, causing Tory to sit up straighter in her seat, her expression wary now as she looked across at her father; his brows were raised ruefully.

She couldn't imagine why; if Jonathan had called just to insult her some more, her father had already heard it once!

There was really no need for Jonathan to have added 'McGuire'; contrary to what he might think of her, she knew no other Jonathans. Besides, that attractive American drawl was unmistakable!

'—owe you an apology,' Jonathan continued tersely. 'I—could you call me once you've received this message?' The call ended with an abrupt click of the receiver.

Could she—?

The man had some nerve calling her at all, after the things he had said to her this morning, let alone expecting her to return the call!

'Tory…?'

She looked across at her father, knew by the slightly reproving look on his face that she was about to hear a gentle lecture on forgiving and forgetting. As in earlier years, the look was enough.

She sighed. 'Dad, if you could have heard the things he said to me this morning—'

'I think I might have been a bit annoyed myself if I were in his shoes,' her father cut in softly. 'Let's face it, Tory. With a famous mother, sister and brother-in-law, the poor man has probably had enough media intrusion in his life already, without encountering it here, of all places.'

He was right. She knew he was right. But—

'He just wants to apologise, love.' Her father once again cut in on her mutinous thoughts, smiling encouragingly. 'I don't suppose it's something he does too often,' he added, obviously having summed the younger man up during lunch on Sunday.

Tory continued to look mutinous for several seconds. And then she began to smile; she never had been able to resist her father's unfailing good humour. 'It might be worth listening to that,' she conceded with a smile.

'You'll call him back, then?' her father encouraged.

'I'll think about it,' she compromised, not sure she could listen to what she was sure would be merely a lip-service apology on Jonathan's part; he probably just didn't want to upset his sister's nearest neighbours!

'That's my girl.' Her father ruffled her hair affectionately on his way to the door. 'Your mother is resting her ankle before tea, and I'm just going outside to check on the chickens before settling down for the evening.'

In other words, she had about ten minutes' uninterrupted privacy in which to return Jonathan's call. Tory acknowledged her father's ploy ruefully.

The thing was, she didn't want to return his call, had no wish to listen to an insincere apology on Jonathan's part and an even less sincere acceptance on her own part; Jonathan had made his opinion of her more than clear this morning.

She paced up and down the kitchen, all the time aware of the precious minutes ticking away.

Oh, damn him, she finally decided impatiently. She would listen to his apology, accept it, and that would be an end to it. Then everyone, including her parents, would be happy.

'Jonathan McGuire,' he answered her call tersely.

Her hand tightened about the phone, antagonism welling up inside her. 'Victory Canan,' she came back challengingly, very aware that he had chosen to call her 'Tory' on the message he'd left on the answer-machine earlier.

'Tory.' His voice softened in recognition. 'You received my message?'

'Obviously,' she snapped.

'Otherwise you wouldn't be calling at all,' he acknowledged dryly.

'No,' she returned curtly.

Jonathan chuckled softly. 'You're still annoyed with me?'

'Yes,' she confirmed abruptly.

'And with good reason,' he conceded with a sigh. 'I owe you an apology—'

'Accepted,' she bit out. 'Was that all?'

'No, it damn well was not all!' he came back furiously. 'I would like to invite you out to dinner.'

Tory became very still, frowning her puzzlement. He wanted to invite her out to dinner…?

'Well, not out exactly,' he went on, almost as if he had heard her thoughts. 'After the way you were recognised on Sunday I'm not sure that would be a good idea. I wondered if you would like to come over here for dinner?'

Over there? But—

Tory was aware she was reacting like a gauche schoolgirl being invited out by the handsomest boy in the school—even worse, she was behaving as if she had never been invited out by a man before!

'Have you forgotten about the media interest in us?' she reminded him. Her father had already dealt very effectively with a couple of reporters who had turned up at the farm. But they were still lurking about at the end of the long driveway to the house.

'No, I haven't forgotten.' Jonathan's voice had hardened. 'But I'm sure from previous experience you must be more than capable of getting past that.'

Getting by nosy reporters, he meant, Tory accepted irritably. And that might be true. She just wasn't sure she wanted to go to all that trouble on Jonathan McGuire's behalf…

'Can you think of one good reason why I should accept your invitation?' she questioned scathingly.

'Because I asked nicely?' he came back.

Yes, he had certainly done that. He had also apologised for his insulting behaviour earlier. Yet Tory still questioned his motives…

'Can you actually cook?' she said slowly. 'Or is this just a ruse to have someone cook dinner for you?'

Jonathan laughed throatily. 'Why don't you come over here and find out?'

Because she wasn't sure she wanted to spend the evening with him! He hadn't only insulted her earlier—he had kissed her, too.

And for a few seconds she had responded…!

She would be lying to herself if she said she didn't find Jonathan attractive. But it was an attraction that was going nowhere. She had already wasted three years of her life—and her love—on Rupert; falling for Jonathan would be even more of a disaster.

'You're taking an awful long time to make your decision,' Jonathan finally drawled. 'Don't tell me you're scared, Tory?'

'Of you?' Her tone was scornful as she bristled defensively.

'Of my cooking,' he came back mockingly.

He hadn't meant any such thing! But, no, she wasn't scared. Not of him. Or anything else, for that matter.

'What time would you like me to come over?' she prompted stiffly.

'Seven-thirty for eight?'

'Fine,' she accepted briskly. 'I'll see you then.' She rang off before he could make any more mocking remarks.

She had been managed, bulldozed, railroaded!

Into spending the evening with Jonathan…

* * *

'You look nice, love.' Her mother, her bandaged ankle resting on top of a stool, raised her head from reading the newspaper, looking over the top of her glasses as Tory entered the room.

Her mother's praise for her appearance was more than welcome. Tory didn't know what it was about Jonathan, but she always had trouble deciding what to wear when she knew she was seeing him!

It wasn't that she didn't have clothes for most occasions; she had a wardrobe full of them. She was just never sure what the occasion actually was when she was meeting Jonathan!

If she had been having dinner with any other man, in other circumstances, then there wouldn't have been a problem, either. But Jonathan already seemed to have the idea that Victory Canan was a siren in leathers, and Tory Buchanan was a jean-clad biker.

Which was why tonight she was wearing a fitted plain dark blue dress—which matched her eyes—sleeveless, knee-length. Her legs were silky in flesh-coloured tights, and two-inch heels on her shoes gave her some height. Her hair was newly washed, falling silkily down onto the shoulders, her make-up light, just blusher highlighting her cheekbones. Her lip-gloss was her only defiant gesture—it was bright cherry-red, giving her mouth a sexily pouting look.

Take that, Jonathan McGuire, she had told her reflection in her wardrobe mirror a few minutes ago; tonight she was neither the Tory Buchanan that Jonathan had come to know, nor the Victory Canan that he didn't want to know!

'Thanks, Mum.' She smiled gratefully at her mother for her confidence-boost. 'Is Dad ready?' she prompted lightly.

'He's strolled outside to chat to the reporters at the end of the driveway, at the same time letting slip into the conversation that he's popping out on his weekly visit to your grandmother's in a few minutes.' Her mother grinned. 'So if you sneak out the side door while he's distracting them, and get into the back of the car, he'll be with you shortly.'

It was ridiculous that they had to go to such subterfuge just so that Tory could go out for the evening. But more reporters had started arriving at the farm in the last hour—keeping a discreet distance at the end of the driveway, but watching every move at the farmhouse nonetheless.

'I'll see you later, then.' She moved to kiss her mother warmly on the cheek.

'Just give your Dad a call when you're ready to come home.' Her mother nodded.

If Jonathan carried on his insulting behaviour of this morning, that shouldn't be too long!

Hiding in the back of the car, a blanket pulled over the top of her head, wasn't the most elegant way to depart for an evening out. But without it, Tory knew from experience, she wouldn't be able to get out at all.

'You can come out now,' her father told her with amusement a few minutes later.

Tory sat up on the back seat, brushing her ruffled hair back into some sort of order as her father turned the car down the drive to the Byrnes' house.

In other circumstances she could have walked over, as she had on Sunday evening. But it was that over-confidence on Sunday that had now made it impossible.

'Have fun,' her father said lightly once he had parked the car in front of the house.

'Give my love to Nan,' Tory replied distractedly, and watched as he drove away, somehow reluctant to approach the front door.

Jonathan's moods were mercurial, to say the least—and she had no idea which one he was going to be in this evening!

'Tory!' he greeted her warmly, seconds after she had rung the doorbell, the speed with which he had answered taking her completely by surprise—it meant he must have been waiting in the hallway for her arrival! 'How did you get here?' he looked out at the deserted driveway.

She looked up at him with wary blue eyes, those insults he had flung at her earlier still very much in her mind. 'My father drove me over. I'll call him when I want to leave,' she informed him pointedly.

Jonathan grinned as he easily picked up on her warning that she might want to leave in the next few minutes if he was as insulting as he had been this morning. 'You're looking very lovely this evening,' he told her huskily.

'Thank you.' Her wariness didn't lessen one iota at his compliment. 'So are you,' she returned archly.

And he was. His grey silk shirt emphasised the muscled width of his shoulders and narrowness of his waist, and was matched with fitted black denims.

He quirked dark brows. 'Pleasantries over, would you like to come inside? Or do you expect me to serve your dinner out here?' he asked mockingly.

'It's such a pleasant evening,' she replied, as she preceded him into the house, 'that it might be rather nice to eat outside.'

'I agree with you.' Jonathan nodded. 'That's why I've set the table out on the terrace.' He walked straight through the sitting room and out of the French doors at the far end.

Tory, following behind him, felt her stomach do a somersault before settling back in place as she took in the romantic setting.

The cane table had been set with cut glass and silver cutlery; a silver candelabra with green candles stood at its centre. Two cane chairs stood almost side by side as they looked out over the garden and distant hills.

She turned to give Jonathan a searching look from beneath lowered dark lashes. The scene was set for seduction…

Jonathan returned her gaze unblinkingly. 'As you said, it's too beautiful a night to sit inside,' he agreed lightly. 'Now, can I get you red or white wine?'

'That depends on what we're eating.' There was no way, when the atmosphere seemed so charged with expectation, that she wanted to mix her drinks, even red and white wine. Ending up more than a little drunk could just convince this man that all her bad publicity was true, after all. If he didn't already believe that…

'Fish to start, steak for main course, so it's your choice.' He shrugged.

'Red, then, please,' she accepted, moving to sit down on the swinging seat, reluctant to actually sit down and embrace the intimacy of that table set for two.

It had been a mistake to come here, she told herself once Jonathan had gone back into the house to get the wine. She didn't know what she had expected when she accepted Jonathan's invitation, but it certainly wasn't this!

Scared, Tory? She asked herself that now. For years she had been regretting the fact that she couldn't have dates and meet men in the way that other women could, and now that she had met one, been invited to dinner by him, she was so nervous her hand was shaking slightly as she reached out to take the glass of red wine Jonathan now held out to her.

'Hmm, Gevrey-Chambertin,' she murmured appreciatively after her first sip. 'Oh, don't look so worried, Jonathan.' She chuckled at his stunned expression. 'I'm not such a wino I can guess a wine just from its taste; I just happen to know that Gideon keeps this particular one in the cellar!'

He sat down on the swing-seat next to her, long legs stretched out in front of him, whereas Tory's feet, even in shoes with two-inch heels, hardly reached the floor!

He turned to look at her. 'Do you see a lot of Maddie and Gideon when they're on the island?' he said slowly.

'If I'm at home, too, yes,' she responded, very conscious of the fact that his arm was stretched along the back of the seat behind her. Not touching her. But she could feel his warmth, anyway.

Jonathan shook his head. 'They've never mentioned knowing you,' he murmured.

She laughed dismissively. 'That isn't surprising; I don't go around telling people that I know them, either!'

Jonathan gave the ghost of an answering smile before turning to look out at the distant hills. 'What do you think of Gideon?'

Tory was taken aback by the question. Gideon was this man's brother-in-law, for goodness' sake; what did he expect her to say in answer to a question like that?

'I think he's a wonderful husband and father,' she answered guardedly.

'I know that part,' Jonathan dismissed impatiently. 'What do you think of him as a man?'

Her frown deepened and she stiffened resentfully. 'Exactly what are you implying…?' After the insults Jonathan had levelled at her earlier today, she didn't like the turn this conversation had taken at all!

'Implying—?' he repeated. 'I'm not implying anything like that, Tory,' he answered impatiently as he picked up on the reason for her indignation. 'I know for a fact that Gideon is head over heels in love with my sister.'

'Then—?'

Jonathan stood up. 'Forget I asked,' he rasped, putting his own barely touched glass of wine down on the table.

'I'll just go and get our first course,' he grated, before striding back to the kitchen.

Tory was more puzzled than ever. Obviously she knew Gideon and Madison, but it was Madison she knew best—Gideon tended to be rather a remote figure. Except when it came to his daughter, Tory remembered with affection. He was a man obviously deeply in love with his wife, but who liked to keep his emotions to himself—except when it came to his baby daughter: he was like putty in Keilly's little hands!

But somehow Tory didn't think that was what Jonathan had wanted to know…

'Here we are.' He arrived back with plates of smoked salmon, placing them on the table before lighting the candles; there was barely a breeze to disturb their flame. 'Would you like some white wine with this, or are you going to stick to the red?'

'Stick with the red. Thank you.' She was still a little disturbed by their earlier conversation. 'Don't you approve of Gideon?' she probed once they were seated at the dining table, having tasted the smoked salmon and found it to be deliciously fresh.

'I told you, I have no doubts of his devotion to Maddie and the baby,' Jonathan answered stiffly. 'His father was John Byrne, you know,' he added abruptly.

As it happened, yes, she did know. She also knew that the legendary actor had died over thirty years ago in a car crash. While drunk. Having apparently left his wife and young son for another woman several months earlier.

'Gideon isn't responsible for who or what his father was,' she said gently.

Jonathan gave her a narrow-eyed look, barely touching his own food. 'You don't believe that we are the genes we inherit from our parents?'

'If you're asking whether I believe Gideon is going to turn into a drunk and adulterer, because that's what his father was, then no, I don't believe it,' Tory answered firmly, shaking her head. 'Things like social background, education, one's own personality strengths and weaknesses have to be taken into account, too. After all, we don't grow up as clones of our parents. No two children in a family, unless they are identical twins, are ever exactly the same. And even twins have different personalities.'

'Perhaps it's easy for you to dismiss. You obviously know who you are,' Jonathan responded harshly, not missing her questioning look.

She laughed softly; this conversation had become altogether too heavy for comfort. 'Do any of us know that? Do any of us really want to know that?' She was deliberately flippant in an effort to lighten the atmosphere between them.

Jonathan sighed. 'That's what I'm here to find out.'

Her eyes widened. 'Who you are…?'

He nodded. 'Amongst other things.'

'You're Jonathan McGuire,' she told him teasingly.

He returned her gaze steadily. 'Am I?'

Tory shrugged. 'That's who you said you were.'

'Then that's who I must be.' He gave an inclination of his head.

Tory raised dark brows. 'Aren't you a little young for a mid-life crisis?'

Wasn't she a little young for that herself? And yet she knew she was going through a similar soul-searching period herself…

He drew in a harshly ragged breath, his smile, when it came, seeming somewhat forced. 'You're right. I am.' He relaxed slightly, eyeing the barely touched food on her plate. 'Eat up, or it will get cold.'

'It's already cold,' she said.

'Just testing,' he came back teasingly. 'And you were right about the wine; I had to raid Gideon's wine cellar earlier, when I realised I had forgotten to buy any.'

'I'm sure he won't mind.' She smiled.

The earlier tension seemed to have abated now. Although Tory wasn't absolutely sure of why it had been there in the first place. Jonathan obviously liked his brother-in-law, approved of him as a husband for his younger sister. And yet…

Jonathan was turning out to be as enigmatic as she knew Gideon to be. In fact, if she hadn't been told Jonathan was Madison's brother, it would have been all too easy to assume he was Gideon's. The two men weren't only alike in temperament, they looked alike, too—both tall and dark, with those grey eyes that revealed so little of their inner thoughts.

Jonathan stood up suddenly. 'I'll just go and check on the steaks.'

'Can I do anything to help?' she instantly offered.

'Did I do anything on Sunday?' he taunted.

She gave that some thought. 'You ate my food without complaint,' she finally remembered.

'For a superstar, you aren't a bad cook!' came his satirical parting shot, before he disappeared inside the house carrying their empty plates.

For a bigoted idiot, neither was he, she discovered a few minutes later when she bit into her first mouthful of steak. The meat had been marinated in something—honey and mustard she could discern, but the rest of it was a mystery to her. It was the most delicious steak Tory had ever eaten!

'This is very good,' she told Jonathan with feeling.

She hadn't been sure she would be able to eat this evening at all, let alone feel like stabbing with her fork the first person who tried to take this steak away from her!

Jonathan grinned at her obvious appreciation. 'Am I forgiven for my rudeness this morning now?' he prompted huskily. 'I was angry—very much so,' he conceded grimly. 'But I really shouldn't have taken that anger out on you in the way that I did. You, and your family, have been extremely kind to me since I arrived here.'

She took another sip of the fruity red wine before answering, aware that he was obviously sincere in his apology. Though some of the things he had accused her of this morning were actually unforgivable. But perhaps—with the last five years of speculative publicity behind her—understandable? that little voice inside her head reasoned.

Maybe, she accepted grudgingly.

'Can I take a raincheck on answering that until after we've had dessert?' she came back lightly.

He gave a rueful smile. 'That depends on how much you like strawberries and cream.' He grimaced.

She gave an impish grin. 'Love them!'

Jonathan gave an inclination of his dark head. 'In that case, I'm happy to wait.'

The evening stayed dry and warm, the flickering candles in the centre of the table their only illumination as it grew dark.

They talked of everything and nothing. Mainly nothing, Tory realised as they lingered at the table after finishing their meal, to drink glasses of port. She was reluctant to talk about her highly charged career, and Jonathan seemed reluctant to talk about anything other than the island and the few places he had managed to see so far on his visit here.

Pretty innocuous stuff, Tory inwardly surmised. But at

least they weren't arguing or, even worse, insulting each other.

She was feeling more than a little mellow from the wine and port she had drunk. Jonathan appeared even more attractive than usual to her glowing gaze, as she admired the strength in the squareness of his jaw, his mouth, which was looking extremely kissable, and as for those eyes—!

Had she really thought they were flinty and cold the first time she saw him? Now they only appeared warmly caressing as he looked at her over the top of his glass, glittering almost silver in the candlelight as his eyes lingered on the fullness of her lips.

'Tory…?' he questioned slowly, even as he put his port glass down on the table.

She swallowed hard. Jonathan was going to kiss her. Again. And she wanted him to!

She moved slightly to accommodate that kiss as his head bent down to hers, her heart seeming to leap behind her breasts as he sipped and tasted at her lips, not touching her in any other way, but seeming to hold her captive anyway.

'You really are a very beautiful woman.' The warmth of his breath stirred the dark tendrils of hair at her temple as he spoke.

And he was a gorgeous man! Everything that tall, dark, and handsome should be. Although she wasn't about to let him know that…!

'Thank you,' she accepted huskily.

'Tell me…' He looked down at her searchingly, one of his hands moving to smooth the hair back from her brow. 'Are you involved with anyone at the moment?'

'Involved with anyone?' she repeated tautly.

He nodded. 'That guy Terry. Or possibly someone else.'

Tory stiffened defensively. '"That guy Terry" happened to be my cousin. The brother of Saturday's bride. Do you think I would be here with you, like this if I were involved with someone else?'

He smiled gently, grey gaze warm on her flushed cheeks. 'I wasn't trying to be insulting, Tory.'

Of course he wasn't, she accepted impatiently; he really didn't have to try! But because she still felt so defensive around this man, it was all too easy for her to feel insulted...

'I'm sorry.' She grimaced.

Jonathan shook his head. 'Your reserve is understandable, Tory,' he conceded. 'I haven't exactly been consistent in my opinions.' He sighed, sitting back in his chair, although one of his arms remained draped across the back of hers. 'The truth is, I don't feel very consistent about anything at the moment!'

Tory felt the loss of his warm closeness, looking at him consideringly now. She had sensed from the first that something was troubling this man; she just wasn't sure how to go about getting him to talk about it. Or if indeed she should!

Jonathan was obviously even more self-contained than she was, and she doubted he would welcome any intrusion into what was, after all, a private matter. In fact, she knew that he wouldn't!

'It's very beautiful here,' he continued heavily, staring sightlessly in the direction of the shadowed hills.

'Very,' she agreed quietly. 'Healing, too,' she added.

Jonathan turned to give her a sharp look. 'And do you think I need healing?' His voice was edged with sarcasm now.

'I don't know. Do you?'

'Maybe.' He sighed heavily, standing up, taking his half-full glass of port with him as he strolled to the edge of the terrace. 'Until a couple of years ago I thought I knew who

I was, where I was going. Damn it, I didn't *think* I knew—I *did* know!' He turned his head, his expression grim.

Tory watched him with narrowed eyes. 'What happened a couple of years ago to change that…?' she prompted.

Jonathan turned back to her with glittering grey eyes. 'On the surface, absolutely nothing,' he bit out tersely.

'But below the surface?'

'Below the surface?' he repeated scathingly, his movements tense. 'I changed,' he revealed heavily. 'Believe it or not, Tory, I've always been a very together type of person.'

Oh, she believed it. Just as she believed that something had happened two years ago to make him less sure of himself, of where his life was going. Whether she now found out what that something was all depended upon whether or not he wanted to tell her…

'This is ridiculous!' he suddenly burst out, moving firmly away from the edge of the terrace, turning back to look at her. 'Here I am, having dinner with a woman millions of men would crawl on their knees to be with—and all I can find to entertain you with is my morose self-pity!' He shook his head self-disgustedly.

Tory gave a wry smile. 'I think crawling on their knees is probably a slight exaggeration!' Although one very determined male fan in Australia had once climbed up to the sixth-floor balcony of her hotel room in an effort to meet her!

Jonathan's gaze moved over her with warm appreciation. 'I don't,' he finally murmured huskily.

She couldn't meet that gaze, turning to look at the shadowed hills herself now. She had allowed this man to kiss her, knew she had returned those kisses. She also knew it was pure madness, on the part of both of them. In a few days she would return to London, and eventually Jonathan would return to America. Theirs was an attraction leading nowhere.

'Can I get you another glass of port?' Jonathan softly interrupted her troubled thoughts.

Considering she still had some in her glass—no.

She didn't find him in the least morose—wished he would tell her what was bothering him. Although she already knew him well enough to realise he wasn't a man who confided his troubles to anyone, least of all to a woman he had only known a few days!

'I don't think so, thanks.' She smiled her refusal, having enjoyed this evening in spite of her earlier misgivings. She glanced at the slender gold watch on her wrist, surprised to find it was almost eleven o'clock. 'It's late, and my father has to be up early in the morning.' So did she! 'I think I should give him a call so that he can come and get me—'

'It isn't even eleven o'clock yet,' Jonathan protested. 'I'll drive you home when you're ready to go.'

It wasn't a case of when she was ready to go; it would be all too easy to just stay here, to know the promise of passion his glittering grey gaze promised, to give Jonathan oblivion for a few hours from his obviously tortured thoughts. That would be oh, so easy to do—because it was what she wanted more than anything at this moment.

It was the thought of the two of them waking next to each other in the morning, of seeing the regret and self-disgust in Jonathan's face, that made even the idea of it impossible.

'I really think I should go now.' She put her glass down decisively on the table as she stood up. 'And I don't think it's a good idea for you to drive me home; there were half a dozen reporters at the end of the driveway when I left earlier.' She grimaced.

He shrugged. 'That doesn't bother me if it doesn't bother you.'

Were they back to the question of her being involved with someone else? Didn't Jonathan believe her when she told him she wasn't?

'Tory...?' He had closed the distance between them in two strides, one of his hands under her chin as he raised her face to his. 'I was referring to the fact that you're obviously here on holiday yourself,' he explained. 'A holiday that has obviously been ruined by the speculation concerning the two of us,' he added grimly.

'The same applies to you,' she reminded him.

'I'm not on holiday,' he told her harshly.

Tory frowned. If he wasn't here on holiday—? What possible work could he be doing here? More to the point, how could he be doing it at the Byrne house? She had suggested he go to the casino while he was here—a business he had told her his family was involved in—and he had very firmly refused to even consider it. So what was he doing here...?

She shook her head, knowing that if Jonathan had wanted to tell her then he would had done so.

'Do I take that as a no to my offer to drive you home?'

She looked up to find Jonathan watching her with narrowed eyes. She had been so deep in thought she hadn't realised he had been looking at her as she shook her head!

'Not at all,' she answered lightly. 'I'm sure my father will be only too pleased not to have to come out again this evening.' And maybe by now, believing that no one was going to leave the farmhouse again this evening, the reporters would have returned to whatever hotels they had booked into for the night! 'Thank you for dinner this evening, Jonathan. You obviously *can* cook!' she said mischievously.

'And I am forgiven for my rudeness to you earlier?'

Once again his closeness became overwhelming. In fact, he was so close to her Tory could once again feel the warmth emanating from his body. 'You're forgiven,' she confirmed huskily.

Jonathan became suddenly still, only his thumb moving caressingly against her lips now as he looked down at her with dark eyes. 'For some reason I'm very reluctant to let this evening end,' he said gruffly.

His words so echoed her previous thoughts that Tory couldn't repress the slight trembling she felt at the gentleness of his thumb against her lips. Although deep inside she ached for the caress of his lips against hers instead!

She swallowed hard. 'I think we both know that it has to,' she said quietly.

'Do we?'

She blinked, looking up at him uncertainly now. 'I think so.' But even to her own ears she didn't sound very convincing!

Jonathan tilted his head to one side as he looked at her consideringly. 'Would you spend the day with me tomorrow?' he asked.

Tory felt what was rapidly becoming a familiar leap of her heart inside her chest. 'I thought you came here to be alone,' she reminded him.

He gave a self-deriding laugh. 'Something else I've discovered since I came here—I'm not too happy with my own company any more!'

'In that case—' Tory grinned '—I suppose I had better rescue you from the boredom!'

Jonathan winced. 'Is that what my invitation sounded like? I'm sorry,' he muttered at her nod of confirmation. 'It wasn't meant like that at all.' He released her, standing back. 'Miss Buchanan, would you do me the honour of spending the day with me tomorrow? There, how was that?' he prompted teasingly.

'It will do,' she assured him dryly. 'And I would love to spend the day with you. What did you have in mind?' Even as she asked the question she could feel the hot colour entering her cheeks; her question had sounded provocative, to say the least!

Jonathan laughed huskily at her self-conscious grimace. Then he stopped laughing as suddenly as he had begun, tersely suggesting he drive her home now, as if the sound of his own laughter had come as something of a surprise to him.

Perhaps it had, Tory speculated as she sat beside him in the Jaguar on the drive back to the farm. Jonathan didn't give the impression he had found too much to laugh about for quite some time. Two years, in fact.

She couldn't help wondering what had happened then to bring about the changes in him that he had mentioned. It must have been something quite serious. Jonathan came over as a very self-confident, self-contained man. But something had happened two years ago that had changed that…

He had asked her earlier if there was already a romantic involvement in her life—perhaps she should have asked him the same question! At thirty-two or thirty-three, as she guessed him to be, it was very doubtful there hadn't been a serious involvement in his life to date. Maybe the breaking up of that involvement two years ago was what had affected the changes in him?

The realisation of that put something of a dampener on her agreement to spend the day with him tomorrow. If Jonathan was still suffering from the effects of a broken relationship two years later, then it must have been a very serious involvement. Perhaps she would be better to stay well away from him?

But it was too late to retract her decision now, without Jonathan demanding an explanation as to exactly why she was doing it. Besides, the part of her that trembled at his touch didn't really want to retract it!

Thankfully, the reporters seemed to have dispersed for the night. There was no sign of them as they turned down the driveway to her parents' house. The lights were still on in the downstairs rooms as Jonathan brought the car to a halt outside, meaning that both her parents had probably stayed up in anticipation of her call to be picked up.

But there was also a car she didn't recognise parked over by the garage…

'Thank you for a lovely evening,' she told Jonathan distractedly as he came round to open the car door for her, her attention still on the other unfamiliar car. Her parents hadn't mentioned expecting visitors this evening, and it wasn't a vehicle Tory recognised as being one of the family's.

'You're welcome,' Jonathan replied ruefully. 'What time shall I pick you up tomorrow?'

'I—' She was prevented from saying more as she heard the crunch of feet on gravel behind her, turning frowningly towards the sound. It had been a long time since her father had hauled her into the house at the end of a date because he considered she had arrived home too late!

'Tory, darling!' a familiar drawl greeted her, before a man stepped from the darkness at the side of the house into the light given off from inside the hallway.

But Tory had known exactly who it was before he did that, had recognised his voice the moment he spoke.

Rupert!

What was *he* doing here?

As she glanced at Jonathan, she could tell by his suddenly cold and bleak expression that he had taken one look at the other man—tall, loose-limbed, extremely good-looking Rupert—heard the way the other man had called her 'darling'—and drawn his own conclusions!

CHAPTER SEVEN

JUST as she could see from Rupert's suddenly speculative expression as he took in her appearance—Jonathan's arm protectively about her waist—that he had also drawn his own conclusions about the situation.

And from the way his expression darkened angrily she could see that he didn't like those conclusions one little bit!

'Darling...' he said again in that over-educated drawl that she had once found so attractive. 'Your parents have been extremely kind to me all evening, but I was beginning to think you were never coming home.' He grasped the tops of her arms before bending his head to kiss her lingeringly on the lips.

Tory at once felt Jonathan's arm leave her waist, whether deliberately or because Rupert had pulled her out of his grasp she wasn't sure.

One thing she was sure of—she did not like Rupert kissing her in this possessive way. In fact, she didn't like him kissing her, full stop!

She pulled sharply away from him, blue eyes glittering in the darkness. 'What are you doing here, Rupert?' she demanded.

He smiled unconcernedly before turning to look at Jonathan. 'As Tory's manners seem to have momentarily deserted her, I had better introduce myself,' he said, keeping a proprietorial hold on Tory's upper arm. 'Rupert Montgomery. And you must be Jonathan,' he added challengingly.

Grey eyes narrowed icily as Jonathan coldly returned the other man's gaze. 'Must I?'

'Oh, yes,' Rupert laughed confidently.

Tory was rigid with anger. Rupert was deliberately giving Jonathan the impression that he knew all about him—an impression Jonathan was obviously far from pleased about. Especially as the only person who could have provided that information was her…

'When did you get here, Rupert?' she demanded, irritably. '*How* did you get here?'

'It wasn't easy, believe me. I'm not sure the powers that be actually *want* visitors on this island,' he answered disparagingly. 'I had the devil of a job getting booked onto a flight this evening at all!'

So he had flown over this evening. But that still didn't tell her why…

'It's TT Fortnight,' Tory dismissed vaguely. 'What are you doing here, Rupert?' she repeated.

'Visiting you, of course,' he answered with brittle affection, his own arm lightly about her shoulders now.

A fact Jonathan wasn't unaware of, Tory noted angrily as she saw his gaze move coldly over their physical closeness. He had obviously assumed—with a lot of help from Rupert!—that her earlier denial of being involved with anyone was far from the truth.

She glared up at Rupert before moving pointedly away from him. 'Wasn't it assuming rather a lot to believe that I wanted a visit from you?' she responded rudely.

'I hope you'll excuse us, old boy.' Rupert smiled boyishly at Jonathan—a man who could only be three or four years his senior at most! 'I'm afraid Tory and I had a little tiff before she came to the island a week ago. Tory obviously still hasn't forgiven me.' He grimaced charmingly.

Apart from their height, the two men were so different,

Tory decided. Rupert had slightly over-long blond hair, laughing blue eyes, and was handsome to the point of male beauty. His body was slim and athletic—and that extreme handsomeness and boyish charm hid a completely selfish and calculating nature. Jonathan, on the other hand, was just as handsome in a darkly brooding way, also physically fit—and yet that arrogantly cold visage hid a much warmer nature, of a man who obviously cared very deeply about his family.

Of the two, Tory knew which one she preferred!

'There's nothing to forgive, Rupert,' she replied. 'You have your ideas on where my future lies, and I have mine—they just happen to be in opposite directions!' She drew in a deeply controlling breath before turning to look at Jonathan. 'I really did enjoy this evening,' she told him, blue gaze pleading for a softening of his coldly set features.

There wasn't one. If anything, his mouth had taken on an even grimmer look. 'You're welcome,' he bit out tersely. 'And now I think I had better leave and let you and—Mr Montgomery—sort out your differences,' he added with a contemptuous curl of his top lip.

Her 'differences' with Rupert were rapidly becoming insurmountable, Tory was quickly realising. Just as she realised exactly what impression Rupert was deliberately giving Jonathan about their relationship. He was making them sound like a couple of star-crossed lovers who had had a silly argument!

She reached out and placed her hand on Jonathan's arm, her fingers tightening as she felt him tense. 'What time shall I meet you tomorrow?' she enquired huskily; after all, he had invited her to spend the day with him. And some time during that day she would find the right time to explain exactly what her 'differences' with Rupert were!

Jonathan raised dark brows, his gaze flickering briefly

over Rupert before coming back to rest mockingly on Tory's upturned face. 'Let's take a raincheck, hmm?' he suggested. 'I'm sure you're going to be—busy, for the next few days. With your guest,' he added with sarcasm.

Rupert was not her guest—a fact he was very quickly going to realise for himself once Jonathan had left, in spite of what arrangements her polite parents might have otherwise assumed!

With a last regretful look at Jonathan's unrelenting expression she removed her hand from his arm. 'Perhaps you're right,' she accepted. 'Enjoy the rest of your stay,' she added evenly.

He gave a sharp inclination of his head before turning to Rupert. 'Montgomery,' he barked, before striding back to his car and getting inside without so much as a backward glance, much to Tory's dismay.

She watched Jonathan drive away, tensing resentfully as Rupert moved to stand at her side, his arm once again moving possessively about her shoulders.

Tory gave an angry shrug to shake off that arm, turning to glare at Rupert once the Jaguar lights had disappeared down the driveway. 'What do you think you're doing?' she asked Rupert furiously.

He looked totally unconcerned, raising blond brows in mocking amusement. 'So that was the elusive Jonathan...' he drawled.

She stiffened. 'Yes?'

'Don't tell you actually find him attractive, Tory,' Rupert scorned. 'The man's like a block of ice.'

Angry colour darkened her cheeks. 'When I want your opinion, Rupert, I'll ask for it! Goodnight.' She turned and strode off towards the farmhouse.

Gravel once again crunched underfoot as Rupert followed her. 'Your parents have invited me to stay the night,' he informed her lightly, his satisfaction with the arrangement clearly audible in his voice.

Tory stopped before opening the back door, turning on her heel to glare at him. 'And I just uninvited you,' she bit out.

He gave a movement of his shoulders, as if puzzled by her unrelenting attitude. 'Isn't that a little rude of you?' he cajoled.

As if she were a child who needed humouring, Tory decided resentfully. 'Call it what you like, Rupert,' she rejoined. 'There are plenty of hotels in Douglas. Admittedly you may have a little trouble getting booked into one this time of year, but you could always try asking one of the TT fans if you can share their tent for the night!' she added with relish, suddenly having a wonderful vision of Rupert in his designer-label clothes having to camp out in a tent. Just the idea of it made her feel more cheerful!

Had she really once thought herself in love with this man? she inwardly chided herself. He was nothing more than an overgrown public schoolboy with a penchant for nice clothes and a comfortable lifestyle.

Something she, with her recent decision to re-evaluate her career, was obviously threatening…

Strange, but until a few months ago she had thought she owed the success of her career to Rupert. A deliberate illusion on Rupert's part, she could now see with hindsight. Because actually it had always been the other way around. Which was why Rupert had suddenly become so attentive. Even to the point of asking her to marry him…

Which brought her neatly round to what she knew had to be the real reason Rupert had hot-footed it over to the island this evening; he had obviously found the reference in the newspapers to her mystery male companion of Sunday night a little too disturbing for comfort. His own!

How it must have annoyed him to arrive here this evening only to find her out once again with the mysterious Jonathan!

Rupert looked irritated now. 'That isn't funny, Tory.'

'No?' she raised dark brows. 'Strange—I find it highly amusing!'

He reached out and grasped her arm as she would have opened the farmhouse door. 'Don't you think you're being a little unfair to your parents?' he pointed out in a hushed voice. Her parents were obviously sitting in the kitchen, where they might inadvertently overhear this heated conversation. 'After all, they were polite enough to make the invitation. It's going to be a little awkward if you now tell them I'm going to a hotel instead.'

'Awkward for whom?' she challenged, although inwardly she had to concede that he had a point. Her parents were going to think Rupert didn't consider their farm good enough for him if he now did an about-face and left to stay in a hotel…

'Stop being childish, Tory.' Rupert sighed his impatience with her attitude. 'It's almost midnight; I can hardly turn up at a hotel at this time of night!'

She arched dark brows. 'I don't remember it stopping you before,' she reminded him softly.

'Back to that, are we?' Blue eyes narrowed dangerously as his charming façade totally slipped. 'I told you, I was upset because you were making me wait before giving me an answer to my marriage proposal—'

'So upset you picked up a woman at the after-show party and took her back to your hotel room for the night!' Tory finished disgustedly.

Although she wasn't sure who she was most disgusted with. Herself, for actually having been considering that marriage proposal. Or Rupert, because she obviously meant so little to him he had gone to bed with someone else on the same night he'd asked her to marry him!

Not that she had needed that extra proof of the shallowness of his feelings for her, but it hadn't stopped it rankling, nonetheless...

'Oh, let's just forget that, Rupert,' she dismissed. 'I suppose if my parents have asked you to stay, and you've already accepted, then you had better stay. But I want you to leave first thing in the morning,' she added firmly as his expression lightened with triumph.

'Deal,' he accepted readily.

Too readily, Tory knew from experience. Rupert was obviously hoping that in the light of day she would relent in her attitude. He was in for a disappointment!

Not that any of that showed as she let them both back into the farmhouse kitchen, her smile light and natural as she answered her parents' questions about her evening. There was no point in unduly worrying them with the problem of Rupert. It was a problem she would ultimately have to deal with herself.

After this evening, she had a feeling it was going to be sooner rather than later!

But at the moment her more immediate problem was Jonathan. They had spent an enjoyable evening together, had arranged to meet again tomorrow—and Rupert's untimely arrival had put an end to all that.

When *would* she see Jonathan again?

More to the point, would she see him again *at all*...!

'Thought I'd find you here,' Rupert said happily as he let himself into her music studio.

Tory barely spared him a glance, concentrating as she was on her guitar work. She was trying to remember the haunting tune Jonathan had been playing last Sunday evening. She had most of what she had heard, but it wasn't complete. And she still didn't know if it had any words to go with it...

Rupert strolled unconcernedly across the room to stand next to where she sat on the sofa. 'Hmm, pretty.' He nodded as she continued to pick out the notes. 'Something new you're working on?' he prompted at her lack of response to his first remark.

'Something like that,' she replied, still not sparing him a glance.

'Your mother has just given me the most enormous breakfast,' he said with satisfaction. 'Perhaps there's something to be said for living off the land, after all.'

Tory's mouth twisted. 'The eggs are fresh, but as we don't keep pigs the bacon came from the supermarket, and my mother stopped baking her own bread years ago, so the same applies to your toast!'

He arched blond brows. 'A little pedantic this morning, aren't we?'

Tory was learning to feel extremely irritated by that lightly cajoling voice! 'Just being honest,' she responded. 'Now, as you've already noticed, I'm busy. So if you have nothing of real importance to say...?'

Rupert's answer to that was to drop down onto the sofa beside her. Tory had no choice but to look at him. As usual, Rupert was impeccably dressed—silvery-grey trousers teamed with a pale grey shirt, his shoes hand-made highly polished black leather. Very suitable attire for wearing on a working farm!

His brows rose ruefully as he saw her assessing glance. 'I can always learn,' he murmured softly.

'Why bother?' she said, not pretending to misunderstand his reference as she stood up to put her guitar back on its stand, very slim in fitted blue denims and a blue tee shirt.

'You won't be staying long,' she assured him firmly as she turned to face him.

'I can't believe you're still angry with me, Tory,' he drawled, not in the least perturbed by her attitude. 'After all, you've apparently been having a minor fling with America's answer to Heathcliff, and you don't see me sulking about it.'

She glared across at him, disliking intensely his description of Jonathan. 'I haven't been having a fling with anyone, minor or otherwise. And even if I had, you aren't sulking about it because, as we both know, you have no right to do so!'

'I have asked you to marry me, Tory,' he reminded her huskily.

'"Tory"?' she repeated mockingly, Rupert having always insisted in the past upon calling her by her full name, Victory. 'And you may have asked, Rupert—but as I recall you have also been given the very firm answer of no!'

He looked at her. 'You were angry at the time—'

Having arrived at his hotel room several weeks ago to be greeted by a very disheveled redhead wearing only a bathtowel, was that so surprising?

'Well, I'm not angry now—and the answer is still no!' she told him emphatically. 'In fact—'

'You know, Victory,' he drawled pointedly, 'you are fast developing a prima donna's temper.'

Her mouth snapped shut at the insult, twin wings of colour in her cheeks as she glared at him.

'In fact,' Rupert continued mercilessly, 'you are becoming the proverbial temperamental pain in the butt!'

'I— You—'

'What's the matter, Victory?' he taunted. 'Or is it that you can't stand hearing the truth about yourself?'

Was it the truth? Had she become one of those egotistical

bores that she had met at so many parties over the last five years? People who could talk of nothing but themselves, and had no interest in anything that wasn't going to further their own career?

Had she…?

'It isn't easy for me to say these things to you, Victory,' Rupert continued, moving closer to her on the sofa, his arm along its back. 'But someone has to do it.'

And it might as well be him! Basically because he was enjoying doing it, Tory knew.

But that wasn't what was important at the moment. Had she become one of those people who believed in their own publicity to such a degree that they became totally selfish and self-motivated?

She looked searchingly into Rupert's handsome face. His expression was bland, blue gaze non-committal.

No, she wasn't like that at all! Rupert was the one who operated on that self-orientated system!

To the point that he would lie to her to achieve his own aims…?

Absolutely, yes!

Her mouth twisted wryly. 'Nice try, Rupert,' she came back at him mockingly. 'You almost had me hooked into believing you again for a moment. Instead of which—' she stood up, looking down at him with cold blue eyes '—you have just finally made my mind up for me. Don't make any more bookings for me other than the ones I'm already committed to—I have other plans now!'

'I've already warned you. You simply can't take a year out at this juncture in your career!' he hissed furiously, sitting tensely forward on the sofa as he looked up at her with glacial eyes.

'Careful, Rupert, your charm is slipping,' Tory taunted.

'Damn my charm!' He stood up in one forcefully fluid movement.

Tory stood her ground. 'My sentiments exactly,' she replied scathingly. 'We had a five-year contract, Rupert,' she told him harshly, pointed chin raised defiantly. 'With an option to renew on both sides at the end of that time. That contract comes to an end in three months' time, fortuitously at the end of the European tour. At which time we will definitely be parting company—personally as well as professionally!'

Cold fury made his narrowed eyes glitter icily. 'You won't last six months without me,' Rupert said nastily, his mouth turned back in a sneer.

In truth, Tory was shaking so badly after her announcement that she had to grasp her hands tightly together in front of her to prevent him from seeing how affected she was.

But, having made the statement, she felt a curious sense of calm spreading through her.

She had enjoyed most of the last five years—the last three of them well at the top of the music tree. But a lot of time lately had been taken up with recordings, the release of albums, appearances on television shows, chat shows. Her personal performances to the audience she loved the best, the fans who went out and actually bought her CDs, were becoming less and less as Rupert involved her more and more in the incestuous world of show business.

'I made you what you are!' Rupert could stand her silence no longer, his face an angry mask, hands clenched into fists at his sides.

'Now that is a bare-faced lie.' Tory shook her head pityingly. 'You helped guide my career. I accept that, and I'm grateful for it—'

'You have a funny way of showing it!' he ground out harshly.

She arched dark brows. 'I am grateful for it, Rupert,' she repeated firmly. 'But you didn't give me the voice that I have—'

'Neither did those two simple souls over there!' He nodded his head in the direction of the farmhouse.

Tory's eyes flashed deeply blue. 'You're going too far, Rupert,' she warned him in a hushed voice, her face very white.

His mouth twisted viciously. 'Why? Because I've dared to mention the fact that the Buchanans aren't your natural parents?' He shook his head scathingly. 'Because, with a birthday in mid-March, you're probably the result of some brief encounter at one of this island's famous TT gatherings?'

Tory's hands were no longer shaking from reaction but from anger—raw, almost uncontrollable anger. Almost. Because that was what Rupert wanted. To hurt her so much she completely lost it. But he was going about it all the wrong way if he thought insulting her parentage—or lack of it!—was going to result in that.

It had never bothered her that she was adopted. She knew that no one could have loved her as much as Thelma and Dan Buchanan, or given her the belief in herself that had allowed her the freedom six years ago to follow her dream.

No, Rupert could never hurt her with the fact that she was adopted. Or with disparaging remarks about who her real parents might be. But he could evoke extreme anger in her by casting any slight on the two people who had *chosen* to be her parents!

'I think you had better go, Rupert,' she told him wearily. 'Before you say something we'll both regret.'

'Oh?' he sneered.

'Oh.' She nodded, meeting his furious gaze unblinkingly.

He drew in a controlling breath, obviously dampening down his own anger with extreme effort. 'Let's not fall out about this, Tory.' His voice had softened to that gentle cajoling again as he realised he really had gone too far. 'We have too much history together to argue now. If you're really set on taking this year out—'

'At least a year, Rupert,' she put in determinedly. 'And I sincerely hope the history you're referring to is our professional one,' she continued tautly, her own anger far from defused. 'Any personal involvement—such as it was!—ended long ago.' Her head went back in challenge.

His mouth curved into a rueful smile. 'I take it that's another no to my marriage proposal?'

He had realised that anger wasn't going to achieve anything, and the charm was on its way back, Tory accepted. But it was too late for that. Far too late!

'I haven't changed my mind from three weeks ago,' she said dully, knowing that where Rupert was concerned she never would. 'My advice to you now is go back to London, and I'll join you there for the start of the tour.'

He moved closer to her. 'Promise?'

Once again Tory stood her ground. 'I have never reneged on a commitment to my fans, and I'm not about to start now!' Even if the thought of spending any length of time in Rupert's company made her flesh creep.

She had realised—too slowly, she acknowledged self-disgustedly—that Rupert was a completely selfish swine, but he had never before personally attacked her parents in the way he had today. That—especially after he had just enjoyed their warm hospitality—she found unforgivable.

She knew that he would use every occasion he could over the next three months to try and get her to change her mind about renewing her contract with him as her manager. It was going to be a very trying three months…!

'Let's go and see if we can get you booked on a flight off the island today,' she said briskly. 'It's much easier to get off than it is on at the moment,' she added. There was racing today and Friday still to come before TT was over for another year.

She was right, and managed to get Rupert booked on an afternoon flight back to Heathrow. She refused to drive him to the airport, ordering him a taxi instead and using the excuse—if she needed one!—that the roads would be clogged enough already this afternoon, with the races on, without having to fight her way back through it as well.

Rupert paused at the open taxi door, his luggage stowed in the boot, the driver already inside, waiting for him to get in the back of the car. 'I'm sorry I lost my temper this morning,' he told Tory quietly.

She was sure that he was. Oh, not because he regretted hurting her with the things that he had said, but because he knew he had simply gone too far.

'So am I,' she said, sounding tired. 'But at least we both know where we stand now.'

Rupert gave a heavy sigh, reaching up to gently cup one side of her face with his hand. 'If it's any consolation, you're the only person that can make me completely lose control like that.' He gave a sad grimace.

That was only because, as the manager of Victory Canan, he had managed to command a lot of respect over the years, and he had wielded that power to his own advantage. In fact, very few people ever stood up to him and said no. If they did, they didn't last very long. It must be galling him very badly at the moment that it was Tory herself who was thwarting him. Besides, with her refusal to keep him on as her manager, she would be removing the power he had wielded so effectively for himself…!

'It isn't,' she replied. 'I— What—?' Her words were abruptly cut off as Rupert suddenly pulled her hard against him, his lips coming down possessively on hers as he moulded her body against his.

What on earth was he doing?

Tory pushed against him. Completely ineffectively. His arms felt like steel bands around her. Damn it, with his easy lifestyle, his love of good food and even better wines, she hadn't realised he could be this physically domineering!

As the kiss went on and on—for what seemed like an eternity because she wasn't enjoying it in the least!—Tory became aware of something else. The sound of a car coming down the gravel driveway…

At last Rupert lifted his head, his expression momentarily triumphant as he looked down at her briefly before turning in the direction of the sound of that approaching car.

A Jaguar.

And a thunderous-faced Jonathan McGuire was sitting behind the wheel…!

CHAPTER EIGHT

TORY turned accusingly back to Rupert, not fooled for a moment by that innocently questioning raise of blond brows. 'You did that on purpose,' she ground out angrily as she heard the Jaguar come to a halt on the gravel several feet behind her.

Rupert grinned down at her unrepentantly. 'I seem to remember you told me Jonathan had left the island. All's fair in love and war, and all that,' he said with satisfaction.

Her mouth firmed. 'As there is absolutely no love between us, I think we just declared war,' she muttered, before turning as she heard the Jaguar car door open and then slam shut.

Jonathan was out of the car now, wearing faded denims and a black tee shirt, sunglasses hiding those normally very expressive grey eyes. But it was obvious from the thin line of his mouth that his mood hadn't improved at all from last night!

Why should it have done? He had just arrived to see her in what looked like a very passionate clinch with Rupert!

'Jonathan,' she greeted him warmly, stepping determinedly away from Rupert's light hold on her. 'You've arrived just in time to say goodbye to Rupert before he catches his plane home,' she announced very pointedly.

'Business commitments,' Rupert put in.

Jonathan turned his head slightly, and Tory could only assume he was looking at the younger man; those dark glasses were a very effective shield. 'Goodbye, Rupert,' he said uninterestedly.

'Jonathan.' Rupert nodded, still looking extremely pleased with himself.

As well he might, Tory inwardly fumed. He had been aware of Jonathan's approach in the Jaguar several minutes before she had, which was why he had been treated to that so-called passionate display.

Rupert would pay for that one later, she decided, smiling at Jonathan now. 'Would you like to come in for coffee?' she invited smoothly, determined to make sure Rupert left with the distinct impression his deliberate sabotage of any relationship she might or might not have with Jonathan hadn't worked.

Even if it had! She and Jonathan, she knew, had reached some sort of understanding last night—a fragile admission of an attraction between them, if nothing else. Rupert's unexpected arrival had damaged that. His deliberate display of possessive passion just now had magnified the situation.

'Sure,' Jonathan accepted brusquely. 'Don't let us keep you, Montgomery; as Tory said, you have a plane to catch.'

Rupert gave Tory a brightly unconcerned smile. 'I'll call you as soon as I get back to London.'

'Don't trouble yourself,' she told him tightly. 'If you go missing, it will be on the six o'clock news!'

Rupert chuckled unconcernedly. 'She's such a joker,' he told the other man appreciatively.

'I wasn't joking,' Tory muttered out the side of her mouth, so that only Rupert could hear.

'I know,' he muttered back, lightly pinching her arm before sliding into the back of the taxi and closing the door.

Tory bent down to the open window. 'Do give my love to Pamela, won't you?' she told him tauntingly.

Rupert's mouth tightened at the mention of the name of the woman who had shared his hotel room three weeks ago. 'I haven't seen her since that night,' he grated, obviously aware of Jonathan, standing only feet away, even if the other man couldn't now hear their hushed conversation.

'Lucky Pamela,' Tory opined.

Rupert looked up at her with narrowed eyes. 'You know, I'm not taking our earlier discussion as an end to that particular subject,' he warned grimly.

She shrugged. 'That is, of course, up to you—but I can assure you, from my point of view, it's well and truly at an end.' Her decision made, she would now stick to it. The irony of it was, it had been Rupert's hounding of her that had made the decision all the easier to make!

She had been approached several months ago by a world-famous producer to star in his new show, which he hoped to put on in London in six months' time, with the added incentive that, as the female lead was actually a singer, Tory could also write the songs that she was to perform.

At the time she had politely thanked Stephen James for the offer but explained she wasn't an actress, that he would be better advised to offer the part to someone who was. But Stephen, bless him, hadn't been willing to accept no for an answer, had explained that he had written the part with her in mind.

Despite her misgivings—after all, she was a singer, nothing else!—Tory couldn't deny she'd been flattered by the offer, and the possibility that she just might be able to do it had begun to grow and then blossom in her mind.

Much to Rupert's disgust. There was no money in it, he had warned her. She would be totally tied to London for the foreseeable future, appearing in the theatre six nights a week until goodness knew when.

But Tory had already known all that, and none of those reasons accounted for her hesitation. She simply didn't want to let Stephen James or her own fans down.

On the plus side of it, however, was the new challenge—

a chance to see if she could be more than she already was. And, after five years at the top of her profession, she acknowledged she was ready for that change. It would also free her, once and for all, from the domineering Rupert…

'We'll see about that once you get back to London,' Rupert told her grimly now, before tapping the taxi-driver on the shoulder and telling him to drive him to the airport.

Tory turned to Jonathan once the taxi had gone, smiling brightly even though she received no answering smile. 'Coffee?' she reminded him.

He gave an abrupt inclination of his head, following her into the farmhouse kitchen. 'Your parents aren't here this afternoon?' he prompted tersely once he had sat down at the table.

Tory's movements were economically efficient as she poured them both a mug of coffee from the constantly fresh brew in the pot. 'Dad has taken my mother to have a check-up on her ankle. Why?' She quirked dark brows as she sat across the table from him. 'Are you frightened to be here alone with me?' She deliberately mocked the image Victory Canan had of being a vamp.

'Hardly,' he dismissed scathingly. 'I telephoned earlier on my mobile before driving back from Ramsey and got the answer-machine again, that's all. Obviously your parents aren't here to answer any calls, and you— Well, you were obviously otherwise engaged!' he observed with pointed scorn.

With Rupert, his derisive tone implied! 'Did you telephone for anything specific?' Tory queried sarcastically. 'Or was it just a social call?' Although what could possibly have been so urgent on a social level that he'd had to telephone on his mobile from Ramsey—a town seven miles away in the north of the island—she just couldn't imagine!

'No, it damn well—!' Jonathan drew in a sharply controlling breath as he broke off the angry reply.

The silence that followed felt just as uncomfortable, Tory decided a few minutes later. What was the matter with the man? He had made it more than obvious the night before that she wouldn't be seeing him today, as planned, and now it turned out that not only had he telephoned earlier, but had actually come over here when he'd received no answer to his call…

The man was in constant contradiction of his own decisions! He had told her when he'd arrived here that he wanted to be alone, and yet he had been to the farm several times in the last four days—had invited her over to his sister's house, too. Now he had arrived here again, after telling her he would take a raincheck on their date for today. She couldn't keep up with the man's unpredictability!

Tory gave a heavy sigh of her own. 'I don't understand you, Jonathan—'

'Nor I you!' He stood up, his chair scraping noisily on the mellow tiled floor as he glared down at her. 'That man—Montgomery—' his mouth turned back in a sneer '—he obviously has some sort of proprietorial claim on you—'

'He's my manager, if you really want to know!' This accusing attitude, after Rupert's recent duplicity, was just too much. Tory glared straight back up at Jonathan as he towered over her.

'Really?' he parried.

'Yes—really!' She couldn't believe they were having this conversation. If she hadn't known Jonathan better, she might have said he was jealous of Rupert—and God knew that was what Rupert had hoped for! Except she *did* know Jonathan better…

He gave a humourless smile. 'And it's obvious in what way he ''manages'' you!'

'Why, you—!' Tory stood up herself now, striding furiously around the table, her arm raised, ready to swing.

Jonathan easily caught hold of it. He pushed her arm back down to her side, long fingers moving down to become entwined with her own, bringing her body up close to his in the process.

His face was very close to hers as they glared at each other. 'Looking at you now, your eyes flashing, face flushed—albeit with anger—I could easily give in to the temptation to manage you myself,' he ground out grimly

'Try it,' Tory muttered, mouth firm, her chin jutting out.

His fingers tightened against hers before he gently bent her arm against her back, his body now moulded against hers. Making Tory fully aware of the truth of his words, his body was obviously aroused.

As her own was rapidly becoming! The warmth and smell of Jonathan set her senses reeling, and her breathing was suddenly shallow as she looked up at the sensuous curve of his mouth.

Longing for it to take possession of hers?

Oh, yes! She wanted Jonathan in a way she had never wanted any man before; she only had to be near him to know that.

But what did he want?

Her, obviously. But what for? A brief fling—as Rupert had called it? Or something more?

Don't be a fool, Tory, she instantly answered herself. Jonathan was a man with obvious troubles of his own. The sort of troubles, she believed, that meant at this time in his life he didn't have the time or space for any other feelings.

Yet he *did* want her…

As she wanted him…!

His free hand moved up to cup one side of her face, fingers curving about her jaw as he held her still to receive his kiss. A fierce, demanding kiss that robbed Tory of the ability to breathe.

Drowning must be like this, Tory decided dreamily as the kiss went on and on, her breath totally gone, a hazy darkness taking over, heightening her senses to an awareness of touch only.

Jonathan felt so good against her caressing hand—his back hard and muscled, shoulders wide, his hair like silk against her fingertips as they became entwined in its darkness.

Jonathan released her hand now, curving her body more intimately with his, his hands moving restlessly against the slenderness of her back.

It wasn't enough, Tory acknowledged achingly. Not nearly enough!

Her breath left her in a sigh of pure pleasure as one of those long, tapered hands moved to cup her breast, easily searching out her roused nipple, stroking its sensitivity as Tory groaned low in her throat.

Her legs felt weak, her head swam. She was aware only of the deep pulsing pleasure of Jonathan's caressing hands. Until she felt the touch of his lips against her bared flesh…!

She had never known pleasure like this. Heat was coursing through her body, every part of her feeling like a liquid flame as she lay limply against him.

His tongue moved moistly against the fiery tip now, circling, teeth lightly biting, before moving silkily against her once again, until Tory began to feel she would explode from the heated pleasure.

'Jonathan, I—' She didn't get to finish what she had been about to say, suddenly finding herself put firmly away from him, her tee shirt pulled down over her throbbing breasts.

He swore darkly to himself, running an agitated hand through his already tousled hair.

Tousled from her own fingers running through its darkness, she acknowledged dully.

Why had Jonathan stopped so suddenly? Why had he put her away from him like that? What—?

'I heard a car outside,' he said grimly as if in answer to her inward query. 'It's probably your parents returning from the doctor's.'

It probably was, Tory accepted, although she had been unaware of any car arriving outside herself.

Because she had been totally lost in the desire Jonathan had evoked in her!

Although if Jonathan had heard the car he couldn't have been as absorbed in passion as she had been…

He looked up impatiently from buttoning his shirt—the shirt Tory must have undone in her arousal! 'Perhaps you had better go upstairs and put on something a little less—revealing, before your parents come in,' he bit out abruptly, giving a pointed glance towards her breasts.

Tory looked down at herself, easily able to see the reason for his concern; her breasts were jutting forward beneath the tee shirt, her nipples still obviously aroused.

As she was herself, though her brain was still befuddled from the passion she and Jonathan had just shared. At least…she had thought they shared it; looking at Jonathan now—his shirt rebuttoned, his hair smoothed back to some semblance of order, his expression grim—it was hard to imagine he had been involved in anything more than drinking a cup of coffee in the last ten minutes!

Jonathan took her firmly by the shoulders and turned her in the direction of the hallway. 'Just go, Tory,' he ordered. 'I'll keep your parents busy here until you come back down.'

Tory stumbled obediently from the room and up the stairs to her bedroom, leaning weakly back against the door as she heard her parents' entrance downstairs, their obvious surprise at finding Jonathan alone in the kitchen.

What had happened just now?

Jonathan had made love to her, and she had undoubtedly responded! But had Jonathan?

Oh, he had been aroused; that was undeniable. But had that arousal come from passion, or had there still been an underlying angry edge to it? Because of what he believed to be her intimate relationship with Rupert?

Of course there had, she berated herself with a self-disgusted groan. Hadn't Jonathan told her before he'd kissed her that he wanted to 'manage' her in the same way Rupert obviously did!

And she had responded anyway! Because she'd wanted to. Because anger had been the last thing on her mind when she was in Jonathan's arms.

She was a fool. A stupid, romantic fool—

Romantic…?

She swallowed hard, feeling the colour drain from her face.

She was in love with Jonathan McGuire…!

How on earth—? Why—? How—?

She walked over to her bed to sink weakly down on top of the duvet. She was in love with Jonathan. It didn't matter why or how—it was a fact!

Well, you've done some pretty stupid things in your time, Tory Buchanan, she chided herself, but this must be the crowning glory of them all!

She could hear the murmur of voices down in the kitchen now as her parents talked with Jonathan. How could she go down there now, behave in the least normally, when she had just realised her love for him?

But, alternatively, how could she *not* go down? Her parents must already think it odd that she hadn't been in the kitchen with their guest when they'd arrived home—although she was sure the more than capable Jonathan would have come up with a feasible explanation for that! She would have to go down, and very shortly, too.

How was she going to face Jonathan again? It would have been bad enough after the way she had melted so passionately in his arms, without the added humiliation of realising she actually loved the man!

But he didn't know she loved him…

Of course he didn't, she told herself briskly. She had responded to him, yes; there could be no denying that. But she hadn't actually told him how she felt about him.

She never would, she decided as she changed her tee shirt for a loose blue denim shirt. There was simply no point in him ever knowing. He certainly didn't love her. But he would only be on the island a few more days at most. There was no reason why the two of them should be alone together again during that time. She would have to make sure they weren't; there was simply no future for them together. She could deal with the problem of her unrequited love once Jonathan had gone back to America…

She could hear the sound of her parents laughing with Jonathan as she approached the kitchen a few minutes later, fighting down the ridiculous feelings of jealousy their shared humour evoked. Jonathan had a whole life in America that she knew nothing about; she couldn't be jealous of everything and everyone else that in any way shared a part of his life!

'Okay, love?' her father prompted as she entered the kitchen. Her parents were sitting down at the kitchen table with Jonathan, steaming mugs of coffee in front of them.

'You didn't burn yourself, did you?' Her father frowned his concern.

Tory shook her head, shooting Jonathan a questioning glance; exactly what explanation had he given her parents for her absence when they'd got home?

'Are you sure?' Jonathan stood up now, coming over to join her where she still stood in the open doorway. 'The coffee was still pretty hot when you spilt it down yourself,' he added pointedly.

So that was the explanation. Pretty good. As lies went! It even covered the fact that she was dressed differently from when her parents left the house...!

'I'm absolutely fine,' she dismissed, avoiding Jonathan's probing gaze as she brushed past him. 'How did you get on at the doctor's, Mum?' Her legs were shaking, her face felt fiery-red, and she was sure her eyes were overbright. She couldn't look directly at Jonathan as she still felt the intentness of that silver gaze on her, but at least she was here, trying to appear normal. Whether or not she was succeeding was another matter entirely!

'Fine.' Her mother grimaced, giving her freshly bandaged ankle a disapproving look. 'I'm still more annoyed at the inconvenience than I am anything else.' She shook her head, smiling ruefully. 'Never mind, love. The doctor said I should be able to get around a lot better by the time you have to leave on Monday.'

'You're leaving?' Jonathan echoed curtly.

Tory shot him another glance. And then wished she hadn't. Just the sight of his grimly handsome face was enough to make her heart leap in her chest and quicken her pulse-rate. The man didn't even need to touch her to have a devastating effect on her. How on earth was she going to be able to stand this?

'As my mother just said,' she confirmed, giving a mocking inclination of her head.

Jonathan looked at her through narrowed lids, a look that it took great effort of will on Tory's part to withstand. But she mustn't by word or gesture, ever let this man know how she felt about him. It would be too humiliating.

He drew in a harsh breath, obviously completely dissatisfied with whatever he could read from her expression. 'Once again, I thank you for your hospitality,' he said shortly. 'I had better be going now. I have some shopping in the car I need to get home and put in the refrigerator.'

That hadn't seemed to bother him fifteen minutes ago, Tory thought uncharitably. Goodness, she was becoming as contradictory as this man was; on the one hand she couldn't wait for him to leave, and on the other she was angry with him for wanting to! Was this what being in love felt like? If it was, she was glad she had never felt the emotion before!

'Would you walk out to the car with me?'

Tory blinked as she realised Jonathan was talking to her. Walk out to the car with him? What on earth for? But then, with a sickening jolt of her stomach, she knew; Jonathan wanted to make sure she knew that what had happened between them a short time ago had meant nothing to him.

Her mouth set mutinously. 'Of course,' she agreed shortly, ignoring the speculative glances passing between her parents as she preceded Jonathan outside.

But she was aware of Jonathan directly behind her as she walked over to the Jaguar, could feel the heat of his body, the intensity of his gaze somewhere in the vicinity of her shoulder blades.

She turned once she reached the car, unable to look at his face for fear of what she might see there. Anger? Mockery? Pity…? Her gaze fixed on the third button down on his shirt. A button she had so recently undone so that she could touch the warm flesh beneath—

No! She mustn't think of that. It would get her nowhere to think of the passion so recently between them. Would only cause her pain.

'Tory—' He broke off abruptly as she flinched from the hand he had raised to touch her cheek. 'Hey, I'm not going to do anything to hurt you!' he rasped harshly.

Just being near him at this particular moment was hurting her! Maybe once she had got used to the idea of loving him, had come to terms with the futility of it, she might be able to at least be in the same room as him without cringing with embarrassment. As it was, she couldn't be near him like this, let alone let him actually touch her!

'Of course you aren't.' She smiled up at him brightly, although she was still unable to meet his gaze.

'Then why—? Never mind,' he dismissed impatiently. 'Tory, I think we need to talk—'

'We are talking,' she cut in hardly, wishing he would just leave.

Perhaps she would be successful as an actress, after all—she was managing to stand here, behaving quite normally, when what she really wanted to do was escape back up to her bedroom and lick her wounds in private!

'Polite niceties because your parents are nearby,' Jonathan protested. 'I meant really talk, Tory.'

She had managed to raise her gaze to the level of that arrogantly jutting chin, could just see his mouth, too. But there was nothing he could say that she wanted to hear from the grimly set line of his lips.

'Some other time, Jonathan.' She gave a careless wave of her hand.

'You—'

'I thought you were in a hurry to put your shopping in the fridge,' she reminded him tautly.

'That was merely an excuse to speak to you alone, and you know it—'

'Do I?' she demanded. 'Well, if you say so.' She gestured unconcernedly.

He drew in a harshly frustrated breath. 'You're being deliberately obtuse—'

'And you are intent on making something out of nothing!' she came back fiercely, glaring straight up into his face now. 'Things got a little—out of hand, earlier. Or do I mean the opposite?' She paused, and then continued, 'It happens. There's no need to make a federal case out of it!'

'"It happens"?' he repeated disgustedly. 'Well, it doesn't happen to me!' he bit out coldly. 'If your parents hadn't returned when they did then we would most likely have ended up making love on the kitchen floor!'

Would they? Tory felt a warm quiver down her spine just at the thought of it.

'Uncomfortable, granted,' she came back coolly, to hide that quiver. 'But not the end of the world, surely?' she added challengingly.

Nowhere near the end of the world as far as she was concerned; to have made love with Jonathan, completely, passionately, would perhaps have been a good memory to look back on when the pain of loving him hurt too much.

Despite what he might think to the contrary, it would have been her very first experience of lovemaking. She hadn't been brought up in a family where brief affairs were part of the norm, had grown up knowing that love was the vital ingredient of a physically loving relationship. The only man she had been close to for any length of time during the last five years had been Rupert, and she had never intended to become just another notch on *his* already very full bedpost!

Not that she thought Jonathan would ever believe that. Although if he had made love to her he would have been left in no doubt; her virginity was an undeniable fact!

Maybe it was as well they hadn't made love, kitchen floor or elsewhere—otherwise how much more intense this post-lovemaking conversation would have been!

'Don't give it another thought, Jonathan,' she replied carelessly. 'Emotions were running a little high, that's all. We were more angry with each other than anything,' she qualified, with some truth.

'Maybe,' he accepted. 'And maybe you're right. We should just forget it ever happened.' He opened the car door and got in behind the wheel, turning on the ignition. The radio instantly blared out. 'Stupid thing,' he muttered as he switched it off. 'I'll see you around, Tory,' he said harshly, before firmly slamming the door shut.

Tory forced herself to remain standing on the gravel drive as he reversed the car before driving off towards the road, even managing a wave of her hand as he drove away.

She only allowed her shoulders to slump once she knew herself totally alone, putting her hands up to her aching temples as she willed herself not to cry. She had come home hoping to find answers to her future, and while she might have decided what she was going to do concerning her career, her personal life was now in a shambles.

How could it be any other way when she knew herself to be in love with Jonathan…?

CHAPTER NINE

'YOU seem a little preoccupied this evening, love...?' Her mother smiled at her encouragingly. The two of them were together in the sitting room. Tory's mother was watching the national news; Tory was completely lost in thought. A fact her mother had obviously noticed!

'Preoccupied' was a serious understatement! Tory was twenty-four-years old, world-famous, had more money in the bank than she would ever be able to spend in one lifetime—and she was hopelessly in love with a man who thought her capable of making love with him while involved with Rupert!

What a mess!

'Would you get that, love?' her mother prompted as the telephone began to ring out in the hallway. 'Your dad's still outside.'

As long as it wasn't Jonathan on the other end of the line! Although there was no reason why it should be; their parting had been pretty final earlier.

'Yes?' she answered the call warily.

'Is that you, Tory?' came the unmistakably cheerful voice of Madison Byrne.

Née McGuire.

Aka Jonathan's sister...

'It certainly is.' She forced lightness into her own voice. 'What can I do for you?'

'You can tell me how my big brother is,' Madison came back with her usual forthrightness.

Tory tensed. How was she supposed to answer that? She

certainly couldn't tell Madison that her brother had seemed just fine earlier, when he'd made love to her!

'Why don't you ask him yourself?' she answered evasively.

'I have. He's about as forthcoming as a clam!' Madison added disgustedly. 'So I thought I would give you a call and ask if you've seen anything of him.'

Too much, Tory inwardly admitted with a groan. Literally!

'He came here for lunch on Sunday,' Tory answered non-committally. 'And he's popped in several times since. In fact, he was here this morning.' All of which was true, but it didn't exactly tell the full story of those visits. But then, she had a feeling Jonathan wouldn't appreciate his young sister knowing the intimate details of his life!

'How does he seem to you?' Madison asked guardedly.

'That's pretty difficult to answer,' Tory came back lightly, 'as I have no idea what he seems like normally!'

'Of course you don't,' Madison sighed. 'Well, until a couple of years ago that would have been easy to answer; he was my big, strong, dependable, good-fun brother.'

Until a couple of years ago… Those two years again…!

'Well, he's still big and strong,' she answered ruefully. 'Dependable, I'll take your word for.'

'And good fun?'

Tory sighed. She had seen glimpses of humour in Jonathan the last few days, also an ability to laugh at himself, but she didn't think that was what Madison meant.

'He seems to have something on his mind,' she finally replied evasively.

'Still?' Madison sighed heavily. 'I'd hoped—'

'Madison, are you sure you should be talking to me about Jonathan,' Tory cut in firmly. 'I don't believe the man I've come to know the last few days would appreciate us discussing him in this way!'

Madison laughed softly. 'That pretty much sums Jonny up,' she acknowledged. 'But as he isn't saying too much himself, what choice do I have?'

'I think Jonathan would consider he's old enough to take care of himself.' Tory grimaced.

'In other circumstances he would be,' Madison accepted. 'But as my marriage to Gideon was partly instrumental in causing these changes in Jonny, I obviously feel responsible for much of his heartache.'

Tory frowned. She had already considered it might have been Gideon Byrne's marriage to Madison that had caused Jonathan to begin the soul-searching he was now going through. But it still didn't make any sense to her…

'He hasn't discussed any of this with me, Madison.' Once again she was non-committal in her reply.

'In other words, neither should I?' the other woman commented dryly.

'Probably not,' Tory agreed brightly.

'Okay, point taken,' Madison accepted, as brightly. 'Oh, just one more thing before I ring off…'

Tory tensed. 'Yes?'

'It was a great picture of you in the newspapers the other day at your impromptu concert.'

'Thanks,' Tory responded warily.

'I don't suppose the mystery man who accompanied you on Sunday evening could have been Jonny, could he?'

She should have known this telephone call wasn't being as casually made as Madison had initially claimed it was!

She should also have remembered that Madison, as well as being an extremely beautiful and talented actress, was also a highly intelligent and perceptive woman; her looks alone wouldn't have attracted, and held captive a man of Gideon Byrne's calibre…

'Why don't you ask him?' Tory returned.

'Because I'm asking you,' Madison reasoned.

Tory gave a reluctantly appreciative laugh at the other woman's perception. 'And he probably wouldn't give you an answer,' she easily guessed.

'It *was* him on Sunday,' Madison said with happy certainty. 'You obviously know Jonny far too well for him to have just ''popped in several times''!' she explained her certainty.

Tory didn't know him at all, not really; somehow, she had just fallen in love with him!

'I repeat what I said a few minutes ago, Madison; Jonathan wouldn't like the two of us talking about him in this way,' she said dully.

'*Jonathan* isn't going to know,' the other woman came back pointedly. 'The family all call him Jonny,' she explained.

'So I believe,' Tory said.

'But not you…?'

'He doesn't seem like a Jonny to me,' she replied—and then wondered if she hadn't said too much. Madison was going to wonder—if he didn't seem like a Jonny to her, what *did* he seem like? 'Just as I've never thought of you as Maddie either,' she added—because that was what the family called Madison!

'Okay, Tory, I've taken up enough of your time for one day,' Madison replied. 'Jonny obviously isn't fading away from lack of food. Or company,' she tacked on softly.

'Madison!' Tory stopped the other woman as she sensed she was about to ring off.

'Yes?' Madison came back innocently.

Too innocently. Tory knew Madison too well herself to

believe she was in the least satisfied with their conversation. Also, the last thing she wanted Madison to do was telephone Jonathan with the intention of questioning him about his relationship with her; Jonathan would jump to the conclusion *she* must have told his sister something about the two of them.

Which she most certainly would never do! After all, what was there to tell…?

'Yes?' Madison prompted again at her silence.

She sighed. 'Madison, don't jump to a lot of conclusions that simply bear no relation to reality. My mother was the one who invited Jonathan to lunch on Sunday—'

'I doubt she invited him into Douglas with you on Sunday evening,' Madison came back teasingly.

'As I remember it, he was the one to do the inviting—' Tory broke off abruptly, realising—too late!—exactly what trap she had fallen into. 'That wasn't very fair, Madison,' she rebuked.

The other woman chuckled her satisfaction. 'Tell me, has Jonny played for you yet?'

'Played…?' she echoed cagily.

'He *has*,' Madison said excitedly. 'What did you think?'

Tory was suddenly overwhelmed by the possibility of having been set up. Oh, not by Jonathan; his surprise—horror!—at her identity as Victory Canan had definitely been genuine. But Madison had known who she was all the time…

'Think?' she repeated distractedly. 'What was I supposed to think?'

'Of his work,' Madison said impatiently. 'Jonny has been writing songs for years. They're good, don't you think?'

Jonathan wrote songs… Had he written the one she had heard him play on Sunday? If he had, then Madison was right; they were good! Was it his songwriting Jonathan had been referring to when he'd told her he wasn't here on holiday?

'Madison, did you know I would be on the island this week?' Tory prompted slowly.

'I had an idea you might be—you once mentioned that you get back to the island during TT as much as possible,' Madison answered vaguely.

'But did you know I would be here this year?' Tory persisted.

'Thelma might have mentioned it before we left the island a couple of weeks ago,' Madison conceded reluctantly.

Her mother might have mentioned it, be damned! Madison had *known* she was going to be at home this week. Just as Gideon had been the one to suggest Jonathan might find the peace and quiet he required on the island…

'You know, Madison, I always believed you to be a very talented and capable woman—I just never realised *how* capable! Just what were you expecting to happen when Jonathan and I met?' she prompted hardly, her hand tightly gripping the receiver.

'Happen?' Madison parroted innocently.

Tory sighed. 'You know, Madison, I'm starting to feel just a little annoyed at what I suspect may have been a set-up on the part of you and Gideon—how much more angry do you think Jonathan is going to feel if he realises the truth?'

'Are you going to tell him?'

After this morning Tory wasn't sure she and Jonathan would ever speak to each other again. But that really wasn't the point!

'Do you think I should?'

'Not if you have any sense,' Madison came back easily. 'And, as I recall, you have a lot of that. Anyway, what's wrong with a little matchmaking?' she added cajolingly.

'Especially as you sing songs and Jonathan writes them. Gideon and I thought the two of you would get on together.'

'I really don't care—!' Tory broke off, breathing deeply to bring her temper back under control. After all, Madison and Gideon were her parents' nearest neighbours. 'For your information, Madison, you're wasting your time where Jonathan and I are concerned. He has made it clear he does not want me to hear any of his songs. In fact, he's let me know in no uncertain terms that he considers Victory Canan to be nothing but a cheap-looking vamp, who may or may not be able to sing!'

'Jonny said that?' his sister gasped disbelievingly.

'More or less,' she said grimly.

'He sounds as if he's still being completely unbearable.' The grimace could be heard in Madison's voice.

'That's putting it mildly.'

'I really am sorry if Jonny has been at all rude to you or your family during his visit there,' his sister apologised wearily. 'I just thought— Well, never mind what I thought; I was obviously wrong. I think I'll give Jonny a call and suggest he goes home; the island obviously isn't doing him any good at all!'

Tory couldn't actually agree with that sentiment. Compared to what he had been like when he'd got off the plane last Saturday, Jonathan was definitely more relaxed and approachable. But as for Madison and Gideon's efforts to matchmake—! What was it about happily married people that made them think they had the right?

'Do that,' Tory advised abruptly.

'Still friends, Tory?' Madison prompted hesitantly.

'Still friends, Madison,' she agreed with a sigh. 'Just leave me to find my own male friends in future, hmm?'

'As long as it isn't Rupert Montgomery!' the other

woman came back with obvious distaste. 'You can do so much better than him, Tory.'

The Byrnes had been in residence on the island during Rupert's last memorable visit to the island—and he had not made a good impression on the couple, either!

'I suppose by much better you're referring to your brother?' Tory observed. 'Well, don't worry, Rupert is definitely out of the picture. But Jonathan isn't even in it,' she stated firmly as the other woman would have spoken.

'Okay, Tory, I get the message,' Madison said. 'I think I'll give Jonny a call, anyway. Take care.'

She rang off.

Leaving Tory staring frustratedly at the now superfluous telephone handset.

She couldn't believe Gideon and Madison had deliberately tried to get Jonathan and herself together!

But they had meant well, she instantly rebuked herself. Even if the two of them hadn't actually come to like each other, there had always been the hope that Tory might like Jonathan's songs.

As she *did* like the one she had partly been allowed to hear. Well…'allowed' was probably overdoing it a bit; Jonathan had been furious when he realised he had an audience.

In fact, she *more* than liked the little of the song she had heard—the wretched thing haunted her! So much so that she wanted to hear the rest of it. 'Pretty', Rupert had called it this morning, when he'd walked into her studio and heard her playing the little she could recall. But it was so much more than that.

And Jonathan was its composer…

Which was a good enough reason for him to refuse to let her hear the rest of it. If she even dared to ask him, that was…!

'…very sad,' her mother was saying. 'It's such a pity that it has to happen.'

Tory had wandered back into the sitting room, still deep in thought about Jonathan's song, and looked up enquiringly now as she had no idea what her mother was talking about.

'There was another accident on the TT course this morning,' her mother explained as she pressed the remote control button to turn off the television, the local news having just finished. 'A young girl in her twenties was killed on the mountain road.' She shook her head. 'It's bad enough when it's one of the competitors; they obviously know the risks they take by taking part. But when it's one of the visiting fans…! They aren't even giving out the poor girl's name yet, as the family haven't been informed. Her poor parents. It's so dreadful for them. I know how I would feel if something like that happened to you,' her mother declared emotionally.

Sadly, it was a fact of the Isle of Man TT Races that, on average, two riders were killed each year, and usually the same amount of visiting fans. Although it didn't seem to deter any of them from returning year after year. Or maybe they all just assumed it would never happen to them…

That was probably nearer the—

Tory became suddenly still, frowning thoughtfully. This morning. A girl in her early twenties. No name yet given out.

Could Jonathan possibly have thought that girl was *her*?

No, of course he couldn't!

Yes, he could, she instantly contradicted herself, as the idea began to take hold. Jonathan had left her in no doubt when they'd parted last night, after Rupert's unexpected arrival, that she would not be seeing him today. But he had then proceeded to telephone from Ramsey this morning, and, when he'd received no answer to that call, he had driven to the farm on his way back home.

She had believed at the time that he was just being his unpredictable self, but now she wasn't so sure…

The radio had been on in his car this morning, when he'd turned on the ignition prior to leaving; she remembered how impatient he had been as he switched it off. Because that was where he had heard the announcement of the accident…?

Maybe she was just being fanciful. Why should it bother Jonathan even if it had been her that was involved in that fatal accident? After all, she meant nothing to him. Did she…?

'Who was that on the telephone, Tory?' her mother asked curiously.

'Madison. Checking up on her brother. I suggested it would be better if she telephoned him and checked for herself.'

Her mother smiled. 'They aren't very alike, are they?' she murmured.

'What do you mean?' Tory tilted her head curiously. Although she knew the answer to that, really—had discovered for herself that not only did Madison and Jonathan look nothing like brother and sister, but their personalities were completely different, too.

'I'm sure you know exactly what I mean, Tory,' her mother chided gently. 'Hard as he tries to hide it, Jonathan is a very troubled man.'

Tory had forgotten just how astute her mother could be!

Her parents were completely happy with their life on the farm, rarely venturing from the island except for the occasional holiday in England, and it was all too easy for people to assume—people like Rupert, that was!—that their minds were as insular as the island obviously was. But they would be very wrong. Her mother was one of the shrewdest people Tory had ever known—could sum a person up after the briefest of acquaintance.

She was right this time, too; Jonathan *was* a troubled man…

'I doubt he would be here at all if he weren't,' Tory conceded heavily. She came to a sudden decision. So sudden she even surprised herself with it! 'Look, Mum, I—I think I'll go out for a walk.'

'This time of night?' Her mother glanced out at the already darkening evening.

She needed time, and space, to think. And if that time and space took her towards the Byrne house, then so be it. There was some invisible force compelling her to go and see Jonathan…

Be honest, Tory, she told herself sternly; you want to see him.

If only to find out if she was right about his reason for arriving here so unexpectedly this morning… Because if she was, surely that must mean Jonathan felt something towards her, too?

'I shouldn't be long,' she told her mother as she pulled on a jacket to ward off the cool of the evening. 'I'll go out the back way so as to avoid any lingering reporters,' she explained; perhaps a couple of die-hards were still lurking about in the hope that they just might manage to snatch a photograph of her with her mystery man!

It was ironic really—because he was actually only yards away!

She could see the lights on in the Byrne house as she strolled along the edge of the field in that direction, so at least Jonathan was at home.

After this morning, Tory had no idea what her reception would be, but her feet kept walking in that direction anyway. Let's face it, she told herself, even if Jonathan keeps me standing on the doorstep, it certainly won't be the first time he's been rude to me in that way!

It felt as if her heart was in her throat as she rang the doorbell and waited for Jonathan to open the door. What was she going to say to him? What could she say to him? How—?

'Yes?'

Tory's breath held, and stuck in her throat, as Jonathan suddenly stood in the open doorway. He looked even more remotely unapproachable than normal—if that were possible!—dressed all in black—black shirt and black denims—his expression grim as he looked at her with questioning grey eyes.

She moistened dry lips, looking up at him from beneath thick dark lashes. 'I— You said this morning that we needed to talk.'

His mouth twisted mockingly. 'As I recall, you told me there was no need,' he reminded her.

Tory's head went up, her chin jutting forward challengingly. 'I've changed my mind.'

Jonathan gave a mocking inclination of his head as he stepped back to allow her to enter. 'That's a woman's prerogative, I believe,' he drawled derisively.

Her cheeks were flushed as she preceded him into the comfortable sitting room. He must have been sitting in here when she arrived; there was a glass of whisky on the coffee table in front of the sofa, his guitar was lying on the latter, with sheets of music scattered over the cushions.

He must have been playing when she arrived! It was the opening she had been hoping for.

She turned to face him, hands tightly clenched together in front of her. 'The song you were playing on Sunday evening…' she began tentatively.

'What about it?' he demanded harshly, his previous almost lazy mockery banished to be replaced with aggression.

Tory held up her hands defensively. 'I only want to know who wrote it,' she soothed. 'You see—'

'But you know who wrote it, Tory,' he cut in accusingly. 'My sister told you during your conversation on the telephone earlier,' he scorned.

Oh! She had hoped Madison wouldn't already have telephoned him!

She gave a deep sigh. 'Okay, so that wasn't very well done. But it doesn't alter the fact that I want to talk to you about that song. And any others that you might have written.'

'Why?'

'Look, Jonathan,' she said, 'it wasn't particularly easy for me to come over here this evening—'

'Then why did you?' he rasped scathingly.

Her eyes flashed deeply blue. 'I'm beginning to wonder,' she bit out through gritted teeth.

But she wasn't really. She was here because she couldn't stay away, knew herself to be in love with this arrogant, pig-headed, hurting man!

'Do you think I could have one of those?' She nodded in the direction of the glass of whisky on the coffee table.

'Why not?' He moved to the tray of drinks on the side-dresser, pouring an inch of whisky into the bottom of a glass before handing it to her. 'Dutch courage, Tory?' he taunted hardly.

'Manx, actually.' She took a swallow of the whisky, gasping as the fiery liquid burnt the back of her throat. 'I've always hated the stuff.' She grimaced as she put the glass down on the table next to Jonathan's.

'Then why drink it?' He shrugged. 'I'll get you a glass

of red wine, instead.' He had gone from the room before Tory could stop him.

Not that she particularly wanted to, feeling as if, with Jonathan's brief departure, she could breathe properly for the first time since her arrival. This meeting was turning out to be as difficult as she had thought it would be.

Or maybe she hadn't thought. Because if she had, she probably wouldn't be here at all!

She glanced across at those strewn music sheets, longing to have a really good look at them, sure they were the songs Jonathan had written himself that Madison had told her about. But if Jonathan should return while she was looking at them—!

She winced just at the thought of the explosion that was likely to follow.

'Here you are.' Jonathan returned to hand her the promised glass of wine. 'I raided Gideon's supply of Gevrey-Chambertin once again,' he admitted unrepentantly. 'Why don't you sit down?' he invited. 'If you do, so can I,' he explained, as she was about to refuse.

Those manners instilled in him by his mother once again! 'I'm fine as I am, thanks. But please feel free to sit down yourself.' They might be on a similar level then, rather than Jonathan towering over her in this ominous way.

'You were saying…?' he prompted pointedly as he sat down in one of the armchairs to look up at her with narrowed eyes.

She swallowed hard. 'I was saying that I would very much like to see some of the songs Madison told me you've written.' The words came out forcefully—before she could change her mind!

'And I asked why?' he returned with deceptive mildness, a nerve pulsing in his clenched jaw.

Tory shrugged. 'I'm a singer, therefore I sing songs.'

Jonathan's mouth thinned. 'You're a bit more than that, I believe,' he drawled again. 'In the light of my scathing remarks to you these last few days, my sister has taken great delight in giving me a complete dressing-down about your vast musical achievements. Most of which I already knew, I might add.'

Which begged the question; if he had known, why had he been so damned rude to her?

She shook her head. 'I'm sorry if you have the mistaken impression that I complained to Madison about your remarks—'

'I don't have that impression at all, Tory,' he interrupted. 'I know Madison well enough to realise she will have made up her own mind about the situation.'

What situation?

She had come here to try and sort out the muddle that seemed to have developed between the two of them—and instead she was just becoming more confused.

'Again I ask what possible reason could the famous Victory Canan have for wanting to look at my pitiful dabblings in songwriting?' Jonathan looked at her with hard grey eyes.

She shook her head. 'If the little I heard on Sunday is anything to go by, then they aren't pitiful,' she told him huskily. 'And I would like to see them because I—I—'

'You what, Tory?' he snapped harshly, standing up abruptly, all pretence of relaxation gone. His face looked as if it were carved from granite; his body was taut with anger. 'I don't care what Madison might or might not have said to you on the subject, Tory; I don't need any charitable gestures from you or anyone—'

'I'm not being charitable, damn it!' she burst out indignantly, eyes flashing deeply blue as she glared across the room at him.

'I don't believe you!' Jonathan came back just as fiercely.

She drew herself up to her full height of five feet two inches. 'I am not a liar!'

'You were lying a short time ago when you pretended you had no idea who wrote that song you heard on Sunday,' he reminded her.

She drew in a sharp breath. 'That wasn't a lie. It was an attempt on my part at being tactful—'

'Then you failed in that attempt,' he rasped. 'Miserably!' he added scornfully.

'Obviously,' she replied. 'My God, Jonathan, are you so wrapped up in self-pity that you can't accept or believe it when someone is genuinely interested—?'

'I'm not wrapped up in self-pity at all.' His voice rose angrily.

She gave a disbelieving snort. 'Then you're doing a damned good job of pretending you are—'

'And just what would you know about it?' he challenged, looking down that long, arrogant nose at her.

'I only have to spend a few minutes in your company to know what your problem is,' she returned gratingly.

'Really?' His voice was dangerously soft now. 'And exactly what *is* my problem?'

Tory was shaking—with anger, and something else. She was angry with Jonathan, yes—very angry—but another part of her wanted to just hold him in her arms, keep him that way until all his hurt and frustration disappeared...!

'I just told you,' she said. 'Self-pity. For reasons I obviously don't understand—'

'Obviously,' Jonathan echoed with hard derision.

'Then tell me,' she implored. 'Jonathan, talk to me!' she encouraged.

He didn't actually move, and yet his emotional withdrawal from her was nonetheless tangible for all that. 'So far in our acquaintance talking doesn't seem to have been too successful between the two of us,' he muttered, his narrowed grey gaze holding her immobile as he did finally move, coming to stand dangerously close to Tory now. 'I think I've come to prefer our other means of communication,' he murmured, before his head lowered and his mouth claimed hers.

Not like this, Tory cried inwardly.

Because as Jonathan drew her close into him, the hard outline of his body firmly pressed against hers, his mouth kissing hers with a thoroughness that left her breathless, Tory knew Jonathan didn't intend stopping this time, that he intended making love to her.

Completely.

Thoroughly.

She also knew that, loving him as she did, she didn't have the strength or will-power to stop him...

CHAPTER TEN

SHE couldn't allow this to happen, Tory cried inwardly.

Not like this.

Not without love!

She pushed against his chest, wrenching her mouth free of his. 'No, Jonathan!' she groaned, shaking her head, tears swimming in her eyes as she looked up at him pleadingly.

There was a dark flush on his cheeks, and his eyes appeared almost black as he looked down at her disbelievingly. 'Why not?' he rasped, his arms still like steel bands about her waist. 'You know that we want each other.'

Oh, yes, she knew that, could be in no doubt of her own feelings—just as she was only too aware that Jonathan desired her physically. It was just that she wanted so much more from him than that. And she knew, even more so after the last few minutes' candid conversation, that Jonathan didn't have anything more than physical desire to give her.

'Do you really think I'm going to leave myself open to the accusation that I made love with you merely to get my hands on your songs?' Her mouth curved derisively, though that derision was directed, she knew, mainly towards herself.

Jonathan looked taken aback, his arms dropping back to his sides as he released her. 'I would never—'

'Oh, yes, you would,' Tory said with certainty, stepping back from the seduction of his physical warmth. 'And probably much more besides!' She was under no illusions concerning Jonathan's opinion of her.

He looked at her wordlessly for several long seconds,

grey eyes icy now. 'You have a very low opinion of me,' he finally murmured.

'Not of you, Jonathan.' She shook her head, her accompanying smile completely without humour. 'Just people in general.' Goodness knew she'd had her own fair share of people using her!

'I have never considered myself to be part of the general populace!' he snapped.

Tory shrugged. 'Nevertheless, I don't want there to be any room for misunderstanding. I'm—I have a need of new material, different from my usual style.' She remained cagey on the subject because she hadn't even told Stephen James yet that she intended taking up his offer! 'Something like I heard you playing on Sunday,' she added determinedly.

Jonathan's gaze remained icy. 'Excuse me if I remain sceptical, Tory, but I sense the interference of my sister and Gideon behind all this.'

'Sense all you like,' she answered impatiently. 'I'm no more a charitable organisation than you are a charity case. If I like your songs—and it's still a big if,' she stated firmly, 'then there would be a contract drawn up between us, with everything done in a completely businesslike manner.'

Jonathan still looked sceptical. 'I can already see a problem with that...'

She eyed him warily. 'Yes?'

He gave a mocking inclination of his head. 'They aren't songs, Tory. I write music; there are no words.'

'But that's even better,' she said excitedly. 'I could put my own words to your music—'

'I don't think so,' he cut in hardly.

'Why ever not?' Tory could hardly contain her impatience with his stubbornness. Why did he bother to write music if he never intended anyone to hear it?

'Because I don't write Victory Canan-type songs,' he told her arrogantly.

'I've just told you—!' She broke off, breathing deeply in her agitation. 'I'm interested in doing something different, Jonathan.' She spoke more calmly; having both of them lose their temper wasn't going to get them anywhere!

He shook his head. 'Not with my music,' he bit out scathingly.

Her eyes narrowed angrily in spite of her earlier attempt to hold onto her temper. 'Do you think Victory Canan might contaminate it?'

Jonathan sighed, moving to stand next to the unlit fireplace. 'Believe it or not, Tory, I write love-songs—without words, granted. But, nevertheless, you only have to listen to them to know they're love-songs.'

'And Victory Canan doesn't sing love-songs,' she acknowledged dryly. 'But that's the whole point; I'm going to!' She had read Stephen James's play, and the underlying theme was most definitely of love. 'I'm thinking of—I've been offered the chance to star in a play, the main female role being that of a singer.' There—she had said it, and it hadn't been so bad, after all. She might even get used to the idea herself eventually!

Jonathan shook his head. 'It isn't what your fans expect of you—'

'Do you think I don't know that?' she replied. 'It's the reason I've taken so long to make my decision.' But, having made it, she now intended seeing it through.

'The reason you're on the island?' Jonathan guessed astutely.

'Partly,' she conceded. 'Isn't it the same for you?' she enquired.

He stiffened, grey eyes enigmatic. 'What do you mean?'

'You obviously came here to wrestle with your own demons—'

'Exactly what has Maddie been telling you?' he demanded harshly.

'—whatever they might be,' Tory finished determinedly, meeting his challenging gaze unflinchingly.

'The implication being that Maddie hasn't told you anything,' Jonathan muttered scathingly. 'Forgive me if I find that hard to believe—'

'No, I don't forgive you,' Tory cut in heatedly. 'Madison is your sister; she would no more break your confidence than she would Gideon's!'

'Why bring Gideon into this?' he demanded again, through gritted teeth.

'Look, Jonathan,' she said wearily, 'I have no idea what your problem is with your brother-in-law—'

'My problem is that he isn't only my brother-in-law!' Jonathan rasped.

Tory looked at him searchingly. But she could learn nothing from his expression—his eyes hard, his face an angry mask.

She shook her head. 'I don't understand you.'

'No?' he replied sceptically.

'No,' she echoed impatiently. 'Jonathan, why do you hate Gideon so much?'

'Hate him?' He looked stunned at the statement. 'I don't hate Gideon, Tory.' He shook his head dazedly. 'How could I?' he protested emotionally. 'He's my brother!'

'I realise that by marrying Madison he has become so, but that doesn't mean you have to like him—' Tory broke off as Jonathan once again shook his head. 'No?' she said uncertainly.

'He really is my brother, Tory,' Jonathan ground out. 'Look at us!' He picked up a framed photograph of

Madison and Gideon that stood on the sideboard, holding it up beside his own face. 'Can't you see the likeness?'

Of course she could. Hadn't she already noted to herself Jonathan's resemblance to Gideon rather than Madison? The two men having the same colouring, the same arrogance of expression? But she had thought at the time it was merely an accidental surface likeness…

Was Jonathan now saying that wasn't the case at all?

Jonathan put the photograph back on the sideboard, face down, turning away to stare sightlessly out of the window. Darkness had fallen completely by this time. 'Until I was eighteen, and my mother told me the truth concerning my birth, I believed Malcolm McGuire was my father,' he said softly.

So softly Madison could barely hear him. But she had no intention of interrupting him, sensing that he needed to talk to someone. Even her!

'Even after my mother had told me the truth it made no difference to me,' Jonathan continued huskily. 'Malcolm had always treated me exactly as if I were his son and my mother obviously loved me. Maddie adored all of us, and was adored in return.' An affectionate smile shattered that hard countenance for a moment. 'It wasn't important, you see.' He turned back to Tory, his eyes that dark grey of their first meeting.

She believed she was beginning to see… That conversation they had here the evening they'd had dinner together, concerning Gideon's father, John Byrne… Jonathan wondering if they were all only the genes inherited from their parents… At the time she had thought it was because Jonathan was concerned Gideon might turn into the drunken adulterer his father had been before his death. But if Jonathan really were Gideon's brother, that made John Byrne *his* father, too…!

'But Madison and Gideon falling in love changed that?' she guessed.

Jonathan gave a humourless smile. 'It shouldn't have done.'

'But it did?' Tory persisted.

He nodded. 'From the age of eighteen I was aware that I had a half-brother—the film director Gideon Byrne—but I was happy with my lot in life, and he was completely unaware of my existence, so I considered things were better left as they were.'

'And then Madison met Gideon.' Tory grimaced—not at the chances of Madison and Gideon meeting—Madison was an actress and Gideon was a film director, there had been every chance that they would meet at some stage in their career—but at the fact they should fall in love with each other!

Jonathan gave a shaky sigh. '"And then Madison met Gideon,"' he echoed heavily. 'Sounds like the title of a film, doesn't it? The really stupid thing about all this is that *I* was the one to talk Gideon out of throwing it all away with Madison, once he had learnt the truth of who my mother was—who I was. And I was right about them. They should be together. It just never occurred to me when I was helping their relationship along that I would end up as the one with the unresolved emotional baggage!'

It hadn't occurred to him, but it was easy for Tory—at least—to see that it had always been a possibility. Easy to see too, now, why Jonathan had seemed to be going through some sort of identity crisis when he'd arrived on the island—what she had teasingly referred to as his 'early mid-life crisis'!

Except that none of this situation was in the least funny to this emotionally confused man…

Malcolm McGuire—to his credit—had always been a

loving father to Jonathan, just as Susan Delaney had no doubt loved her son. But none of that changed the fact—for Jonathan, at least—that his real father was a man he had never known, a man he never *could* have known. Because he had been killed in a car crash before Jonathan was even born. And, despite the twelve or thirteen years of uninterest in the subject that had elapsed after Jonathan had been told about his real father, it must nevertheless have brought the situation to a head for Jonathan once he had actually met his half-brother—two years ago…

Because he hadn't just *met* Gideon; he had welcomed him into his own family as his brother-in-law!

'Have you talked to Gideon about his—your—father?' Tory prompted.

'No,' Jonathan replied harshly. 'Why should I?' His eyes glittered resentfully.

'Because you need to?'

He shook his head. 'That's ridiculous—'

'Why is it?' Tory persisted.

'Because John Byrne has no bearing on my life. The man has been dead for over thirty years—'

'But you didn't even know of his existence as your father until you were eighteen,' Tory reasoned.

'What the hell does that have to do with anything?' Jonathan rasped coldly.

'You don't really need me to tell you that,' she said gently.

His eyes narrowed icily, his mouth a grim slash in a face that looked carved out of granite. 'Since when did you become a psychologist? Even an amateur one!' he bit back scathingly.

Tory refused to rise to the insult, knowing that was exactly what Jonathan wanted. In fact, he wanted to keep everyone at a safe emotional distance from him at the moment!

'I didn't,' she acknowledged lightly. 'I just know that if I were in the same position—'

'But you aren't,' he scorned. 'You had your safe island childhood, with your safe, loving parents. Now you have your safe, successful career—what can you possibly know of questioning the very fabric of who and what you are?'

Was this the time to tell him of her own adoption? Of the fact that she had never needed to know who her real parents were, what they had been like as people, because the parents who had chosen her as their child had given her all the security and confidence in herself that she could ever need?

She looked searchingly at Jonathan, saw the strain, the pain, the uncertainty—and knew that the parallel of her own adoption was not something he would welcome at this moment! It was his own parentage he was concerned with, no one else's!

'I said *if* I were in the same position,' she pointed out gently.

'Which you aren't!' he responded forcefully.

'Don't you think you're going about all of this from the wrong angle, Jonathan?'

His eyes narrowed to icy slits. 'What does *that* mean?'

She sighed. 'It appears to me— It appears to me,' she repeated as he gave a disparaging snort, 'that it's who you are, what you've done with your own life that's important, not who and what your parents were or are. I very much doubt you've ever expected to succeed on the fact that your mother is Susan Delaney—'

'Certainly not!' he rasped.

Tory nodded. 'Just as you shouldn't expect to fail because your father was John Byrne!'

Jonathan looked at her wordlessly for several long seconds, mouth tight, eyes still glacial. 'Back to the amateur psychology again?' he finally murmured derisively.

'If you like.'

'I don't like,' he rejoined insultingly.

Tory sighed, realising that she wasn't getting through to this man at all. 'Tell me, Jonathan,' she said quietly. 'How do you think Malcolm feels about all this?'

He looked startled. 'Malcolm? I don't think—'

'No, you obviously don't,' she accepted. 'But you said yourself the man has always treated you as his son—something he had obviously known you weren't from the beginning of his marriage to your mother. It seems to have made no difference to his love and pride in you as his own son. As evidenced by the fact that you run his family business,' she pointed out. 'How do you think all this soul-searching on your part, since Madison married Gideon, is affecting him?'

She watched the emotions chasing across Jonathan's normally guarded expression, clearly saw the confusion, the pain, the dismay, as the full import of her words struck home.

Despite encouragement by her adopted parents, Tory had never had any interest in knowing who her real parents were, and she had seen the relief and love on Thelma and Dan's faces when she'd told them that. Obviously Jonathan couldn't meet his real father, but she could well imagine Malcolm McGuire's hurt confusion at Jonathan's behaviour the last couple of years.

'My feelings concerning Gideon as my brother and John Byrne as my father have no bearing on the love and respect I have always felt for Malcolm,' Jonathan finally said stiffly.

'Does he know that?'

'You—'

'After all, you're here, not there,' she continued determinedly, knowing that Jonathan was going to hate her—even more than he already did—for bringing this painful truth home to him. But if Jonathan couldn't love her in the way she loved him, she could at least try to reconcile him with his family. 'And Malcolm is presumably running the casino business himself.'

'Like anyone else, I'm entitled to a holiday,' Jonathan snapped.

She gave an acknowledging inclination of her head. 'Anyone else would have told their family where they were going. If only so that they shouldn't worry,' she went on, as he would have interrupted. 'Okay, so Madison and Gideon know, but you weren't even happy about the fact that Gideon had told his own wife—your sister—that you were staying here in their home.'

'I'm thirty-three, Tory, not three; long past the age where I have to tell anyone where I'm going!' Jonathan exclaimed.

She shook her head. 'I'm twenty-four, but I'm still not selfish enough to consider my parents have no right to worry about me.'

'So I'm selfish as well as inconsiderate?' Jonathan said with sarcasm.

'In a word—yes,' she confirmed.

Jonathan drew himself up to his full height—well over six feet—grey eyes as cold as ice, his expression grim. 'I don't remember asking for your opinion,' he told her scathingly.

Tory took a deep breath. No, he hadn't asked for her opinion, and she would rather it had been anyone else other than herself who had told him these home truths—but, in the circumstances, she couldn't think of anyone else who could have done it. Only Madison and Gideon knew exactly where he was, and they were both just too close to the situation to dare to say these things to Jonathan: one his half-sister, the other his half-brother. It was such a muddle of a situation!

'No, you didn't,' she conceded with a sigh. 'But, as I've already told you, I'm very fond of Madison and Gideon.'

His mouth quirked mockingly. 'Exactly the opposite of how you feel about me!'

She swallowed hard. Jonathan's emotions were far too much in turmoil at the moment for him to really know how he felt about anything; he certainly didn't need the complication of hearing that Tory Buchanan, aka Victory Canan, was in love with him!

'Not at all, Jonathan,' she dismissed lightly. 'I have just tried to put myself in your family's shoes. All of them—including yours.'

'And your conclusion?'

He didn't want to hear her conclusion! It was there in that slightly challenging tone, that arrogant tilt to the squareness of his jaw. No, Jonathan didn't really want to hear her opinion…

'Perhaps you should be grateful for what you have, Jonathan; a loving sister and brother, an adorable niece.' Her voice softened affectionately as she thought of Keilly. 'A mother who obviously loves you very much, and a step-father who, although I have never met him—' nor was she ever likely to, either! '—is a man much to be admired.'

'Of course I admire Malcolm,' Jonathan said huskily.

'Then perhaps you should try looking at how he must feel about what happened two years ago,' Tory encouraged pleadingly. 'I realise it must have been difficult for you when Madison and Gideon were married, but how much more difficult it must have been for Malcolm. He suddenly became a complete outsider within his own family.' She frowned at the thought.

As did Jonathan. He had obviously never looked at the complicated situation from this point of view before.

But she could see that he was now! And, if she knew Jonathan half as well as she thought she did, once he had thought about this deeply enough he would come to the right decision; that of going back to America and making his peace with his family.

'I have to get back now, Jonathan,' she told him decisively. 'They'll wonder where I've got to; I told my mother I was just going out for a short walk.'

His mouth twisted mockingly as he followed her out into the hallway. 'And you don't want them to worry about you!'

'Exactly.' She turned at the front door to give him a rueful smile. 'I sincerely hope you come to the right decision, Jonathan,' she concluded, before turning to leave.

Even if that decision meant he went away from her, back to America. Never to be seen again!

She had slept badly, Tory acknowledged bad-temperedly as she staggered down the stairs the next morning, the smell of freshly brewing coffee drawing her down to the kitchen. Her father was obviously up and about already, despite the fact that it was only six-thirty.

It wasn't too difficult to know the reason she had slept badly: Jonathan!

Once in bed the previous evening she hadn't been able to think of anything but Jonathan, and the tangle his life had suddenly seemed to become two years ago.

She sincerely hoped he had listened to her the evening before, for all of his family's sakes, but she somehow had the feeling that all she had succeeded in doing was alienating him from herself, too!

Her father looked up with a smile as she came into the kitchen. 'You're up early, love...'

'You know I never could resist the smell of your coffee.' She poured herself a mug of the strong brew before sitting down opposite her father at the kitchen table, slightly slumped over the steaming mug.

Her father quirked a questioning brow. 'Is that the only reason?' he prompted softly.

Tory frowned. What did he mean? Did she look that bad? A little pale when she'd looked in her bedroom mirror before coming downstairs, but then, it was only six-thirty in the morning!

She shrugged dismissively. 'What else could it be?'

'Jonathan was here earlier,' her father told her.

Tory looked across at him sharply, her frown deeper than ever. 'Jonathan was...?'

He must have had as much trouble sleeping as she had. She only hoped it was for the right reasons!

Her father nodded, grimacing slightly. 'About a quarter to six. I had just got up to check on that ewe I have in the barn.'

Quarter to six! Tory's stomach gave an apprehensive lurch; what on earth had Jonathan been doing here at that time of the morning? Normally an early riser, even her father wouldn't normally have been awake at that time. Only the fact that he had a sick ewe to check on had caused him to rise earlier this morning than his usual six o'clock.

'Jonathan has gone, Tory,' her father continued gently.

'Gone?' she echoed sharply. 'Gone where?'

'To London. On the seven o'clock plane.'

Tory felt her cheeks pale even more as she stared across at her father disbelievingly.

Jonathan had gone!

Left the island!

Just like that. 'Without even saying goodbye?'

'No, not without saying goodbye,' her father said, making Tory aware of the fact that she must have spoken her protest out loud. 'That was the reason he called in here on his way to the airport. He also brought back your mother's clean pie dish,' he said wryly, standing up. 'And he asked me to give you this.' He picked up a large bulky brown envelope from the worktop near the sink.

Tory stared at the envelope unseeingly. Jonathan really had gone…!

She had hoped, once he'd had time to consider some of the things she had said to him the previous evening, that he would return home to America. But not like this! Not without even saying goodbye!

'Aren't you going to open it, Tory?' her father prompted as she made no effort to take the envelope from him.

She stared at the bulky envelope as if it might bite her. As indeed she almost felt it might! What on earth could Jonathan have left for her in the envelope? It looked a bit too large for a goodbye note!

Her hands shook as she took the envelope from her father, fumbling slightly as she ripped open the seal to tip the contents out onto the kitchen table.

Music sheets! Dozens of them!

'Here.' Her father held out a smaller envelope that had fallen out with the music.

Tory stared dazedly at the white envelope. Jonathan seemed to have left her all his music. What would he have written in the letter?

Goodbye, certainly.

But what else?

CHAPTER ELEVEN

'HAVE my parents arrived yet?' Tory asked Stephen huskily as she looked at his reflection behind her in the dressing room mirror, checking her own appearance one last time before she had to go out on stage.

Anyone less like Victory Canan it would be hard to imagine!

The play began with the aging singer lying on what was obviously going to be her deathbed, her thoughts drifting back to memories of her life and career. At the moment Tory's make-up made her look like a seventy-year-old woman.

Which was one of the reasons she had asked her parents not to come backstage before the play. Only one of them! Her main reason was that she was so nervous at this first venture away from her career as a rock star that she could barely speak her teeth were chattering so much!

What if she fell flat on her face as soon as the curtain rose? Not literally, of course; unless she actually fell out of bed! But what if she froze? What if all these months of rehearsal turned out to be a complete waste of time—her own as well as everyone else's? What if she let Stephen down?

She had come to know the portly fifty-year-old quite well over the last six months, knew him as a loving husband to Dorothy, his wife of the last thirty years, as a wonderful father to his son and daughter, and grandfather to six. But she also knew him as a perfectionist where his work was concerned, a man who wouldn't accept anything less than the best. She hoped he still considered her that at the end of their opening evening!

'Your parents are in their box,' Stephen assured her, moving forward to place his hands firmly on her shoulders. 'And don't worry, Tory; you're going to be wonderful,' he told her.

She turned to smile up at him, grateful for his confidence—and sincerely hoping it wasn't going to be misplaced.

The last six months had been the most gruelling Tory had known in her career so far. For one thing, she hadn't appreciated the work that went into a production of this size. Stephen, although one of the most charming men Tory had ever met, was also one of the most exacting. But as director, as well as author of the play, he had a right to be!

'Has— Is there anyone else in the box with them?' she pressed, unable to meet Stephen's gaze now.

'Not yet.' He gave an understanding squeeze of her shoulders. 'But there's still time; the curtain doesn't go up for another ten minutes.'

She was grateful for his comfort, but they both knew they were probably empty words. Jonathan had left her his music six months ago, on the morning he'd left the island so abruptly, but there had necessarily been communication between their lawyers once Tory had decided on the music she wanted to use; there had been no way she could just take it, as his short note had told her to do. Tory had also sent Jonathan two tickets for this evening's show, but a part of her had always known he wouldn't come.

Although that hadn't stopped her hoping!

The last six months hadn't just been gruelling because of the work involved in the play—in fact, the hours she'd had to spend rehearsing, perfecting, had probably been her saviours during those months; less time to sit and brood over Jonathan, and the heartbreaking love she felt towards him.

Rupert, too, had proved a slight diversion, trying every trick he knew to get her to change her mind about this play, to get her back on the road. But the last six months of staying in one place, of knowing exactly where she would be tomorrow, the day after, a month later, had proved one thing to her; she was tired of travelling, of never being in one place long enough to call it home.

When bullying hadn't worked, Rupert had tried to cajole. But even though she had agreed to have dinner with him one evening, had listened to all he'd had to say, she had been totally immune to the Montgomery charm. And remained so!

Jonathan had never needed to use charm, had just been his arrogant if vulnerable self, and even though she hadn't seen or heard from him personally for six months, she still loved him.

But he hadn't even accepted the invitation of those two complimentary tickets to her opening night!

She hadn't realised how much she'd been depending on his being here tonight until Stephen told her he hadn't arrived, and that sinking feeling in her stomach now owed nothing to first-night nerves.

Why hadn't he come? She had thought—

'Your flowers are nice,' Stephen told her almost questioningly as he looked at the colourful blooms that covered most of the dressing table.

There were flowers as well as cards from well-wishing fans, orange roses from her parents, a bouquet from the ever-hopeful Rupert, a wonderful display from Madison and Gideon, who had written to say they couldn't be here because they were filming in Morocco—but not even a card from Jonathan.

Jonathan again! She had to put him out of her mind if she were to get through this complete sell-out of a first night…!

'Five minutes, Tory,' Stephen told her as he stepped back. 'I had better get out front. Don't worry, you're going to be wonderful. Break a leg, hmm?' he added affectionately.

She gave a choked laugh. Tonight was what she had worked so hard for, and yet without Jonathan… She had thought, really believed, that he would put any antagonism from the past behind him, that he would at least want to hear his own music being performed on stage.

She had been wrong…

But her parents were here, she told herself firmly as she walked on stage behind the still drawn curtains, arranging herself in the hospital bed. She owed so much to her parents. She would do this for them.

All her nerves disappeared as the curtain went up, professionalism taking over as she became Marion. It was an exacting role, with Marion's age ranging from twenty to seventy as the play progressed. But as the minutes, and then hours passed, Tory forgot everything but being Marion.

The emotional ending—Marion at seventy, sick and dying, finally reunited with the man she had loved fifty years earlier but given up in favour of her career—left the audience momentarily stunned. And then the thunderous applause threatened to take the roof off the theatre!

Curtain call after curtain call followed, with Stephen joining the cast on stage, and the audience unwilling to let any of them go.

A huge bouquet of mixed flowers, and another of red roses were presented to Tory before she was finally allowed to leave the stage, her tears of happiness blending with the fragrant blooms as she at last allowed herself to look up into the box that contained her parents.

Pride was too mild a word to describe the expressions on their faces. Her mother was openly crying; her father's beaming smile was threatening to split the sides of his mouth.

Tory waved to them before she finally left the stage. All of the cast were kissing and hugging each other now that their first night was over.

'You did it, Tory!' Stephen swept her up in his arms, swinging her round and round in his jubilation, the flowers becoming crushed between the two of them.

'*We* did it,' she corrected laughingly. 'None of us could have done it without you!'

'We all did it!' Stephen released her. 'We're going to run for months, Tory. Months and months!'

She had done it! Really, really done it! She had never known such exhilarated happiness in her life before. Only one thing could have increased her happiness—

No, she mustn't think about Jonathan now! He hadn't even sent a card or telephoned, let alone arrived here himself. Obviously his time on the Isle of Man was an interlude in his life he would rather forget.

As she must forget it…

Easier said than done, she realised as she at last escaped to her dressing room, not putting on the main lights, just staring at her own reflection in the mirror in the illumination of the single lamp. It seemed like only a matter of minutes had passed since she'd left here to go out on stage, whereas in reality it was over two hours ago. Two hours of nerve-racking bliss!

A small scream left her throat as a shadow moved in the darkness reflected behind her. One hand moved to clasp her throat, her eyes widening apprehensively as she turned to confront the intruder.

'Don't be alarmed, Tory,' drawled an achingly familiar voice. Jonathan stepped out of the shadows. 'I come in peace.'

Tory stared at him as if he were the ghost she had first imagined him to be. Where—? How—?

Jonathan gave a lop-sided smile, grey eyes light and smiling, the black evening suit and snowy white shirt he wore suiting his elegant masculinity.

His gaze moved to the array of flowers on the dressing table, his mouth quirking ruefully as he saw the crushed roses. 'You didn't like my flowers?' He raised one dark brow.

Tory blinked, still totally dazed by his unexpected presence here in her dressing room, then glanced at the crushed roses. She had assumed—but Jonathan had sent the red roses?

'You didn't think I would let your first night pass unrecognised, did you?' he said teasingly.

First, second, third and last, if she were honest with herself! But Jonathan was here, after all…

'You saw the play?' She at last managed to find her voice, although it sounded strangely disorientated even to her.

He nodded. 'I sat in the box with your parents.'

She shook her head, frowning. 'I didn't see you.'

'I should hope not,' Jonathan laughed softly. 'Your attention should all have been on stage!'

It had been. Only at the end had she looked up at her parents, and Jonathan hadn't been in the box with them then.

'I came backstage while you were enjoying your much deserved applause.' He seemed to guess some of her thoughts. 'I wanted to give you my congratulations in private,' he added huskily.

She swallowed hard, still totally unnerved at finding him here waiting for her. 'You should have been on stage with us, taking your own bow,' she murmured gruffly.

He shook his head. 'It's your night, Tory. Totally. Absolutely. Your parents are so proud of you,' he declared emotionally. 'As they have every right to be. Your decision to take the risk of a career change paid off, Tory,' he told her happily. 'You were wonderful!'

She drew in a ragged breath, feeling on the verge of tears again. She still couldn't believe he was here!

'How about you?' she prompted quietly. 'Have things worked out for you?' Her own schedule had been so busy the last six months that she hadn't even spoken to Madison on the telephone, let alone actually seen the other woman. Which meant she had heard no news of Jonathan, either…

'I—'

'Tory, you were wonderful!' her mother cried as her parents burst excitedly into the room, bringing Stephen and several other members of the cast in with them. The noise from outside indicated that the celebrations had already begun!

Tory hugged her mother, and then her father, all the time keeping an eye on Jonathan; if he should just leave now, without any further conversation between them—!

'Stephen!' She grabbed his arm as she saw Jonathan edging towards the door. 'That's the composer of our music over there.' She nodded in Jonathan's direction. 'I think he should stay and join the party, don't you?' she encouraged desperately. Jonathan was actually standing in the doorway now, preparing to leave.

'I certainly do,' Stephen agreed in understanding, before crossing the room to talk with the younger man.

Tory didn't see what happened after that. Her few minutes of what she had thought would be peace and quiet were obviously at an end, and more of the ecstatic cast spilled over into her room, blocking the door from view.

Glasses of champagne were thrust into her parents' hands, as well as her own, and the next half an hour was filled with everyone congratulating everyone else, all of them utterly convinced the show was a hit.

Jonathan seemed to have completely disappeared, but as Stephen was missing too Tory decided to think positively, rather than negatively. Jonathan simply couldn't have come all this way just to disappear again before the two of them had had time to say more than hello! Could he...?

'Time we all got changed, I think,' she decided firmly after that half an hour of jubilation. Her curiosity concerning Jonathan was turning to anxiety as the minutes passed without any further sign of him. 'After all, we have a party to go to!' she encouraged lightly as the rest of the cast slowly moved out of her room.

It wasn't until Tory was alone again in her dressing room that she realised she still had on her make-up for playing seventy-year-old Marion—a terminally ill Marion, at that!

What must Jonathan have thought? she groaned inwardly. He hadn't recognised her on the island as Victory Canan when she'd been dressed as Tory Buchanan, but with this aging make-up on, and her hair coloured grey, she wasn't recognisable as either of them—simply looked like an old woman. No wonder Jonathan had decided to beat a hasty retreat!

She reached out a hand and lightly touched the petals of one of the deep red roses Jonathan had had presented to her on stage—crushed red roses, she corrected sadly. Red roses, she knew, meant love, but she mustn't read too much into that. After all, Jonathan hadn't been able to wait to escape once he had given her his verbal congratulations…

The party was in full swing when she arrived at the club half an hour later with her parents, and the three of them were quickly pulled into a crowd of celebrating people.

'I only hope the critics agree with them,' Tory groaned, as Stephen brought his wife over to introduce her to Tory's mother and father.

'How could they possibly do otherwise?'

She turned sharply at the sound of Jonathan's voice, her heart leaping happily at the sight of his dearly familiar face. He had come to the party after all! 'That's the second time this evening your sudden appearance has almost given me a heart attack!' she teased.

He chuckled. 'Then let's hope it's the last time, too. And you need have no fear of the critics, Tory—you were sensational!'

To Tory it seemed as if they were the only two people in the room; all the surrounding noise and chatter faded into the background, only Jonathan was real to her. After dreaming about him for so long, it was a wonderful feeling!

She gave an inclination of her head. 'Thank you.'

He smiled. 'You're more than welcome,' he assured her warmly.

Tory didn't know what else to say to him. In her daydreams concerning him she had said all manner of things to him, explained so much, told him of her love for him. But, faced with the flesh and blood man, she felt completely tongue-tied. She couldn't say any of those things when she had no idea how he now felt about her!

'Didn't Tory do a wonderful job with your music, Jonathan?' Stephen joined them, putting a brotherly arm about her shoulders as he smiled at her beamingly.

Tory saw the way Jonathan's gaze narrowed as he took in that arm about her shoulders, her heart giving a leap as she realised he was not at all pleased by the familiarity.

'There will be a CD of the music released in the next few weeks, of course,' Stephen told the other man conversationally, completely unconcerned by that narrowed grey gaze. 'I hope you're ready for fame and fortune as a songwriter, Jonathan!'

'I doubt it will come to that,' the younger man drawled. 'After all, it's Tory who is the star here.'

'But you're clearly named in the programme as co-writer of the songs,' Stephen told him.

Tory felt the colour enter her cheeks as she saw Jonathan's eyes on her now. Well, what had he expected? That she would take all the credit for the music herself? Though the brief letter he had included in the parcel of music that morning on the island six months ago, had ordered, 'Keep them, Jonathan', that did not mean she had literally taken him at his word!

'Didn't you read the contract before signing it?' She looked concerned.

'I left my lawyers to deal with the details. I gave you the music, Tory, to do with what you would.' His eyes narrowed again as an idea occurred to him. 'Was it because of the music that you sent me the tickets for tonight's show?'

'I—'

'Excuse me, won't you?' Stephen cut in distractedly. 'There's a couple of reporters over there that I have to talk to.'

The silence left behind by Stephen's departure was even more uncomfortable than before. Earlier, Tory just hadn't known what to say to Jonathan—now she feared she had said too much!

'I thought you understood about the music.' She looked up at him frowningly, glad she no longer looked like an old woman in her stage make-up. Now her hair was loose and darkly shining, her black knee-length sequinned dress clinging lovingly to her slender curves.

'Understood what?' Jonathan rasped.

She shook her head. 'I couldn't just *take* it.'

'But I gave it to you.'

Tory gave a glimmer of a smile. 'To use, yes. I accept that. But I wouldn't take credit for something that I didn't do. And Stephen is right. When the album comes out you're going to be famous.'

'Great!' he muttered, his tone implying the opposite.

'Jonathan—' She broke off, biting her lip. 'How are things at home now?'

'"Things"?' he echoed dryly. 'Say what you really mean, Tory. The real question is—have I stopped feeling sorry for myself?'

She shook her head. 'No, I—'

'The answer to that is a definite yes!' he replied. 'You were one hundred per cent right about how my behaviour was affecting Malcolm. He is my father. He always has been. Despite the fame that you now say is imminent, I'm back in the family business where I belong. I have you to thank for showing me that,' he added warmly.

'Me?' She swallowed hard. 'Why me?' She looked up at him warily.

'Why didn't you tell me that night that you're adopted?' he probed softly.

She couldn't quite meet his gaze now. 'Who told you?'

'I read it somewhere—'

'Where?' she interrupted sharply; her adoption had been made much of at the beginning of her career, when fans had wanted to know everything about her, from what she ate for breakfast to what she wore in bed. But no one mentioned her adoption nowadays…

'Somewhere,' Jonathan repeated firmly. 'I must have sounded like a spoilt child to you that night, going on about what I didn't have and never could have—a personal knowledge of my real father—when all the time you had no idea who your father *or* your mother really were!'

'I never wanted to know. But I realise not everyone is the same.'

'I've made my peace with Malcolm and Gideon. I was a fool ever to have let that strained situation develop in the first place. But I was just so caught up in my own self-absorption; it took someone independent of the situation to tell me that.'

'Me!' She grimaced as she remembered the things she had said to him that night.

'You. Don't look so worried, Tory,' he grinned at her. 'You did me a big favour by talking to me so—'

'Bluntly?' she put in apologetically.

'Truthfully,' he corrected. 'So, your change of career is obviously going to be a success, Tory,' he continued briskly. 'I suppose we can also expect to hear wedding bells in the near future, too?'

'Wedding bells…?' she echoed dazedly.

Jonathan looked around the crowded room. 'I must say I'm surprised Montgomery isn't already here, helping you celebrate. I expect he'll be along later—'

'He hasn't been invited,' Tory said firmly. 'I can't imagine what made you think he would be. Our parting was—acrimonious, to say the least!' She pulled a face at the memory of the slanging match that had ensued on the one occasion she had agreed to meet Rupert after beginning rehearsals for the play.

'Parting?' Jonathan repeated. 'But I thought— I saw a

photograph of the two of you together in the newspapers about four months ago. You were just leaving a restaurant together.'

Minutes before the slanging match had begun!

She remembered those photographs: Rupert and Tory smiling for the cameras, neither of them willing to add fuel to the fire of the rumour that the two of them hadn't parted company on the best of terms. It hadn't occurred to her that Jonathan would have seen those photographs, too—and put a completely different interpretation on them!

'I—'

'Tory, the press would like some photographs,' Stephen came over to tell her a little breathlessly, obviously overwhelmed by the positive reaction to his play. 'You too, Jonathan.' He smiled.

'I think I'll give the photo-call a miss, if you don't mind,' Jonathan drawled.

'But I do mind.' Stephen grasped Tory in one hand and Jonathan in the other, walking them determinedly over to where the press waited for them.

Tory was grateful for her director's doggedness, though barely aware of the photographs being taken, the interview that was given. All her chaotic thoughts centred on Jonathan. Had he really thought she and Rupert were still an item? Could that possibly be why she hadn't heard from him personally during the last six months?

She accepted it was rather a big leap in her thought processes, but now that she had actually seen Jonathan again, realised her love for him was as deep as ever, that hope was all that she had!

'Let's go and grab some champagne,' Jonathan whispered when they were at least free to escape and go and sit down.

Minutes later Tory eyed him curiously over the rim of

her champagne glass. 'You hated all that, didn't you?' she said slowly; his impatience and uncomfortableness during the taking of the photographs and the interview had been more than obvious.

'Was it that obvious?'

'I'm afraid so.'

'Strange, really,' he reflected wistfully. 'Part of the problem I've had the last two years—since Madison married Gideon,' he began to explain, 'with the necessity of coming to terms with John Byrne as my father, Gideon as my brother—was that I suddenly felt a partial outsider. They're all so damned artistically talented—'

'But so are you,' Tory protested. 'Your music is beautiful,' she added with feeling.

'Thank you,' he drawled self-mockingly. 'The irony is, Tory, now that I've actually achieved some sort of artistic recognition, according to you and Stephen, I could as well do without it!'

'Don't just take our word for it,' Tory said in reply. 'When the reviews come out tomorrow the musical score is going to receive as much acclaim as the play itself.'

Jonathan paused before taking a much-needed sip of his own champagne.

'When do you return to America?' Tory asked as lightly as she could manage—his answer meant so much to her! If he was going back home to America in the near future, then she doubted there would be much opportunity for them to meet again. But if he was staying on for a few days—or weeks!—she might, by using the play as a talking point, be able to persuade him to at least have lunch with her. Anything would be better than her totally lacking-Jonathan life of the last six months!

Jonathan's expression was suddenly guarded. 'Not for some time,' he answered abruptly.

'Oh?' God, how difficult it was for her to keep her excitement in check!

'We've recently taken over a casino in England, and I'm in charge of making the changes and refurbishments needed,' Jonathan explained casually. 'Tory, the tickets you sent to America, for me to come to the play this evening, were forwarded on to me here; I've been living in London for the last two months.'

Strange how that bubble of excitement could so easily be burst!

Two months!

Jonathan had been in London for two months, and he hadn't so much as telephoned her...!

She moistened suddenly dry lips. 'I see.'

He looked at her with narrowed grey eyes. 'Do you?'

'I think so,' she sighed.

'Somehow I doubt that.' Jonathan shook his head disbelievingly. 'Tory, I behaved very badly during that week on the Isle of Man. I was arrogant, insulting, judgmental, prejudiced,' he concluded self-disgustedly.

'And?'

He laughed huskily, laughter lines beside his eyes and mouth now. 'Isn't that enough to be going on with?'

She shook her head, her hair moving silkily on her shoulders. 'I didn't mean it that way! Possibly you were all of those things—I'll take your word for it,' she said brightly as he would have spoken. 'But, in the circumstances, those emotions were understandable.'

Jonathan shook his head. 'No, they weren't,' he insisted grimly. 'And it's because they weren't that—' He broke off abruptly, scowling darkly.

'Yes?' Tory was sitting on the edge of her seat now, desperate for him to say something—anything!—that would give her the courage to say the things she wanted to.

'You've obviously been busy with the play the last six months—'

'Even so, I've had some leisure time,' she protested.

'I thought that was spent with Montgomery!'

'And now that you know it wasn't?'

Jonathan exhaled sharply. 'I had no right—'

'You had every right!' she cried emotionally, tense in her seat now. 'Jonathan, I don't believe that you know me so little, that you're so caught up in my Victory Canan persona, that you aren't well aware of the fact that I do not go around making love with men I care nothing about!'

'We didn't make love,' he denied.

'As good as!'

'No, Tory,' he gave a wistful smile. 'Believe me, if the two of us had made love, there would be no "as good as" about it!'

It was that wistfulness that gave her the courage to say her next words. 'I have no idea, Jonathan,' she told him. 'You see—' she raised her head to meet his gaze unflinchingly '—my parents brought me up to believe that love is the most necessary ingredient to any intimate relationship. Which is why the closest I've ever come to making love with any man was that one time with you.'

The jolt her words had given him was clearly visible. He was obviously taken aback, his gaze searching on her now flushed face. 'Tory...?' he finally managed gruffly.

'Jonathan.' She physically couldn't say any more than his name—wondered if she had already said too much.

He swallowed hard. 'I—will you meet me tomorrow? Have lunch with me?'

Her breath caught in her throat, her pulse racing as she gambled everything on the next few words. 'Every day of my life, if you want me to.' Tears swam in her deep blue eyes.

Something like pain flashed across Jonathan's face, his eyes dark with that same pain. 'Tory, what have I done to us these last six months?' he groaned achingly.

Well, at least he hadn't openly rejected her! 'Wasted time?' She looked at him tearfully.

He looked around them, obviously suddenly impatient with the noise and people that surrounded them. 'Are you going to mind if I take you out of here for a while?' he asked throatily. 'I have an urgent need to kiss you until neither of us can stand up!' He put his champagne glass down on the table before reaching out and taking both her hands in his. 'Tory, I believe I have been incredibly stupid the last six months, but I would dearly like to rectify that!'

She gave a choked laugh. 'Rectify away,' she invited emotionally.

He stood up, pulling her close against him. 'Before I do that, I would like to accept your earlier offer.' He gazed down at her intently. 'Marry me, Victory Buchanan!'

Tory gulped, staring up at him disbelievingly. 'Do you mean it?' she finally managed to gasp.

'With every breath in my body!' he assured her vehemently, his arms tightening about her. 'These last six months have been a living hell. A time when I didn't dare even begin to hope that you might return my feelings for you.'

'Feelings...?' she repeated wonderingly.

'I love you, Tory,' he told her fiercely. 'I think I have from the moment I saw you at the airport!'

'You were furious when you realised I was there to meet you at Madison's request!' she protested half-heartedly. Jonathan loved her! It was more than she had ever hoped for...!

'That wasn't the first moment I saw you, Tory.' He rested his forehead on hers, grey eyes gazing into hers. 'I noticed you the moment I came through from baggage reclaim, and I was totally bowled over by the way you looked. That's probably the reason why I didn't see the huge placard you were holding up with my name on it!' he groaned with self-derision.

Tory looked up at him with love-filled eyes. 'No one would ever have guessed,' she said, her heart singing, her pulse racing. Jonathan loved her!

'No, well...' He gave a self-conscious grimace. 'I had come to the island to think—not be totally mesmerised by a black-haired, blue-eyed witch called Tory Buchanan!'

She laughed, her arms about his waist as she rested her head against his chest, instantly aware of his own racing heartbeat. 'That morning you came to the farm, as Rupert was leaving— He isn't important to me, Jonathan. He never has been,' she assured him as she felt the sudden tension in his body. 'We heard on the television later that evening that a girl rider had been killed that morning. Did you—?'

'God, yes...!' Jonathan confirmed raggedly. 'I heard it on the radio. They weren't giving out the woman's name until the family had been informed, and when I telephoned the farm to see if you were there, there was no answer. My imagination went into overdrive! I was terrified it might have been you!' He began to shake at the memory.

'And then when you arrived at the farm it was to find Rupert kissing me,' Tory acknowledged disgustedly. 'That kiss was solely for your benefit, Jonathan. Rupert considered me to be a piece of property that he owned.' She shuddered. 'The photograph you saw of the two of us in the newspaper four months ago was the last occasion on which I saw him—and told him exactly what he could do with the new contract he wanted me to sign with his agency.'

'I'm glad.' Jonathan's arm tightened about her. 'You haven't answered my question yet, Miss Buchanan,' he reminded her.

'Question?' she repeated lightly, wondering if she had ever felt this happy in her life before, and knowing with certainty that she hadn't. 'Well, if I'm going to have lunch with you for the rest of my life, I think it would be nice if we were married to each other first—don't you?' She looked up at him glowingly.

'I can't promise to wait that long—'

'Tory! Jonathan! Come and join the party,' Tory's father invited happily as he strolled over to join them.

'I can wait if you can,' Tory told Jonathan, knowing her parents would be very disappointed if she were to disappear now.

He nodded. 'I've waited all my life for you—I can wait a few hours more!' he murmured, before turning to face her father. 'There's something I need to ask you, Dan...' He turned to wink at Tory before turning his attention back to the older man.

Tory grinned as she stood at his side while he asked her father for her hand in marriage.

Marriage!

She was going to marry the man she loved!

This truly was the happiest night of her life.

So far...

[illegible]

[illegible] mingled [illegible]

[illegible] She repeated [illegible] wandering [illegible] had [illegible]

[illegible]

VIRGIN MISTRESS

by
Kay Thorpe

Kay Thorpe was born in Sheffield in 1935. She tried out a variety of jobs after leaving school. Writing began as a hobby, becoming a way of life only after she had her first completed novel accepted for publication in 1968. Since then, she's written over sixty books and lives now with her husband, son, German shepherd dog and lucky black cat on the outskirts of Chesterfield in Derbyshire. Her interests include reading, hiking, and travel.

CHAPTER ONE

'I'M AFRAID that's it,' said the solicitor with regret. 'The house is mortgaged up to the hilt, and what's left of the contents can be worth very little.'

'So I'll get a job,' Erin declared, grasping at straws. 'We'll manage!'

'At nineteen, with no particular qualifications, you'd find it difficult to obtain any employment that would provide you and your sister with an adequate living,' came the wry reply. 'It's fortunate that I was able to trace your uncle's whereabouts. He—'

'Samantha's uncle,' Erin cut in. 'I'm only a stepdaughter.'

'In the eyes of the law, that still makes you family. I'm sure Mr Carson will see it that way.'

If Nicholas Carson was anything at all like his brother, Erin reflected, he would probably be reluctant enough to assume responsibility even for Sam, who was at least his own kith and kin, much less herself, who was no relation whatsoever. Not that she wanted *anyone* assuming responsibility for her, if it came to that.

Mr Gordon was right, though, she was bound to concede. Even if she could find a job, there was little if any chance of her being able to provide for the two of them. The thought of being parted from her half-sister was distressing, to say the least, but Sam's welfare had to come before any other consideration. If her uncle had refused point-blank to be involved in his late brother's affairs—as he might have done after so many years estrangement—she could possibly have been taken into care. Anything had to be better than that!

Watching the play of expression across the young face opposite, John Gordon could only admire the girl's apparent fortitude. A typical teenager, he had judged on first seeing her—fair hair long and loose about features bare of makeup, slender body clad in jeans and sweater. Widely spaced and thickly fringed, the vivid blue eyes belied that impression, registering a strength of character in advance of her years.

'I don't think the receivers will be pressing for an immediate vacation of the house,' he added, getting back to the matter in hand, 'but the sooner you start sorting things out the better. It would probably be easiest to bring in a house clearance firm to give you an overall price on what's left of the furnishings, though Mr Carson will want to go through his brother's personal belongings himself, I imagine. He'll be here before the end of the week.'

By which time she would need to have some idea of her own movements, Erin concluded, although quite what she was going to do she had little real notion as yet. Somewhere to live would be a first priority.

Unexpected though it had been, her stepfather's death had left no particular void in her life. They had never been close at the best of times, and since her mother had gone they'd become even further apart. Not that he'd given his own daughter that much attention either. So far as David Carson had been concerned, the two of them were a liability he could well have done without.

'How did you manage to find Mr Carson?' she asked curiously. 'So far as I know, there hadn't been any contact between him and my stepfather for years.'

'The gallery where he exhibits in town put me in touch with his agent, who then got him to contact me.

Unfortunately, by the time he did, it was too late for him to make the funeral.'

'I don't suppose he felt it mattered whether he was there or not,' Erin murmured, trying to be impartial about it. 'He's quite well known, isn't he?'

'More than quite, I'd say,' returned the solicitor. 'I'm not into art myself, but his work is considered exceptional by those who are. He's still only young too.'

Maybe to him, thought Erin, but from her viewpoint thirty-four was already more than halfway over the hill! The ten years between the two brothers could have had a lot to do with the bust-up, she supposed. Nicholas wouldn't have been all that much older than she was now when he took off on his own. From what little she knew about it, there had been money involved. No surprises there. Money no doubt played as important a role in his life as it had in her stepfather's. It was losing it all that had caused the latter's heart attack, she was sure.

'Do you think Barbados is going to be a suitable place for a fourteen-year-old to live?' she asked. 'I mean, there's school, for instance.'

'By all accounts, schools on the island are as good as you'll find anywhere.' John Gordon hesitated. 'On the other hand, Mr Carson might see a good boarding-school as a better solution. After all, at his age, and unmarried, he's hardly in an ideal position to take on full-time supervision of a fourteen-year-old. I'm not even sure Barbados is his permanent home.' His voice briskened. 'Anyway, those are things to be decided when he gets here. I'm sure he'll do what's best all round.'

Erin only wished she could be as sure. Sam would hate boarding-school. Not that being transported thousands of miles to a new home among total strangers would be any picnic for her either. But there was no point getting in a twist about it at this stage, she told herself staunchly. No point getting in a twist about anything until they knew what was in store.

Held up by traffic, she was ten minutes late reaching the school, and was relieved to find her sister still waiting. Left to her own devices, Samantha was capable of begging a lift from any likely-looking source rather than take the somewhat roundabout bus route home, heedless of any possible danger.

Like Erin herself, she took after their mother in looks, fair hair caught up in a swinging ponytail, blue eyes vivid in a face just beginning to reveal the fine boning beneath. Erin had done her best to make up for the lack of parental caring, but there was no real substitute, as she knew to her own cost.

'I thought you were never going to get here!' the younger girl complained lightly, climbing into the car they were soon to lose along with the rest. 'What did Mr Gordon say?'

'Nothing we hadn't already worked out for ourselves,' Erin acknowledged, seeing no point in being anything but straight about it. 'It's all gone, Sam. House, money—everything.'

'Well, Dad never gave us much money, so that isn't going to make a lot of difference,' came the unperturbed response. 'Melanie says her mum gets money from the post office every week, and the council gave them a house. We could do the same, couldn't we?'

If it was only as simple as that, thought Erin wryly.

'I don't think our situation is quite the same,' she said. 'In any case, we have to find out what your uncle has in mind when he gets here. Officially he's your guardian. That means we have to do whatever he says.'

Samantha looked mutinous. 'I don't need a guardian! You've always looked after me. Why can't you now?'

'I don't have the means,' Erin acknowledged with an inner sigh. 'Your uncle has.'

'If he's got lots of money, he could buy us a new house!'

'There's a bit more to it than that, I'm afraid.' Erin sought an upbeat note. 'How about calling at Halson's for some chocolate eclairs?'

Blue eyes lit up. 'Can we afford them?'

'No, but who cares?' declared her sister recklessly. 'Let's live for the moment!'

They bought six, and devoured the lot at a sitting on reaching the house they could no longer regard as home. A five-bedroomed detached in this area should fetch a fair price, Erin considered as she washed up the tea things after they'd finished eating. Whether whatever it did fetch would be enough to clear her stepfather's debts was another matter. Hardly her concern anyway, thank heaven. She had other things to worry about.

The two of them spent a quiet evening watching television. Samantha took herself off to bed around ten without being urged for once, leaving Erin to mull over those same concerns without reaching any useful conclusions. In the words of one of her favourite fictional heroines, tomorrow was another day, she decided philosophically in the end. A good night's sleep, and everything would look better.

As so often happened, by the time she had got herself ready for bed she was wide awake again. With the idea that a cup of hot chocolate might help her sleep, she went down to the kitchen to heat some milk, not bothering to put on a dressing gown over her short cotton nightdress.

It had started to rain, she realised, hearing the patter against the kitchen window. Good for the garden, which was suffering from the unusually dry spring. Not that it was going to be her problem for very much longer, of course.

She had her foot on the bottom tread of the stairs when

she heard the sound of a car engine, along with the unmistakable crunch of tyres on the gravel drive. Headlights flashed across the glass panes of the outer door as the vehicle took the curve to draw up in front of the house.

There was a short pause, the sound of voices, then a dark shape loomed beyond the glass and the bell push was depressed with what Erin considered a totally unnecessary vigour, considering that a light was still on. There was only one person this caller could be, only one person they were expecting—though not quite this soon, it had to be admitted.

Setting the mug of chocolate down on the flat square top of the newel post, she padded across the carpet to open the door, fingers already sliding the bolt before caution took over and halted the motion. The figure out there was certainly male, but that was all she could be sure of.

'Who is it?' she asked.

'Nick Carson,' came the anticipated answer. 'Open up, will you? I'm getting wet out here.'

Rain tends to do that, it was on the tip of her tongue to retort, but she bit it back. This was no time to get smart. She finished sliding the bolt, and turned the key, drawing the door towards her with more than a little reluctance to admit the man who held Sam's immediate future in his hands.

He signalled to the taxi to go before stepping forward into the light, towering over her for a moment as he brushed past to deposit a suitcase on the hall floor. Closing the door again, Erin turned with her back to it in a stance instinctively wary as she viewed strongly carved features. Taller by two or three inches than her stepfather, who himself had been close to six feet, he resembled him only in the colour of his eyes, which were grey, and the thick dark hair. A stronger personality altogether, she judged, meeting the penetrative gaze. Whether that meant stronger in fibre was something else.

'Taking it that you're a mite older than fourteen,' he remarked, running an assessing glance over her, 'who exactly are *you*?'

'I'm Samantha's half-sister,' she said. 'Didn't Mr Gordon tell you about me?'

'I'd hardly be asking if he had,' was the dry response. 'All I got from him was that my brother had died, leaving a fourteen-year-old daughter without a penny. Half-sister, you say?'

'My mother married your brother when I was four. Sam was born the year after.'

He studied the dewiness of her skin, the soft curve of her mouth and the long, straight curtain of fair hair, his lips taking on a slant. 'I'd have gone for maybe sixteen rather than nineteen. Do you usually wander about the house in your nightdress?'

'Only at night,' she said, refusing to be self-conscious about a garment she knew was no more revealing than the average mini-dress. 'Lucky I came down for a drink. Otherwise I'd have probably been asleep by now.'

'In which case I'd have had to waken you.' He made an abrupt movement. 'There's obviously a whole lot I haven't been told. Supposing we go somewhere more comfortable? I've been travelling most of the day.'

'If you're tired, we could always leave things till morning,' Erin suggested hopefully, looking for a reprieve.

'We'll sort it out now,' he stated unequivocally. 'I need to know just what's expected of me.'

'So far as I'm concerned, nothing,' she assured him. 'I can take care of myself.' She started forward, pausing as a thought struck her. 'Did you want something to eat?'

He shook his head. 'I ate on the plane.' His glance

shifted to the mug resting on the newel post. 'Better bring that along before it goes cold.'

Erin went to retrieve it, toes curling into the carpet pile. She rarely wore shoes around the house, much less slippers, but she regretted the lack right now. Children ran about barefoot, not adults. No wonder this man doubted her age.

Stripped of all items of any real value, the living room looked denuded. Nick Carson made no comment, though his expression spoke volumes. Erin switched on a couple of lamps and turned off the overhead light in an effort to soften the effect, curling into a chair the way she usually did, with bare legs tucked under her, as her step-uncle—if there was such a title—took a seat on the sofa.

He was dressed fairly casually, she noted, though not in any arty fashion, the dark tan trousers and lighter cord jacket conservative, if anything, in cut. On the surface, not at all what she had anticipated, but there was a lot more to people than their outward appearance.

'What exactly do you intend doing about Sam?' she asked.

The directness of the question drew a lift of one dark brow. 'Not backward in coming forward, are you?'

'Not backward in anything, I hope,' she retorted, with no intention of allowing herself to be browbeaten. 'I'm naturally concerned about what's going to happen to her.'

'And what about you?'

'I've told you, *I* can take care of myself.'

'Does that mean you already have plans made?'

Erin lifted her shoulders in a gesture meant to convey a total lack of concern. 'Nothing specific as yet.'

'You have money of your own?'

'No,' she was bound to admit, much against her will. 'But I can always get a job.'

'Doing what exactly?'

'Children's nanny, for instance,' she improvised, unable

to think of anything else on the spur of the moment. 'A live-in nanny,' she added, warming to the idea.

'Without qualifications or experience?'

Blue eyes held grey unwaveringly. 'I've had plenty of practice looking after Sam.'

'There's a lot of difference between keeping an eye on a kid sister and taking care of a child or children full-time,' Nick pointed out. 'You're hardly more than a kid yourself, if it comes to that.'

A spark lit the blue. 'It isn't just a matter of years. And kids, by the way, are young goats.'

'I stand corrected.' There was a hint of amusement in the brief widening of the firm mouth. 'Is Samantha as self-assured as you?'

Erin kept her tone easy with an effort. 'We can both stand up for ourselves, if that's what you mean. And you still didn't say what you intend doing about her.'

'I'm hardly going to be making any hard and fast decisions at this point,' he returned. 'As I said, there's a lot I need to know first. About your mother, for instance. What—?'

'She was killed in a plane crash a few years ago,' Erin interjected without emotion. 'Along with the man she was running off with, who was piloting it. I left school to keep house.'

'Your own idea, or my brother's?'

Slender shoulders lifted in another brief shrug. 'There wasn't much alternative.'

'He could have hired a housekeeper and allowed you to complete your education.'

'At a cost. Anyway, I didn't like the idea of some stranger taking over.' Still don't, she could have added.

'At least with me there's a blood tie,' he said, apparently able to read minds. 'Not that I'm in seventh heaven myself over the situation. I'm surprised David would have bothered to name me as next of kin to start with.'

'He had to name someone, I suppose, and you're all there is.' Erin hesitated, wondering if it was too soon to voice the suggestion she had been turning over in her mind all evening. Better sooner than later, she decided, though a little subtlety wouldn't go amiss.

'I can understand how difficult it would be for you to have Sam to live with you,' she began. 'I mean, being on your own, and all that.'

There was a quizzical expression in the grey eyes. 'What makes you so sure I live alone?'

'Mr Gordon said you weren't married.'

'And I'd have to be, of course, to have a woman living with me?'

Erin bit her lip, feeling a complete idiot. How naive could you get? She made an effort to cover up the momentary embarrassment, voice as toneless as she could make it. 'So would your…partner be willing to accept a fourteen-year-old addition to the household?'

'I didn't say I had one,' he returned. 'I've yet to meet the woman I could live with full-time.'

'The problem might be finding a woman who could live with *you* full-time!' Erin flung at him in sudden surging antagonism.

'Possibly,' he agreed with infuriating calm. 'You were saying?'

Erin took a hold of herself, already regretting letting fly that way. There was something about this man that made her feel all keyed-up and on edge, but giving way to it was hardly going to help convince him of her fitness to be left in full charge of his niece.

'I'm sorry,' she got out. 'I shouldn't have spoken to you like that.'

'Why not?' he asked. 'You're entitled to say whatever

you like, providing it isn't slanderous.' The pause was pointed, the grey eyes too perceptive by half. 'You were going to suggest I consider leaving Samantha in your care, I believe? With some financial aid to boot, of course.'

'For her, not me.' Erin set herself to recover lost ground. 'And only until I was in a position to support us both. She's doing well at school,' she said, mentally crossing her fingers. 'It would be a shame to uproot her. We could rent a furnished flat for the time being—there are always plenty advertised in the paper.' Legs uncurled, she was poised on the edge of her seat, eyes fired with enthusiasm for her cause. 'It would be better for Sam, and for you too. It *has* to be!'

There was a certain calculation in Nick Carson's regard, as if he were weighing up what she had said. When he spoke, it was with dry deliberation. 'I think this would be better discussed in the morning after all—without the distractions.'

Having totally forgotten how she was dressed, it took Erin a moment to glean his meaning. Colour tinged her cheeks as she looked down to see the way her nightdress had ridden up, exposing a length of slender thigh.

'You do have *some* inhibitions, then,' he commented as she pulled the material hastily down again. 'I was beginning to wonder.'

'There wasn't much point in my coming all over coy when you'd already seen me,' Erin responded with what sangfroid she could muster. 'Anyway, I shouldn't have thought you'd find a bit of bare leg so hard to ignore—especially when it belongs to someone you see as little more than a kid!'

'I shouldn't have thought so either.' Nick sounded amused again. 'Nothing throws you for long, does it?'

'Not unless it's important.' She put up an automatic hand

to push the hair back from her face, wishing she had something handy to tie it with. 'So what do you think?'

'About what?'

Erin drew a hard breath, suspecting him of playing with her. 'About what I was saying just now, of course!'

'Oh, yes, your considered plan for the future.' He shook his head. 'No go, I'm afraid.'

'Why not?' she demanded, hopes crashing about her ears. 'If it's the cost, I'd guarantee to pay you back as soon—'

'It isn't about money.' His tone was peremptory. 'What you're proposing is a long way from what I'd consider a suitable solution to the problem.'

Erin looked at him helplessly, recognising adamancy when she heard it. Sitting there, broad of shoulder and square of jaw, he looked the proverbial immovable object, with her force, it seemed, far from irresistible.

'So what *would* you consider a suitable solution?' she asked.

The shrug was brief. 'We'll talk about it in the morning, after I meet Samantha herself.'

He got to his feet in one smooth movement, the open jacket revealing a lean hipline and taut waist. Gazing up at him, Erin was aware of a sudden stirring deep down in the pit of her stomach. She wasn't backward enough not to recognise physical chemistry at work, although she would never have anticipated feeling any attraction whatsoever towards a man of Nicholas Carson's age. He was almost old enough to be her father, for heaven's sake!

'I just realised I don't even know your name,' he said, snapping her out of it.

'Erin,' she told him. 'Erin Grainger.'

The dark brows drew together. 'Was it your own choice to keep your father's name?'

'Mother's name,' she corrected impassively. 'I never knew who my father was.'

'David could have adopted you.'

'He didn't want to. At least he never made any attempt. I imagine he felt he'd done enough marrying Mum.'

Nick's expression was difficult to judge. 'He must have had some feeling for her.'

'I suppose.' Erin rose abruptly, unwilling to discuss the matter any further. 'I'll need to make up the bed for you. Like I said, we weren't expecting you before the weekend. It will only take a few minutes.'

'I may as well come up with you, then,' he said. 'It isn't exactly a welcoming atmosphere down here.'

Erin could hardly deny it. She led the way, self-conscious as she climbed the stairs with him close at her back. The room he was to have was next door to her own. She paused on the way to take clean sheets and a duvet cover from the linen cupboard on the landing.

'I'm afraid there's little more than the basics left in here either,' she said apologetically, opening the bedroom door. 'I didn't know whether you'd want to go through your brother's things yourself, so I left everything as it was. His personal papers are in that suitcase in the corner. The study furniture went to auction.'

'So long as there's a mattress on the bed, I dare say I can manage,' Nick advised. 'I'll have a look through the paperwork in the morning, but the rest can go straight to charity.'

He dropped the travel bag he was carrying on the floor as Erin shook open the bottom sheet to spread it across the double bed, moving forward to take the far side and pull it straight meeting her surprised glance with an ironic smile. 'I'm not above lending a woman a hand with household chores on the odd occasion.'

'A woman now, am I?' she retorted, sensing ridicule. 'That's what I call quick promotion!'

'General terminology,' he returned smoothly. 'Sling the duvet cover across and we'll each tackle our own corners.'

Erin did so, irritated beyond measure when he completed his part of the task before her. Having had no help in the house these past three years, she was used to doing things her own way, and resented his interference. Resented his being here at all. They would have managed somehow without him.

Leaving one of her corners unfilled, in what she knew was a thoroughly childish gesture, she straightened to indicate the other door leading from the room. 'That's the *en suite* bathroom. You'll find towels in the cupboard.' She hesitated before adding, 'You do realise that apart from a few odds and ends there isn't going to be anything left?'

Nick inclined his head. 'I gathered as much. My brother was always one for putting his eggs in one basket. He was lucky to last as long as he did without coming to grief.' He left it there, lifting his shoulders in a dismissive gesture that suggested regret over having said as much as he had. 'I'll make a start in the morning. Right now, I'm all for getting my head down.'

It was gone midnight, Erin realised, catching a glimpse of the bedside clock that hadn't been deemed worth enough to bother with by the bailiffs. Sleep was the last thing on her mind all the same; there was far too much to think about.

'I'll leave you to it, then,' she said shortly. 'I'm usually up by seven, but don't feel obligated to do the same.'

She moved to the door, pausing there as a thought struck her. 'About Samantha? Did you want her to stay home from school tomorrow?'

'It might be an idea,' Nick agreed. 'Give us an opportunity to get to know one another.'

A day was hardly going to be long enough for that, it was on the tip of Erin's tongue to observe, but she bit it back. There was still a glimmer of hope that he would come round to seeing things her way in the end—especially after meeting Sam and realising she was far from the pliant little thing he probably visualised. Acting like a responsible adult herself would be a good start.

'We can both of us only be grateful that you didn't decide to opt out altogether,' she said. 'Some men would have done.'

Hoisting the travel bag onto the bed to open it, Nick gave a short laugh. 'You knowing so much about men, of course.'

Erin caught herself up before the pithy reply could take shape on her lips; she had a feeling she might be exercising more and more restraint over the coming few days.

'I count myself a fair judge of character,' she said levelly instead. 'I'm sure you must have had good reason to part company with my stepfather. See you in the morning,' she added swiftly, and closed the door before he could answer.

She'd left the hot chocolate downstairs after all that, she realised on the landing. Not that it would be hot any longer. She briefly contemplated going down again to reheat it, but doubted if it was going to help her get to sleep anyway.

What she needed to do was replan her whole approach—to convince that doubting Thomas in there that she was capable of making a life right here for Samantha. He didn't really want her himself; that was obvious. She couldn't blame him for it either. What confirmed bachelor in his thirties *would* welcome the idea of taking on a fourteen-year-old?

There was no sound from Sam's room. Finding her uncle already in residence when she got up was going to be a surprise, but she wasn't easily thrown. He might get a surprise himself when he met her, and realised just how adult she could be for her age.

Always providing, of course, that she didn't take an instant dislike to her only living blood relative and act accordingly. She could, Erin was forced to acknowledge, be a total brat when the mood came over her. An early warning might be advisable.

In her own room, she stood for a moment by the door, listening for any sound from the next room, but none reached her. He would be in the bathroom on the far side, she guessed. At least that was still fully equipped. She had a sudden mind's-eye vision of that tall, lean body stripped of all clothing, and felt that same curling sensation deep down in the pit of her stomach. She had seen the naked male form in art works, but this was a different feeling altogether.

He's old enough to be your father, a small voice reminded her. Unlikely, maybe, but certainly possible. She dismissed the image forcefully, settling instead on what she knew of his background. The brothers had been left equal shares in their father's estate. David had wanted the younger man to join him in business ventures, but Nick had refused and gone his own way. Erin couldn't lay any blame at his door for that; given the choice herself, she would have done the same. What she could neither understand nor condone was the total lack of contact between the two of them since.

For her stepfather to have failed to appeal for financial help during the final crisis was beyond understanding too; he had certainly tried every other avenue. Unless he had, of course, as a last resort, and been turned down. That thought hadn't occurred to her before.

Was the man next door capable of refusing to help his own brother out of desperate straits? Erin cogitated. He came across as a tough nut to crack, but would he really be that ruthless? Without asking him outright, she was hardly likely to ever know.

In bed, though far from sleep, she lay listening to the rain on the windows, wondering what the fates had in store. Life would be simpler, she supposed, if Nick Carson did take Samantha back to Barbados with him, but the parting would be hard.

Not that worrying about it was going to make any difference, she concluded wryly. The ultimate decision rested entirely with him.

CHAPTER TWO

THE alarm jerked Erin from a sleep that had held a quality of exhaustion. Stretching out a hasty arm, she switched the sound off, hoping it wouldn't have disturbed the occupant of the room next door. She needed to warn Sam before Nick put in an appearance.

As always, her sister was still dead to the world, head burrowed deep beneath the covers. She came awake with reluctance when urged, pulling an indignant face when she saw the time.

'It's only just gone seven!' she exclaimed grumpily. 'I don't get up till half past!'

'Usually,' Erin agreed. 'Today's different. We have a visitor.'

Samantha looked at her blankly for a moment, then in dawning realisation. 'He got here already?'

'Late last night.'

The younger girl sat up, all thoughts of sleep flown. 'So what's he like?'

'Tall, dark, and bossy.'

Samantha grimaced again. 'Sounds just like Dad!'

'Well, they are brothers.' Erin kept her tone light. 'He wants you to stay off school today so you can start getting to know one another.'

Blue eyes brightened immediately. 'Things are looking up already!'

Don't count on it, Erin wanted to tell her, but some things were better left unspoken. Sam would find out what was in store for her soon enough.

'It will look better if we're both of us up and dressed by

the time he surfaces,' she said instead. 'I'll take first shower, then I can be fixing breakfast while you get yourself organised. Just don't use the day off school as an excuse to go back to sleep again,' she added, knowing her sister only too well. 'If you're not out by the time I finish, I'll throw a jug of water over you!'

'You're the one who'll finish up with a load of wet bedding to deal with if you do,' was the prompt response.

Which was true enough, Erin conceded. She left her to it, and went back to her own room to collect some clothes before making for the bathroom. The master bedroom door was firmly closed. She hoped it would remain that way a good while longer.

It was a fine sunny morning after last night's rain. Erin felt her spirits lift when she opened the bathroom window to admit the myriad of scents of an English spring. Perhaps Uncle Nick would prove a little more amenable to suggestion after a good night's sleep. He might even have come to recognise the advantages for himself.

There was still no sign of movement from the newcomer's room when she emerged. Samantha, she was pleased to find on popping her head round the door, was actually out of bed and ready to take her place in the bathroom.

'Make it quick as you can,' she urged. 'I want to be finished eating before your uncle puts in an appearance. He'll probably want the works.'

'You could present him with the frying pan and let him do his own.' Samantha grinned at the look on her sister's face. 'Start as you mean to go on—isn't that what you're always telling me?'

Erin grinned back. 'Telling and doing are two different things. Anyway, he's hopefully not going to be here long enough for any patterns to be set.'

She clung to that thought as she headed for the stairs.

The last thing he was surely going to want was an extended stay. Time was in short supply in any case. The house had to be cleared before it was put on the market, and the bank wasn't going to wait much longer.

With breakfast the first thing on the agenda, she made straight for the kitchen, coming to a disconcerted stop in the doorway on seeing Nick Carson seated at the central table with a mug of coffee to hand and the daily newspaper she hadn't yet got around to cancelling propped against the coffeepot.

He looked up from his perusal of same on her entrance, taking in every aspect of the slender young body revealed by close-fitting jeans and a pale blue T-shirt.

'A bit more circumspect than last night's outfit,' he commented.

'People who drop in unexpectedly have to take as they find,' Erin returned, struggling to retain an outer composure at least. 'I didn't think you'd be up yet.'

'I was awake at six.' He looked beyond her. 'What time is Samantha likely to surface?'

'She'll be down in a minute.' Erin stirred herself to move on into the kitchen. 'Assuming you didn't eat yet, what would you like?'

'Cereals, fruit, and yoghurt, if you've got it, will do me fine.'

'I don't mind cooking you something, if you'd prefer it,' Erin offered. 'Your brother always had the works.'

'I'd prefer to live a little longer than he did.'

'You mean you're a health nut?'

A spark of humour lit the grey eyes. 'No, I'm not a "health nut," as you so elegantly put it, just not too fond of fry-ups—especially first thing in the morning. The coffee's still hot if you want some to be going on with.'

He took her agreement for granted, reaching for a clean mug from the tree by his elbow. Seating herself on the far side of the table, Erin watched him refill his own mug, unable to restrain a faint snort when he spooned in sugar.

'We all have our weaknesses,' he said drily. 'Cheers!'

The coffee was a little too strong for Erin's taste, but she refrained from saying so. She was supremely aware of his comparative closeness—of the possibility of catching a foot against his outstretched ones. He was wearing jeans and T-shirt himself this morning, the latter revealing the muscular structure of chest and shoulders. For the first time since she had learned to speak, she found herself totally tongue-tied.

Nick regarded her with lifted brows as she continued to sit there mute. 'Not so much to say for yourself this morning!'

'I was waiting for you to start the ball rolling,' she claimed. 'There must be all kinds of things you need to know.'

The shrug was brief. 'I'd say you filled me in pretty well on the detail last night.'

Erin eyed him hopefully. 'Did you come to any definite decision yet?'

'With regard to what?'

'What I asked you to consider. I realise you'd be subsidising me too for a while, but I'd honestly—'

'I told you that idea was no go,' he said flatly. 'Nothing happened overnight to change my mind.'

She gazed at him in frustration. 'Then what *do* you plan on doing? Sam won't settle at boarding-school, I can tell you that now!'

The grey eyes acquired a suddenly steelier glint. 'She'll do whatever's decided for her.'

'I wouldn't bet on it!' Erin was too inflamed by the tone to pay any further lip service to diplomacy. 'You can't push a fourteen-year-old around!'

'Calm down.' It was said quietly enough, but the inflection left nothing to misinterpretation. 'You're doing neither of you any favours.'

Erin took a grip on herself. For a moment there he had reminded her so much of her stepfather. 'I'm concerned about her, that's all,' she said stiffly, unable to bring herself to apologise. 'Send her away to school and she'll probably finish up running away.'

Nick drew an impatient breath. 'I hadn't even thought about boarding-school till you threw it in my face just now.'

'So what's the alternative?' she demanded. 'As a bachelor, you can hardly have her to live with you on her own. Imagine how people would talk.'

'Tell me about it.' He paused, expression hard to read. 'I'm not going to try making out I'm over-enthused about acting as surrogate father to a fourteen-year-old, but, as you pointed out last night, I'm all there is, so it seems it's needs must—for the time being, at any rate. I'll be relying on you for support.'

Erin stared at him in silence for a lengthy moment, the wind taken completely out of her sails. 'You're suggesting that I come to Barbados too?' she got out.

The strong mouth slanted. 'Why the surprise?'

'It's supposed to be only women who answer one question with another,' she said, and saw the slant increase.

'When it comes to prevarication, your sex wins hands down! If you don't want to come, say so.'

'It isn't that simple,' she protested. 'Sam's kith and kin; I'd just be a…charity case.'

'You'd save me the trouble of finding someone else to act as nursemaid—or whatever you like to call it. That has to be worth your keep. As to the rest, you could always get a job.'

'Doing what? As you pointed out last night, I'm not qualified for anything.'

'Qualifications can be gained.'

'Given time. Up until then—'

'Up until then you could make yourself useful around the house if you feel that strongly about it.'

'*I'm* not going unless you come too,' stated Samantha from the doorway.

'*You* don't have any choice,' replied her uncle.

Blue eyes took on extra sparkle. 'Erin said you were bossy!'

'Erin doesn't know the half of it.' Impatience had given way to amusement. 'Hallo, Samantha. Easy to see which side you take after.'

She regarded him consideringly. 'Do I have to call you uncle?'

'Nick will do fine,' he said. 'Let's all be adults together.'

Her grin registered approval. 'Okay, Nick. I prefer Sam, by the way.'

'Now in that you *do* have a choice,' he returned equably.

'I'll get breakfast,' Erin declared, still unable to get her mind round the idea he'd just outlined to her. 'Juice, everybody?'

'You didn't give me an answer yet,' Nick reminded her. 'And, yes, I do want it now,' he added, guessing what she was about to say. 'I like things cut and dried.'

Considering that the only alternative was to wave goodbye to Sam for the foreseeable future and apply for support from the State while she looked for work, she'd be a fool to say no, Erin conceded. 'Then I suppose it's yes,' she said, with some hesitation still. 'And…thanks.'

The dark head inclined with a mockery directed as much at himself as at her. 'You're welcome.'

'So, having settled that much,' said Samantha, pulling out a chair for herself, 'when do we go?'

'At least it seems I can count on unmitigated enthusiasm

from one side of the family,' came the dry comment. 'Monday, if we can get a flight.'

Erin almost dropped the cereal bowls she had just taken from the cupboard. 'We can't possibly have everything done by then!'

'What doesn't get done gets left. All you need worry about is your personal stuff.'

'It isn't just the house. We neither of us have passports, for one thing.'

'A detail. We'll take a trip into town this morning.' Nick lifted a sardonic eyebrow as she made no move to carry on with what she was doing. 'Anything else?'

Erin attempted to get her thoughts in order. 'There's the school.'

'They'll be informed.'

'Considering it's Friday tomorrow, does that mean I needn't go back at all?' asked Samantha hopefully, giving vent to a cheer when he signified assent. 'Great stuff!'

'Don't get too carried away,' her uncle advised. 'You've still got a few years to go.' He turned his attention back to Erin again. 'That it?'

'More or less,' she acknowledged, unable to come up with any further delaying factor. 'I'm just not used to things happening so fast,' she tagged on lamely. 'You're very...decisive.'

'An improvement on "bossy," I suppose.'

Erin had to smile. 'You did come across a bit that way last night.'

'Put it down to jet-lag.' Nick looked meaningfully at the bowls she was still holding. 'Do we get to eat at all?'

'Right away.' Erin slid the bowls onto the mats already laid out, and turned to open another cupboard. 'Cornflakes okay?'

'Fine.'

Which was just as well, considering it was the only cereal they had in right now, she reflected. She would need to pay a call at the supermarket to gather supplies to tide them over the next few days. Hopefully, she had enough cash to hand.

She took the same chair opposite Nick to eat her own flakes. Seated beside her, Samantha kept up a lively conversation throughout the meal. Erin wished she could feel as much at ease with the situation.

While her presence might be needed in order to stop any possible gossip, there was no getting round the fact that she was going to be living off this man's charity for some time to come. It said a lot for his character that he was prepared to do what he was doing. From living alone to having two females he scarcely knew in his home would be no minor disruption. The very least she could do by way of return was to make life as easy as possible for him.

What little she knew about Barbados had been gleaned from television holiday programmes, but it certainly looked a beautiful place. She felt a sudden anticipatory ripple at the thought of seeing it in the flesh, so to speak. It would be the first time either she or Samantha had even been on a plane, much less crossed the Atlantic!

With a trip into town in the offing, she went back up to her room after they finished breakfast and exchanged jeans and shirt for the grey skirt and jacket that was the one really smart outfit she possessed. She even managed to find a pair of unladdered tights. With her hair hanging loose about her shoulders, she still looked less than her age, she acknowledged disconsolately, studying herself in the dressing table mirror.

On impulse, she rooted in the drawer to find an elasticated hair-binder, fastening the heavy length back into her nape. Not a vast improvement, she had to admit, but the best she could do for the moment.

Having changed his own clothing for the trousers and

cord jacket in which he had arrived, the white T-shirt replaced by a creamy-beige one bearing the same up-market logo, Nick was waiting in the living room.

'Amazing what a pair of high heels and a touch of lipstick can do,' he commented, looking her over.

'I'd no more go into town in jeans than you obviously would,' Erin responded swiftly, sensing derision. 'I thought I heard Sam come down.'

'She did. Several minutes ago. She's waiting in the car.'

'We never take the car into town,' she protested.

'*You* won't be doing now,' he returned. 'I will.'

Erin bit back the smart retort. If anyone owned the car, it was the bank, she supposed—or they would very shortly. 'Be it on your own head,' she said instead. 'The traffic will be murder!'

It was, though it didn't appear to bother him. He even managed to find a spare parking meter within easy walking distance of the Passport Office. Before presenting themselves, they obtained the necessary photographs via one of the machines, finishing up, as Samantha was moved to observe, looking like a couple of escapees from a lunatic asylum. Par for the course, according to Nick.

It was gone noon by the time they had the paperwork finished and the passports issued. With little food in the house at present, Erin was relieved when Nick suggested they had lunch here in town. It might be necessary to seek a sub in order to get in enough to see them over the weekend anyway, but she would cross that bridge if and when she came to it, she told herself. Right now, she intended enjoying being waited on for once.

Given the option, Samantha would have opted for the nearest burger bar, though she settled with reasonably good grace for the Italian restaurant that was Nick's choice of venue. Erin relished every mouthful of the chicken in red wine sauce she chose from an extensive menu, following it with a chocolate concoction that was nectar from heaven.

'I couldn't eat another crumb,' she admitted when Nick asked if she would like anything else. 'That was absolutely wonderful!'

He eyed her shrewdly. 'How long is it since you last ate out?'

'I can't remember,' she claimed, unwilling to go down that road.

'Dad didn't believe in it,' chimed in Samantha. '"Why pay somebody else to do what can be done at far less cost at home?" he always used to say. He used to go to restaurants himself, though.'

'With clients,' Erin corrected. 'Legitimate business expenses.'

'I don't think all of them could have been. I heard him telling somebody on the phone that the Inland Revenue was investigating him.'

'Not something you need worry about anyway,' Nick observed before Erin could make any further comment. 'Coffee?'

'I'll have a brandy,' said Samantha, responding to her uncle's glance with innocent eyes. 'That woman over there just ordered one.'

'When you're her age you can do the same,' he said.

The guilelessness increased. 'How do you know how old she is?'

'Call it an educated guess.'

'Stop playing silly games, Sam,' instructed Erin, wondering how long it would take for her sister's brand of humour to turn tolerance into irascibility. 'Do you want coffee or not?'

The younger girl pulled a face, drawing a shrug from Nick.

'I'll take that as a negative.'

They left the restaurant at two, but not, as Erin had anticipated, to go straight back to the house. He had a call of his own to pay first, Nick advised in the car.

Once again, he managed to find a parking place on a side street close by where he wanted to be. The luck of the devil, thought Erin, a little unfairly considering he'd been anything but to the pair of them so far.

'We'll wait here for you,' she said when he opened the door to get out. 'Assuming it isn't going to take long, that is?'

'I shouldn't think so,' he returned. 'The gallery's just round the corner there.'

Her interest perked up immediately. 'They have some of your stuff?'

'One or two, yes.'

'May we come with you?' she asked tentatively.

There was a slight hesitation before he nodded. 'No reason why not, I suppose.'

Its two windows draped in lemon silk and bearing just one easel-supported landscape in each, the gallery looked as exclusive as the area suggested. It was more spacious than it had appeared from outside, its subtly-lit depths partitioned into different areas. Apart from one wealthy-looking couple studying a work Erin couldn't see from this angle, they appeared to be the only callers.

The middle-aged man with long blond hair tied back in a ponytail who emerged from behind a curtain off to one side was something of a shock. Wearing a velvet suit in a brilliant burgundy, with silk ruffles at both neck and sleeve-ends, he looked more nineteenth than twentieth century. White teeth showed in a sparkling smile as he viewed the newcomers.

'Nicholas, *darling*, what a *wonderful* surprise!' he exclaimed extravagantly. 'Why didn't you let me know you were in town?'

'An unexpected visit.' Grinning, Nick held up a hand as the other advanced. 'Try kissing me, and I'll floor you!'

The smile turned into a pout, accompanied by an exaggerated sigh, fingers splayed over heart. 'Oh, the brute!'

'Aren't I always?' Nick glanced at the two girls. 'Meet Miles Penhalligen. My nieces, Erin and Samantha.'

Miles shook the hands both girls extended in turn, his clasp unexpectedly firm. 'There isn't much of *you* there,' he remarked, looking from one to the other. 'Far too pretty!'

'We both take after our mother,' Erin supplied. 'It's only Sam who's related anyway. We had different fathers.'

'Had?' Miles looked swiftly back to Nick.

'My brother died,' the other confirmed. 'How are things going?'

Miles took the hint, becoming suddenly businesslike. 'Gone. Your stuff is snapped up as soon as it's put on display. A real investment, considering the price one fetched at auction the other day. We might give some thought to upping the ante.'

'Does this mean we don't get to see any of your paintings after all?' asked Samantha.

'Not here and now,' her uncle confirmed.

'You can come and see the portrait he did of me and Rummy,' offered Miles, flicking a fastidious finger at a speck of fluff on his lapel. 'Not his best work, I'm afraid—he quite failed to capture Rummy's spirit—but better than nothing, I suppose.'

'That cat of yours doesn't *have* any spirit worth talking about,' Nick retorted, and drew an indignant look.

'He's aloof with you because he recognises your lack of empathy, darling. Do you like cats?' he asked the girls.

'Apart from the odd stray, I'm afraid we've never had much to do with them,' answered Erin, fighting to stay serious. 'But I'm sure we'd both love to meet Rummy.'

'And so you shall, if you can get this insensitive soul to bring you to my home.'

'It's doubtful if there's going to be time,' said the latter. 'We're leaving Monday.'

Miles looked intrigued. 'All three of you?'

'That's right.' Nick's tone was bland, his expression giving nothing away.

'Nicholas Carson bringing home a pair of lovely young nieces nobody knows about. That's really going to set the island buzzing! I'd give a whole lot to be a fly on the wall when the news hits the fan in certain quarters!' Miles broke off with a theatrical sigh as a man further down the gallery signalled for attention. 'Duty calls, I'm afraid, chickens. I'm all on my ownsome today.'

He kissed both girls continental-style, on both cheeks, contenting himself with a touch of lips to fingertips in Nick's direction. Samantha gave way to the giggles as they left the gallery.

'He's priceless!' she exclaimed. 'An absolute hoot!'

'He's also one of the most astute art dealers in London,' Nick advised drily, 'so don't let that act of his fool you. It amuses him to camp it up.'

Erin had guessed as much. Nick's whole attitude had suggested it. She stole a glance at the hard-boned face, wondering just which quarters Miles had been referring to with that 'fly on the wall' remark. Instinct suggested a woman.

The strength of her reaction to the idea of his being involved with someone shocked her. It was ridiculous to have any such feelings about a man not just fifteen years older than her but Sam's uncle to boot! She concentrated on the paving stones under her feet as if her life depended on not stepping on any lines.

Nick not only insisted on accompanying her into the supermarket on the way home, but paying the bill too.

'Something you're going to have to accept for the time being,' he observed on the way back to the car, when she made some only semi-joking remark about feeling like Orphan Annie. 'You don't have money, I do—ergo, I pay. It was my brother who got you into this fix in the first place.'

They had left Samantha listening to the radio in the car. Erin took a chance on asking the question she had been wanting to ask since his arrival. 'Did he try contacting you at all during the last few months?'

The lean features tautened a fraction. 'Yes,' he admitted. 'And, yes, I refused to help him out.'

'Which you feel guilty enough over to make amends by taking the two of us on,' Erin murmured, and received a cool hard glance.

'Don't try psychoanalysing me. I feel no guilt whatsoever where David's concerned.'

Erin didn't believe him. If he was as hard as he was making out, he wouldn't be doing what he was doing. She wished suddenly and fervently that she was older—able to meet him on level footing. He treated her like a child because to him that was all she was, but he didn't make her feel like a child.

'You've been absolute ages!' Samantha complained when they got to the car. 'We only needed enough to last over the weekend!'

'We don't know for sure yet that we'll be going on Monday,' Erin pointed out mildly, getting into the rear seat.

'Yes, we do.' Having stowed the bags in the boot, Nick slid behind the wheel. 'I booked the flight this morning, while I was waiting for you to get ready. Ten-twenty from Heathrow. We'll spend Sunday night at the Hilton to save any rush.'

Erin left it to Samantha to make the appropriate noises,

telling herself she wasn't yet fully committed; reservations could always be cancelled.

But she knew deep down that it was beyond her to pull out now.

CHAPTER THREE

APART from odd wisps of cloud drifting across from time to time, there was nothing to mar the view straight down to a sea that looked flat calm from this height, the occasional ships like toys in a bathtub.

Samantha had long ago grown bored with looking at it, and been only too happy to exchange seats. Flying, she had declared with lofty disdain, was no big deal.

It certainly was for her, Erin reflected, nose pressed against the glass; more especially flying first class. From the moment of reaching the airport this morning they had been treated like Royalty, with drinks and snacks served in the VIP lounge, and an escort to take them to the plane.

Nick had taken it all in his stride, of course, obviously well accustomed to treading the red carpet. Erin had begun to wonder just how affluent he really was. Artists she had read about seemed to have spent much of their lives struggling to keep body and soul together.

He was seated right behind her; if she turned her head just a fraction she could catch a glimpse of him from the corner of her eye. The book he had been reading appeared to have been laid aside in favour of a sketchpad.

Supple and sensitive, those long-fingered hands were the only part of him that fitted the artistic image. The rest was pure masculinity. All through dinner at the hotel last night she had been aware of the interest he was drawing from other women in the restaurant—especially one seated at the adjoining table. If he'd noted it himself—which he could hardly fail to have done—he'd paid no heed. No doubt he was well accustomed to that kind of attention too.

As if in direct response to that assessment, one of the stewardesses paused by his seat to ask if there was anything she could get him, following the query with a gratified-sounding exclamation.

'Would you like it?' asked Nick.

'I'd love it!' she sparkled. 'I've never had a portrait done before.'

He laughed. 'Hardly a portrait.'

'As good as, to me,' came the response. 'Would you sign it for me?'

'Sure.' There was a brief pause, followed by the sound of a page being torn from the pad. 'Here you are.'

'I'll treasure this,' the recipient assured him. 'My very own Nicholas Carson!'

'Don't you wish!' murmured Samantha. She looked up with bland expression as the stewardess moved on to direct the same question at the pair of them. 'Can we have a look?'

An extremely attractive brunette in her late twenties, the woman smiled and offered the sketch for appraisal. It was, Erin acknowledged, an excellent likeness.

'Nice,' Samantha commented, handing it back.

'Isn't it!' the other agreed, directing another smile at the man seated behind. 'It's very flattering to be considered worth the trouble.'

'No trouble,' Nick assured her easily. 'Bone structure like yours is an artist's dream!'

If the woman's chest swelled any further, her boobs were going to burst her blouse buttons, thought Erin uncharitably. Talk about laying it on with a trowel!

Never backward in coming forward, Samantha turned to direct a grin between the seats at her uncle as the stewardess moved on. 'Great chat-up line!'

'You're too young for such cynicism,' came the equable response. 'She does have good bone structure.'

'So do I,' claimed Samantha promptly, 'but you haven't offered to sketch *me*.'

'Would you like me to?'

'I thought you'd never ask!'

'So come and sit back here where I can see you.' Nick was obviously amused.

She did so with alacrity, plumping into the empty seat at his side. 'Full-face or profile?'

'Whichever, so long as you keep reasonably still.'

'Profile, then,' she decided. 'I might start laughing if I'm looking at you.'

Listening, Erin doubted if she could ever bring herself to be as much at ease with him as her sister was. The physical thing aside, much of the problem still lay in the fact that while with Sam there was at least a blood factor, she had no claim on him whatsoever. Taking the costs already incurred on her account, she was in debt to him for more than she could ever hope to repay.

The sketch was completed at what seemed lightning speed, to be viewed with a critical eye by its subject.

'You've made me look like a kid!' she complained.

'You *are* a kid,' Nick returned drily. 'Do you want it, or shall I tear it up?'

'I'll take it,' she condescended. 'How about doing one of Erin now?'

'Another time,' he said, before Erin could frame a rejection. 'I'd like to get back to my book.'

Sam took the hint, returning to her seat to toss the sketch into Erin's lap with a deprecatory air. Regardless of what her sister might think, Nick had captured the youthfully pretty face to perfection in Erin's estimation. She hoped he didn't think she was disappointed by his refusal to comply with Sam's suggestion. Having herself portrayed on paper was the *last* thing on her mind.

From the first glimpse of the green-clad jewel of an island, fringed by beaches of pure white sand, she was too much in thrall to think about anything else. The sun was still high in the clear blue sky when they landed, the sheer quality of light a revelation in itself.

Nick was greeted by airport staff with smiling familiarity, the speculation regarding her and Samantha obvious. On an island the size of this one, the news would spread like wildfire, Erin imagined. What might be made of it was something else.

They took a taxi from the airport, disappointing Samantha who had been expecting some fancy limousine to be waiting for them.

'The inland roads aren't suited to limos,' said Nick, when she asked if he had one. 'I use a Jeep as a general runabout myself, but there's a Mercedes 190 in the garage. If you drive, I can get you put on the insurance,' he added to Erin.

'Yes, I do, but I'll be perfectly happy using the bus when I need to go anywhere,' she assured him swiftly. 'I imagine there's a service?'

'It would be a pretty fair walk from the house to the nearest pickup point. If it's independence you're after, you could always learn to ride a moped.'

Hardly a hardship in this climate, Erin conceded, looking out on gently undulating landscape and rioting colour, though buying such a machine was a long way from being a viable proposition. Not that she found the thought of walking to a bus stop off-putting.

'It's all so utterly beautiful!' she exclaimed, transport problems thrust aside. 'I've never seen so many different flowers!'

'You'll soon get used to it.' Nick sounded tolerant. 'A month, and you'll be taking it all for granted.'

'Never!' She could say that with certainty. She turned back to look at him, too euphoric to be reticent. 'I can imagine how different it's going to be for you, having the two of us around, but I'll do everything I can to keep things running smoothly. Anything at all I can do for you, you only have to ask.'

The smile was more than a touch ironical. 'I'll bear it in mind.'

Seated, at her own request, up front beside the driver, Samantha was chatting away as though she had known the man for years. There was one who was going to have no trouble at all adjusting to her new life, reflected Erin. Hopefully, her wayward streak wouldn't surface too often.

Its faded pink walls covered in creeper threaded through with bougainvillaea, lower reaches shaded by wide white-railed verandas, the house they eventually reached via a curving driveway edged with flamboyant was a delight to the eye. A place like this must cost the earth! thought Erin dazedly. She was forced to revise her estimate of their benefactor's possible worth once again as she viewed smoothly manicured emerald-green lawns edged by majestic Royal Palms, the eye-dazzling profusion of blooms and shrubs. Maintenance of the grounds alone had to be a full-time job!

'You must be absolutely rolling in it!' exclaimed Samantha enthusiastically, echoing her own thoughts. 'Is there a swimming pool too?'

'Out back,' Nick acknowledged. 'It was being cleaned when I left, so it might not be useable yet.'

'I'll go take a look!' she said, and headed off along the path leading round the side of the house.

Erin eyed Nick uncomfortably, thankful that the taxi driver wasn't still around to witness her sister's appalling lack of manners. 'Sorry about that.'

'About what?' he asked.

'The comment Sam made. It was totally out of order!'

'On the premise that it's vulgar to refer to money?' He lifted his shoulders. 'I'd hardly be living here if I were a pauper.'

'I realise that. It's just—' She broke off, spreading her hands in a wry little gesture. 'I'm feeling a bit overwhelmed by it all, I suppose.'

Nick made no reply, studying the smooth young face upturned to his with an unreadable expression in his eyes. Looking back at him, Erin felt the familiar tingle run down her spine, and found it hard to maintain a steady gaze. Not only would it be downright embarrassing to have him guess the effect he had on her, but possibly disastrous, in the sense that he might consider the situation untenable. It was only a temporary attraction anyway. It *had* to be.

The screened double doors at the rear of the veranda were flung back suddenly to frame an ample figure in a bright orange dress, her face split almost from ear to ear by a sparkling white smile.

'Mr Nick! I thought that was a car I heard!'

'Hallo, Bella,' he said. 'My housekeeper,' he added, for Erin's benefit. 'The finest on the island!'

'None of that soft talk!' she chided, exchanging the smile for a frown as she viewed the newcomer. 'Why didn't you let me know you were coming home—and bringin' a visitor too!'

'Two visitors,' he corrected imperturbably. 'The other one went to take a look at the pool. This is Miss Grainger.'

'Erin,' said the latter, managing a smile of her own. 'Nice to meet you, Bella. I'm sorry to land on you unexpectedly.'

'What's done's done,' came the unmollified response. 'I'll need to get some rooms ready.'

'Let me help,' Erin offered, and received an affronted shake of the head.

'I don't need no help! And Joshua will do that,' she scolded her employer as he bent to lift the two suitcases. 'You just come and sit while I fix you some tea.'

'I may as well bring these in with me now,' said Nick

mildly. 'Josh can take them up. Make that tea for two,' he added, ushering Erin ahead of him through the doorway as the housekeeper shifted her not inconsiderable bulk to make room. 'I'll have a whisky.'

'It's too early to be drinkin' that stuff!' declared Bella.

'Probably.' Nick hadn't altered his tone, but the message apparently got through all the same, lifting the housekeeper's shoulders in a resigned shrug.

'Some folk just don't listen to reason.'

She went off, grumbling under her breath, her movements surprisingly light for someone her weight. Dropping the suitcases to the coolly tiled floor of the spacious entrance hall, Nick caught Erin's eye and grinned briefly.

'You'll need to stand up for yourself with Bella. She considers it her duty to keep everybody on the straight and narrow.'

'Obviously she doesn't have too much success with you,' Erin returned, still trying to come to terms with it all.

'I'm past redemption.' He indicated an archway off to the right. 'Let's go and find your sister.'

The room into which he took her was sumptuous by any standards—a vast expanse of pale cream carpet, warm woodwork and fresh tropical colour. Glass doors gave onto the rear veranda, with a view out over more landscaped gardens containing a free-form pool complete with a central island.

Turning from her contemplation of the latter, Samantha waved a cheery hand as she spotted them through the glass. Nick crossed to open one of the doors, admitting a subtle fragrance.

'Come on in,' he invited.

She obeyed, stepping across the threshold to view the room appreciatively. 'Some place!' she commented. 'Must have cost you a bomb!'

'Home to you for the next few years at least,' her uncle advised, cutting across Erin's remonstrance.

'I feel completely at home already,' she returned chirpily. 'I always knew I was destined for the high life!'

Nick gave a short laugh. 'You won't find things so very different once you're acclimatised. Schools tend to be much the same wherever you are.'

She pulled a face. 'You would have to remind me! Still—' on a cheerier note '—I'll hardly be going right away, will I?'

'Depends how soon it can be arranged,' he said. 'I'll get onto it first thing in the morning.'

The rattle of crockery heralded the approach of Bella, pushing a loaded trolley. She regarded Samantha with even greater disconcertion.

'You didn't say nothin' about no child,' she accused. 'Come to it, you haven't said nothin' about anythin'!'

'An omission about to be corrected,' returned the master of the house. 'This is my brother's daughter, Samantha. Erin is her half-sister. They're going to be living here.'

'You mean all the time?'

'That's the idea.'

The woman looked from one to the other girl as if she could hardly believe what she was hearing. 'You plannin' on adoptin' them both?'

'I'm a little past adoption age,' Erin cut in hastily. 'We'll do our best not to cause you any extra work, Bella.'

'I'll even make my own bed every morning,' offered Samantha magnanimously. 'You won't know we're here!'

'I already know you're here.' Bella was unamused. 'You best get your tea while it's still hot.'

'I'll be mother, shall I?' said Samantha brightly as the housekeeper went off.

Nick gave her a quelling look. '*You* can sit down and behave yourself. Erin can do the honours.'

He left them to it, crossing to a cedarwood cabinet to pour himself the promised whisky. There were three cups and saucers on the trolley, Erin noted; obviously Bella wasn't one to accept defeat easily. Her reaction to the news that she and Samantha were to be permanent fixtures was hardly to be wondered at. Nick could surely have given some kind of warning via the phone rather than simply dropping them on her out of the blue this way!

He came back to take a seat opposite her own, lifting one leg casually across the other.

'I need this,' he said, catching Erin's eye as he raised the heavy glass to his lips. 'It's been quite a week!'

'For all of us,' she returned meaningfully, and saw his lips slant.

'Point taken. Maybe you'd like something stronger yourself?'

She shook her head. 'The tea will do me fine, thanks.'

'I wouldn't mind something stronger,' declared Samantha, already halfway through a succulent fruit tart. 'I was never very keen on tea anyway.'

'Just drink it,' Erin said shortly, tolerance running out. 'Think yourself lucky to be here at all!'

The blue eyes so like her own flashed in swift resentment. 'I've more right than you, at any rate!'

'Cut that out!' Nick hadn't altered his position, but the sudden snap in his voice left no room for misunderstanding. 'You apologise to your sister—now!'

'She didn't...' Erin began, voice petering out in face of the glance he briefly turned her way.

Looking a little shell-shocked, Samantha did as she was told, subsiding into aggrieved silence. Erin wanted to tell her it was okay, that she knew she hadn't really meant what she'd said. Nick had jumped so hard and fast, stunning them both with the swift metamorphosis.

He drained the glass and put it down on the lamp table

by his elbow, expression still verging on the flinty. 'You owe Erin some respect,' he said. 'She sacrificed a lot to be dogsbody for you and your father this last few years.'

'That was hardly Sam's fault,' Erin protested. 'And a little housework and cooking hardly merits the term "dogsbody"!'

Nick gave her an exasperated look. 'There's a damn sight more than that to running a household, and well you know it! I saw the way Sam here took it for granted that it was *your* place to see to everything the last few days, so don't try making out you had help from any quarter.'

'Sam had school, and Dad had business affairs to deal with,' she said.

'You should have been in school yourself.' He shook his head as she started to form a response. 'You don't owe my brother any loyalty. Judging from the amount of luggage you've brought between you, I'd say he kept a pretty tight grasp on the purse strings all round.'

'We just brought what we thought we were going to need,' Erin defended. 'There didn't seem much point in packing winter things for this climate.'

'We don't have all that many summer clothes either,' Samantha chimed in, recovering her spirits.

'No problem,' said her uncle. 'There are plenty of good boutiques in Bridgetown.'

'Charging plenty too, I'd imagine.' Erin gave him back look for look. 'You must do as you see fit where Sam's concerned, of course, but I can manage well enough with what I already have.'

Nick lifted an eyebrow. 'That depends on what you *do* have. I've a position to keep up in this community.'

'I'm hardly going to be going places where it matters what I'm wearing.'

'That pride of yours could become wearing.' He sounded

as if that time might already have come. 'Will you get it through your head that you're not here as a charity case?'

'I'm certainly not here for the reasons you led me to believe,' she returned shortly. 'With a resident housekeeper, you're already safeguarded against defamatory gossip.'

He made an impatient movement. 'I don't give a damn about ''defamatory gossip''! You're here because Sam needs you.'

'Yes, I do!' The younger girl both looked and sounded eager to convince. 'I didn't mean what I said just now. You know I didn't! I'd be lost without you.'

Erin doubted it. Not in present surroundings. 'I'm sorry,' she said hollowly. 'I must appear very ungrateful.'

'I don't want your gratitude.' Nick's tone was curt. 'Malvern is as much home to you as it is to Samantha, so stop acting the poor relation!'

Erin's chin lifted, a spark lighting her eyes. 'I'm not *acting* anything! If I'd known how you lived—'

'Just what kind of lifestyle did you imagine I lived?'

'One where I could at least make myself useful. You never mentioned staff.'

'It didn't occur to me to mention them. As to making yourself useful, I've a mountain of paperwork that could do with sorting. I don't want to hear another word on the subject,' he added as she once more made to speak.

There was nothing much else she *could* say, Erin concluded heavily. With little or no means of her own to fall back on, she was stuck with the situation. Some people might call her a fool for carping about it.

Bella returned to say that their rooms were ready. Accompanying her up the lovely balustraded staircase, Erin attempted to engage her in light conversation, giving up when her overtures elicited no more than monosyllabic replies. She didn't blame the woman for her attitude. Having two permanent additions to the household thrust upon her without warning was reason enough for grievance.

Judging from the initial reaction, any offer to help around the house was obviously going to be taken as a dire insult, but that didn't mean she had to accept being waited on hand and foot. There must be things she could do that wouldn't get up Bella's nose. All it needed was a little tact and diplomacy.

Both bedrooms were at the rear of the house, overlooking the pool and gardens and allowing a distant glimpse of the sea through the far trees. Each had its own beautifully appointed bathroom and sitting area, with French doors giving onto an upper balcony running the whole length of the house.

'It's really cool!' Samantha proclaimed. 'Just imagine living here all the time!'

Expression dour, Bella left them to it, muttering beneath her breath as she went. Erin sat down on the edge of the double bed, feeling as limp as a wrung-out wet rag. Her sister eyed her curiously.

'You really didn't take what I said a bit back seriously, did you?' she asked.

Erin forced a smile. 'Of course not. It was my fault for coming the big sister the way I did. I'm just finding it a bit hard to take in, that's all.'

'I'm not,' claimed the younger girl. 'It's *exactly* what *I* expected!' She performed an exuberant twirl, ponytail swinging, eyes sparkling like twin sapphires. 'I'm going to love every minute!'

A very large proportion of which would be spent in school, it was on the tip of Erin's tongue to remind her, but she held it back. It could be several days—even a week or more—before Nick managed to get her enrolled in one. Why burst the bubble now?

'We'd better unpack,' she said instead. 'Not that we're

either of us going to fill more than a fraction of those.' She glanced in the direction of the walk-in closet on the far side of the room.

Samantha gave a dismissive shrug. 'I'll be having lots of new things anyway. You should too. You heard what Nick said about keeping up appearances.'

'I'm sure he spends sleepless nights worrying about it.' Erin hesitated before adding cautiously, 'Try not to go overboard, Sam. There has to be a limit.'

'I don't see why. He's hardly short of a dollar or two, as Dad used to say.' Viewing her sister's expression, Samantha laughed. 'Stop being so stuffy, Rin! He's our uncle, after all.'

'*Your* uncle, not mine,' Erin replied firmly. 'I dare say he'll set his own limits anyway.'

For all the notice taken, she might as well have held her breath. Samantha was too well ensconced on cloud nine to be fetched down by words. 'I'm going to find a cossie and have a swim before anything else,' she announced. 'The pool awaits!'

It was going to be up to Nick himself to establish some ground rules, thought Erin resignedly as the door closed in her sister's wake. He had made something of a start earlier, but Sam had soon bounced back. He hadn't even begun to experience the worst.

Unpacking her one suitcase and travel bag took no more than fifteen minutes. As anticipated, her things looked lost in the huge closet. She had a long, slow shower, unable to avoid her image in the mirrored walls as she towelled herself down. Her breasts were so small, she thought disconsolately. No man was ever going to be turned on by the sight of them.

She left it there, unwilling to acknowledge that the one man she might want to turn on was unlikely to be stirred by anything *she* could offer.

Back in the bedroom, she donned clean underwear and got into a blue cotton tunic that owed its length more to the fact that she had grown since acquiring it than any fashion statement. Darkness had already fallen, stirring the crickets to vibrant life. Erin went out onto the balcony, leaning on the rail to draw in great breaths of the fragrant night air as she looked at a sky strewn with stars twice as big and bright as back home.

Despite everything, she couldn't help being glad she was here. Who wouldn't prefer to live in this lovely place? There had to be some kind of work she could get. Bridgetown sounded the right place to start looking. Tomorrow, she reminded herself ironically, was a whole new day.

Supper was served out on the veranda by a cheerful West Indian whom Nick introduced as Bella's husband, Joshua Parish. They had their quarters in a converted stable block some short distance from the main house, he advised, with a sardonic glance in Erin's direction, so the three of them would have the house to themselves at night.

'What made you buy a place this size in the first place?' Erin queried, refusing to react to the taunt.

Broad shoulders lifted. 'I like space. Anyway, you never know when people might drop in.'

'Do you have lots of visitors?' asked Samantha.

'Lots, no. Some, yes.'

'We'll make sure not to get in the way when they do come,' said Erin, and received another mocking glance.

'I'm sure you will.'

Samantha spooned up the last of her flamed banana with a sigh of pure bliss. 'Scrumptious! I love it here!'

You haven't been here five minutes, Erin wanted to say, but she held her tongue, conscious of the grey eyes still resting on her. Wearing a casual white shirt and tan chinos, dark hair still slightly damp from the shower, he had set her heart racing again the moment she clapped eyes on him. It was no use reminding herself about the age gap—it made absolutely no difference to her responses. Where Nick Carson was concerned, her body had a will of its own.

'How soon can we make that trip into Bridgetown?' Samantha asked next, thoughts turning from inner to outer gratification. She smiled the sweet smile that deceived so many people into believing her thoroughly angelic. 'It's going to be wonderful to have new things! This—' casting a wry downward glance at the dress she had on '—barely fits me any more—and the others are even worse!'

'I guess we'd better make it tomorrow, then,' said Nick. 'I've business of my own to attend to, so it's going to be up to you to kit her out with whatever she needs,' he added to Erin. 'Naturally you'll be provided with the wherewithal.' He paused, lip tilting at the corner as he viewed her expression. 'Don't worry, I'm not about to suggest you take advantage yourself.'

'Good,' she responded, rallying her forces. 'If it's going to be down to me, I'll need a set figure to work with.'

'All you'll need is my card as authority to charge.'

Erin gave up. It was hardly her place to try dictating how much—or little—he should spend on his own niece. That Samantha herself would take full advantage of an open-ended arrangement was without a doubt. It would serve him right if she ran up some astronomical bill.

The blue tunic seemed to be revealing a great deal too much bare leg when she rose from the table in response to Nick's suggestion that they adjourn to the wickerwork chairs grouped about a low table further along the veranda for coffee. She was conscious of him looking at her—sensed the derisive smile. So what? she thought defiantly. Her legs were probably her best feature anyway.

Both low and deep, the chairs were designed for relaxation rather than decorum. Erin stopped even trying to keep her lower thighs covered, concentrating on the sounds and scents and wonderful velvety warmth of the Caribbean night instead. Moths of all shapes and sizes fluttered about the lights, but there appeared to be no biting insects around. One of the few places in the world devoid of snakes of any kind, she had read somewhere. That had to be a plus in itself.

'Where do you have your studio?' she heard herself asking.

'It's behind the old mill. I like to be right away from it all when I'm working.' Leaning back in his seat, legs stretched, hands clasped comfortably behind his head, Nick both looked and sounded relaxed. 'Did you ever do any painting yourself?'

'Only in school.'

'Were you any good?'

'Brilliant!' interposed Samantha before Erin could answer. 'Everybody said so!'

Erin gave a deprecatory little laugh. 'Stop exaggerating, Sam!'

'Who's exaggerating?' she said. 'You were set on going to art college until Dad blackmailed you into taking over Mum's job. Not that she ever did all that much to start with.'

'Don't talk about her like that!' Erin remonstrated sharply. 'Your father either. Blackmail's a ridiculous word to use!'

Samantha stuck out a stubborn lip. 'No, it isn't. He said you owed it to him for giving you a home in the first place, *and* letting you stay after Mum went off. I heard him!'

'Did he?' Nick's jaw had tautened. 'Don't flannel me,' he admonished as Erin hesitated. 'This is *my* brother we're talking about.'

'He was experiencing some financial difficulties even

back then,' she defended. 'I was happy to help any way I could.'

'Why make excuses for him? He acted deplorably.'

'No worse than you refusing to help him out,' she flashed, instantly regretting the hasty rejoinder as she saw the grey eyes harden.

'I've told you before, that's my affair!'

'I know.' She spread her hands in a contrite little gesture. 'I've no right to make any judgements. Especially when...'

'Especially when you owe *me* so much,' he finished drily as she let the words trail away. 'It goes against the grain to be beholden to anyone, doesn't it?'

'When I've no way of paying back, yes.' She was doing her best to stay on even keel. 'As I'm obviously not going to be allowed to do anything much around the house, I aim to find a job.'

'Offering what kind of experience?'

'I can cook, and clean.'

'So can hundreds of others. As an alien, you'd only be allowed to take a job no resident could be found to fill, which limits the choice even further.'

'It looks like you'll have to settle for being a kept woman after all, Rin,' observed Samantha blandly.

Face warming, Erin saw Nick's lips twitch. At that precise moment, she could cheerfully have wrung her sister's neck.

'I don't think it need come to quite that,' he said. 'As I mentioned earlier, there's a whole lot of paperwork needs sorting out for starters.'

She hesitated. 'I wouldn't want to know your affairs.'

'You wouldn't glean all that much if you did.' Nick was beginning to sound a mite exasperated again. 'Do you want the job or don't you?'

Anything, Erin decided, was better than just sitting back

and accepting a life of leisure at his expense. 'I want it,' she said. 'Along with anything else you can find me to do.'

'I'll give the matter some serious thought.'

She said no more, conscious of the underlying impatience in his tone. She could to a certain extent understand his attitude. What she couldn't do was allow it to influence her own attitude. Pride was all she had.

Samantha gave a sudden yawn. 'I can't possibly be tired yet!' she complained. 'It's not even ten o'clock!'

'Almost two in the morning by your body clock,' Nick reminded her. 'Why don't you go on up? You'll need to be fresh and bright for all this shopping tomorrow.'

The thought alone was enough to convince her. Erin made a move to get to her feet along with the younger girl, subsiding again with some reluctance in answer to Nick's gesture. The last thing she wanted right now was to be alone with him.

CHAPTER FOUR

IF SAMANTHA had seen the gesture, she made no comment, taking herself off with a cheery, 'Night, all!'

Silence reigned for several moments after her departure. Erin was the first to break it. 'You wanted to say something?'

Nick gave an easy shrug. 'I just thought it would be nice for the grown-ups to have half an hour on their own.'

'Another promotion?' she asked a little more tartly than intended.

'It wasn't meant sarcastically,' he returned on a mild note. 'Just as a matter of interest, when do you get to be twenty?'

Erin modulated her tone. 'October.'

'Now there's a coincidence! Same month as me. We'll have to plan a double celebration.'

'It's a long time yet,' she said.

'You're thinking you might not even be here still by then?'

'I...suppose.'

He made no immediate reply, studying her reflectively. Erin put up an automatic hand to rake the heavy fall of fair hair back from her forehead, serving to lift the tunic hem even further up her thigh. She saw the grey eyes drop the length of her body to linger for an interminable moment on the silky expanse of bare flesh, and was hard put to it to stop herself from showing discomposure.

'I'd like you to sit for me some time,' he said unexpectedly, throwing her into even more confusion.

'Why?' she got out.

The mobile left eyebrow lifted. 'I don't normally need to give a reason.'

Erin could imagine. Most people would be only too flattered by the interest. 'Do you specialise in portraits?' she asked.

'No. I paint whatever or whoever I'm moved to paint.'

'Like the airline stewardess?'

A hint of a smile flickered across his lips. 'Like the airline stewardess.'

'You weren't interested in drawing me on the plane,' she reminded him.

'You call for rather more care and attention than I'd put into any quick sketch,' he said. 'I knew it the first time I saw you standing there, with your back to the door, all legs and eyes like a wary young gazelle. That's the way I want to paint you.'

'In a nightdress?'

The smile came again. 'What did you think I might want—a nude study?'

'Of course not,' she denied hastily. 'I hardly have the...attributes.'

'You reckon large breasts are an essential factor? Not so, I can assure you.'

'I'll bet!' she slung back, losing what little was left of her composure. Eyes brilliant, spots of colour burning high on her cheekbones, she got to her feet. 'I'm going to bed.'

Nick didn't stir, amusement replaced by an expression much harder to define. 'If you won't sit for me by choice, you can do it as part of the ''anything I can find'' you asked for. A fairly painless price to pay, wouldn't you say?'

Erin made her escape with a muttered goodnight, still unable to convince herself that he wasn't simply making fun of her. A gazelle indeed!

She prepared for bed quickly, donning one of the cotton nightdresses she always wore. Like the walls, the bathroom door was fully mirrored. Leaving the room, she was faced with a view that had, she realised, to be very similar to the one she must have presented the night Nick arrived. It was certainly true that she was showing a great deal of long, slender leg, but her eyes looked ordinary enough—as did the rest of her.

On impulse, she lifted both hands to cup the modest curves for a moment, testing the consistency. They were firm enough, but hardly a handful for her, much less...

This had to stop right here and now! she told herself forcibly. Nick's interest in her was purely artistic.

She slept fitfully, coming wide awake at six to a morning too glorious for despondency of any kind. Dressed in her usual uniform of jeans and practical cotton shirt, she crept downstairs to let herself out via the French doors from the living room, feeling the air like soft silk on her skin.

The sound of voices came faintly to her ears, although there was no one in sight. She headed away from the sound, rounding the far end of the pool to follow a path meandering through lush shrubbery. Colour danced before her eyes wherever she looked, ranging through delicate pinks and blues and yellows to the exotic red-orange of the flamboyant. Bougainvillaea spilled over old stone walls and arches.

Paradise must be like this, thought Erin whimsically, breaking off a small spray of frangipani to inhale the sweet, tantalising scent. Other matters aside, it was certainly going to be no hardship living here.

She emerged upon a grassy clearing backed by the creeper-covered remains of the old mill Nick had spoken of last night. Jutting out from the rear was a glass-roofed extension that could only be the studio.

About to turn and head back the way she had come, Erin hesitated. There was surely nothing wrong with just taking a look through the windows while no one was about?

The area within was far more spacious than it looked from outside. There were racks of canvasses stacked against the rear wall, protected by covers. An easel held yet another, also covered, the palette and other tools of trade on a nearby table suggesting a work not yet completed.

Finding the door unlocked when she tentatively tried it gave rise to further hesitation, but the temptation was too strong for her. Just a quick peep, she promised herself.

No quick peep was going to be enough, she realised at once on easing back a cover to reveal a stormy seascape so wonderfully executed that the towering waves seemed about to leap from the canvas and engulf her. She forgot about trespassing, forgot about everything over the following minutes, lost in admiration of a talent greater even than she had been led to expect.

It took movement from the doorway to jerk her out of it. Leaning against the doorjamb, thumbs hooked into the pockets of his jeans, Nick viewed her with enigmatic expression.

'How long have you been here?' he asked.

'Just a few minutes,' she said uncomfortably. 'I'm sorry. I know I shouldn't have come in, but the door was unlocked and I couldn't…I didn't—' She broke off, lifting her shoulders in a wry little shrug. 'I don't have any excuses.'

'You don't need any excuses,' he returned. 'I'm sure you can be trusted not to damage anything.' He paused, making no attempt to come further into the room. 'So what's the verdict?'

Erin looked at him suspiciously, but there was no telltale curl at the corner of the strong mouth. 'For what it's worth, I think they're exceptional,' she said.

This time his lip quite definitely did curl. 'You consider your opinion of no great importance?'

'I only meant I'm no art critic,' she parried.

'According to Samantha, you've a talent of your own.'

Erin forced a laugh. 'I wouldn't take anything Sam says too seriously. I can draw a bit, that's all.' She let the cover she was holding up fall back into place. 'Are all these going to be for sale?'

'Eventually, yes. They're due for shipping out the end of the month.'

'To Miles Penhalligen?'

He shook his head. 'To New York. You can help pack when the crates arrive. One more job to add to the list.'

'Still nowhere near enough.'

'A matter of opinion. Which brings us back to where we started.'

He straightened from the doorjamb in one lithe movement, bringing her heart into her throat as he came over to where she stood to take her by the shoulders and turn her further into the light.

'You've no idea how lovely you are, have you?' he said. He drew a fingertip down the side of her cheek, tracing the delicate line of her jaw with a featherlight touch that stimulated every nerve ending in her body. 'Wonderful bone structure!'

'Me and the stewardess both,' she managed with creditable flippancy, and saw his lips curve.

'With her it was something of a line, with you it's a fact. Sam has it too, although it hasn't fully emerged as yet. Your mother must have been a very beautiful woman.'

Erin steeled herself not to move as he ran both hands into her hair, to smooth it back from her face, eyes narrowed in concentrated assessment. Flattering that he found her worthy of his artistic interest at least, she thought wryly.

'It might have been better if she hadn't been,' she said, not a bit surprised to hear the unsteadiness in her voice.

'Because it drew men to her?'

'Like moths to a candle-flame, your brother used to say.' He had actually used a far cruder term, but she had no intention of repeating it. 'The man she ran away with was a business acquaintance of his.'

'That must have been tough on him.'

The expression in the grey eyes had altered subtly. She could feel the tremoring response spreading through her body, and knew he must feel it too. She wanted him to draw her closer, to know what it was like to be in his arms, his lips on hers, his hands caressing her—possessing her.

'I'm not the one to take you down that road,' Nick said softly, letting her go. 'Tempting proposition though it is.'

Erin drew in a mortified breath, the warmth rushing up under her skin. 'I don't know what you're talking about,' she said, attempting to infuse a genuine-sounding bewilderment.

The smile was brief. 'Yes, you do. It was coming from you in waves. Considering your lifestyle up to now, I'm probably the first male you've ever been in close enough contact with to light the spark. You'll soon get over it.'

'I'll take your word for it,' she said thickly, abandoning any further face-saving denials. 'I'm sorry to have embarrassed you.'

'You haven't.' There was a certain irony in his voice. 'We'd better get back to the house.'

He made no attempt to converse on the way, just strolled at her side as if nothing of any note had happened. She should be grateful, Erin supposed, that he had let her down so gently. Another man might have taken advantage of her girlish passions. A temptation, he had said; she wondered if he had really meant it or was simply pandering to her ego.

Either way, she had to stop thinking of him in any sense other than as Sam's uncle, she told herself bleakly. There was no future in anything else.

It was a surprise to find Sam already up and dressed when they got back to the house.

'I've been awake ages!' claimed the girl. 'I was going to have a swim, but I wasn't sure what time we'd be setting off for town?' The last directed at her uncle.

'I want to be in town by nine,' he said, 'so we'll be leaving eight-thirty.'

'Great!' she enthused, sobering to add plaintively, 'When's breakfast? I'm starving!'

As if in direct response to the question, Bella appeared round the corner of the veranda, pushing a loaded trolley.

'If it's late it's because you're early,' she berated, obviously having heard the remark. 'Breakfast is *always* eight o'clock.'

'Apart from when I ask for it earlier,' said Nick mildly. 'We'll be back for lunch the usual time.'

'That's somethin' I s'pose.' Not noticeably appeased, the housekeeper transferred the trolley contents to the already laid table, and departed, her head-up carriage only too indicative of her frame of mind.

'Why do you let her speak to you like that?' asked Samantha. 'She's only a servant.'

Grey eyes turned suddenly steely. 'Bella isn't *only* anything. You'll treat her with the respect she's due!'

'I don't think Sam meant—' Erin began.

'Yes, she did,' he cut in. 'And I'm not having it. Is that clear?'

'What about the respect *we're* due?' retorted his niece, sticking out the stubborn underlip. 'It isn't nice being made to feel like intruders.'

'She'll come round,' he said. 'She's just annoyed that I didn't consult her first.'

'Why didn't you, then?'

Erin held her breath, waiting for the explosion, letting it out again slowly when he failed to react the way his expression had indicated he might.

'An oversight, I have to admit.' He moved abruptly. 'Let's eat.'

Erin took her place at the table, feeling anything but happy. There was a limit as to how much Nick was going to be prepared to take from her sister, and she had very nearly reached it a moment ago. Between the two of them, he must be fed up to the back teeth already.

One thing he didn't do was indulge in displeased silences, keeping up a light conversation throughout the meal.

'Before I forget,' he said at one point, fishing out a small square card from a back pocket and sliding it across the table to where Erin sat, 'you'd better have this. I suppose I'd be wasting my breath suggesting you take advantage of it too?'

'Totally,' she confirmed, wondering even as she said it just what she was going to wear for this shopping trip. She had travelled in the grey suit, but it was far too warm for here. 'Not that I don't appreciate the offer,' she tagged on.

'Taken as read,' he said drily.

Completely recovered from any chastening effect, Samantha was overflowing with enthusiasm for the coming expedition. Erin wished she had just a fraction of her sister's ability to dismiss past discomfitures. The humiliation she had suffered earlier still burned within her, and would continue to do so for a long time to come. She felt so unutterably gauche.

She made her escape as soon as possible to go and riffle through the all too few garments in her closet, settling in the end on a multi-coloured skirt and a white blouse that had both come from a charity shop. Scarcely worn when she'd acquired them, her sandals were from the latter too. Even at charity shop prices, she had been unable to afford more than the occasional foray, but what she did have was at least of good quality.

Nick made no comment this time when he saw her. He had changed his own jeans and T-shirt for a pair of white trousers and a rust-coloured shirt open on the strong brown column of his throat, creating more havoc. She couldn't stop herself from feeling this way about him, Erin acknowledged dispiritedly. All she could do was learn to conceal it. Starting right now.

Bridgetown was bustling with traffic of both the motorised and pedestrianised kind. Nick parked the car close by the Careenage, where inter-island schooners unloaded cargoes of plantains, heading back along the wharf to Trafalgar Square with its picturesque coral stone fountain and colourfully uniformed traffic policeman.

'Try Broad Street to start,' he advised, indicating the main avenue running away to the left. 'I'll meet you back here at noon.'

'I'd still prefer it if you gave me some kind of figure to work with,' Erin asserted.

'*I'd* prefer it if you just did as you're told.' Nick glanced at his watch. 'You've got three hours.'

She watched him stride away, wondering who he was going to meet. No teenage infatuant for certain. One was more than enough for any man to deal with.

Samantha tugged at her arm. 'Come on,' she urged. 'We only have three hours!'

Erin stirred herself, adopting a light note. 'I don't imagine you'll be restricted to just this one expedition.'

'I don't intend being restricted to anything,' the younger girl returned airily. 'You heard what Nick said. I'm to have whatever I want.'

Perhaps not in so many words, but that had certainly been the implication, Erin was bound to concede. Who was she to worry about his bank balance, anyway?

Three hours had seemed a reasonable length of time at the outset, but it proved nowhere near long enough for

Samantha to reach saturation point. The presentation of Nick's card brought them instant attention wherever they went. Erin did her best to ignore the obvious curiosity when it became plain that this was strictly a one-sided buying spree. It was impossible, however, not to feel just a little covetousness when faced with such a plethora of choice.

One particular dress, with narrow shoulder straps and softly draped skirt in her favourite blue, really took her fancy. Samantha urged her to at least try it on, but she wouldn't, knowing how much harder it would be to say no once she saw herself in it. Fine feathers, she reminded herself, did not make fine birds. What she had already would suffice until such time when she could come shopping with her own money—far in the future though that might be.

By eleven-thirty she could take no more. Samantha had flatly refused any offers to deliver the goods, leaving the two of them so loaded with bags they could barely hold them together.

'We've just time for a drink before we go to meet Nick,' she said, pausing outside a café. 'I'm so dry, it's either this or the fountain! Anyway, we can't possibly carry any more.'

'I suppose not,' agreed Samantha with some reluctance. 'Although there are one or two places we didn't get to look at yet. Still,' she added on a cheerier note, 'there's always another day!'

Erin made no comment. She had long since given up even attempting to keep a tally on what they'd spent this morning, although it had to be astronomical by any standards. Nick's own fault for failing to lay down a limit, she told herself, but still felt accountable.

The café was crowded. Looking around for somewhere to sit, Erin saw one of the two youths seated at a table for four by the window wave a hand in invitation, and looked hastily away again. Samantha knew no such hesitation, ploughing her way between the intervening chairs with scant regard for the people occupying them. Erin followed behind, murmuring apologies which were for the most part accepted with smiles. One of these days, she thought wrathfully, she was going to really blow up!

The lemon trouser suit Samantha had insisted on wearing from the shop added at least a couple of years to her age. Both youths looked her over appreciatively as she dumped all her bags down by the side of one of the spare chairs and collapsed into it with a gamine grin.

'Thanks for the invite. We're just about ready to die of thirst!'

'Hopeless waiting for service,' said the blond-haired young man who had issued the invitation. 'I'll go and fetch some drinks. What do you fancy?'

Not yet seated, Erin put up a staying hand as he started to rise. 'It's all right, thanks. I can go myself.'

'Quicker for me to do it,' he returned easily. 'Tourists tend to get pushed aside.'

'We're not tourists,' said Samantha. 'We live here.'

The interest increased. 'Yeah? How come we never saw you around before?'

'We only got here yesterday,' Erin supplied, reluctantly accepting the offer to buy drinks on the sudden realisation that she didn't have any Bajun currency anyway. 'It's very nice of you,' she added lamely.

'Call it an aloha,' he grinned.

'Wrong island, dummy!' scoffed his companion. 'Wrong ocean, in fact.'

'At the risk of sounding pedantic, the Caribbean's actually a sea not an ocean,' said Erin, dropping her own load of bags and taking a seat. 'Just so we know where we are.'

'Got ya!' chortled the one on his feet. 'I'll be back!'

'I'm Reece Brady,' proffered the other. 'He's Tim Wyman. We live here too.'

'Born and bred?' asked Samantha.

'Tim is. My folks moved here from Michigan when I was a kid.'

He was probably no more than seventeen now, Erin judged. A very good-looking seventeen, she had to admit, with his thick thatch of reddish brown hair and laughing green eyes.

Samantha performed introductions from their own side, drawing a sudden enlightenment when she mentioned Nick's name.

'So you're the ones everybody's talking about!' Reece exclaimed. 'Is he really your uncle?'

'He's my father's younger brother,' said Samantha before Erin could speak. 'Dad didn't leave any money when he died, so we've come to live with Uncle Nick.'

'And relieve him of some of his?' With a meaningful look at the bags strewn about their feet. 'Guess he can afford it. He's loaded!'

'How would *you* know?' demanded Erin brusquely, and received a derisive glance.

'Everybody knows!'

'Knows about what?' asked Tim, returning with a precariously balanced tray.

Reece filled him in on the detail as he set out the glasses, eliciting a gleeful chuckle.

'Dione's going to get a real shock when she gets back!' he exclaimed.

'Who's Dione?' queried Samantha.

'My sister. She helps run the family store—leastways, she does when she's here. She's in New York right now.'

Wyman. Up until now Erin hadn't connected the name with that of one of the stores they had visited this morning. A very up-market store, she recalled.

'What does she have to do with Nick?' she asked on

what she hoped was a casual note, already pretty sure of the answer.

Her use of his name minus the prefix brought a certain speculation to both pairs of eyes, though no comment was made.

'Not quite as much as she'd like,' said Tim. 'Having two gorgeous blondes *in situ* is really going to cramp her style!'

Samantha giggled. 'You don't sound very brotherly.'

'She's not very sisterly. Twenty-six, and full of it! Can't imagine what Nick sees in her.'

'Yes, you can,' Reece grinned. 'The same thing all the guys see in her. A couple of nieces aren't going to make any difference. What Dione wants she goes after, regardless!'

From what had just been said, it was likely that this Dione was the 'certain quarters' Miles Penhalligen had been referring to, thought Erin. If the woman was involved with Nick, she could well imagine her reaction on returning from New York to find this new situation.

His own fault, she told herself defensively. *All* his fault, in fact. If he'd done as she suggested in the first place he wouldn't be faced with any problem at all.

Reaching for the glass of orange juice she had requested, she caught sight of the clock on the far wall and let out a dismayed exclamation.

'We have to go. It's almost twelve!'

'You sound like that fairy-tale character,' scoffed Reece as she began hurriedly to gather the bags together. 'Going to leave us a glass slipper?'

'It surely doesn't matter if we're a bit late,' Samantha protested, making no secret of the fact that she for one was reluctant to abandon their new friends. 'He'll wait.'

'It's been nice talking with you,' Erin told the two boys, ignoring the objection. 'And thanks for the drinks.'

'You've hardly touched them,' Tim pointed out on a disgruntled note.

'I know. I'm sorry.' Unable to offer to pay for them, it was the only thing she could say. 'Come on, Sam.'

She was outside and heading in the direction of the square before the younger girl caught up with her.

'That was real bad manners!' she accused. 'You could at least have let me finish *my* drink, even if you didn't want yours!'

'Nick said he'd see us at noon,' Erin reminded her. 'It would be even more bad-mannered to deliberately keep him waiting. We owe him a lot. More even than we realised.'

Samantha slanted a glance. 'You mean because of what they said back there about Tim's sister? So what? She's only his girlfriend, not his wife. Too bad if she doesn't like us being here.'

Erin had gathered the impression that 'girlfriend' was rather underplaying the relationship. If not Nick's wife—as yet—this Dione was almost certainly his lover. She hated her already.

'It's about time you started showing a little more appreciation,' she said tautly. 'Nick's turned his whole life upside down for our sakes. Not many men in his position would do the same.'

'Most men would think themselves lucky to have two *gorgeous* blondes sharing their home,' came the tongue-in-cheek response.

Erin was unable to stop her lips from curving into a smile, unwilling though she was to give way to it. She only wished she really *was* a gorgeous blonde—preferably one around twenty-six!

It was coming up to a quarter past the hour when they finally reached the square. Nick was waiting by the fountain.

'Sorry we're late,' proffered Erin, surprised by the easy shrug.

'I've known worse time-keeping. Did you get everything you wanted?'

There was no hint of sarcasm in his tone; not that Samantha would have taken any note if there had been, Erin suspected.

'Not *everything*,' she said airily. 'But enough to be going on with.'

'Good.' This time there was a definite dryness. 'No problems?'

'None at all,' Erin confirmed. 'Your name was recognised everywhere.'

He made no comment to that. The surprise would have been, she reflected, if someone had failed to recognise the name.

It was a relief to dump the bags in the car boot—an even greater one to get out of the midday heat. Samantha opted to sit in the back this time, leaving Erin with no choice but to take the front passenger seat. She steeled herself not to draw away when Nick slid in beside her, although his shoulders seemed almost to be brushing hers. The lesser-sized cars might be more sensible for use on the narrow inland roads, but they were too closely confining for comfort.

'We met a Tim Wyman in town,' Samantha imparted when they were on their way. 'Him and his friend, Reece. They bought drinks for us.'

'Non-alcoholic in your case, I hope,' Nick returned. 'They should have been in college, the pair of them.'

'How old are they, then?' she asked.

'Seventeen. They both attend Peterson—the same one you'll be going to come Monday.'

'That soon?' On a disgruntled note.

'The earliest I could arrange. Gives you five full days of freedom.'

Five full weeks wouldn't be enough, Erin could have told him. She waited for Dione's name to come up, but Samantha had other matters on her mind. Erin could almost hear her thinking that if Tim and Reece could get away with playing truant, there was no reason why she shouldn't do the same on occasion. She'd done it often enough back home.

It would be a whole lot better if she were only fourteen herself right now, Erin thought disconsolately. She certainly wouldn't be thinking the way she was about this man at her side. On the other hand, he might see her in a different light if she were older. Nineteen was so betwixt and between. Maybe in October…

She felt a tremor go right through her as her mind leapt ahead to visualise the two of them together, those long, clever fingers exploring every inch of her body, the grey eyes devouring her, wanting her, his shoulders so wide, his body so hard, her arms sliding up about his neck as he…

She put out the tip of her tongue to dampen lips gone suddenly dry, desisting abruptly when Nick glanced her way. This really did have to stop! she thought desperately. The whole thing was getting out of hand.

CHAPTER FIVE

BELLA mellowed a little as the days passed, chiefly due to Erin's efforts to keep both her own and Samantha's room spick and span. As anticipated, the latter's bed-making lasted no longer than the first morning, while the idea of actually tidying up her abandoned clothing never even occurred to her. Erin knew she was as much to blame for the lack of consideration as her sister. It had always been both quicker and easier to do things herself rather than attempt to lay down the law.

Sorting out the build-up of paperwork in the little office at the rear of the studio took no more than a few hours. Inexperienced as she was in business matters, Erin couldn't fail to glean that the sale of art works constituted only a part of Nick's income: he also appeared to have a vast investment portfolio. Not that it made any difference so far as she was concerned. She had known he was wealthy; the degree was of no importance.

His presentation of bank account books and corresponding chequebooks made out in hers and Samantha's names was another matter. The balances added together had to be far in excess of the sum he claimed to have received from the house-clearance firm he had called in that last weekend back home.

Faced with it, he made no attempt to deny it.

'The only way of giving you both a little independence,' he said. 'And no arguments,' he added as she began to form a reply. 'If you don't want to use it, don't, but it's staying right there.'

Erin had collared him in the studio, where he was finishing off the work she had first seen covered on the easel. It was a study of cane cutters at work in the fields, backs bare, muscles gleaming with sweat under the baking sun, the heat almost palpable. Watching the seemingly casual brushstrokes, she envied him his talent. Given all the teaching in the world, she could never have come anywhere close.

'Me aside,' she said, forced to recognise the futility in further protest, 'I don't think it's a very good idea to let Sam loose on this amount of money. She'll probably squander it.'

'On what? More clothes? I'd have thought she had enough to stock a shop already.'

Erin bit her lip. 'I know. I shouldn't have let her spend so much.'

'That wasn't what I meant.' Nick stood back to view the painting, then laid down his brush and palette. 'One of these days,' he continued hardily as he wiped his fingers on a rag, 'you're going to stop reading criticism where there's none intended.'

About to apologise, Erin stopped herself. Right now it would be adding fuel to a fire already smouldering. She half turned to go, pausing as he said her name on a slightly softer note. She could see him in her mind's eye, muscle and sinew contracting, standing there so tall and lean, a comma of dark hair falling across his forehead.

'This is the last of the New York consignment, so we may as well get started on you while you're here,' he said.

'I'm not wearing a nightdress,' she pointed out, and he laughed.

'Preliminary sketches only. I like to do several. Come and sit over here in the light.'

Glad of any legitimate excuse to stay, she did as she was bid, perching on the chair indicated. Nick shifted the easel, setting up another smaller one along with a stool for himself. Erin tried to appear relaxed as he assessed the angles before putting pencil to paper, though it was impossible to feel it under that all-too perceptive gaze.

The paint-spattered T-shirt he was wearing fitted close about the taut swell of his biceps: she could see the movement of muscle beneath the light coating of dark hair on his forearm as he shifted the pencil through both horizontal and vertical axis lines. He was so utterly and devastatingly male: a real man—so different from the boys she had known back home. Not that she'd had much opportunity to meet the opposite sex at all since leaving school.

'Try thinking about something else,' he suggested, obviously aware of her lack of tranquillity. 'Something you'd like to be doing right now.'

There was no trace of irony in his voice. She must stop reading innuendo into every word and gesture, Erin told herself.

All the same, she couldn't stop the images conjured by the words from forming: Nick putting down his pencil and getting to his feet, coming over to lift her bodily from the chair, his face taut with desire, his lips seeking hers. There was a chaise longue over in a corner of the studio. He was carrying her there and laying her down on it, standing back to peel off his shirt and reveal the muscular span of his shoulders and chest, fingers reaching for the buckle of his belt…

She jerked out of it to find the grey eyes viewing her with an expression that brought the hot colour rushing up under her skin. He had a good idea of what had been going through her mind, she realised. It must have been written on her face.

'You've all the time in the world,' he said. 'Don't be in too much of a hurry. And don't bother trying to make out you don't know what I'm talking about either. Just wait for the right man to come along.'

It was too late for denials, Erin conceded in a sudden rush of blood to the head. 'He already did,' she declared. 'I love you, Nick!'

'No, you don't.' His voice had roughened. 'What you're feeling is simple sexual arousal, nothing more. I'm flattered to be the object of it, but that's as far as it goes. Now, be a good girl and forget it.'

'Don't patronise me!' she flashed back. 'I'm not a child. I don't need anyone to tell me what I feel!'

'*I* don't need *this,*' he snapped back. 'Are you going to sit for me, or do we call it a day?'

Trembling with anger and humiliation, her throat too tight for words, Erin got to her feet. Nick made no move to stop her as she headed for the door.

It was several minutes before she could pull herself together sufficiently to take proper stock of what she had said back there, even then unable to believe she could have been so idiotic as to tell a man she had known just one short week that she loved him. What had she expected—reciprocation?

How could she face him again after this? she thought wretchedly. If it were only possible to go home—back where she belonged.

If she used the money in her account, it was possible, she realised. There had to be more than enough for a one-way ticket. She'd be practically destitute when she got there, but anything would be better than staying on here.

And what about Sam? came the reminder. Was she really prepared to turn her back on her sister simply because she'd made a fool of herself? The answer had to be no, of course, leaving her with no alternative but to stick it out the best way she could.

It was gone six when Nick returned to the house. Watching him from her bedroom window as he rounded the pool, Erin wished it were only possible to turn off emotion like turning off a tap. It might not be love, but it was still overwhelming. She had never felt so utterly downhearted in her life.

Dinner was an ordeal. Having spent the last few days just lazing around the pool, Samantha was becoming bored, and making no effort to conceal it.

'There's not much point in my having all these new things just to wear around here,' she complained. 'I didn't even get to see a beach yet!'

'There's no reason why you shouldn't,' Nick responded. 'Try Paradise on the west side,' he added to Erin. 'It's only a mile or so outside Bridgetown. I'll highlight a route avoiding town on the map. It will be good practice for the school run next week.'

Blue eyes held steady by sheer force of will. 'You're going to trust me with the car?'

'Why not? You hold a valid licence.'

At least they still drove on the left, was Erin's first thought—although the roads between here and the main highway were hardly wide enough for sides to have much meaning. She would have to take careful note of the turns: one cane-bordered lane looked much the same as another.

'You're lucky,' Samantha exclaimed morosely. 'I'm going to be stuck in class for two more years while you're out enjoying yourself!'

'Don't count on leaving at sixteen,' said Nick. 'Erin lost out on extended education. You're not going to do the same.'

'You can't *make* me do anything once I'm sixteen,' she retorted smartly.

'Want to bet?'

Over the course of the past few days, Erin had learned to stay out of any battle of wills between uncle and niece. Nick was more than capable of holding his own. He was doing it now, the spark in his eyes quelling any further outspokenness on Samantha's part—for the time being, at any rate. She applied herself to her dessert with a mulish look on her pretty face.

There was no lingering over coffee tonight. Nick left as soon as he'd finished. Erin wasn't surprised to hear a car departing some twenty minutes later. He had obviously had enough of the pair of them.

It was a long evening, made even longer by Samantha's disgruntlement over Erin's refusal to take the other car and drive down to town.

'I can't see why not,' she said. 'It only takes about twenty minutes.'

'In daylight, and for someone who knows where they're going,' Erin pointed out. 'We'd probably finish up thoroughly lost.'

'Even that would be more exciting than just sitting around out here night after night!' The younger girl shoved herself to her feet. 'I'm going to watch television!'

So far as Erin was concerned, the Caribbean evening was one of the best parts of the day, but she could understand Sam's frustration. Luxury living was no substitute for the action-packed lifestyle she had anticipated.

At least she would have school to occupy her come Monday. What she herself was going to do with her time Lord only knew. Sitting for Nick was definitely out. He'd probably lost interest in painting her anyway.

She felt sorry for him, stuck with a situation no man his age could possibly relish. He had done what he considered the right thing in bringing them to his home, but he had to be regretting it by now.

He still hadn't returned when she turned in at ten. Not that she would have expected it. Samantha was in her room reading a magazine, her mood considerably lighter.

'We'll make our own fun,' she declared when Erin popped her head round the door to say goodnight. 'Starting tomorrow when we go find that beach. It's Sunday. We might even run into Tim and Reece down there.'

'We might at that,' Erin agreed, too relieved to find her sister's flag flying high again to point out the unlikelihood of their choosing the same stretch of sand. 'See you at breakfast.'

Undressed, she found herself too restless for sleep. There were chairs on the balcony. She went out to take one, propping her legs on another to contemplate the moonlit scene below. If this afternoon's episode had achieved nothing else, it had made her grow up at last. From now on she kept her feelings under lock and key.

It was hot tonight, the trade winds no more than a waft of warm air against her cheek. The pool looked so inviting, twinkling out there beneath the stars. On impulse, she got up again and went back indoors to seize her one costume from the shower stall where she had hung it to dry this morning, only now remembering that it had split right along the side seam as she'd taken it off.

One of Samantha's new ones would probably fit her okay, but it went against the grain to go borrowing—especially if she had to wake her up to ask.

So what was wrong with skinny-dipping? she thought recklessly. Bella and Josh were over in their own home, and Nick probably wouldn't be back for ages—if he came back at all. It could even be that Dione had returned to the island, hence his hurry to depart. If the woman had her own place—and it seemed more than likely that she would—then he might well spend the night with her.

Erin shut off that train of thought abruptly. The house was silent as she crept downstairs, her bare feet making no sound on the thick carpeting. It was quickest and easiest to let herself out via the French doors from the living room. Reaching the pool, she dropped the towel she had brought from the bathroom and stripped off her nightdress before she could change her mind, letting herself down into the water instead of diving in, so that she wouldn't cause a splash.

The water felt like silk against her bare skin. She swam slowly round the island, relishing the wonderful sense of freedom in being at one, so to speak, with Nature. A dozen different scents tickled her nostrils, more emotive by night even than by day.

The sky was cloudless, the stars brilliant in their setting of coal-black velvet. Erin floated on her back to gaze at them, mind emptied of everything but the sheer delight in being so totally unrestricted. She could spend eternity like this, supported in the soft caress of the water, her hair spread like a butterfly's wings about her head, her limbs boneless.

A shadow blocked out the moon, resolving itself into a tall dark figure standing on the pool-edge watching her. Erin continued to float there, too far under the spell of the night to recognise reality.

'It's heaven!' she murmured. 'You should try it.'

Face in shadow, Nick made no verbal reply. When he moved it was with almost robotic purpose, unbuttoning his shirt and shrugging it from his shoulders, flicking open his belt to slide the zip and discard his trousers. He was wearing black jockey shorts beneath, but only for a moment. The ripples when he let himself down into the water spread into a widening fan as he forged a passage to her.

It was only when he seized hold of her that Erin knew this was no dream. He felt too devastatingly real to be a figment of imagination. She shut out everything but the messages reaching her through her senses, fingers sliding up over smooth wet muscle to lock behind the dark head as he found her mouth with his in a kiss that rocketed her from girlhood to womanhood once and for all.

The water was shallow enough here for him to stand.

Erin felt the tremoring start deep as he brought the lower half of her body into closer contact with his. He was already fully aroused; instinctively, she opened her legs a little, to fit herself even closer, feeling him slide between her thighs, her insides turning liquid—molten fire reaching down into every extremity.

He hadn't so far said a word; nor did she want him to for fear of breaking the spell. Black as the sky above in this light, his eyes held a glitter to rival the stars. She clung to him as he lifted her legs about his waist, tensing momentarily at the first pressuring touch but too far gone to resist the urge coursing through her.

He claimed her mouth once more, parting her lips with the tip of his tongue to taste the inner sweetness. She gave a muffled gasp as the pressure between her thighs increased to almost unbearable proportions for a fleeting moment, then the pain was gone and they were wholly and wonderfully together, his body possessing her, filling her, beginning to move, his hands cupping her buttocks to move her in tune with him, his lips sealing her involuntary cries—all thought suspended as the world spun crazily about her head…

She awoke to early-morning light, disorientated for a moment until memory came flooding back, bringing with it a sense of fantasy. Had last night really happened?

Erin put out the tip of her tongue to touch her lips, conscious of a pleasurable ache in her lower regions, a tenderness no dream could have produced. It had happened all right. Every last sensational moment! She closed her eyes again, the better to savour the memories: seeing Nick standing there, so lean and powerful in his nudity, feeling the excitement rising in her at the mere thought of all he'd done to her. She wished he was here right now, ready to do it all again. Never in a thousand years could she have enough of him!

The euphoria faded a little as she recalled the change in him when he'd brought her indoors. He'd packed her off to bed with scarcely a word, much less a goodnight kiss. Not that he had anything to regret. If anyone was to blame for what had happened between them it was her, for enticing him. Men were notoriously weak when it came to resisting temptation.

Anyway, *she* had no regrets. Neither would he once he realised she wasn't going to go all clingy on him now. Not that she wouldn't be over the moon if he did come to feel the same way about her that she felt about him, of course. At any rate, there was nothing to stop them from sharing a bed some nights. No one else need know.

It was still very early. She was tempted to slip along to his room right now and waken him with a kiss. She could visualise the way he would look with his hair tousled, his jaw bristly. His chest would be bare; she didn't see him wearing a pyjama jacket. After last night, it hardly mattered if he was wearing nothing at all.

She was out of bed as she thought about it, too stimulated by the prospect of seeing him again to lend an ear to any cautionary voice. Bella wouldn't be over for at least another hour. All the time in the world for whatever might happen.

Nick's bedroom lay at the far end of the landing. It was most unlikely that Samantha would be awake at this hour, or that she would hear footsteps on the thick carpeting if she was, but Erin found herself tiptoeing past just in case. Nick's door wasn't locked. Gingerly depressing the handle, she eased it open, peeping round it to see a king-sized bed across a wide expanse of dark green carpet.

He lay on his stomach, face turned away from her towards the window, arms curved around the pillow. The single sheet was pushed down below his waistline, confirming her guess that pyjamas were not his style. A shaft of sunlight outlined the powerful shoulders.

Erin damped down the excitement swelling inside her and ventured further into the room, closing the door softly behind her. It seemed to take an age to cross the yards of carpet; any moment she expected him to waken up and roll over. Reaching the bed at last, she allowed herself a moment of delicious contemplation, running a slow gaze from the dark head down the line of his back to the firm swell of his behind. There was no surplus flesh anywhere, just hard muscle. But she already knew that, of course.

As usual, she hadn't bothered to put anything on her feet. Without pausing to consider, she slipped off her nightdress and lifted the sheet to slide very gently into the bed beside him. He stirred, and murmured something, then settled again. Erin put her face closer, to inhale the emotive masculine scent of his skin, unable to stop herself from pressing a feather-light kiss to his nape.

She froze for a moment when he rolled over to face her, relaxing when his eyes remained closed, his breathing regulated. It was too late to start changing her mind now anyway, she told herself. She was bound to waken him getting out of the bed again.

His face in close-up was just as she had imagined it, tanned skin smooth over brow and cheekbone, jawline dark with morning stubble. Never having had the luxury of studying him in such detail before, she hadn't fully realised how long his eyelashes were, or just how well shaped his mouth.

The sheet had slid even lower when he turned. She dropped her gaze down the strong column of his throat to a chest lightly coated in dark hair that tapered away to merge with ridged stomach muscle. Dormant, he was still impressive. Pulses racing, insides on fire, Erin reached down a hand to gently enclose him, thrilled to feel an immediate pulsing response.

Nick drew in a long, slow breath, mouth curving. 'Good morning to you too,' he said softly.

Erin formed a smile of her own as the grey eyes opened. 'Hi!' she said.

For a brief moment there was no reaction, then he thrust himself upright, face darkened, eyes blazing. 'What the hell do you think you're doing?' he demanded.

Shaken to the core by the force of his anger, Erin sought refuge in sarcasm. 'You didn't say that last night!'

The anger died, the expression that replaced it no more encouraging. 'It shouldn't have happened,' he admitted wryly. 'I thought I could handle it.'

'Handle what?' she asked.

'Wanting you.' His voice was suddenly savage again. 'Wanting a nineteen-year-old kid!'

'I'm not a kid,' she protested. 'I wanted you too. You know I did.'

'You didn't even know *what* you wanted.'

'Yes, I did. I've known the facts of life since I was about ten.'

Nick said something short and sharp under his breath. 'I'm not talking about basic biology!'

'Neither am I.' The words formed themselves. 'I was telling you the truth yesterday, Nick. I love you. Wanting is a part of loving, isn't it?'

His lips curved in a mirthless smile. 'Not always.'

'If you're saying you don't love me, I already know, and it doesn't matter.' That was a downright lie, but she wasn't about to admit it. 'I'm happy just being with you.'

'It *isn't* going to happen again,' he declared. 'Once might still be one time too many.'

'If you're worried I might get pregnant, you needn't,' she said. 'I've been on the Pill for the last three months.'

His brows drew together. 'Why?'

'Women's problems.'

The scowl deepened. 'Don't get clever with me!'

'I'm not trying to be clever,' she denied. 'The doctor put me on it for "regulatory purposes"—to use his own words. You're the only one I've ever made love with.'

'I already gathered that.'

'Then you'll know how special you are to me. I really do—'

'Don't start trying to tell me you love me again,' he cut in roughly before she could voice the words. 'You've no idea what love is.'

Blue eyes flared. 'Will *you* stop telling *me* what I do or don't feel! What are you afraid of—that I'll expect you to marry me? Well, you needn't be! I'm no more interested in marriage than you are!'

'So exactly how *do* you see yourself?' he asked with obvious scepticism. 'As my live-in lover?'

'If you want me to be.' Erin softened both expression and voice. '*Do* you want me, Nick?'

The tell-tale muscle jerked in his jawline as he surveyed her slender curves. 'Get out of here,' he said thickly. 'Now!'

Her smile was slow, her confidence fully restored by what was happening to him regardless. 'You don't mean that.' She raised her arms to slide both hands behind her head beneath the spread of sun-kissed fair hair, seeing the effect on him as her breasts lifted into pert prominence and aware of a wholly new sense of power. 'Do you?' she whispered.

His teeth came together with an audible snap. When he moved it was with controlled violence, rolling to the far edge of the bed to sit up with his back to her.

'You've got ten seconds,' he said grimly. 'I'm serious, Erin. I want you out!'

She came to a sitting position herself, eyeing the tapering back irresolutely. She could take the coward's way out and obey him, or defy him and accept the consequences—whatever they might be.

He stiffened when she slid a fingertip down the ridge of his spine. 'It already happened,' she murmured. 'What difference is it going to make if it happens again? I told you there's no danger of my getting pregnant.'

'There's no such thing as a hundred per cent guarantee, you little fool,' he gritted.

'There was no guarantee at all so far as you knew beforehand,' Erin felt moved to point out. 'It didn't stop you then.'

He gave a short, hard laugh. 'The way you looked floating in that damned pool, wild horses couldn't have stopped me! That's something I have to live with.'

'If you used something yourself this time, there wouldn't be any risk at all,' she said, trying to sound practical about it. She bent to put her lips where her finger had been, extending the tip of her tongue to taste the faint saltiness of his skin, the clamour mounting by the second inside her. 'I'm not leaving,' she stated recklessly, 'so you'd better reconcile yourself. I *want* you, Nick! Now! This minute!'

For a moment or two, when he made no attempt to remove the hands she slid over his shoulders, she really thought she'd won through. The sudden jerk as he stood up tore her hands from him and left her kneeling there numbly watching as he moved with purpose over to the nearby chair to take up a silk robe and slide into it.

When he turned, he was in control, face taut. 'It isn't me you want,' he said. 'It's just sex. My fault, I admit, for giving you the taste, but this is as far as it goes. Now, are you going to go, or do I have to put you out?'

It was on the tip of Erin's tongue to issue a challenge,

but she held it back. He still wanted her, and they both knew it, but there was no doubting his adamancy.

Unselfconscious in her nudity until this moment, she felt herself flushing beneath the hardened gaze as she slid back across the bed to find the nightdress she had discarded. She was glad of the curtain of hair falling forward about her face as she pulled it on. The boldness had flown; all she felt now was rejected.

'Are you going to send me back home?' she asked in muffled tones.

'It would be the sensible thing to do,' he said. 'Better from both points of view.' He added tersely, 'Though not until I can be sure there are no repercussions.'

Erin forced herself to say it. 'And if there did turn out to be?'

The pause seemed to stretch for ever. 'Something we'd have to deal with,' he said at length. 'Don't you have any slippers?'

She shook her head, avoiding any direct contact with the grey eyes for fear of losing what little self-respect she still had and begging him not to send her back. 'I'll try and stay out of your way,' she declared stiffly. 'Sorry to have been such a nuisance.'

She made her escape before he could respond—if he'd intended responding at all—closing the door on him in a welter of self-disparagement. If she hadn't made a fool of herself before, she'd certainly done the trick this morning.

Nick was wrong about one thing, though; it was more than just sex. The thought of never seeing him again if he really did make her leave Barbados was unbearable.

CHAPTER SIX

THE school run down to St Thomas proved no great problem. By the end of that first week Erin felt she could almost have done it blindfold.

Samantha settled down surprisingly quickly once over the initial strangeness. As schools went, it wasn't bad, she admitted. Everyone was being really friendly. Three years above her, Tim Wyman had taken it upon himself to introduce her around the very first day, which had certainly helped.

Life would be a whole lot simpler if she was in the same age group, thought Erin with some envy, listening to her sister relate the week's happenings over breakfast on the Saturday morning. It was probably true that schooldays were the happiest days of one's life, even if it didn't always appear so at the time.

She stole a glance at Nick, seated opposite, wondering what was really going on inside the dark head as he gazed out past her at the sun-bathed landscape. He'd taken care to keep contact between them to a minimum this past week, which might have been best from his point of view but had simply served to increase her hunger.

The nights were the worst time: she would lie there for ages, unable to sleep, her whole body aching for the touch of those supple, sensitive hands, her mouth yearning for his kisses. If only he would forget the circumstances and just let things happen the way they were obviously meant to happen!

He switched his gaze suddenly, meeting her eyes with

inscrutable expression. Heart jerking, Erin said the first thing that came into her head.

'I was thinking of driving down to town. One or two things I need to get.'

'You don't need to explain,' he returned. 'The car's there whenever you need it.' He paused. 'You might consider getting yourself at least one new outfit while you're down there. We'll be going out tonight.'

Samantha's interest perked up. '*All* of us?'

'All of us,' he confirmed.

'To where?' asked Erin, quelling the urge to say she wasn't going anywhere with him while he kept up this pretence that nothing had happened between them.

'The Wymans' place down on the coast. Yes, that Wyman,' he added before Samantha could frame the obvious question. 'I know Tim's father.'

'He must be a piece older than you are to have a daughter of twenty-six,' observed Erin with deliberation, and saw the grey eyes sharpen.

'How do you know about the daughter?'

'Tim told us about her when we met in town that first day,' Samantha chimed in, looking at her most innocent. 'You know her quite well too, don't you?'

Nick gave no sign of having registered the nuances. 'Val's in his early fifties, if it matters. There's another son in between Dione and Tim. Harley's twenty-three.'

Samantha giggled. 'They must have run out of ideas when it came to naming Tim!'

'Why would the two of us be invited?' asked Erin bluntly.

'They want to meet you.'

'Why?'

Nick drew an impatient breath. 'Are you trying to rile me?'

Blue eyes widened in bland imitation of younger ones. 'Why would I do that?'

'If I hear that word once more—' He broke off, shaking his head as if in repudiation of what he had been about to say. 'You're invited, that's it. We'll be leaving here around eight.' Abruptly pushing back his chair, he got to his feet. 'I'll be in the studio.'

The crates had arrived yesterday. She could have been over there helping him pack them if she hadn't chosen to go skinny-dipping that night, thought Erin. Not that she would be without the memory; it was all she had to sustain her.

'What's with you and Nick?' asked Samantha curiously. 'I thought he was going to let go with something really nasty just then!'

Erin forced a smile, a light shrug. 'Just a difference of opinion. Are you coming into town with me?'

'You bet!' Successfully sidetracked, the younger girl pushed back her own chair. 'I'll go and change. You never know who we might meet!'

Erin watched her go, too lacking in enthusiasm to make any immediate move herself. Nick's suggestion that she buy a new outfit had been more in the nature of an order. While what she wore round here was of no importance to him, he obviously didn't want her looking like the poor relation in front of his friends.

It would be discourteous to refuse the invitation, so a new outfit it had to be. If the dress she had seen before was still available, and it fitted okay, she would settle for that. Probably not a patch on what others would be wearing, but who was going to notice?

The dress was not only still available, it fitted as if it was made for her. Samantha clapped her hands when she saw it on.

'You look absolutely super!' she exclaimed generously.

'Don't ever try to tell me that nice clothes don't make a difference! It's added at least three years for a start!'

Whatever hesitation Erin had still entertained, that latter statement clinched the decision for her. And the wisp of a high-heeled sandal Samantha urged her to try on with the dress gave her a poise she had never possessed before. Viewing herself in the long dressing mirror, she felt a stirring of excitement at the thought of Nick seeing her like this. She even had cleavage!

'You'll wow them all tonight,' Sam declared with confidence when they emerged onto the street again. 'I wonder what this Harley's like?'

Erin didn't care. The only person she was interested in wowing was Nick. If she failed to make him want her again, it wasn't going to be for lack of trying, she vowed.

He didn't put in an appearance for lunch. He'd left soon after they had themselves this morning, Bella advised. No, she didn't know where he'd gone. She didn't go asking the master his business.

'You really think of him as "the master"?' asked Samantha, tongue tucked well into cheek.

'It a courtesy title,' replied the Bajan woman severely. 'It be good for you to show some respec' too.'

'He'd think I was being the dead opposite if *I* started calling him that!' Sam laughed. 'Lighten up, Bell! It's the twentieth century now!'

Muttering, Bella swept off along the veranda. Erin gave her sister a reproving frown.

'You shouldn't tease her like that.'

Samantha pulled a face back. 'Don't be such a grump! You're getting more like Bella every day!' She gave another laugh. 'I wonder what "maulsprigging" means.'

Erin had a very good notion. There were times when she too thought her sister might benefit from a well-placed smack.

They spent the afternoon around the pool. At the last moment Erin had added a yellow bikini to her purchases. Wearing it now, she felt slightly conspicuous, aware of the faint demarcation lines about her midriff and hoping they would soon fill in. At least with Sam there were no detrimental comparisons in other departments; her sister's breasts were still in the earlier stages of development.

Not that the smallness of her own had appeared in any way off-putting to a certain party, she conceded, thoughts harking back as always to that tumultuous occasion. Her nipples started tingling at the very memory of how it had felt to be enclosed within those firm lips, his tongue a flickering flame against her skin. Making love was the most wonderful sensation in the world! She wanted, needed, *yearned* for it to happen again. Only not just with anyone, of course. If she couldn't have Nick, she would stay celibate for the rest of her life!

Opening her eyes to see him poised on the pool-edge in the act of diving in, it was almost as if she had conjured him up by the very power of her longing. She watched avidly as he cleaved the water with scarcely a splash, the strong, clean lines of his body imprinted on her retinae. The black trunks he was wearing were brief enough, but she had seen him minus even those. Her inner thigh muscles went into involuntary spasm just thinking about the way he had looked then.

'Show-off!' said Samantha, watching him too as he executed a fast crawl down the length of the pool and around the little island. 'Not that he hasn't got a lot to show off,' she allowed. 'Dad never had muscles like that for sure!'

'Your father didn't have the time to exercise,' Erin felt bound to defend.

'You mean he didn't have the inclination,' came the unimpressed return. 'He might have lived a lot longer if he'd kept himself fit.'

Erin couldn't argue with that. In the years after her mother's death, her stepfather must have put on at least twenty pounds. If genes had any bearing at all, Nick might be expected to have a battle with weight gain himself as he got older, but she doubted if he would ever allow it to get out of hand.

She could imagine him at fifty, hair silver grey at the temples, perhaps a few lines radiating out from the corners of his eyes. When he was fifty, she would be thirty-five—a mature woman—maybe even a mother. Two children, she thought dreamily: a boy and a girl, in that order. The boy would look just like his father; the girl would take after her.

Nick hauled himself out of the pool, snapping her back to reality. There was about as much chance of that particular daydream coming to fruition as the world coming to an end next Tuesday, she reflected wistfully.

'Terrific style!' applauded Samantha as he ran both hands through his hair to squeeze out excess moisture. 'Not a bad bod either, for an old man.'

'All reassurances gratefully received,' he grinned. 'I hope you're wearing plenty of sun lotion.'

'We both are,' she confirmed, not in the least fazed by the oblique reference to the brevity of her bikini. 'I finally got Erin into one.'

'So I see.' The smile was still there as the grey eyes shifted to the other reclining figure, though altered a little in character. 'Very fetching too.'

'You wait till you see her tonight!' Sam enthused, still in a generous mood. 'You'll have to fight all the guys off!'

'I'll do my best,' he said, registering Erin's discomfiture. 'Either of you fancy a drink? Non-alcoholic,' he added as Samantha started to reply.

'As if I'd ask for anything but,' she retorted in wide-eyed indignation. 'Iced pineapple juice for me, please.'

'I'll have the same, thanks,' said Erin, having difficulty in thinking straight about anything at the moment.

Nick moved off towards the house, the moisture drying on him as he went. Erin tore her eyes from the departing back to find Samantha looking at her with a sly smile on her face.

'You like him, don't you?' she said. 'I mean *really* like!'

Erin kept her voice level with an effort. 'Of course I like him. He's been very good to us both.'

'That's not what I mean, and you know it! You've got the hots for him.'

'Where did you pick *that* little gem up?' Erin demanded, using disgust as a shield.

Sam grinned again. 'Don't come over all high and mighty. It only means—'

'I know what it means. I just don't like hearing you say it.'

'All right, then, I'll put it another way. You'd like to go to bed with him, wouldn't you?'

Erin could do nothing to stop the tell-tale colour from flooding her cheeks. Her, 'Don't be ridiculous!' sounded weak even to her own ears.

'It's nothing to get in a strop about,' her sister returned imperturbably. 'I might even fancy him a bit myself if I were your age.'

Erin sat up abruptly. 'You shouldn't be thinking about fancying anybody at your age!'

'Oh, come on! I'm fourteen, not nine! I fancy Tim like mad.'

'You watch far too much television.' It was all Erin could come up with on the spur of the moment. Sam had always been a bit precocious, but this was reaching new levels! She added hesitantly, 'You wouldn't do anything…foolish?'

'I'm not stupid either.' The tone was derisive. 'I'm not going to finish up like Maureen Bailey back home!'

There was a chance yet that *she* might, thought Erin, recalling what Nick had said about the lack of fail-safe. A very small chance, she assured herself, aware of a part of her that actually wished it would happen.

She made no further comment, too afraid of what she might inadvertently give away. Nick returned bearing three tall frosted glasses on a tray, setting it down on the low round table between the two girls. There was a spare lounger laid out on Erin's far side. Taking up his own glass, he moved round to seat himself on it.

Sam took a single long swallow from her glass, then put it down and got to her feet.

'I'm going in again,' she announced. 'I want to wash my hair before we go out.'

'Me too,' Erin agreed, seizing on the excuse. 'I suppose I'd better get started, in fact. It takes ages to dry!'

'In a minute.' Nick spoke quietly but with purpose. 'We have to talk.'

Erin subsided with mixed emotions, waiting until her sister was in the water before saying tonelessly, 'We've had all week to talk.'

'Don't make this any harder than it has to be,' he admonished. 'I'm not here to make excuses for what I did the other night. It was totally—'

'Wonderful!' she interjected, throwing caution to the winds along with any last remnants of pride. 'You don't need to make excuses. You didn't take advantage of me. I knew what I was doing. *And* I'd do it again,' she added boldly.

His lips twitched at the corners. 'You just don't know how to take no for an answer, do you?'

'I would if I knew it was really meant,' she said, emboldened still further by the flash of humour in the grey eyes. 'You might regret it happening, but it doesn't stop you wanting me. That's why you've steered clear all week, isn't it? You're afraid you might let yourself be tempted again.'

Humour gave way to a swift-growing intolerance. 'You've no idea what you're talking about,' he said grimly. 'You're—'

'Only a kid?' she cut in again, determined not to give way. 'If I was, I stopped being one a week ago, so please stop treating me as one! It's too late to go back.'

'Do you think I don't realise it?' he growled. 'I started something there's no going back on!'

Erin shook her head emphatically. 'You didn't start it, it was already there—just waiting for the right person to come along at the right time and let it out.'

Nick didn't answer immediately, regard narrowed to her face, framed within the fall of bright hair. When he did speak it was with deliberation. 'Except that it was the wrong person and the wrong time.'

'Why?' Erin demanded.

'I'm too old for you, for one thing.'

'No, you're not!' she denied fiercely. 'Lots of men have relationships with younger women.'

The dark brows lifted sardonically. 'You've seen it happen so often, of course.'

He was laughing at her now, she sensed, and not in any kind way. 'I don't need to see it to know it happens,' she said with what dignity she could marshal. 'I'm going to wash my hair.'

This time he made no attempt to stop her as she got up from the lounger, nor did he say anything more, laying himself down with an air of resignation. So much for talking, Erin reflected wryly.

She spent a long time over her hair. It was coming up

to seven-thirty before it was fully dried. Falling loose about her shoulders, it made her look depressingly young.

Rooting through her things, she came up with a packet of hairpins she had acquired some time ago and never yet used, and managed to secure a thick coil on top of her head. Neck and shoulders bared, the slightly dipped front of the blue dress revealing a glimpse of lightly tanned curves, she looked very different from the girl who had arrived here almost two weeks ago. An improvement for certain.

If she'd had any doubts at all left on that score, they were banished by the look in Nick's eyes as she descended the stairs to where he waited in the hall.

'Sam wasn't exaggerating,' was all he said, but it was enough.

He looked devastating himself, in a pale cream tuxedo that made his shoulders appear even broader. It took every ounce of control Erin possessed to keep her emotions from visibly surfacing.

'You didn't say it was a formal affair,' she managed with creditable lightness.

'It isn't,' he said. 'Not the way you mean, at least. Val and his wife believe in making the most of any occasion, and like their guests to follow the same code. I didn't want you to feel uncomfortable.'

Which she would have done, Erin was bound to admit, in any of her other garments. She'd been acting like an idiot in refusing to replenish her wardrobe. Nick had every reason to consider her an ungrateful wretch. First thing Monday she would go down into town again and settle that situation at least. As to the rest…

Sam's arrival broke off the thought before it crystallised. Wearing a short, off-white tunic that exposed rather too much leg, her eyes and lips emphasised with make-up, she looked not only older than her years but a bit tarty to boot, in Erin's estimation. She expected Nick to order an immediate removal of the eyeliner, if nothing else, but he made no comment, leaving her with the impression that such matters were her province if anyone's.

'Shall we go?' he said while she was still trying to come up with some unhurtful way of putting it across. 'It's gone eight already.'

Built in Spanish style, with arched entrances and fretted iron window grilles, the Wyman villa lay in a private cove near Holetown on the west coast. The huge lounge occupying the greater part of one jutting wing already held a regular throng of people, most of them older than Nick, all of them well dressed.

The dark-haired woman who came to greet them was in her late forties, at a guess, her smile purely social as she welcomed the two girls. Erin had the distinct impression that *her* appearance had come as something of a surprise.

'You'll find Tim out on the patio,' she said to Samantha. 'He'll look after you.' Her expression warmed as she turned her attention back to Nick. 'I imagine you already knew Dione was planning on cutting her New York visit short?'

'As a matter of fact, no,' he returned. 'When did she get in?'

'Just an hour ago. She's still in the process of deciding what to wear. You know how long that can take!'

Nick laughed and shrugged. 'I'll expect her when I see her. Are your in-laws here tonight?'

'They are,' she confirmed. 'I don't think you've met Shirley's daughter and her husband. I organised this affair to welcome them back as full-time residents at last. They own Bay Marris.'

Nick looked interested. 'Lovely place!'

'Isn't it, though! It's been run as a country club for years, of course, but they're turning it back into a private residence now—although they'll still allow the golf course to be used. Bryn's a top-flight construction consultant—or he was. Tessa's spent most of her married life chasing all over the world after him, poor dear!'

'I suppose she felt it worth it just to be with him,' said Erin, knowing she certainly would if she were ever in that position.

Pamela Wyman gave her a condescending glance. 'The same romantic notion Tessa had. She was about the same age as you when she married Bryn. They never found time to have children.' The last in the complacent manner of one who had found time to produce three. 'Shirley will introduce you. They're all of them outside at the moment. Val too, I think.'

She turned on the smile again to greet the couple just entering the room. 'Paul—Melissa! How lovely to see you!'

Nick put a light hand beneath Erin's elbow and steered her clear of the welcome pad. 'Let's find the younger element for you.'

'I'd like to meet these other people,' she said, with no intention of being ditched. 'They must have led a fascinating life!'

'A pretty hard one at times, I'd imagine.' He sounded tolerant. 'Come on, then.'

A loggia laced through with bougainvillaea gave onto a broad patio with an oval swimming pool at its centre. Beyond that, through a curtain of palm trees, lay the beach itself, both sand and sea shimmering in the moonlight. The cicadas were loud and fluid, rising even above the combined chatter and laughter issuing from the various small groups of people scattered about.

Still holding her elbow in that same light grasp, Nick led Erin to one of the nearer groups seated about a slatted wooden table, bending to kiss the cheek of a silver-haired woman whose looks belied the age she had to be if she was the mother of the younger version seated next to her.

'Good to see you, Shirley,' he said. 'You too, Roland,

Val.' He looked across at two men with roughly the same age difference between them. 'I'd like you to meet my niece—or one of them, at any rate. This is Erin. Samantha is over there with Tim.'

Shirley Wyman's smile put her daughter-in-law's in the shade. 'How do you like Barbados, Erin?'

'I love it!' she said, smiling back. 'Both Samantha and I are *so* grateful to Uncle Nick for letting us come to live with him!'

The other, younger woman bit her lip as if to control a laugh, her eyes dancing. 'You must be,' she said. 'I'm Tessa Marshall. This is my husband, Bryn.' She indicated the man who had risen from his seat on the arm of her chair to stretch out a hand in greeting to the pair of them. 'It's so unusual to find a man your age willing to take on such a responsibility,' she added to Nick.

'It poses no problem,' he returned easily. 'Erin takes care of her sister, the way she's always done.' The hand still under her elbow had tightened its grasp, as if in warning against any further facetiousness. 'She's eager to hear all about your travels.'

Tessa laughed. 'It'll have to be the potted version. Life isn't long enough for all the detail.' She patted the empty chair at her side. 'Come and sit by me.'

'You don't know what you're letting yourself in for,' warned her husband on a humorous note as Erin obeyed. 'She'll have *your* life story out of you before you know it.' He turned his attention to Nick. 'I'm a great admirer of your work. Do you take on commissions?'

'He's going to ask if he'll do a portrait of me to hang at Bay Marris now we're home for good,' said Tessa wryly. 'I hope Nick won't mind being collared so soon. Bryn doesn't believe in hanging back.'

'I'm sure Nick would be only too pleased to paint you,'

Erin assured her. 'You're a very beautiful woman. So is your mother.'

'Yes, you'd never believe she's in her seventies, would you?' Tessa sounded gratified. 'You remind me very much of myself when I was your age, Erin. I had long blonde hair and a slinky figure too back then.'

She had a good figure still, from what she could see, Erin considered, but decided it would sound a mite sycophantic to say so. 'Mrs Wyman said you were about my age when you married Bryn,' she said instead.

'Sweet nineteen,' the other confirmed. 'Bryn's twelve years older, although you wouldn't guess it now. Men are so fortunate that way. Greying hair just makes them look distinguished. He and Nick share a certain similarity, wouldn't you say? Allowing for the years between, of course. How old is he?'

'Thirty-four.' Erin was watching the two men as they talked, realising that Bryn did indeed quite closely resemble the image she had created in her mind that afternoon. 'Fifteen years,' she murmured, only becoming aware that she had said it out loud when she looked back to meet a pair of comprehending green eyes.

'Not unsurmountable,' Tessa said softly. 'In fact, the way he was holding onto you just now, I'd say the odds were very much in favour.'

There was no point, Erin decided ruefully, in trying to deny what she had made so patently obvious. 'That was just to stop me calling him Uncle Nick again,' she admitted. 'I'm not really his niece, of course. His brother was my stepfather.'

Tessa smiled. 'I'd gathered it was something like that from the way you reacted. I suppose it's simpler for him to introduce you that way rather than go into explanations—although it could make things a little difficult for you both.'

The others were all engrossed in their own conversations—Nick himself too far away now to overhear anything they were saying anyway. Erin lifted her shoulders in a wry little shrug, feeling drawn to this woman who had known what it was like to fall in love with an older man. 'It's hardly likely to matter.'

'That's defeatist talk!' Tessa kept her voice low, but the cogency came through loud and clear. 'Age doesn't have any bearing on how you feel about someone. I fell in love with Bryn when I was fourteen.'

'Did he feel the same way?'

'Yes. He waited five years for me to grow up.' She gave a reminiscent smile. 'Not that it was plain sailing even then, but we've had twenty-seven wonderful years together—and plenty more to come.'

Erin did a quick mental calculation, her eyes widening. 'That makes you forty-six and Bryn fifty-eight! I can hardly believe it!'

'Love keeps the wrinkles at bay.' Tessa was obviously appreciative of the compliment. 'There might be a few men who can look at a young and lovely girl without wanting her, but I doubt if your Nick is one of them.' Catching the fleeting expression in Erin's eyes, she gave a sage nod. 'You're halfway there already.'

Erin bit back the instinctive denial, recognising the unlikelihood of being believed. 'You're not shocked?' she asked.

Tessa smiled again. 'The way you obviously feel about him, there's nothing to be shocked about. I once pushed Bryn fully clothed into a swimming pool in the hope that he'd lose the control he was exercising at the time and do what I wanted him to do.'

'And...did he?'

'No, much to my disappointment. A bit *too* strong on will-power at times, my husband.'

Glancing his way in quick appraisal, Erin could imagine. Nick was strong-willed too, but she had managed to undermine him in little more than a week, which surely had to mean something.

Tessa was right, she decided in sudden surging determination: she *was* halfway there. Whatever it took to go the rest of the way, she was up to it!

A cheer went up from the group gathered nearest the house, followed by laughter and greetings as some newcomer emerged from within to join the party. Erin saw Nick look across, his expression altering.

Turning her head to follow his gaze, she felt her heart drop like a stone as she viewed the woman making her way towards him. If this was Dione, the battle was over before it had begun!

CHAPTER SEVEN

JET-BLACK hair drawn back from a smooth oval of a face, voluptuously curved body poured into a classic black tube of a dress, the new arrival had just about every male eye in the vicinity riveted to her, but her smile was directed only at one.

'Surprise!' she said.

'Not any longer,' Nick returned equably. 'Why the change of plan?'

'I just couldn't stay away any longer darling!' She kissed him lightly on the lips. 'Missed me?'

'Some,' he allowed, eliciting a provocative pout.

'I'll be looking for a little more enthusiasm later.'

'In vain, if he's any sense,' said Tessa *sotto voce*. She returned her husband's meaningful glance blandly.

If Nick had heard the comment, he gave no sign, and Dione had already moved on to greet some other people. Erin felt as flat as a burst balloon. Why would Nick want her any more when he had all that for the taking? Dione obviously didn't mind who knew what their relationship was.

'I have to find the bathroom,' she murmured.

'I'll show you,' offered Tessa, rising with her. 'Those seats are reserved,' she declared to the company at large. 'No pinching them while we're gone.'

Erin felt Nick's eyes on her, but she couldn't bring herself to look at him for fear of what he might see in her face. Jealousy was a soul-destroying emotion.

Tessa led the way back indoors and out through the far side of the lounge, answering all greetings on the way with a smile and a promise to make the rounds in a little while. The corridor beyond had doors opening off it from both sides. Choosing one, she ushered Erin through into a luxuriously furnished bedroom.

'There's an *en suite* if you really need it,' she said. 'I got the feeling that you just wanted out for a few minutes.' She paused, viewing the younger face shrewdly. 'If you're half the girl I think you are, you won't let that *femme fatale* out there put you off. If your Nick is half the man I think *he* is, he can see right through her anyway.'

Too downcast to even try dissembling, Erin lifted her shoulders. 'Does it make a difference?'

'Of course it makes a difference. Men being the way they are, they're likely to be physically stirred by someone like Dione, but if they've any sense at all, that's as far as it goes.'

Erin looked at the older woman curiously. 'I gather you don't like her very much.'

'You gather rightly. Dione's a predator. She feeds on male attention. She even tried it on with Bryn when we were here last year.' Tessa gave a short laugh. 'He found it amusing. I was more inclined towards murder. It would be great to see her deposed! What's more,' she added, 'I think you're the one to do it.'

'I wish I could share your confidence,' returned Erin on a doubtful note. 'I just don't have the same pulling power.'

'Don't be so self-deprecating.' Tessa took her by the shoulders and turned her about to face the full-length wall mirror. 'Just look at yourself! You've got everything it takes to have Nick eating out of your hand! If you want him, fight for him! Show Dione he's taken!'

Looking from her own reflection to the zealous green eyes of the woman at her back, Erin felt her mettle beginning to firm again. If Nick was worth having he *had* to be worth fighting for, regardless of the odds!

'Attagirl!' encouraged Tessa, registering the change of expression. 'Get back out there and give 'em what for!'

Nick was still talking with Bryn when they got outside again. Refusing to allow herself time for reflection, Erin put a proprietary hand on his arm, smiling up at the older man.

'You won't mind if I steal him away to dance? They're playing our favourite tune.'

If Bryn was taken aback he didn't show it. 'Not at all,' he assured her. 'In fact we might join you.' He glanced his wife's way. 'Feel like dancing?'

'Such finesse!' she sighed, and he grinned.

'Take it or leave it.'

Face unrevealing, Nick slid a hand about Erin's narrow waist to guide her around the intervening groups to the cleared area where several couples already gyrated to the piped music. Reaching it, she moved directly into his arms, sliding both hands over his shoulders to lock her fingers loosely together at his nape and look up into the ironic grey eyes.

'Since when did we have a favourite tune?' he asked.

'Since now,' she said. 'You obviously weren't going to ask me to dance, so I decided to take matters into my own hands.'

'With a vengeance,' he agreed drily. 'What makes you so sure I didn't have it in mind to ask you anyway?'

'Because if you'd asked anyone it was probably going to be Dione, and she's the one I don't intend to let near you.'

His mouth took on a slant. 'Is that a fact?'

'Yes,' she said firmly, determined not to give way to any undermining doubts. 'She doesn't have the same claim on you that I do.'

'And what exactly is that?'

'You're *my* first.' She paused, holding his gaze, heart

fluttering like a trapped bird. 'I don't want anyone else making love to me—ever.'

'Thinking of joining a convent?'

Erin shook her head. 'You know what I'm saying. I want to be married to you. I want to have your children. I want—'

'Whoa!' Nick sounded less than amused. 'I thought you weren't interested in marriage?'

'I lied. Of course I'm interested. You might not love me the way I love you yet, but you will. I'm going to make sure of it. I'll even let you paint me in the nude if you want to. After all, you wouldn't be seeing anything you haven't already seen.'

'That's enough,' he said on a brusque note. 'Joke over!'

'Who's joking?' She pressed herself closer to him as they moved, elated to see the sudden spark leap in his eyes. 'I want you, Nick. And you want me. *Don't* you?'

'One more word, and I'm taking you home!' he threatened.

'Great!' she said. 'That means we can be alone.'

The hands at her back were hard. 'Stop it,' he gritted. 'Now!'

'Or you'll do what?' she queried, too far along the line to consider backing down. 'Spank me?'

Humour fought a brief and losing battle with anger in the lean features. Reaching up, he took hold of her hands and dragged them down from about his neck, pressing her far enough away to clear a limited space between them.

'I said cut it out!' he clipped. 'I don't know what's got into you, but—'

He broke off as she hoisted an eyebrow in faithful imitation, letting out his breath with explosive force. Turned about and propelled ahead of him off the floor, Erin kept a smile on her lips for the benefit of those about them, even now rejecting any inclination towards withdrawal. Perseverance paid in the end. She clung to that thought.

Nick made no attempt to steer her indoors, making instead for the shelter of the trees edging the beach. He came to a stop in the shadow of a coconut palm growing obliquely across their path, his face hard set in the filtered moonlight.

'Whatever game you think you're playing, it stops right here!'

'It's no game,' she said steadfastly. 'I love you, Nick. If you'd let yourself, you could love me too. You're halfway to it already.'

'Because I made love to you?' There was cynicism in the tilt of his lip. 'It's only the very naive who see the two as synonymous.'

Blue eyes refused to flicker away. 'So I'm naive. Preferable to being over-practised. Dione will let you down sooner or later. I wouldn't. That has to make me the better proposition when it comes to taking a wife.'

Nick gave a short laugh. 'It might, if a wife was what I was looking for.' He studied her pure young features, cynicism increasing as his eyes followed the smooth line of her throat to linger for a timeless moment on the tender curve of her breasts. 'I was weak enough to let myself be overcome by a lovely face and body, but there's no way I'd consider marrying you.'

'Even if I turned out to be pregnant?' she asked softly.

The grey eyes narrowed. 'Are you trying to tell me something?'

Erin shook her head again, wondering at her ability to stay calm and collected in such circumstances. 'It's too soon to know one way or the other. And you didn't answer the question. Would you marry me if I was having your baby?'

There was a pause, an expression she couldn't decipher

in his eyes. 'It would have to make a difference,' he conceded.

'Then I hope I am!'

Anger flared once more, tautening the lean features into a grim mask. 'The last thing you need is to be tied down with a baby at your age!'

'What does age have to do with it?' she demanded. 'What does age have to do with anything? Did you ever see a better suited couple than Tessa and Bryn?'

Nick eyed her in dawning realisation. 'She put you up to this, didn't she? Just what did you tell her?'

'I didn't tell her anything,' Erin denied, aware even as she said it how unlikely it was that he'd believe it. 'She guessed how things were.'

'Oh, sure! One look at the two of us and she had the whole picture!' He spoke with a clipped quietness more telling than if he'd ranted and raved. 'I can't really complain, can I? If I hadn't—' He broke off, lips compressing. 'That's enough!'

Erin shot a hand out to grasp his arm as he started to turn away, pulling him back round to face her with a strength that surprised them both. 'It isn't enough,' she said forcefully. 'Not nearly!'

Sliding both arms about his shoulders, she put passionate lips to his, willing him to respond, for his arms to enclose her, moulding her to the hard angles of his body. For a brief moment it seemed as if he might do just that as his mouth softened a fraction and began to answer, his hands sliding down her back to draw her closer the way he had done in the pool that night. The deprivation when he suddenly and roughly jerked her away from him was all the more brutal for that delay.

'It isn't going to happen,' he gritted.

This time there was no stopping him as he turned back the way they had come—no breaking the grip he had on her upper arm. Erin went along because she had no choice, but she wasn't beaten yet, she vowed. Tessa had sown too strong a seed.

Dione happened to be looking their way when they emerged from the shadow of the trees. The look that crossed her face gladdened Erin's heart. If nothing else, she had shown the woman that Nick wasn't her exclusive property.

The youngest by a couple of years at least, Samantha was over in a corner of the patio with a small group. Nick steered Erin over to them and left it to Tim to introduce her to his brother Harley.

'I've been waiting to meet you,' said the latter with a keenness that might have been flattering if she hadn't had her sights set on other goals. 'Mother said you were pretty, but I didn't realise just *how* pretty!'

Tim gave a derisive snort. 'How corny can you get!'

'Let's leave the children to play,' suggested his brother, not a whit put out. 'It's impossible to hold an intelligent conversation with this lot.'

'Thanks!' exclaimed Samantha indignantly, and received a condescending smile.

'Excluding newcomers, perhaps. I'll leave it to you to teach them some English manners.'

'I wouldn't rely on it,' said Erin jokingly as he drew her away from the group. 'There are times when my sister forgets all she ever knew about good behaviour.'

'She's in bad company with Tim, then. Father despairs of him doing anything worthwhile with his life.'

'He's only seventeen,' Erin defended, sorry now for having made the remark. 'There's plenty of time for him to make good.'

'Not while he spends nearly as much time out of school as in it. Being buddy-buddy with Reece Brady doesn't help. His folks have no control at all.' He made a dismissive gesture. 'Anyway, that's enough on *that* subject. I'm far more interested in you. Where have you been all my life?'

Tim had a point, Erin reflected, keeping a straight face with an effort. 'Growing up, I suppose,' she said.

Harley laughed. 'Very smart! I like a woman with a quick wit! Shall we dance?'

About to refuse, Erin spotted Nick taking to the floor with Dione, and abruptly changed her mind. 'I'd love to.'

'The music's a bit dated, I'm afraid,' he apologised, providing unnecessary guidance via a hand at her back. 'Father's a sixties fan.'

'I quite like that era too,' Erin returned lightly. 'You look a lot like your father. You and Tim both.'

'And he looks very much like Grandfather. It's a strong male line. Dione, of course, takes after Mother.'

It hardly took a degree in genetics to work that one out, thought Erin drily. Harley might be both closer to her own age and extremely good-looking, but he left her totally unmoved. After Nick, she would never be satisfied with her peers.

Except that there wasn't going to be any 'after Nick' she reminded herself, reinforcing her purpose. Whatever it took, they were going to be together.

She caught his eye over Dione's shoulder as Harley urged her ahead of him onto the floor, directing a challenging gaze that met with little response. He could chill her out all he liked; it wasn't going to work.

'Shirley obviously isn't your real grandmother,' she said when she and Harley were moving in slow unison to the music, unable to come up with any more riveting conversational gambit.

'No,' he confirmed. 'She and Grandfather were married the week before Bryn and Tessa. This was their house then, but they moved to a smaller place up the coast when Father and Mother married.'

'Do you see much of them? Bryn and Tessa, I mean?'

'I dare say we might see more of them now they're going to be here full time. He's much older than she is, of course.'

'Twelve years isn't much!' said Erin, a little too emphatically, and drew a surprised glance.

'It's a great deal more of a gap than I'd want myself. I think four is just about right.'

'You're looking for someone around your sister's age, then?'

Harley gave a laugh. 'As I said, a woman of wit! You and I are going to be spending a lot of time together from now on, Erin.'

It was the sheer assumption that riled her the most. Putting him down was uppermost in her mind at that moment, the consequences ignored. 'I don't see Nick allowing it once we're married,' she returned. 'He's very possessive.'

In any other circumstances Harley's expression would have made her want to laugh. 'Dropped on from a great height' was the nearest description.

'He's your uncle, for God's sake!' he spluttered.

'No, he isn't. Sam and I are only half-sisters.' Erin kept her voice steady by sheer force of will, aware of having gone too far, and seeing no way out. She made an attempt all the same. 'This is just between the two of us, Harley. We don't want it broadcasting around yet.'

'I'll bet *he* doesn't!' Harley sounded savage. 'He should be ashamed of himself, taking advantage of a girl half his age!'

'Why should age make a difference?' Erin protested. 'It didn't with Tessa and Bryn.'

'Not to them, maybe. Nobody else approved.'

'How would you know that? You weren't even born when they married!'

'My father was. He'd already—' Harley caught himself

up, obviously regretting what he had been about to say. 'That's all in the past. We're talking about you and that...*artist*!' The amount of invective he managed to get into the word gave it a whole new connotation. 'I suppose he talked you into posing for him in the nude—the way he did Dione. The man's a pervert!'

There were only three couples left on the dance floor at present, neither of the other two close enough to overhear what was being said—especially with Harley gritting everything through his teeth. It had to be obvious to anyone looking their way that something was wrong, though, thought Erin, not caring to glance in Nick's direction.

The very idea of his painting Dione in the nude set her own teeth on edge. She had a vivid image of those voluptuous curves reclining on the chaise longue in the studio—of Nick putting down his brush to go to take the woman in his arms. Taking what Tessa had said into consideration, Dione would probably know every trick in the book when it came to pleasuring a man—unlike herself, who could only rely on instinct. Her virginity had been her only real asset. Without it, what did she have to offer?

'I think I'd like to sit down,' she said huskily.

Harley made no attempt to dissuade her. He was probably coming to the conclusion that she deserved all she got, Erin reflected.

'I hope I can rely on you to forget what I told you,' she said as they moved away from the dance floor, without much hope at all. 'It's really no one else's business anyway.'

There was no verbal reply, just a shrug that could mean anything, followed by an abrupt departure. Tessa was beckoning, the chair at her side still empty. Erin made her way over to slide into it with a wry grimace in response to the questioning look.

'I've just done something very stupid,' she admitted. 'I told Harley Nick and I are going to be married.'

Comprehension was immediate. 'A chat-up stopper if ever I heard one! I take it Nick hasn't actually asked you as yet?'

'No.' Erin paused. 'I asked Harley to keep it to himself. Do you think he might?'

'Doubtful, I'm afraid. He'll have had his nose put out of joint. That isn't going to go down too well. He's used to having girls falling over themselves.' Tessa gave a dry little smile. 'A chip off the old block! His father found it hard to take when *I* turned *him* down.'

'So I gathered.' Erin glanced over to where Bryn stood talking with another couple of men. 'Was there much opposition?'

'Not so much opposition as lack of appreciation in some quarters. ''Autumn weds spring'' was how one idiot put it, which was totally ridiculous; Bryn was only thirty-one. And, no, I don't consider another few years of any consequence. You'll find you grow closer in every sense of the word.'

Erin found a weak smile. 'Providing I ever get the chance.'

'It's too late to start backing out now. You're going to have to see it through.' The green eyes were encouraging. 'It will work out, just see if it doesn't. Nick will be the envy of every able-bodied man on the island when news gets around.'

If Harley's reaction was anything to go by, he'd as likely be vilified, Erin reflected ruefully. How could she have been so utterly irresponsible?

It soon became apparent from the glances cast her way that Harley had lost little time in spreading the tidings. Nick had disappeared, as had Dione—whether together or not there was no telling. With neither courage nor desire to go and help herself from the vast buffet supper laid out under the loggia, Erin picked without appetite at the plateful Tessa brought back for her, wondering how long it was going to take for word to reach Nick's ears. If he was with Dione in private somewhere, it could be quite some time.

Bryn asked her to dance when the music started up again. Held loosely in his arms, Erin thought again how like Nick he was in many ways. Not so much in actual looks, perhaps, but in his unequivocal masculinity, his ability to assert without arrogance. She could well understand why Tessa had fallen in love with him all those years ago—why she was so obviously crazy about him still.

'I believe congratulations are in order,' he proffered. 'Although I should really be saying that to Nick, of course.'

Erin gave a small resigned sigh, seeing no point in trying to keep up the pretence when Tessa was already in possession of the true state of affairs. 'I'd rather you didn't say anything to Nick. It's all a mistake.'

'I had an idea it might be.' He paused, looking down at her with quizzical expression. 'These things have a way of getting out of hand. Especially with help from my wife.'

'It doesn't have anything to do with Tessa,' Erin denied quickly.

He smiled. 'I'd very much doubt that. The two of you have had your heads together since you got here. Tessa remembers the difficulties we went through ourselves by not being forthright with each other. It would be like her to try giving your situation a helping hand.'

'There is no situation.'

'No? That wasn't the impression I had when Nick towed you off the floor a while back. He looked like a man with quite a lot on his mind.'

'Still has,' said a grim voice. 'You'll excuse me if I cut in?'

'Sure.' Bryn yielded his hold and moved unhurriedly

away, leaving Erin to face a pair of steely eyes. With two ways to go, she opted for the boldest, chin lifting.

'So?'

Nick drew her to him, holding her in a crushing grip as he started to move in time to the music. She could feel the tension in him: a coiled spring held in check by sheer will-power.

'Just what did you hope to achieve?' he clipped. 'Did you really think I'd be so overwhelmed with shame I'd feel forced into marrying you?'

Erin stiffened her backbone, adopting a taunting tone she knew was asking for trouble, and suddenly not giving a damn. 'Smile, darling, or people are going to think we're having a row already!'

She hadn't thought it possible for his arms to tighten their hold on her any further, but they did, shortening her breath as her breasts came up hard against his chest. 'People are going to think a hell of a lot worse if you keep this up!' he threatened.

'I told you how I feel about you,' she said, ignoring the injunction. 'If Mohammed won't come to the mountain, then the mountain has to shift for itself. I was a virgin before you. Marriage is the price you have to pay for the privilege.'

Nick was silent for a lengthy moment, anger giving way to some other less easily identifiable emotion as he studied her upturned face. 'I can't believe this is you talking,' he said at last.

Erin could hardly believe it either. The words just kept coming. 'I love you,' she said, and kissed him on the lips. 'There's nothing you can say that's going to alter that. If you marry me I'll be the best wife any man ever had! I'll wash your shirts, darn your socks, cook all your favourite meals!'

An unwilling smile touched the corners of his mouth. 'I

don't need any socks darning, and Bella does everything else.'

'Not *every*thing.' Erin softened her voice, drawing on some hitherto untried feminine artifice. 'I'd be there whenever you wanted me, Nick—for whatever you wanted. I'd love and honour you—even obey!'

He gave a dry laugh. 'Don't let's get too carried away!'

'I mean it!' Right then she would have promised him anything. 'You can't marry Dione! I won't let you!'

'I never had any intention of marrying Dione,' he said with convincing certitude. 'I'd no intention of marrying anyone.'

Erin seized on the past tense implication. 'That was before we met. I knew the first minute I clapped eyes on you that no mere boy would ever be able to make me feel what you made me feel. I hardly slept a wink that night for thinking about you.'

The smile came again, tinged with more than a little irony. 'Ditto—though I'd doubt that we were thinking along quite the same lines.'

'Don't be too sure. I might not have had the experience back then, but I had all the feelings.' She paused, searching the lean features. 'Did you really feel that way about me even then?'

'I'd have had to be made from stone not to. You were—' He broke off, jaw hardening again. 'I should never have brought you back here with me.'

'I'd have died an old maid if you'd left me behind.'

'No, you wouldn't. You'd have met someone—'

'If you're going to say someone nearer my own age, don't!' she cut in. 'They're boring. Take Harley. He's so full of himself he thinks his company alone is enough to make a girl happy!'

'It would be with most.'

'Why? Because he's a good catch?'

'One of the island's finest.'

'Well, whoever he finishes up with, they're welcome to him. All *I* want is *you*!'

Nick gave a long drawn sigh, anger no longer a factor. 'You might think you do now.'

'I don't think; I know.' Having got this far, Erin wasn't about to give ground. His arms had loosened their hold on her; she closed the slight space between them again, relishing the movement of his thigh muscles against her—there was a lot to be said for high heels when a man was so much taller. 'Whatever arguments you come up with, you're not going to change anything,' she whispered against his cheek. 'I love you!'

He was silent for a lengthy moment, though he made no attempt to put her from him. When he did finally speak he sounded resigned. 'We'd better make it known you're not really my niece.'

Heart leaping, Erin drew back her head to search his face, not finding quite the confirmation she sought. 'I already told Harley I'm not.'

'That will have to do for now.'

'For now?' Her spirits had plummeted again.

The grey eyes offered no comfort. 'Short of forcing you to make a public retraction, I don't have much choice. In a few weeks' time—providing nothing else occurs—we can call the whole thing off. Until then, you don't say anything to anyone. Is that clear?'

The music had come to a stop, Erin realised. People were moving off the floor. Those who hadn't already heard the news would soon be put in the picture, only it still wasn't going to be for real.

'I think we'll call it a day,' Nick said firmly, turning her about. 'It's gone midnight.'

Erin was too downcast to even think of resisting. Catching Tessa's eye across the patio, she summoned a smile, reluctant to show her defeat. It was obvious from the way people were looking at the two of them that the rumour had gone all the way round. Obvious too, as Nick led her towards the house, that he had no intention of taking the least notice.

They were almost there when Dione put in an appearance, ignoring others in the vicinity, including Erin herself, her face a study as she confronted the man she had believed was hers.

'Is it true?' she demanded.

'That depends,' Nick said levelly, 'on what you've heard.'

'Harley just told me you're planning on marrying your niece!'

'There's no blood relationship. Erin and Samantha are half-sisters. He was already informed of that. Is your mother inside?' he added. 'I'd like to thank her for the hospitality before we go.'

'You can't be serious!' Like her brother, Dione found rejection impossible to accept. 'She's just a...kid!'

'*She* is more than old enough to speak for herself!' Erin cut in before Nick could answer, losing sight of everything he'd said in the searing heat of the moment. 'Wedding invitations will be in the post shortly.'

There was a laugh from somewhere behind them; probably Tessa enjoying the younger woman's comeuppance, thought Erin fleetingly. Mouth set like a trap, eyes sending out lightning bolts, Dione stepped aside to let them pass as Nick urged her forward with an ungentle hand at her back.

Erin could feel the anger in him, but she couldn't find it in herself to regret what she'd just done. It was time everyone—including Nick himself—realised she was no wilting violet ready to accept anything thrown at her. The fight wasn't over yet by a long chalk!

CHAPTER EIGHT

PAMELA made no effort to conceal her feelings when they took their leave of her.

'You could at least have told Dione what was going on in private, instead of leaving her to find out this way!' she berated.

'That was my fault,' Erin claimed swiftly. 'I let it slip to Harley. I did ask him not to spread it around.'

'That's hardly the point.' Pamela was giving no quarter, her anger directed at Nick. 'You should be ashamed of yourself!'

'You're probably right,' he agreed without expression.

Samantha barely waited till they got outside before letting fly with her own indignant reproofs.

'You're a real pair of dark horses! Why didn't you tell me what was going on? I felt an absolute idiot back there!'

'Don't exaggerate,' Nick said shortly.

Erin slid into the front passenger seat when he opened the car door for her, avoiding looking at him directly. That there were going to be ructions over that scene with Dione there was no doubt. She had put him in a cleft-stick, with no way out other than to show her up for the liar she was. Most men, she had to admit, would probably have done exactly that.

'So aren't you going to say anything about it at all?' demanded Samantha plaintively, after five minutes during which no one spoke.

'Such as what?' asked Nick.

'Such as when you came up with the idea in the first

place. Rin was making out she didn't even fancy you this afternoon!'

'I wasn't ready to talk about it then,' Erin claimed.

'You'd only just met Harley, but you were ready enough to tell *him*!'

'That was...unintentional.'

'Hooey! He said you couldn't wait to tell him!'

Out of the corner of her eye, Erin saw Nick's hand tauten on the wheel. 'It wasn't at all like that,' she denied.

'So how else was it?'

'Let it drop.' Nick spoke quietly enough but the undertone brooked no debate. 'You'll be told what you need to know when you need to know it.'

Affronted, Samantha thumped back in her seat. 'Pardon me for breathing!' she muttered.

Nick ignored the comment. Glancing sideways at the impassive profile, Erin rallied her flagging spirits. There was to be no backing down, out, or in any other direction. If she wanted him, it had to be an all-in effort.

Reaching the house, he bade the two of them to go on indoors while he put the car away. Still sulking, Samantha made no answer when Erin wished her goodnight, swishing off up the stairs without a backward glance. Erin sat down on the bottom step to wait. Tomorrow might be another day, but tonight was the time to get things sorted.

Nick looked unsurprised to see her there when he came in. 'We'll go to the library,' he said curtly.

The lovely book-lined room where Erin had spent many enjoyable hours was at the side of the house farthest away from the bedrooms in use—although it was doubtful, she thought, that Sam would have heard anything even if she had been directly overhead.

'I know what you're going to say,' she started in as Nick closed the door, 'but I couldn't help it.'

'Yes, you could,' he retorted. 'You thoroughly enjoyed shoving it down Dione's throat!'

'I was entitled to resent being treated like some trashy kid!' she declared. 'All right, so I enjoyed it. She obviously thought she owned you!'

'Maybe she had some reason.'

Erin drew in a lip, by no means deaf to the nuances. 'However many times you've slept with her, it doesn't give her any rights over you. You said you'd never had any intention of marrying her.'

'True.'

'So she was sticking her neck out going for you the way she did—which means you should have chopped her down to size yourself instead of leaving me to do it for you.'

Still not moving away from the door, Nick eyed her contemplatively. 'Dione isn't the only one in need of chopping down to size!'

Erin took fresh heart from the hint of humour in the line of his mouth, faint though it was. 'As the woman you're going to marry, I've every right to be uppity. Yes, I know what you told me; it doesn't mean I have to accept it.'

'What other course did you have in mind?'

She drew a steadying breath. 'Everyone believes we're going to be married. If you try to wriggle out of it now I'll sue for breach of promise!'

'I'll make sure to hire a good lawyer.'

'I mean it, Nick!' Erin put all the certitude she was capable of into that statement. 'I'm *not* giving up!'

There was a pause, an expression she couldn't be sure of in the grey eyes. 'It wouldn't work.'

'Yes, it would!' She was eager, sensing a certain weakening. 'I might not be experienced, but I can learn to be everything you need. All you have to do is show me.'

'There's more to marriage than sex.' His voice had gained a rough edge again. 'I'd be doing you no favour in marrying you, Erin. You're infatuated with the idea of it, that's all.'

'Not true. I know the difference between love and infatuation.'

'Of course you do.'

The satire lit flares in the blue eyes. 'If it was just infatuation, I'd be turned off by that kind of thing for a start! You can be a real pain at times.'

'That makes two of us,' he returned drily. 'Hardly a recipe for a harmonious marriage.'

'Total harmony would be downright boring,' she retorted. 'There's nothing like a good row for getting the adrenalin flowing!'

Nick looked as if he were fighting to stay on top of a situation fast getting out of hand. 'Where did you hear that bit of philosophy?'

'I probably read it somewhere,' she admitted, 'but it's true enough. Married couples who claim they've never had a single row must either be lying their heads off or too bovine to make the effort. Just imagine missing out on the making up afterwards.'

There was no controlling the laugh this time. 'You paint an alluring picture!'

'Private sale only,' she flashed back. 'You're going to say yes in the end, Nick, so why not save a lot of time and trouble and say it now? I'll be—'

'I know—the best wife a man ever had.' He studied her standing there, piled hair gleaming under the overhead light, shoulders bared in the blue dress, legs long and slender beneath the softly draped skirt, his lips twisting. 'I'd have to reserve judgement on that.'

Erin hesitated no longer, unable to control the urgent need to be close to him. Nick slid his arms about her supple young body as she raised an eager mouth, the look of a man driven beyond endurance in his eyes. The kiss was everything she'd hoped for. She savoured every moment of it, loving the taste of him, the scent of him, the overwhelming contact with that lean hard body.

'You wouldn't regret it,' she murmured against his lips. 'You wouldn't *ever* regret it!'

'You'd better get to bed,' he said, putting her gently away from him. He shook his head at the look on her face, his expression resolute again. 'Sleep on it. You'll probably feel differently in the morning.'

She could sleep on it from here to Christmas without it making a scrap of difference, Erin could have told him, but she had a better idea.

'All right,' she agreed, feigning resignation. 'Are you coming up?'

'I'm in need of a cooling-off period,' he said with a certain irony. 'You've got me so I'm not sure whether I'm standing on my head or my heels!'

Erin doubted it. She might have undermined his resistance but she'd by no means fully conquered it as yet. That was something she had to work on.

She went upstairs quietly, passing her own bedroom to slip into his, and standing at the doorway for a moment to calm herself before crossing to switch on a single bedside lamp.

She was wearing nothing but a pair of lace panties beneath the blue dress. Leaving both garments where they fell, she slid between the crisp cotton sheets, recalling with shuddering anticipation the last time she had done this. Nick wasn't going to kick her out tonight—or any other night, if it came to that. So far as she was concerned, they were married already. The wedding was merely trimming.

It seemed an age before he came up. She had turned out the lamp again, and he didn't bother to put on a light. The moon had either gone down or out, leaving the bed in deep shadow. Erin listened to the sound of his movements, hoping he wasn't planning on taking a shower. She wanted his lovemaking so badly she could barely contain herself.

The butterflies in her stomach increased their fluttering tenfold on his approach to the bed. He saw her only when he was a couple of feet away, coming to an abrupt halt.

'This wasn't what I meant by sleeping on it,' he said.

'It's my interpretation,' she claimed, senses clamouring on sight of his naked outline. 'We're not going to argue over a definition, are we?'

With eyes grown accustomed to the darkness, it was possible to see the struggle going on as he stood there looking at her. Erin threw off the sheet and held out her arms invitingly, willing him to give in, to stop thinking about possible future problems and do what he so obviously wanted to do right now. She didn't care *how* she got him, only that she did get him. Her life was worth nothing without him.

His move to open the top drawer in the bedside cabinet took her by surprise for a moment, until she realised what it was he was after. She didn't care about that aspect either, but if it made him feel safer then so be it.

She welcomed the impact of his body as he came down over her. The touch of his lips at her breast was agony and ecstasy rolled into one, his tongue searing a path around her areola, the potent weight pressuring her thighs apart. She wrapped her legs about him, too hungry for the tumultuous fulfilment she knew was to come to wait a moment longer for the sensation of him inside her. All man, and all hers—and woe betide *anyone* who tried to take him away from her!

Like that other morning, she woke up in her own bed, only this time it was in the safe and sure knowledge of even better things to come. She hadn't wanted to leave Nick at all, but he had insisted. Until they were married, they continued to occupy separate rooms, he'd said. Erin really couldn't see what difference it made now.

Mrs Nicholas Carson. It sounded so impressive. There was no reason to wait any longer than absolutely necessary for the wedding. After what she'd said to Dione, everyone would be expecting it to be soon, anyway. Lying there, luxuriating in the thought of it all, she even found an element of sympathy for the older woman. Losing any man to another woman would be hard enough for someone like Dione to take; losing Nick was obviously beyond all reckoning.

The tentative knock on the door brought her starting upright in anticipation, until common sense pointed out the unlikelihood of it being Nick out there—a guess confirmed when the door slowly opened to reveal Samantha's face peering round it.

'I thought you might have company,' she said, coming all the way in. She closed the door and rested her back against it, viewing her sister's tumbled hair with open speculation. 'I suppose he went back to his own room.'

'He never left it,' said Erin truthfully. She hesitated, not at all sure how best to approach the subject. 'I'm sorry you had to learn what you did the way you did,' was the best she could come up with. 'It's just the way it happened.'

Samantha looked sceptical. 'The way you planned it, you mean. Was it my saying how Dad blackmailed you into giving up school that gave you the idea?'

'I didn't *blackmail* Nick!' Erin denied hotly.

'Near enough, letting Harley spread it around like that. It would take somebody even harder than Nick can be to force you to stand up in front of all those people and admit to making it up.'

There was too much truth in what she was saying for comfort, Erin acknowledged wryly—rallying her spirits with the thought that she had only hastened the inevitable. Nick wouldn't have agreed to marry her if he hadn't had the idea in mind himself—even if only tentatively.

'I love him,' she said. 'He's the best thing that ever happened to me.'

'You never had a proper boyfriend to compare with,' the girl protested. 'Why don't you go for someone like Harley Wyman?'

'Even if I could have him I wouldn't want him,' Erin assured her. 'Or anyone else, for that matter. Nick is everything I could ever look for.'

'But he's old! *And* he's my uncle. If you marry him, he'll be my brother-in-law too. Have you thought about that?'

Erin hadn't. She found the notion quite intriguing. 'I suppose I'll be your aunt as well as your sister,' she mused. 'Quite a tangle!'

'The whole thing's disgusting!' Samantha burst out. 'You've got to stop it, Rin!'

Erin bit her lip, hardly knowing what to say. 'You didn't seem to think it so disgusting yesterday when you were teasing me about wanting to go to bed with him,' she appealed.

'That was just talk. You know it was! And it's not just my opinion either. You should have heard some of the comments last night!'

'I'm not interested in what other people think,' Erin countered. 'Neither is Nick. You didn't meet Tessa and Bryn Marshall, did you? If you had, you'd realise that love knows no barriers.'

'I'll bet you read that somewhere!' Samantha was not to be pacified. 'Don't expect me to be a bridesmaid, that's all! I shan't even come to the wedding!'

Erin sat gazing at the door for several moments after it closed on the departing figure, trying not to allow her sister's disapproval to affect her too deeply. Sam would come round. She had to come round. Nick would talk to her.

He was already seated at the breakfast table when she

went out some half an hour later, though there was no sign of Samantha as yet. Erin slid her arms over the broad shoulders from behind to press a kiss to the upper point of his jaw.

'Good morning, lover!' she laughed.

There was a sudden clatter of crockery as the trolley Bella was pushing towards them along the veranda collided with a potted palm.

'What are you about, girl?' she exclaimed in scandalised tones.

'I'm saying hallo to my fiancé,' Erin answered blithely. 'We're going to be married, Bella. Isn't it terrific?'

From the expression on the wide black face as her glance went from Erin to the man still seated, Bella had other adjectives in mind. 'She's just a child, Mr Nick! What are you thinkin' of?'

'Right at this moment, a cup of strong black coffee,' he returned wryly. 'I didn't intend dropping it on you quite this way, Bella, but it will be all round the island before the day's out, anyway.'

'Be pleased for us,' Erin pleaded. 'We know what we're doing.' She slid round and across Nick's knees, to plant another kiss on none too willing lips, refusing to allow his lack of response to undermine her ebullience. 'Don't we, darling?'

'That's enough,' he said in a low tone.

There was no ignoring the look in the grey eyes. Not anger, exactly, but a long way from ardour for sure. Sobering, Erin transferred to a chair, aware of a very great difference in mood from that of the night before. It was too late to start having doubts again. If they hadn't been committed before, they were now. They had to be!

Bella finished serving up breakfast in disapproving silence, and took herself back to the kitchen. Erin waited until the scarlet-clad back had disappeared around the corner of the veranda before giving voice to the concerns circling in her head.

'Have you changed your mind?' she asked.

'No,' Nick answered with reassuring promptitude. 'I'd just prefer you to keep your feet on the ground.'

'All the time?' she queried innocently, and saw his mouth start to crease at the corners.

'In public, at any rate. We're going to be running into a whole lot of reactions like Bella's.'

Samantha's, for one, she could have told him. She hoped her sister would have had second thoughts by the time she put in an appearance.

'It's ridiculous!' she exclaimed. 'You'd think there were fifty years between us! Not that it would make any difference if there were,' she added. 'I'd still feel the same way about you.'

'At sixty-nine, I might have found it difficult keeping up with you,' he said drily. 'I've a feeling I might anyway.'

'Rubbish!' She could say that with certainty. 'You're as virile as they come!'

His grin was good to see. 'You wouldn't know how they come.'

'I can guess.' She was laughing, eyes sparkling with pure, unadulterated happiness—the latter fading a little as her eyes went beyond him to where her sister stood framed in the doorway. 'Sam…'

The younger girl turned abruptly on her heel and vanished back inside again. Nick looked round in time to catch a glimpse of her retreating figure, turning back to direct a questioning gaze.

'What was that about?'

Erin adopted a flippancy she was far from feeling. 'She's been mixing with too many Wymans.'

'I see.' It was apparent that he saw all too clearly. 'I was under the impression she was just piqued last night because she hadn't been told in advance.'

'She probably was, to start with. She's had all night to think about it.' Erin hesitated. 'She came in to see me earlier. She said some people had made nasty remarks.'

'As I told you, it's to be expected.' Nick had sobered too. 'I don't personally give a damn, but you might not find it all that easy to handle. It's more than just the age gap. You're my brother's stepdaughter. A lot of people will see it as not all that far removed from incest.'

'Anyone stupid enough to think like that isn't worth bothering about!' she dismissed scathingly. 'At least we can rely on Tessa and Bryn for support. They've been through it themselves.'

Nick refrained from pointing out that they had been far away from island gossip for the most part. Viewing the angular features, Erin felt a nigh on irresistible desire to get up and go to him again—to feel the security of his arms about her, the delicious tingle of his lips against her skin. The last thing she wanted right now was food.

'Did you finish packing the crates yet?' she asked, pouring coffee for them both as a means of taking her mind off her urges.

'I didn't even get started,' he admitted. 'Too many other things on my mind.'

She looked at him through her lashes. 'Me being one of them, I hope.'

'You being all of them.'

'Really?' Erin was highly gratified. 'And what conclusions did you reach about me?'

'That the best thing all round would be to send you to art college back home—providing there were no complications.' The smile held an element of self-mockery. 'I didn't reckon on finding myself engaged to be married before the day was out.'

'But you don't regret it now?' she asked with a trace of anxiety. 'You really do want me?'

Nick eyed the lovely young face, his mouth curving again. 'There isn't a man alive who wouldn't want you.'

It wasn't quite what she'd asked, and was a great deal less than she'd wanted to hear, but it was obviously all she was going to get right now. He hadn't once used the word 'love,' Erin realised, thinking back. Not even last night in the throes of passion, although she must have said it a dozen times or more. According to magazine problem pages, she wasn't alone in finding romantic wordplay in short supply. A man's emotions were far more physically orientated than a woman's.

'I could give you a hand with the packing,' she offered, dismissing the matter for now. 'I'd be very careful.'

'I'd be very grateful,' he said. 'It has to be done today. The carrier's due in the morning. If we finish by lunchtime we can drive over to Bathsheba this afternoon, if you like. You'll find the Atlantic coastline very different.'

Erin hesitated. 'Do you mean all three of us?'

'If Sam wants to come. The way she acted a few minutes ago, I'd say it was doubtful.'

Erin doubted it too. 'Couldn't you have a word with her?' she suggested tentatively.

'Telling her what? I can't alter the factors she's upset about.' Nick shook his head decisively. 'She'll have to come round to it in her own time.'

There was sense in what he was saying, Erin had to concede. Sam wasn't going to be swayed by words. What they had to do was show her how right they were together—how unimportant the years between them were. In the meantime, she would just have to put up with the situation.

She was still missing when the two of them finished breakfast. Over at the studio, Erin concentrated on the job in hand. Each canvas had to be fitted into a protective cover before insertion in the padded crate, two of them so large it took a concerted effort to get them safely secured.

'Do you ever paint to order?' she asked, regretting the lost opportunity this last week to study the works in more detail. 'I mean general subjects?'

'Occasionally,' Nick confirmed. 'The cane cutters was a commission from someone who used to live here and wanted a reminder. It will go up for exhibition along with the rest, but with a ''Sold'' sticker already attached. Not a bad incentive.'

'From what Miles said, the public don't need any incentive.' She added lightly, 'Tessa thought Bryn was asking you if you'd do a portrait of her to hang at Bay Marris now that they're here for good.'

'That's right, he did.'

'Are you going to do it?'

'Why not? She'd be an interesting subject.' Nick gave her an oblique glance. 'You in thirty years' time, maybe?'

'Tessa's only forty-six,' Erin corrected pedantically, drawing a grin.

'I'll make a note of that. You never know when it might come up in conversation.'

He was sealing up the last crate, his back half turned to her. Erin allowed her eyes to drift the length of his body, lingering on the firm hemispheres in mounting excitation. Giving way to an ungovernable urge, she moved in behind him to slide both arms about his waist, leaning her cheek against his shirt.

'I want you,' she said softly.

Nick grasped her exploring hand before it could reach its target, the smile there in his voice. 'Behave yourself, or I'll put you across my knee!'

'Whatever turns you on,' she murmured, giving vent to

a squeal as he swung to sweep her up off the floor with an unholy glint in his eye. 'Pax!'

'You,' he said, 'are going to have to learn to wait till you're asked!'

She widened her eyes at him. 'So ask me.'

The glint became a gleam, but only for a moment, damped down by an iron will. 'Not here.'

'Why?' she pressured. 'There's no one likely to turn up unexpectedly, is there?'

'It isn't unknown.' He deposited her back on the ground. 'Not that I don't appreciate the enthusiasm.'

Erin looked at him uncertainly, sensing a subtle alteration in mood. 'It isn't *just* sex I want you for,' she said, trying to make a joke of it. 'It's just that you're so good at it.'

'I do my best.' He was smiling still, but the amusement was definitely edged. 'I need to fetch some more tape. You might start tidying up the debris while I'm gone.'

She watched him go, wondering disconsolately what more he wanted from her. She'd told him time and time again how she felt about him. Surely he could see that sex was only a part of the attraction?

A very good part, admittedly, but not the be-all and end-all.

He hadn't returned by the time she'd finished clearing away the packing remnants. The New York consignment had left a number of the racks empty, but there were still some occupied.

Erin went over to leaf through a stack, pausing in particular admiration of a study of Bella in her red dress. Nick had caught the Bajan woman in an unusually pensive mood, her attention concentrated on the sprays of frangipani she was arranging in one of the big floor vases. Unposed almost certainly, so probably fleshed out from a snatched sketch—and obviously never intended for sale.

Exposing the next canvas in the rack, she came to a

stomach-churning halt, knowing in her heart of hearts that this was what she had really been looking for. Dione reclined, as anticipated, on the chaise longue, one arm draped elegantly over the cushioned end, the other resting along her thigh, a sultry half-smile on her face. She had a superb body, Erin had to acknowledge, full-breasted and hipped, with a waist almost as slender as her own. Her legs maybe weren't quite as long, but that was small consolation. What mattered was that Nick had put the portrait with those he apparently regarded as special.

But then it was, of course. The woman had been his lover. For all she knew he had other similar studies stashed away—a regular pictorial diary, in fact.

If he had, she didn't want to know about it, Erin told herself staunchly. She was going to be his wife. That was more than anyone else had achieved. One thing she wouldn't be doing was allowing him to paint her in the nude, though. After seeing this, she would feel totally inadequate.

CHAPTER NINE

POUNDED by huge Atlantic rollers, the eastern coastline was spectacular. Nick did some lightning sketches of the surfers, and one of Erin herself absorbed in watching them, her hair tossed by the wind.

'Sneaky!' she commented on seeing it. 'I didn't even realise!'

'I didn't want you to,' he said. 'You don't belong in any studio pose. I realised that last week. Too much like trying to capture a cat on a hot tin roof!'

'Frustration,' she returned flippantly. 'You were still playing hard to get.'

Nick gave a dry smile. 'Amazing what a little moonlight can do.' He eyed her consideringly. 'Did you know I was back when you decided to go in the pool that night?'

'No,' she said. 'I hadn't heard the car. I'd torn my one and only suit earlier, that's why I wasn't wearing anything. I thought you were an illusion.'

'One I lost little time in dispelling.'

'You only did what I wanted you to do, so stop castigating yourself!' Erin admonished, and saw his lips widen.

'I'll make every effort. Why don't you show me what you can do while we're sitting here?'

He was offering her the sketchpad and pencil, the glint in his eyes daring her to come up with any saucy retort. Erin took them from him with reluctance.

'I'm very amateur.'

'A gifted one, if Sam's to be believed. Just draw what you see.'

Blue eyes acquired a sudden glint of their own. Holding

the pad so he couldn't see what she was doing, she executed a few swift strokes, finishing off with a scrawled signature across the bottom of the page.

'Portrait of an artist,' she said, handing the pad back.

Nick took one look and burst out laughing. She had done a wicked caricature of him standing before an easel, a huge brush in his hand and a lascivious leer on his lips. She had actually contemplated adding a reclining nude in the background, but decided there was too much risk of his recognising the source of that particular piece of inspiration.

'You,' he said, 'are asking for trouble!' He handed back the pad. 'Let's try for something a little less defamatory.'

She took a great deal longer over the drawing, eyes narrowed against the light, brow furrowed in concentration. Nick stayed silent until she finally handed over the pad with a self-critical little shrug.

'It's not very good. The eyes are wrong.'

She had drawn him again, but in strictly realistic vein this time: a three-quarter facial study showing the strong clean lines. He studied it without comment for several seconds, expression impossible to define.

'You don't have to be kind,' she said at length, unable to stand the suspense. 'I'm not going to fall apart if you tell me it's rubbish.'

'It's a long way removed from being rubbish,' he returned. 'Although I agree with you about the eyes. They're always the most difficult feature to capture. You have talent, for certain. All you need is to work at it. I'll be happy to give you what help I can.'

Erin looked at him suspiciously. 'You're not just saying that?'

'It would be cruel to give you false hopes.' His lips curved. 'It will be an extra facet of interest on honeymoon, if we need it.'

Suspicion melted into sudden entrancement. 'Honeymoon?'

'It comes after most weddings. You might start thinking about where you'd like to spend it—unless you'd rather it was a surprise?'

'Yes. Yes, I would!' Looking at him lounging there on the sand, dark hair tousled, eyes full of dancing amber lights, Erin felt full to overflowing with emotion. 'I must have been born under a lucky star!' she said softly.

She leaned over to kiss him, wishing they were alone. However many times he made love to her, it could never be enough!

It was almost six o'clock when they got back to the house. Bella met them at the door, concern written large on her face. Sam had been missing for the last four hours. The grounds had been searched twice, but there was no sign of her.

'I'll drive around the area in case she went for a walk,' said Nick decisively.

If she had, it wouldn't be just for walking's sake, Erin could have told him. The main road was over a mile away through cane fields not yet cut. If Sam had set out in the hope of hitching a lift down to town, she could quite easily have taken a wrong turning and finished up thoroughly lost. It would be dark before too long. That would vastly reduce the chances of finding her.

'I'll come with you,' she said, trying to curb her anxiety.

They spent half an hour traversing the narrow routes without success. Nick headed for Bridgetown without comment when Erin suggested it on the off chance that Sam had actually made it there, though his expression more than adequately reflected his thoughts. If they did find her down there, she was going to be in serious trouble, Erin gathered. For herself, she only cared about finding her.

With no cruise ships in dock, and most people at supper,

the town was relatively free of tourists. Nick made a slow detour of the main streets, while Erin kept a sharp look-out.

There were plenty of young people around, either gathered in laughing, chattering groups or parading in their Sunday best. Samantha was with one of the former, Tim's arm about shoulders bared by the black boob tube she was wearing, her red skirt so short it only just covered the curve of her behind.

Neither of them items purchased in her company, Erin knew for sure.

Nick drew up at the side of the group, putting a restraining hand on her arm as she made to get out.

'I'll see to it,' he said grimly.

Her back to the road, Samantha was totally unaware of his approach, almost jumping out of the boob tube when he spoke.

'Get in the car,' he ordered. 'And *you'd* better make yourself scarce,' he added to Tim.

'Hey, man, what's all the aggro?' drawled the latter, making no attempt to drop the embrace. 'We're just hangin' out.'

It was obvious that he'd been drinking. Obvious that the girl at his side had too, as she staggered a little in turning to direct an insolent, liner-emphasised blue gaze.

'I'm not coming with *you!*'

Nick wasted no more time on words. Seizing her by the arm, he yanked her out of Tim's grasp and opened the rear door of the car to put her forcibly inside, slamming it closed on her furious protests. Neither Tim nor anyone else in the group moved or made a sound as he strode back round the front to slide behind the wheel, sober enough to recognise a man operating on a dangerously short fuse.

Much as she felt like giving the younger girl a piece of her mind, Erin deemed it wiser to stay mute for the time being and let Nick handle it himself. If Sam had any sense left at all, she would keep her own mouth shut.

Sense, it seemed, was in short supply. Either that, or alcohol was fuelling a false bravado.

'You've no right to do this!' she raged. 'I *hate* you!'

'Keep that up, and you'll have reason to!' Nick said tautly. 'When did you get that damned outfit?'

'When do you think?' came the scathing retort.

'Not when I was with you,' Erin felt moved to cut in. 'Have you been cutting school?'

'So what if I have?'

'You've only been there a week,' Nick snapped. 'What kind of an impression is that supposed to make?'

'It was only one lunchtime.' Samantha was beginning to sound just a little on the defensive side. 'You gave me the chequebook so I could be independent, didn't you?'

'An obvious mistake, if that's the use you're going to put it to!'

There was a lengthy pause while he negotiated the one-way system. When he spoke again it was on a controlled note. 'How did you get down here in the first place?'

'Tim picked me up at the gates.' Samantha rallied to add defiantly, 'Why should *I* have to hang around the house?'

'You didn't have to,' Erin pointed out. 'You could have come to Bathsheba with us.'

'I didn't want to be with you! I still don't! It's horrible!'

'That's enough!' Nick sounded suddenly weary. 'From now on you steer clear of Tim Wyman.'

There was no reply from the rear, but Erin could visualise the mutinous set of her sister's pretty face. Nick was being very forbearing under the circumstances, only Sam wouldn't see it that way.

He bade her go and change her things on reaching the house, refusing to accept her claim not to want any dinner.

'You need something in your stomach to soak up whatever it is you've been drinking,' he stated, viewing her somewhat unsteady progression towards the stairs. 'Just what *have* you had?'

'Can't remember,' she flung back over a shoulder. 'Don't care anyway!'

Erin held her breath, but Nick let it go. 'I could do with a shower myself before we eat,' he said. 'I'll go and tell Bella to hold dinner for another half an hour.'

Mounting the stairs in her sister's wake, Erin fought back the despondency threatening to overtake her. It was no use telling herself she was hardly to blame for Sam's behaviour when it was so obviously a direct result of her own. Nick must be beginning to regret ever having responded to Mr Gordon's call.

There had been no legal obligation. Had he chosen to, he could quite legitimately have washed his hands of the whole affair. Instead, he was now stuck with a forthcoming marriage he hadn't asked for, and a teenager problem most parents would find hard enough to handle.

Feeling very little better after showering, she put on an Indian cotton skirt and sleeveless blouse and went to knock on Sam's door, guessing that in this mood the latter would drag things out to the very last moment.

Opening it when there was no reply, to see her sister sprawled across the bed and apparently fast asleep, she at first didn't believe it. Only when she went right over and heard the heavy breathing did she accept that the sleep was genuine. Not quite a drunken stupor, perhaps, but too close for comfort.

'You're going to spoil everything if you keep this up,' she whispered, pushing the fair hair back from the younger face. 'Not just for me, but for you too. Please, Sam, try and understand. I can't help the way I feel about him.'

The only answer was a faint snore. Erin left her to sleep

it off, resolving, without too much hope, to try again in the morning on the way to school.

Nick was already down and waiting, a whisky to hand.

'Drink?' he asked.

Erin shook her head. 'No, thanks. Sam's asleep,' she added. 'Genuinely. I hope she doesn't wake up with a hang-over.'

'It might teach her a lesson if she did,' Nick returned hardily. 'Playing the heavy father isn't exactly my scene.'

'You must be sick of the two of us,' she said, low-toned. 'We've been nothing but trouble to you.'

'You could say that.'

Erin gave him a swift glance, finding little reassurance in the ironic expression. 'It's not too late,' she steeled herself to say. 'If you want rid, you only have to—'

'Forget it.' His tone was brusque. 'What I start, I finish.' He drained the whisky glass and put it down. 'Let's go and eat.'

There was little conversation at table. Nick obviously wasn't in the mood for small talk, and Erin was too miserable to even attempt to dissemble.

If Bella recognised any untoward atmosphere, she kept her own counsel. Erin waited until she'd made a final departure before forcing herself to say what was on her mind.

'I really would understand if you decided to make other arrangements for the pair of us, Nick.'

'Such as what exactly?' he asked without particular inflection.

'Well, boarding-school for Sam, for a start.'

'Where she wouldn't stay, according to you.'

'She might. I suppose it would depend on the school.'

The grey eyes were unrevealing. 'And what other arrangement would you suggest for yourself?'

'You mentioned art college.' Erin's throat hurt so much

she could hardly get the words out. 'I realise it would cost a lot, but—'

'For God's sake, will you stop thinking in terms of cost!' Nick exploded. 'I don't give a damn about money!'

'You would, if you didn't have so much of it.' She went on doggedly, 'It wouldn't just be the college fees. I'd need somewhere to live too. It wouldn't have to be high-class, of course. I'd be more than happy to share a room.'

'You're not going anywhere!' Nick sounded as if he was fast reaching the end of his tether. 'Neither of you. I'll deal with whatever your sister comes up with as and when. As for you...'

He got to his feet, crossing the small space between them to yank her up into his arms, crushing her lips beneath his in a kiss that held little tenderness, eyes glittering with an anger she didn't fully understand.

'You're not going anywhere,' he repeated.

'I don't want to go anywhere,' she assured him thickly. 'I just thought—'

'Then don't think.' He was in control of himself again, the anger giving way to wryness. One hand came up to smooth back the tumbled hair from her face in much the same way she had done with Samantha's. 'We'll work it out.'

Erin ached to hear him say he loved her, but he obviously wasn't going to. He was marrying her because she'd played on his guilt. Oh, he still wanted her—last night proved that much—but how long before her unsophisticated responses became downright boring?

There were books one could learn from, she believed. If she could get hold of some such, she might at least stand a chance of maintaining his interest in that direction, and the rest could come in time. Meanwhile, she would just have to make the most of what she did have.

'Let's go to bed,' she said on a husky note, unable to

withstand the urges his touch and her thoughts combined were arousing in her.

Nick gave a faint smile. 'One of these days, I'll get to call the tune myself.'

Whatever else might be lacking, his lovemaking left absolutely nothing to be desired. Waking at daybreak to find herself still wrapped in his arms, Erin lay without moving a muscle, reluctant to relinquish the warm security of his embrace.

They were in her bed this time, not his. So far as she was concerned it didn't matter which room they shared, just so long as they were together. Waiting until they were married to see the whole night through was ridiculous on the face of it. She wanted to waken every morning like this, his arm heavy across her waist, his hand at her breast, his breath ruffling the hair at her nape. What difference was a piece of paper going to make?

She held her breath as he stirred, torn between conflicting desires.

'You awake?' he asked softly.

'No,' she said, and heard his low laugh.

'It's late. I should be going.'

The feel of his lips as he gently kissed the sensitive hollow was enough to reduce her to quivering jelly. She rolled onto her back, reaching up blindly to pull the lean face down to hers and kiss him with all the pent-up emotion of the last fifteen minutes.

'I won't let you go!' she whispered fiercely.

Supporting himself on an elbow, Nick looked down into passionate blue eyes with a smile that didn't quite reach his own. 'Much as I appreciate the enthusiasm, there's such a thing as moderation. Go back to sleep.'

There was no chance of that, she thought desolately, as he slid from the bed.

Samantha had still been out to the world when Erin had

made a last check on her. Finding her not only up but already dressed when she went to call her was quite a shock.

'No headache this morning?' she asked, prepared to be sympathetic.

'No,' her sister replied shortly. 'I didn't have *that* much to drink. And I don't need you checking up on me every five minutes either! It was bad enough last night, being dragged off in front of everybody like that! *He* had no right!'

Erin kept her tone reasonable. 'He's responsible for your welfare. Tim had no right to take you down there in the first place—especially without anyone knowing where you'd gone. Bella was going frantic when we got back.'

'It's none of *her* business what I do!'

'She was concerned that you might have got yourself lost.' Erin was having trouble hanging on to her temper. 'You should be grateful that people care enough to be worried—especially ones we've only known such a short time.' She paused, waiting for some easement in the mulish expression, giving vent to a sigh when it failed to materialise. 'You can't expect Nick to just let you do whatever you want, Sam.'

'Why not?' she retorted. 'You're the only one he cares about. I'm just in the way!'

'That's not true!' Erin took a step towards her, desisting in face of the fierce blue glare. 'You're his niece—his brother's only child. Of course he cares. Why else would he have brought you here when he could quite easily have sent you to some boarding-school and let others look after you?'

'He only did it because you wouldn't have come without me. I heard him persuading you that very first morning. He'd got the hots for you right away!'

'Will you stop using that stupid word!' Erin burst out.

'He needed me here to stop anyone getting any wrong ideas, that's all.'

'People were more likely to get them over you than me.' Sam was not to be pacified. 'I bet he got started on you that very first night when I left the two of you on your own!'

'Not true.' Erin was too upset to be angry any longer. 'It was me who made all the running. Me who told Harley we were going to be married. You said it yourself only yesterday, it would have taken someone a lot harder than Nick to make me tell everyone I was lying my head off.'

'He would have done it if he'd really wanted to.'

It was like batting her head against a brick wall, Erin acknowledged dispiritedly, viewing the set expression on her sister's face. Sam had got it into her mind that she was just a means to an end so far as Nick was concerned, and nothing was going to shake that conviction.

'We'd better get down for breakfast,' she said. 'You still have to go to school.'

'At least it gets me away from here!' was the only response.

Nick made no reference to the previous evening, and appeared not to notice his niece's uncustomary silence. The carriers worked to Caribbean time, he advised, when Erin asked when they were expected to come for the crates. It might even be tomorrow before they got here.

'I thought I might go straight into Bridgetown after I drop Sam off at school,' she said. 'Is there anything you need?'

'You could get me some shaving foam. I'm almost out.'

The idea of him wet-shaving was somehow far more alluring than if he had used an electric razor. Erin had a fleeting mental image of him standing before the bathroom mirror, a towel slung over one bare shoulder in readiness, each razor-stroke exposing smooth, firm skin. There was more than one kind of marital intimacy.

'Before I forget,' he added, 'Tessa rang while we were out yesterday. Her brother and his wife arrived yesterday. She wants us to go over to Bay Marris for dinner tonight and meet them.'

It was unlikely that the invitation included Sam. Unlikely that she'd want to come in any case. Erin felt none too keen on the idea of meeting more new people herself.

'What about Sam?' she asked when the latter went back upstairs to fetch a book she had forgotten. 'We can't leave her on her own for the whole evening.'

'We can't revolve our lives about her either,' Nick returned levelly. 'Bella and Josh will stay around till we get back.'

'To make sure she doesn't kick over the traces again?'

Her tone drew a cynical glance. 'You reckon I was too hard on her last night?'

'No.' Erin spread her hands in a wry gesture. 'I've never known her quite like this before.'

'She's never had Tim Wyman behind her before. If Val would put a curb on him we'd all benefit. Anyway, I'll see you when you get back.'

Samantha came back downstairs in silence, got into the car in silence, and kept her mouth tightly shut the whole journey. Reaching the school, she joined the incoming flow without so much as a glance, much less a goodbye.

It was all her fault, Erin acknowledged ruefully, heading for town. Even if it was true that Nick had been physically drawn to her, he would probably never have done anything about it if she hadn't thrown herself at his head.

She'd been lying to herself as well as to him in denying that she'd heard the car returning the night she went nude bathing in the pool. She'd wanted him to find her there. Sam was right in accusing her of using emotional blackmail. The price he had to pay, she'd told him; she couldn't have put it any plainer.

Still, if he wanted out he would have seized the opportunity she had offered him last night, she assured herself. And while it might take Sam a little while to get used to the idea, she would accept it in the end. She had to accept it. Everything was going to work out just fine!

CHAPTER TEN

WITH two cruise ships in dock, Bridgetown was thronged. Erin went back to the same boutique where she had bought the blue dress and purchased two more, along with some tailored shorts and a pair of white cotton trousers.

Enough for the present, she decided, already nervous over the amount she was spending. Wedding finery she refused to even contemplate until definite plans were made. She would prefer a church ceremony herself, but if Nick proved set on a quiet register office affair she was prepared to go along. The most important thing was the marriage itself, not where it took place.

Daydreaming about a rosy-hued future, she wandered through the stores. Most brides-to-be had to think about furnishing a home, but Malvern wanted for nothing—though she might at some point consider changing the colour scheme in the bedroom she and Nick would be sharing. This fabric she was looking at right now would make the most wonderful drapes. Outrageously expensive, of course, but cost was something she didn't have to worry about any more.

'I wouldn't make too many plans for spending Nick's money before you get that ring on your finger,' said a chilly voice at her back. 'He might come to his senses yet.'

Erin put a smile on her face as she turned to look at the last person she would have wanted to run into, feeling the corrosive impact of Dione's regard.

'He already did,' she said, and couldn't resist adding tauntingly, 'To the victor the spoils!'

The acrimony increased. 'You really think you've got it made, don't you?'

Erin made a rueful gesture, ashamed of the malicious remark. 'No, I don't. I shouldn't have said that. I wouldn't care if Nick didn't have a penny in the world!'

'Don't take me for an idiot,' came the scathing retort. 'I've been following you around this last twenty minutes, watching you finger your way through the stock. It's obvious you can hardly wait to get spending!'

Up until that moment Erin hadn't even realised that she'd wandered into Wyman's, of all places. She rallied with an effort.

'I'm surprised you've nothing better to do. Anyway, I have, if you'll excuse me.'

'You're living in a dream world if you imagine you can keep a man like Nick satisfied for long,' Dione thrust at her as she made to pass. 'He might have lost his head temporarily, but don't run away with the idea that a marriage licence is going to keep him chained to your bed!'

'I don't regard a marriage licence as any kind of entrapment,' Erin rejoined, hanging onto her dignity by a thread. 'As I said, if you'll excuse me.'

She walked away with head held high, aware of a trembling reaction in her lower limbs. The intimation had come across loud and clear as intended: when Nick got bored with her, then Dione would be there to offer solace. So it was going to be up to her to see that he didn't get bored.

The first bookshop she found had sections covering just about every subject under the sun barring the particular one she sought. She had to visit another two before discovering a solitary hardbacked manual on a bottom shelf.

The male assistant gave her a knowing look when she presented the book at the pay desk. Erin stared him down, not about to let him see any discomfiture. From her brief perusal of the contents, there was a whole lot she had to learn; she hadn't even realised there were more than a couple of positions in which to enjoy sex. Some of them looked more like wrestling than lovemaking, she had to admit, but if that was the way to keep a man stimulated then so be it. There were no lengths to which she wouldn't go to make this marriage work.

Nick had gone out when she got back. To where, Bella either genuinely didn't know or was deliberately acting dumb. Considering her general attitude since yesterday's announcement, Erin suspected the latter.

'I know you don't approve of what we're doing,' she said, deciding there was no point in beating about the bush, 'but I don't understand why.'

'Mr Nick needs a woman in his bed, not a child,' came the unequivocal return.

'I'm nineteen,' Erin protested. 'I'm sure a lot of Bajan girls are married at my age, or even younger!'

'You're not Bajan.'

Erin wanted to ask what the difference was, but doubted if a reply would be forthcoming. Like Sam, Bella would just have to come round to the idea. Nick's was the only opinion that mattered. He didn't *have* to marry her—ergo, he must really want to. What more did she need?

All the same, she had a struggle to stop herself from demanding to know where the devil he'd been when he finally put in an appearance halfway through the afternoon—especially when he made no attempt to tell her.

'I thought you wanted to be here in case they came for the crates on time,' she said by way of a hint.

'They did, for once,' he confirmed. 'Did you get everything you wanted?'

'For the moment, yes. I put the shaving foam in your bathroom. Three canisters.' Erin hesitated, unable in the end to stop herself from mentioning the name. 'I saw Dione in town.'

The grey eyes remained steady. 'Whereabouts in town?'

'The store. She was...rather nasty.'

'She probably thought you'd gone in there deliberately to provoke her.' Nick spoke calmly enough, but there was a certain tension about his mouth. 'Did you?'

'Of course not!' The denial was overheated; Erin made haste to tone her voice down. 'I didn't even realise I was in Wyman's until she spoke to me. I was looking at fabrics.'

'You reckon the house needs doing over?'

The irony stung, but she stood her ground. 'Not all of it, obviously, but I wouldn't mind getting rid of all those dark colours in your bedroom—assuming that's the one we'll be using?'

'Replacing it with what, exactly?'

It was time, Erin decided, to introduce a little humour into this conversation before it got out of hand. 'I rather fancy pink and gold myself,' she said blandly. 'With some animal prints thrown in for interest, perhaps.'

'Over my dead body!' Nick was smiling again, recognising the ploy for what it was.

Sitting there on the veranda, face bronzed by the sun, body leanly muscled beneath the tautly stretched white shirt, he made her ache. Fired by a need she couldn't have controlled if she'd wanted to, she got up and went to him, sliding down onto his knees to put her lips to his—breathing in the heady masculine scent of him.

He slid his fingers into the thickness of her hair to draw her closer, mouth taking over, pressuring hers apart, tasting the sweetness of soft inner flesh, his free hand seeking the tender curve of her breast. There was a growing heat radiating from the very pit of her stomach, a dampness between her thighs. She wanted his touch there too—the feel of him inside her.

Recalling something she had read in the book she had

bought, she abandoned his lips in order to run the tip of her tongue very, very lightly and slowly around the outer rim of his ear, feeling his immediate response. 'Let's go to bed,' she murmured. 'I want you, Nick!'

'Wrong time, I'm afraid,' he said after a moment. 'I'm expecting a phone call.' He kissed her again, more lightly this time, and put her back on her feet, registering her expression with a dry smile. 'If it's worth having, it's worth waiting for.'

'In other words, *you'll* decide where and when?' she flung at him, lacerated by the rejection. 'That's sheer chauvinism!'

'Prudence,' he corrected. 'I need to conserve my energies.'

Erin caught herself before she could let fly with a pithy rejoinder. It was good, according to the book, for the woman to take the initiative, but obviously not too often. Male pride was such a fragile affair!

'You know what they say about the first flush of enthusiasm soon wearing off,' she said, opting to make a joke of it. 'You'll have something to complain about when I start having headaches!'

'I'll keep a good stock of aspirin.'

There was a pause while he studied her as she leaned against the veranda rail. When he spoke again it was on a cogitative note. 'I believe you have to stop taking the Pill for a week every month in order to have your period. How many more days before you're due to take the break?'

Erin hesitated, unable to stop a guilty flush from staining her cheeks. 'I'd have to check,' she mumbled.

The grey eyes narrowed a fraction. 'What are you hiding?'

'Nothing,' she denied. 'Like I said, I'd have to—' She broke off, lifting her shoulders resignedly. 'All right, I've gone a few days over. There's no harm in it.'

'Scared of nothing happening when you do stop?' he asked softly.

'Of finding I'm pregnant, you mean?' She shook her head emphatically. 'It's a remote chance anyway, but it wouldn't worry me.'

'Then why—' It was Nick's turn to break off, his lips twisting. 'It didn't fit in with your plans for the weekend, right?'

'It wasn't like you're making it sound,' Erin protested. 'I wanted you to make love to me again, yes, but I didn't plan what happened Saturday night. It just...did. I'm not even capable of concocting a plot like that!'

'Not until you got together with Tessa Marshall, at any rate.'

'Don't blame Tessa,' she pleaded.

'I don't,' he said. 'I blame myself.' He paused, eyeing her dispassionately. 'You'd better take the break now. This time next week we'll be married. I already made the arrangements. Sorry if you were counting on a lavish affair. I'd prefer to keep it low-key.'

Erin dropped to her knees beside his chair, laying her cheek against his bare arm. 'I don't care how low-key it is! I just want us to be together.'

The burr of the telephone cut off any reply he had been about to make. She lifted her head as he reached for the extension at his other elbow, watching his face for some indication of who the call might be coming from.

'Isn't it time you were going to pick Sam up?' he asked, covering the mouthpiece for a moment.

It was indeed, she realised, looking at his watch. She got reluctantly to her feet. 'See you when we get back,' she said in the ridiculous way one did.

'I'll be here,' he returned easily.

'Tomorrow will be fine,' he told the listener on the other end of the line as she went indoors. 'Let's make it eleven.'

A business meeting, Erin told herself firmly, and wished she could wholly believe it.

The flood of emerging students had already dried to a trickle when she reached the college. Sam wasn't waiting at the gates. Nor was anyone Erin asked able to tell her where her sister might be.

About to go in to make further enquiries, she was torn between relief and exasperation on seeing the girl come strolling out, as if time was of no importance, Tim Wyman at her side.

'I've been waiting nearly ten minutes!' she exclaimed. 'What on earth have you been doing?'

'Not a lot, compared with you,' came the smart retort, bringing a grin to Tim's face. 'Anyway, you don't need to come and pick me up any more. I'll be getting a lift.'

Erin forced a milder note. 'Thanks Tim, but it isn't necessary. Come on, Sam.'

'Better do as big sister tells you,' Tim advised derisively as the younger girl hesitated. 'We don't want Uncle Nick on the warpath again. See you tomorrow.'

Sam got into the Mercedes as he moved away, pretty face set. 'You're just as bad as *he* is!' she fumed. 'Why can't you both just leave me alone?'

'You know why.' Erin had had enough of diplomacy. 'You can't be trusted to act responsibly.'

'And you can, of course! I bet it's true what people are saying!'

The best thing would be to ignore the comment, Erin knew, but she couldn't. 'What *are* they saying?'

'That he's got to marry you because you're pregnant!'

No such thing as a hundred per cent guarantee, Nick had said, but the chances were infinitesimal, Erin was sure.

'Well, they're wrong,' she rejoined flatly, starting the engine. 'I'm not.'

Sam looked unconvinced. 'Why else would he choose you instead of Dione? Tim says they were a regular item.'

'That doesn't mean he wanted to marry her.'

'It means he was doing it with her before he did it with you!'

The crudity of it set Erin's teeth on edge. Those were Tim's words, not her sister's. 'I wouldn't let Nick hear you coming out with things like that,' she said, trying not to let her thoughts dwell on the implications. 'He'd wash your mouth out with soap!'

'I'd bite his fingers off if he tried!' There was a pause, a sly glance. 'You have, though, haven't you?'

Erin kept her eyes fixed firmly on the car ahead of them on the narrow road. 'Have what?'

'Done it.' She used the phrase with deliberation. 'What's it like?'

'Stop it, Sam—please!' Erin was past being angry. 'Try and understand. I love him!'

The plea struck deaf ears. 'If you marry him I'll never speak to you again!' declared the younger girl fiercely. 'I mean it, Rin!'

Erin let it lie. For the time being at least. Much as she loved Sam, she couldn't contemplate doing as she demanded—if Nick would agree to it to start with. The arrangements were made, the date set: a week hence they would be man and wife. Between then and now she had to somehow talk her sister into accepting things the way they were.

She'd forgotten about the Marshalls' invitation, and was on the verge of making some excuse not to go until she realised that by doing so she would be giving Sam the wrong impression. They left her watching television in sullen silence, with Bella to keep an eye on her from time to time.

'I'm getting close to losing patience with that young

lady,' Nick admitted in the car. 'A boarding-school might be the best answer after all.'

'She'll be okay,' Erin assured him hastily. 'I think she's just a bit jealous, that's all.'

The dark brows drew together. 'Of what?'

'Not what. Who.' Erin crossed her fingers in her lap. 'She has a crush on you herself.'

Nick tilted a sardonic lip. 'Sure she has!'

'It's true.' Having said it, Erin felt bound to follow through. 'It's part of growing up.'

'You being past that stage yourself, of course.'

She gave the lean, hard profile a swift glance. 'Way past. I'm truly, madly in love with you!'

'So you keep telling me.'

More than he ever told her, came the thought, swiftly thrust aside. 'I'm going to keep right on doing it too,' she said, 'so you'd better get used to it.' She put a hand on his thigh, feeling the muscle tense as she slid it slowly and tantalisingly upward. 'It's going to be a long week!'

'Cut it out,' he ordered, sounding anything but lover-like. 'You'll have us off the road!'

She withdrew the hand immediately, appreciative of the reason if not the tone. 'Sorry, I wasn't thinking.'

He made no reply, expression austere. Erin made a silent vow to be a little more circumspect in her behaviour. It was just so darn difficult to resist the urge to touch him. Her fingers itched even now to smooth their way along his freshly shaven jawline. His very maturity excited her. Who would want a boy when they had a real man?

Shaded by tropical evergreens, the old plantation house that was Bay Marris welcomed them with open doors and a revitalised decor.

Erin was glad she had worn the deceptively simple little black dress the saleswoman had persuaded her was worth every penny of its cost on seeing the equally simple but obviously expensive outfits Tessa and her sister-in-law were wearing. With her hair taken up again, and poised on high heels, she felt able to hold her own with anyone.

Tessa's brother, Oliver, proved to be around Nick's age, Elizabeth a couple of years or so younger. They had a son of ten and a daughter of eight, both of them at present being looked after by their maternal grandparents back in Los Angeles.

Ten years from now, she and Nick could be in a similar position, Erin reflected, caught up in a familiar daydream. He would still only be in his mid-forties, while she would be a mature twenty-nine. Tessa was right: the gap did narrow.

It was an enjoyable evening all round. Oliver kept them entertained with a fund of amusing stories about the advertising business. Erin was impressed to learn that he was the producer of a number of major TV advertisements.

'We've sometimes had American ads in England,' she said, talking with him later. 'There was one particularly funny one with a couple of men trying to repair a car and everything going wrong.'

Oliver shook his head. 'Not one of mine. What was the product, anyway?'

'To be honest,' she confessed, 'I was always too busy laughing to take much notice.'

'The client was wasting his money, then.'

'I suppose so. I never thought of it like that before.'

'Neither do many of the writers. Too intent on the visual impact.' He paused, a smile on his face as he studied her. 'Nick's a lucky man.'

Nick was talking with Bryn down the other end of the veranda. They could almost be father and son, Erin thought fleetingly.

'I'm the lucky one,' she said.

Oliver laughed. 'I can remember Tessa saying the same thing about Bryn.'

'How did you react when you found out she was going to marry him?' asked Erin with some diffidence. 'You'd only be about seven or eight at the time, I imagine?'

'Eight,' he confirmed. 'I wasn't too impressed at first.'

'But you obviously came round to it?'

'I had a whole new life of my own to think about. We used to live just down the hill. Bryn inherited Bay Marris from his grandfather and decided to turn it into a country club as he wasn't going to be around a great deal owing to his job. He bought our house and land to form part of the golf course when Mom married Roland and we moved down to his place. A house with its own private beach and boat was pure paradise to an eight-year-old.' His gaze was shrewd. 'Your sister giving you trouble, is she?'

'Some,' Erin admitted.

'She'll accept it once you and Nick are married—even more so when you make her an aunt. You do plan on having children?'

'Definitely. Two at least.'

'Well, I wouldn't leave it too long to get started. Nick might not find the patter of little feet all that appealing in his forties.'

There was still a chance, no matter how remote, that they'd already started, Erin reflected. Even after leaving off the Pill, it was going to be a couple of days before she knew for sure.

Tessa joined them, addressing her brother with sisterly candour. 'Go and keep your wife company while we talk women's talk.'

'I can't tell you how happy I am that it all worked out for you,' she continued, sliding into the chair he'd obligingly vacated. 'I loved the way you put Dione down Saturday night!'

Erin lifted her shoulders in a rueful little gesture. 'I shouldn't have said it.'

'Of course you should. She asked for it. Anyway, you weren't all that premature.'

'It's going to be a very quiet affair,' Erin felt bound to emphasise. 'Apart from you and Bryn, I'm not even sure who'll be coming.' She shrank from admitting that so far she didn't even know the venue. 'It will have to be word of mouth, in any case. There isn't going to be time to get invitations printed.'

'Well, the Wymans won't be there for certain—though my mother will certainly be rooting for you. Roland too, if I know him at all. Val was always the self-important one. As you haven't any family apart from your sister, and you don't really know anyone else on the island, then I suppose it has to be up to Nick to decide who else he wants to invite.'

Erin supposed so too. It wasn't important anyway. The only thing she cared about was the wedding itself.

'It's a pity Oliver and Elizabeth are only here until Sunday,' she said in the car going home. 'It would have been nice to have someone our own age group.'

'My age group, at any rate,' Nick rejoined. 'Apart from Sam, I'm afraid that's as close as it's going to get to yours. One of the penalties of marrying an older man.'

'Not so far as I'm concerned,' Erin assured him. 'I've told you before, people my age are boring. All most of them are interested in is having a good time.'

'You've never had the opportunity to do the things most teenagers do,' Nick pointed out. 'How do you know you'd have found it all so boring?'

'I just do, that's all. And I did have the opportunity. I wasn't a prisoner.'

'You lacked the funds to be anything else but.'

There was some truth in that, Erin had to admit. And,

yes, there had been times when she would have liked to get dressed up and go out somewhere. Only never to discos and pubs; that scene hadn't interested her one iota.

'You'll just have to take my word for it that I don't see myself as having missed out on anything,' she declared. 'And I'm not doing it now either. I'm as happy as Larry! I wonder who Larry was?' she tagged on with genuine curiosity.

'Probably a galloping depressive,' he said.

'It's a good job I know you're not the cynic you make yourself out to be,' she mocked back, and saw his mouth take on a different slant.

'You reckon you know me so well?'

'Well enough,' she said firmly. 'I wouldn't want to know you through and through—any more than I'd want you to know everything there was to know about me. There'd be no surprises left.'

He gave her a quizzical glance. 'Something else you once read somewhere?'

'I do have *some* original thoughts,' she retorted in mock indignation. 'You're not marrying some dumb blonde!'

'That I can vouch for,' he agreed drily.

Erin was silent for a moment. When she spoke again it was on a subdued note. 'You said that very first night that you'd never met a woman you could contemplate living with full time. Do you still find it difficult?'

'The idea's growing on me. Given time, I may even get to like it.'

Erin had to laugh, although it was far from the answer she would have liked. If she hadn't come on the scene, Nick might well have opted to stay a bachelor for life. He wouldn't have been deprived of feminine company, for certain.

It was gone midnight when they reached the house. Erin

demurred when Nick attempted to kiss her goodnight at her bedroom door.

'It's going to be two or three days before I start,' she said softly. 'You already turned me down once today. If you do it again, I'll start to wonder if you really want me at all!'

'You're too forward for your own good,' he remonstrated lightly. 'I've half a mind to turn you down just to emphasise who wears the trousers round here.' Looking at the lovely young face upturned to his, he gave a wry smile. 'Unfortunately, the flesh is weaker than the spirit. We'd better go to my room.'

'I'm already as protected as I need to be,' Erin protested, guessing the reason. 'I want you as Nature intended, not covered in cling film!'

Nick hastily stifled the involuntary laugh, eyes dancing. 'You,' he said, 'are an out-and-out hussy! Get in there!'

'Age before beauty,' she returned blandly, inviting him ahead of her.

It was her turn to muffle laughter as he swept her up and bore her into the room, burying her face in his jacket lapel. So thrillingly assertive, this man of hers. So thrillingly *everything*! A lifetime spent with him wasn't going to be nearly long enough.

Tossing her down on the bed, he stood up to slough both jacket and shirt, shoulders silvered against the moonlit window at his back. 'I'll do the undressing,' he said possessively when she sat up to reach for the fastening at her nape.

'You're the one wearing the trousers,' she responded demurely, lying down again to watch with mounting anticipation as he stripped them off along with everything else.

He came down on the bed-edge, supporting his weight on hands placed either side of her as he bent to put his lips to hers with a tantalising, infinitely light brushing motion that sent her pulse-rate soaring.

'A regular hussy,' he repeated softly. 'I can see I'm going to have real trouble with you in time to come.'

'I'll look forward to being dealt with,' she murmured, hungry for more. 'Any way you like!'

Something flared deep down in the grey eyes. This time his lips were less gentle, demanding not asking a response. Erin gave it without restraint, fingers curling into the crisp thickness of his hair, every sense tuned to the feel of him, the scent of him, the roughened sound of his breathing.

She had already kicked off her sandals. Lifting one bare foot, she slid her toes slowly and sensuously down the side of his calf and back again, bringing her body into more intimate contact where it mattered most—pressing herself against him with an urgency impossible to resist.

The black dress gave at the seam as he lifted it over her head without bothering to unzip it. As before, she was wearing nothing but a pair of skimpy lace panties beneath. Nick took those off too, kissing his way down the length of her body to the shadowed joining of her thighs. It was only the sudden memory of Sam in the very next room that kept her from giving way to the sounds jerked from her throat at the sensations conjured by the marauding mouth. It was almost too much to bear. If he didn't stop, she would explode!

When he did stop, that was almost too much to bear either. She reached for him, allowing her instincts to guide her as she mastered the movement, seeing the lean features contort, hearing his breathing roughen, stimulated even further by the pleasure she was affording him. There was so much she still didn't know, but she was learning. All the time she was learning! She was going to make sure he never had need to seek other women for satisfaction. Never, never, never!

She was more than halfway to the peak already when he moved over her, supporting himself on his elbows to join his body to hers. Erin stifled her cries against the dark curls of hair on his chest as the long, slow strokes gathered momentum, unable to fully let go for fear of the girl next door overhearing the sounds. They should have done as Nick wanted in the first place, and gone to his room!

It was her last coherent thought for some time. Emerging slowly from total enervation, she found herself still wrapped tight in Nick's arms, although lying on her side now, facing him.

His eyes were open, looking directly into hers, the smile on his lips reflecting her own sentiments.

'Better and better!' he said.

'You mean it wasn't all that good the other times?' she asked, only half joking.

He gave a low laugh. 'I mean you're a source of constant revelation. You almost had me over the top back there!'

'Your own fault for being too good a tutor.'

'I don't have to be. Your instincts are sound enough.' He kissed the end of her small straight nose, making no attempt to let her go. 'It seems I have a lot to thank David for.'

'Me too,' she whispered. 'I didn't want him to die, of course, but I might never have known you if he hadn't.' She put her fingers to his lips. 'Please don't start on about my meeting someone else. It could never have been like this!'

'You'll never know,' he said. 'Unless you ditch me at some later date, of course.'

'Not in a million years! Well, the next sixty or so, at any rate!'

'In sixty years I'll be ninety-four, if I'm here at all,' Nick observed drily.

'You'll still be the same man.' She stirred uncomfortably. 'I need to go to the bathroom.'

He released her with obvious reluctance. 'Hurry back. The night's still young.'

Sleep was the last thing on her mind too, she could have told him, but he would know soon enough. The fact that he wanted her again was a boost in itself. The book wasn't needed. As he had said, her instincts were sound enough. She would give free rein to them from now on, she thought exultantly.

CHAPTER ELEVEN

NICK was sitting up in bed with the bedside lamp on and the book she had left lying carelessly on the cabinet top open in his hands when she came out from the bathroom. The expression on his face as he looked across at her was more than a little disquieting.

'Where did *this* come from?' he clipped.

'I bought it.' Unable to understand his attitude, Erin found herself stumbling a little for words. 'I wanted to know how to keep you...satisfied.'

'And you think sexual acrobatics are going to do it?'

'Well, no, not on their own.' She became suddenly and self-consciously aware that she was standing there without a stitch on, with nothing in the least lover-like about the way he was looking at her. 'I thought it might help if I knew a little more about what men like, that's all.'

'Well, you obviously studied the right page for tonight's performance.'

The sarcasm hurt. Even more so because it wasn't true. 'That was nothing to do with what I'd read,' she said huskily. 'I'd already realised there are things no book can teach.' She made a gesture of appeal. 'I love you, Nick! I just want to make you happy.'

There was no relaxing of the ironically tilted lips, no softening of tone. 'You could get what I give you from any man.'

'No!' Oblivious now both of her nudity and the possibility of listening ears next door, Erin went to him, snatching the book from his hands and hurling it across the room.

'You're the only man I want! You're the only man I'll *ever* want!'

The grey eyes were veiled. 'I'm the only man you've known in any intimate sense. Maybe we should hang fire until you've some basis for comparison.'

'What do you plan on doing?' she countered in outrage. 'Hiring someone to provide it for me?'

The veil lifted, revealing a steely glint. 'Your sister's next door. Do you want to waken her?'

Erin bit her lip. It was very likely already too late. The cotton wrap she had bought on a last-minute impulse that morning was draped over the bottom of the bed. She reached for it, dragging it about her with numbed fingers, the painted image looming too large in her mind's eye to withstand the need to cover herself. Nick already had a basis for comparison.

'All this over a stupid book!' she said, trying and failing to keep her voice steady. 'I hadn't even got round to more than just leafing through it.'

'It isn't just the book.' Nick sounded suddenly weary. 'It's the whole affair. I need my head examining for ever letting things get this far!'

Eyes dark, mouth vulnerable, she stood there like a statue as he threw back the sheet and slid from the bed. Her impulse was to throw herself at him and refuse to accept what he appeared to be telling her, but pride held her back.

'I suppose it's lucky you came to your senses in time,' she got out through a throat that felt as if it were coated with sandpaper.

He finished pulling on his trousers before answering, his back to her. 'In time for what?'

'To cancel the wedding arrangements.'

'There's no question of that. I told you before, what I start, I finish.'

Erin gazed at the broad bare back, hardly knowing what to feel. 'Supposing *I* decide to cancel it!'

'You won't.'

The surging anger was a refuge from the hurt inflicted by that flat statement. Scooping up the small china clock from the bedside table, she flung it at him, missing his head by inches to hit the wall beyond with a crash that jerked the back of her hand up to her mouth in realisation of what she might have achieved.

'Nick, I'm sorry!' she said shakily as he turned. 'I could have killed you!'

'Not with an aim like that.' If he was angry, he was concealing it well. He studied her flushed young face with a certain wryness in the line of his mouth. '*Do* you want to cancel?'

'You know I don't. You just told me so.' Erin made an effort to inject certainty into her voice. 'I really do love you, Nick.'

The smile was faint. 'You have a very forceful way of showing it.'

'I never did anything like that before in my life,' she said ruefully. 'I never will again either.'

'Never's a long time—although I wouldn't count on quite the same tolerance in future. Just make sure to gather up the bits before Bella sees them,' he added. 'She'll notice the thing's missing, so you'll have to say you dropped it. It's well insured.'

Blue eyes widened in dismay. 'Was it *very* valuable?'

'Fairly.' Nick lifted a quizzical eyebrow. 'Would it have made a difference?'

'I don't suppose so,' she conceded. 'I was too wound up to think about it.' She gave an involuntary little laugh. 'No pun intended!'

Her smile faded as Nick picked up his shirt. 'You're still going?'

'Considering the likelihood that Sam's wide awake and all ears by now, I think it might be the best policy,' he said. 'Anyway, it's time we both got some sleep.'

They could sleep together, Erin wanted to point out, but knew she would be wasting her breath. He was right too: Sam couldn't possibly have slept through the noise the clock had made crashing against the party wall. Considering the circumstances, there was every chance that they wouldn't be making love again at all until after the wedding. A whole week to wait. She didn't think she could live that long!

It took every ounce of self-control she had to hold back when Nick kissed her goodnight.

'Sweet dreams,' he said softly, and went.

Erin took off the wrap and got back into bed, burying her face in the pillow he had used. She wasn't going to sleep a wink without the warmth and comfort of his arms about her. Not a solitary wink!

The confirmation a couple of days later that she wasn't pregnant gave rise to mixed feelings. On the one hand regret, because it would have been wonderful to be having Nick's baby, on the other relief, because he might not have wanted to make love to her at all when she got fat. He certainly showed no regrets when she told him the news.

Despite what Oliver had said, there was plenty of time anyway, Erin assured herself. They could well afford to wait another year or two.

In the meantime, relations with her sister were little improved. Samantha had made no mention of being woken up the night of the clock-throwing incident, but her attitude the next morning had made it obvious, to Erin at least, that she had not only heard the noise but put her own interpretation on it.

Nick's tolerance was beginning to wear very thin. If she

didn't stop acting the brat, he was going to start treating her like one, he threatened.

'You wouldn't dare!' she retorted, with a contempt that made Erin wince. 'It's against the law for you to lay a finger on me!'

Grey eyes sparked. 'It might be in England. Don't count on it being the same here. It doesn't matter what you think of me. Erin's the one you're hurting.'

He might have been talking to a brick wall for all the difference it was making, thought Erin unhappily, viewing the stubborn set of her sister's mouth. Sam was heading for a fall if she pushed him much further.

It was all on her head, of course. She'd had no one's interests but her own at heart when she'd set out to get her man. Nick himself had been trapped into making a commitment he wasn't wholly ready for.

She could put everything to rights by backing out on the marriage, but the strength of mind that it would take to do that was beyond her. Sooner or later Sam had to realise that no matter how much she played up she wasn't going to change anything. Hopefully it would be the former not the latter.

The lovely old church in St Andrew where the wedding was to take place was set on a hilltop with wonderful views of the Atlantic coastline. Nick had taken her to meet the pastor, and then down to view the very up-market Sandy Lane Hotel where he had arranged a reception for the dozen or so people invited, most of whom Erin had still to meet. The friend he'd asked to be his best man was due to fly in from New York on Sunday.

With Tessa's help, Erin extended her wardrobe to take her through a honeymoon in some definitely warm but otherwise unknown location. The dress she chose to be married in was a simple affair in white broderie anglaise. No veil or hat, she decided, just a small spray of flowers to match the one she would be carrying.

'You're going to look positively angelic!' Tessa stated after whisking her off to lunch at the Hilton. 'You should leave your hair down on the day, spread over your shoulders like a golden cape!'

'I'll probably look more like Alice in Wonderland if I do,' Erin rejoined laughingly. 'I think Nick would rather I added a year or two.' She sobered a little. 'I still feel guilty about the way I conned him into this.'

'I very much doubt if he would have gone along with it if he hadn't wanted to,' said Tessa reassuringly. 'All right, it might not have happened as soon, but it would have happened eventually, I'm certain. It's obvious to everybody that he's crazy about you!'

'Not to me. At least, not in the way you mean.' Erin hesitated before saying it. 'He's never once told me he loves me.'

'Well, men don't find it all that easy a word to use. Not really macho, and all that. Wait till you're on honeymoon. It's surprising how much more emotional they become once they get to the bridal suite. Something to do with having finally plighted their troth, maybe.'

Erin had to smile. 'I'll take your word for it.'

There was a pause while they both sampled the wine. When Tessa spoke again it was on a different tack.

'Oliver told me you were having trouble with your sister. Has she come round to it yet?'

Considering that Sam was still adamant about not coming to the wedding, there was no point in putting up a pretence, Erin acknowledged. 'No,' she admitted. 'She thinks the whole thing is utterly revolting.'

'How is Nick coping with it?'

'Well enough, up to now, but I'm afraid he's going to finish up really losing his temper.'

'Might be the best thing for her.'

Erin shook her head emphatically. 'She'd hate him for ever!'

'Then you'll just have to wait for her to grow up enough to recognise that she isn't the only axis your world turns on.'

Easily said, not so easily done, Erin reflected. No one could force Sam to attend the wedding, as Nick had already said. All she could hope was that, come the day, she would at least relent that far. It certainly wouldn't be the same without her.

It was no help to get to the college later that afternoon and learn that Sam had defied her and gone off in Tim's car. If Nick found out about this he was really going to blow his top! she thought worriedly.

With no idea at all of where else they might have gone, she headed for home in the hope of finding them somewhere along the way, breathing a sigh of relief when she came on the bright red open-top parked some quarter of a mile from the gates.

Neither of the occupants looked in the least bit discomfited when Erin drew up alongside. She suspected they'd been kissing, although as college rules forbade the wearing of lipstick there was no actual proof of it.

'You won't be so pleased with yourselves if Nick gets to know what you're up to!' she said searingly. 'You'd better get in here, Sam. And *you'd* better take warning, Tim!'

His grin mocked her anger. 'I'm shaking in my shoes! See you tomorrow, honey,' he added as Sam slid from the car.

She gave him a smile and a wave before getting into the Mercedes, the former disappearing as Erin put the car into jerky motion.

'I told you you didn't need to come for me any more.'

'And I told you no go,' Erin retorted. 'Tim Wyman is far too old for you!'

'Listen who's talking!' came the scathing response.

'It's different for me.'

'You're not kidding! Nick's nearly old enough to be *your* father!'

It was what she had told herself once, Erin acknowledged, but only in defence from the emotions he had aroused in her. 'I mean it's different because I'm of an age to be sure of how I feel,' she said. 'There's nothing wrong with having a boyfriend at fourteen, but not someone like Tim Wyman. He's just out to score points.'

'You don't know him! You don't know anything!' The younger girl was beside herself with anger. 'Why don't you go and ask Tim what your precious Nick gets up to when he goes out on his own?'

They had nearly reached the gates. Erin drew to a stop at the roadside to sit gazing blindly through the windscreen for a slow, ticking moment.

'What are you talking about?' she got out.

'He's been meeting Dione. Tim saw them together yesterday afternoon, driving down to Frame Cove. It's nice and private down there, especially in the week.'

Some time soon, Erin knew, the pain had to start, but right now all she felt was numb. Nick hadn't been home when she'd got back with Sam yesterday afternoon, and he'd offered no explanation when he did put in an appearance around six-thirty.

'Rin?' The belligerence had gone from her sister's voice, replaced by something approaching abashment. 'Say something.'

'What would you like me to say?' Erin asked tonelessly.

'I don't know. Call me a liar. Anything!'

A spark momentarily lit the dullness of the other blue eyes. 'Are you lying?'

Sam hesitated before slowly shaking her head. 'It could have been perfectly innocent, though.'

And pigs might fly! thought Erin, feeling the numbness vanish as her imagination began filling in the picture. She had never been to this Frame Cove herself, though Sam obviously had—the question of how and when still to be resolved. Unlikely to be visited by others during the week, which made it the ideal place for a tryst. She could see the two of them lying together under the shade of a palm tree, the sunlight filtering through the gently waving fronds onto bare bronzed skin. Dione would have no need of books to tell her what a man might like; she would know it all!

'We'd better get back,' she said, unable to bear any further envisaging. 'Bella will have had tea ready for ages.'

They were through the gates and heading up the drive before Sam spoke. She sounded subdued. 'What are you going to do?'

'I don't know,' Erin responded hollowly. 'Face him with it, I suppose. Give him a chance to explain.' Sensing the reaction from the girl at her side, she gave a wry little shrug. 'You're right. What's the point?'

'You wouldn't still marry him, would you?' asked Sam as they drew up at the house. 'I mean, you *can't* still think you love somebody who'd do that to you!'

Lack of trust in itself was no basis for marriage, Erin reflected. Nick had been prepared to go through with it because she had brought unfair pressure to bear on him, but there was no way she was ever going to be able to give him what a woman like Dione could give him. It was better for them both that they called time on the whole relationship.

'No, I shan't be marrying him,' she confirmed in the same expressionless tones. 'I'll tell him I changed my mind. But in my own time,' she added. 'You're not to say anything about this to anyone!'

'Of course not.' Sam sounded subdued again, as if only just beginning to realise what she'd set in motion. 'What about all the arrangements?'

'They'll have to be unarranged.' Erin thought of the bags piled up in the car boot, and steeled herself. 'It's only Thursday. There's time enough.'

Bella's appearance in the house doorway put paid to any reply Sam might have been going to make.

'I got tea set ready!' she scolded. 'What are the both of you doin'?'

'We're just coming,' Erin answered, opening the car door. 'Sorry, Bella.'

The housekeeper's annoyance faded as she surveyed the pale young face and lacklustre eyes. 'You got a bad feelin' in your stomach, child?' she asked on a sympathetic note.

'Must be something I've eaten,' Erin answered, seizing on the excuse as a way of giving her time to think. 'I'm going to go and lie down for a bit.'

'You do that. I'll tell Mr Nick where you're at.'

'It's best if I just try and sleep it off,' Erin said hastily, nowhere near ready to face Nick as yet.

'I'll come up and sit with you,' offered Sam.

Erin shook her head. 'I need to be on my own.'

It was obvious from her expression that Sam was reluctant to face Nick herself. Erin almost relented, but self-interest won the day for once. She *had* to be on her own.

The bedroom she had shared more than once with Nick proved no retreat. She went out onto the balcony, to sit gazing down at the pool where it had all begun, heart and mind heavy as lead.

Bella must have served tea on the veranda, she realised, hearing the sound of her sister's voice, although not the words themselves. Nick replied in even quieter tones, eliciting a sudden rise in Sam's decibel level.

'It's *you* she's sick of! She doesn't want to marry you any more! She told me so!'

Erin sat frozen, waiting for Nick's reply, but none came. She heard the sudden scrape of chair legs on wooden boards, the sound of footsteps heading indoors, then silence. He would be coming up here, she thought in panic, and she wasn't ready for him! Thanks to her loud-mouthed little sister, she hadn't even had time to consider what she was going to say to him.

The door had a lock, of course. For a fleeting moment she contemplated rushing across and turning the key. But what was the use? No matter how long she put it off, it had to be faced in the end. Best to get it over with now.

She was sitting in one of the easy chairs when Nick came in without bothering to knock. He closed the door quietly and stood looking across at her, face impassive.

'Feeling better?' he asked.

Erin moved her head in slow negation, fighting for the control to see this through without giving way to the urge to throw the whole thing in his face. 'Not so you'd notice.'

There was a lengthy pause. Nick made no attempt to advance further into the room, nor did he reveal what he might be thinking.

'I understand you might have something to tell me.'

'Yes.' She swallowed the hard lump forming in her throat, forcing herself to carry on. 'I've...changed my mind about marrying you.'

'Just like that?'

'No, not just like that.' She cast around for some plausible reason. 'I suppose not being pregnant after all had something to do with it.'

'You never really believed you were to start with,' he returned in the same unemotional tones, 'so why would it make a difference to how you feel?'

'I don't know why, it just did,' Erin said doggedly. 'I

realised today that I'd been living in a dream world the last few weeks—a romantic dream world. I thought because I liked having you make love to me that I had to be in love with you.'

'But now you know you're not?'

'Now I know I'm not.' It was all she could do to force the words out, because they weren't true. Love didn't die because the recipient of it turned out to be unworthy. That was something else she had learned. 'I'm…sorry,' she tagged on lamely. 'I realise how much trouble I've put you to—to say nothing of the expense. I—'

She broke off, seeing the sudden glitter in the grey eyes, the hardened line of his jaw.

'Better you came to your senses now than after the ceremony. I'll take care of everything. You just concentrate on what you want to do from here on in.'

Do? She hadn't got that far. One thing she couldn't do was stay on here, though. Nick himself would probably be glad to see the back of her.

'I want to go home,' she said. 'Back to England. Only not at your expense—or at least, no more expense. I charged everything today, like you said, so I still have the majority of the money you put to my account. That will buy me my return ticket, and tide me over for a few days while I get things sorted out. Social Services will find me somewhere to live.'

'Do you really think I'm going to agree to that?' Nick demanded harshly.

'You don't really have a choice,' she said. 'I was never your responsibility.'

'Sam is,' he reminded her. 'You're willing to leave her?'

Erin braced herself against the anguish. 'I can hardly take her with me, can I?'

'No,' he agreed hardily. 'She'll just have to manage without you.' He straightened away from the door. 'It might be best if we stay out of each other's way for the present. I'll get Bella to bring you up a tray later. She'll be glad to hear you're on the road to recovery.'

She would no doubt be even more so to hear that the wedding was off, thought Erin painfully, willing herself to defy the urge to call him back as the door closed in his wake. Even if she had faced him with what she knew it would have made no difference to the outcome. Once he got over the anger he must be feeling inside over all the trouble she had caused him, he could only be relieved to have his life back in order again. Dione would see to it that he didn't lack satisfaction—or, if not her, there were plenty of other women around.

One thing he definitely wouldn't be doing from now on was taking an interest in teenage girls. They were far too prone to cause problems.

Arriving with the promised dinner tray some couple of hours later, Bella fussed over her like a mother hen.

'You eat up now!' she admonished as Erin listlessly picked over the chicken casserole. 'That'll make you feel better.'

'I'm sure it will,' Erin answered. 'I'm just not very hungry, that's all.'

'Just try, then,' encouraged the woman. 'You've still some growin' to do, chil'.'

Not any more, Erin reflected, alone again. She had seen the very last of her girlhood.

Had she, though? asked an inner voice. Would a full-grown woman have reacted the way she had reacted over what to all intents and purposes was purely and simply hearsay? Sam hadn't seen Nick and Dione together herself; she only had Tim's word for it. Supposing he was lying?

She was grasping at straws, she told herself wearily. Tim had no reason to lie. It was too late anyway.

The evening wore on, every minute an hour, every hour

a lifetime. Erin dreaded the night still to come, yet even that was going to be easier than the morning. He'd take care of it all, Nick had said, but there were things she had to see to herself. The packages still out in the car must be returned to their various points of origin for a start—embarrassing though it would be to do it. She would also book a seat on the next available flight to Heathrow while she was in town. Hopefully it would be before Monday. Flying home on what was to have been her wedding day would be too much to bear.

Despite everything, her heart leapt when the door opened again, sinking back into its pit when the visitor turned out to be Sam.

'Nick says you're going back home!' she burst out. 'You can't, Rin! I'm not staying here without you!'

Erin made a wry gesture. 'I'm afraid you have to. Even if Nick would allow it, I couldn't take you with me. It's going to be difficult enough as it is.'

'You don't *have* to go! Nick says it's your decision, not his. Everything will be all right again now you're not going to marry him. Things will just go back to the way they were.'

'They can't. Not now.' Erin could hardly bear to even think about it. 'It's no use, Sam. There's no way I can stay on here. You have to see that.'

'You could find somewhere else to live. I bet Mrs Marshall would help if you asked her.'

'Even if she could, I wouldn't want it,' Erin denied. 'The only way I'm ever going to be able to get over Nick is to go where I'm never likely to see him again.'

Samantha was silent for a moment, a variety of expressions chasing across her face. 'You still love him, don't you?' she said on a defeated note.

'Yes,' Erin admitted. 'I know I probably shouldn't, after what he's done, but I can't help it.'

'He hasn't.' Her sister's voice was so low it was scarcely audible. 'It was all Tim's idea.'

Eyes dark, heart plummeting to new depths, Erin said thickly, 'What was?'

'Telling you he'd seen them together. He knew I wanted to stop you from marrying Nick.'

'I see.' Erin struggled to contain the anger welling up inside her. 'Well, you certainly succeeded.'

'I'm sorry, Rin.' Sam looked on the verge of tears. 'I was so jealous of you! Nick's *my* uncle, but he wouldn't have bothered with me at all if you hadn't been there. He doesn't even like me!'

'That's nonsense!' Erin thrust everything else aside for the moment to go and put her arms around the girl, hugging her close. 'Of course he likes you, dummy! You've just been making it a bit difficult for him to show it, that's all.'

'I've ruined everything!' Sam was crying in earnest now. 'I'm really, really sorry, Rin.'

'Don't,' Erin pleaded. 'It's all right. I understand.'

'How can it be all right? You've told Nick you don't want to marry him now, and it's all my fault.' She lifted a tear-streaked face. 'Couldn't you say you'd made a mistake and you'd changed your mind again?'

Erin kept her tone carefully neutral. 'I don't think so. I've got a box of tissues in the bathroom. Sit down while I fetch them.'

The detachment was surface only. Reaching the bathroom, she stood for a moment or two to gather herself, aware that it was going to take everything she had to restrain the urge to hit out at the girl who had cost her everything she held dear.

Except that she hadn't, had she? came the unwelcome thought. Not wholly. If she had given Nick the opportunity to speak for himself, instead of simply accepting Sam's word, then none of this need have happened.

It took her several minutes of talking and cuddling to convince her sister that she bore no grudge.

'I'm as much to blame, if not more, for wading in the way I did,' she said. 'Love and trust are supposed to go hand in hand. Anyway,' she added, forcing a lighter note, 'it's time you were in bed. You still have school in the morning.'

'I'll not be having anything to do with Tim Wyman again, for certain!' Sam vowed. 'I wouldn't be surprised if Dione put him up to it to start with.'

The same thought had crossed Erin's mind. Not that it altered anything.

Sam looked back tentatively from the door. 'Do you really mean to go back home, Rin?'

'I have to,' she said.

Her sister nodded as if in resignation, and went, leaving Erin to face the effort of getting ready for bed herself.

She was lying there, far from sleep, when the door once more opened some immeasurable time later. Nick didn't switch on any lights, coming over to the bed as Erin lifted herself on an elbow.

'Sam told me what she told you,' he said. 'Did it occur to you to ask me if it was true?'

Erin shook her head, keeping a tight rein on her emotions. 'Not then. I was too busy saving face.' She hesitated, unable to see his expression all that clearly, and not at all certain why he was here. 'I'm sorry, Nick.'

'Sorry for believing it, or for telling me you'd changed your mind about marrying me?'

'Both.' A cautious warmth was beginning to uncurl deep inside her. 'I thought you might be relieved to be rid of me.'

'Did you now?'

'Yes.' She made an appealing gesture. 'I've behaved pretty appallingly all round.'

'You certainly have,' he agreed. 'Utterly outrageous from start to finish!'

'Most of it purely involuntary,' she claimed. 'You obviously bring out the worst in me.' She paused again, still not wholly sure. 'Am I forgiven?'

'For doubting me, yes. Not for what you've put me through these last few hours.'

'What have I put you through?' she whispered.

'Hell,' he said simply. 'I really thought I'd lost you.'

The warmth had permeated her whole body. 'It mattered that much?'

'More than anything I'd ever known.' He sat down on the edge of the mattress, taking her face between his hands to kiss her with a tenderness that spoke more loudly than any words. 'I love you, Erin. I've loved you since the first moment I saw you. Oh, I wouldn't let myself recognise it at first. I even managed to convince myself I was just being philanthropic, bringing you out here with Sam—for a little while, at any rate. Finding you in the pool that night finished me.'

'If you felt like that about me, why were you so rotten to me next morning?' she murmured, still finding it difficult to realise that everything was coming out right after all.

'Guilt,' he said. 'I'd not only taken a girl nearly half my age, I'd opened up a sex drive she wasn't capable of handling.'

'I was so!' Erin disputed. 'I was handling it just fine until you turned all holy on me!'

His lips curved. 'I remember. Beats an alarm clock any day of the week!'

'You thought it was someone else, though, didn't you?' she said, and saw the smile fade a little. 'It doesn't matter,' she tagged on swiftly. 'Really it doesn't.'

'Nothing that happened before I met you matters,' he

said on a roughened note. 'You're the only woman I want in my life.'

Erin widened her eyes at him. 'I was still a girl a minute ago.'

'Figuratively speaking.' He was smiling again, though a certain tension still lingered. 'I know what you feel for me is probably still little more than infatuation at present, but you'll have plenty of time to learn what love's really about when we're married. One thing I can't do is risk you falling for someone else.'

'As if I ever could,' she said softly. She put her hands to his face in turn, running the balls of her thumbs along the firm line of his jaw. 'It isn't just infatuation, Nick. I love you so much it hurts! If I'd gone back to England, I'd have spent the rest of my life pining for you. I can't wait to be married to you. And just to prove that sex isn't the only thing I'm interested in, I'm ready to stay celibate for the whole first year—well, a month, at any rate.'

Nick's laugh was good to hear, the light in his eyes good to see. 'You know there's as much chance of my taking you up on that as the two of us sprouting wings!'

'I thought it unlikely,' she admitted. She sobered again, to add with force, 'Don't you ever try telling me I don't know what love is really about again! I'm as capable of it as you are—probably more so because I'm a woman, and it's a well-known fact that women feel emotion far more deeply than men.'

'We might do a deal less talking about it, but that's the only difference.' Nick stroked back the tumbled hair from her face the way he had done that very first time, studying her as if to commit every last, minute feature to memory. 'You're lovely now, but you're going to be even more so in years to come. I want to paint you at every stage of your life—girl, wife, maybe mother too, in time.'

In not too much time if she had anything to do with it, thought Erin mistily, her cup overflowing.

'You know I'm...indisposed,' she added, coming down to earth again as Nick stood up to start removing his clothing.

'I hadn't forgotten,' he said. 'We've all the time in the world to make love. Tonight, I just want to hold you close.'

Erin relaxed again, secure in the knowledge that sex wasn't his only need either. The honeymoon could wait.

EPILOGUE

'I PRONOUNCE you husband and wife,' intoned the pastor, drawing recollective sighs from one or two members of the congregation.

Erin's prime reaction was one of relief. It had been a pretty hectic few days. Now, at last, she could relax, secure in the knowledge that last-minute hitches were a thing of the past. The dress fitted like a dream again, after Tessa's quick nip and tuck last night when the final trying-on session had revealed the loss of a pound or two. Just the reception to get through, then it would be time for bride and groom to be on their way.

'Where are you going?' piped up a voice as she made to follow Nick out into the aisle.

'Hush, now!' admonished Bella, holding the small, squirming figure firmly on her ample lap. 'Your mama and papa have to go and see Aunt Samantha and Uncle Alan sign the big book to say they married now.'

'We shan't be long,' promised Erin, turning back to direct a smile at the child. 'You stay with Bella, Ryan.'

'I'm thankful Sam decided against having him as a pageboy,' she murmured as she joined Nick. 'I think it could have proved a bit of a disaster.'

'I'm sure of it,' he returned drily. 'That son of ours is mischief personified!'

'No more than any other three-year-old,' she claimed, drawing a grin.

'I wouldn't want to take a bet on it. Lucky our first-born is so well-behaved.'

They were coming into the vestry. Erin sought and found

the diminutive figure of their daughter amidst the group of bridesmaids gathered about the happy couple. Pretty as a picture in her lilac and white crinoline dress, blonde hair cascading down her back, Francesca displayed a poise far in advance of her six and a half years. 'She been on this earth before,' Bella had declared more than once.

It seemed a lot less than eight years since she had sat where Sam was sitting now to sign the register, Erin reflected. At forty-two, Nick looked very little different from the man she had fallen in love with on sight, lean and fit as ever in the formal morning attire, dark hair showing the merest hint of silver at the temples.

They'd been wonderful years all round. Not totally without dispute, it had to be admitted, but then what married couple didn't have the occasional disagreement? What mattered was the balance achieved.

He had given her so much, not least the ability to express herself on canvas the way she had always yearned to do. While she would never match his talent, Miles Penhalligen had been impressed enough with her work to offer her a minor exhibition a couple of years ago, since when she had achieved a fair degree of success in her own right. Not the most important accomplishment of her life, but satisfying all the same.

The children were their joint pride and joy. Nick was a brilliant father, never too busy to spend time with them, just enough of a disciplinarian to counteract her own tendency towards over-indulgence at times. A brilliant lover still, too, came the thought, curving her lips into a reminiscent little smile. A good sex life might not be the only factor necessary to a happy marriage, but it surely helped.

'You've done a great job putting all this together,' Nick said quietly, viewing the serenely lovely face beneath the wide white brim of her hat.

'No more than you did for us,' she responded.

'Hardly on the same scale. Trust Sam to want the full works!' He paused, eyes reflective. 'Do you ever regret not having had the same?'

'Not for a minute,' Erin returned truthfully. 'My memories leave nothing to be desired. My life neither,' she added softly, and saw the greyness take on a deeper hue.

'Nor mine,' he said. 'No man could ask for more.'

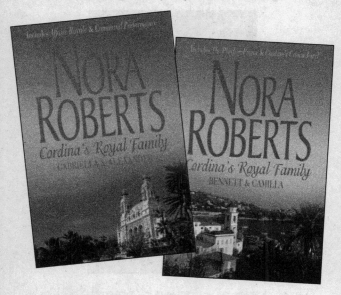